IN THE
SHADOW
OF THE
FURIES

A Novel of the Second Punic War

Cary Reed

ISBN: 978-1-64953-033-2

Printed in the United States of America

Second Printing, 2020

For my wife, who has shown me how to live life in full color

Table of Contents

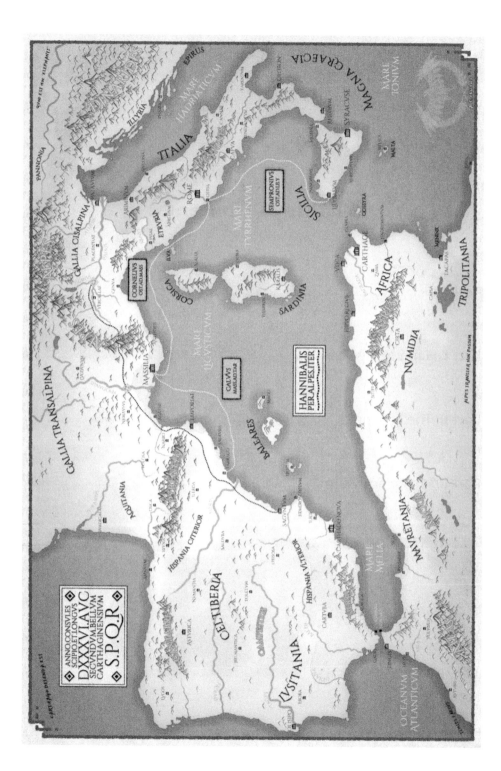

Prologue

Hannibal was bathed in the light of thousands of fires. Behind him, the campfires of his sixty thousand-strong army of Carthaginians, Numidians, and Celtiberians—men unified not by culture or language, but by obedience to Hannibal's will alone. Beside him, the fires at the tips of the archers' arrows and giant round clay containers that were filled with oil and loaded into catapult buckets, ready to shatter and spread flames on impact. Before him, the fires that marked the beginning of the end of his three-month siege of Saguntum.

For Hannibal, the road to Rome—the enemy against whom he'd spent all thirty of his years on Earth preparing to face—ran through Saguntum. He had to take this city, and he had to do it now—for nothing short of destroying an ally would so provoke Rome into war with the resurgent Empire of Carthage, and nothing short of a Roman declaration of war would convince the royal family in Carthage to finally commit to total war with the Republic.

Despite all Hannibal's efforts, the royals simply didn't understand the true nature of Rome's threat. They supported Hannibal only when he used his military prowess to rebuild Carthage's empire and confidence, both of which Rome shattered twenty years before in the most calamitous war Carthage had ever fought. Rome's power had grown like a cancer every year from then until now, and Hannibal knew that it would only expand if left unchecked, until it enslaved the world. But here, at Saguntum, was the beginning of the end of Rome. This was the first step to fulfilling the oath he made to his father and destroying the most pernicious state the world had ever spawned.

A firing catapult captured Hannibal's attention. The whiz of the unwinding restraining rope, the clunk of the arm hitting the frame as it propelled its burning payload toward the city, and the creak of the frame as the catapult rocked back into place were the drumbeats of beautiful music.

"General..." he heard a voice call to him.

Hannibal peered down from his personal war elephant, Surus, to see his cavalry commander, Maharbal, looking up at him.

"The cavalry is ready," Maharbal told him. "Behind the elephants, as you ordered."

"Bring up the tortoises," Hannibal ordered.

Maharbal called the battering ram crews forward, and soon Hannibal heard the unmistakable lumbering of their wheels under the great weight of their wooden and iron frames. Their arms were capped with great iron heads of rams—animals sacred to the god Baal Hammond. Each was protected with a wooden roof, earning them the nickname "tortoises"; but Hannibal knew they were far from indestructible. He had at least two for every gate he planned to breach, presupposing one would be destroyed by enemy fire.

Hannibal looked over the opposite side of his rumbling elephant to see his standard-bearer waiting patiently with bow in hand. One of his personal guards stood next to him, holding a torch.

"Signal the infantry," Hannibal told him.

The standard-bearer immediately readied an arrow and

dipped its head in a small jar of oil at his feet. After the guard lit it with his torch, the standard-bearer aimed it nearly straight up in the air, drew, and fired it. Almost immediately, Hannibal heard the war cries of thousands of infantrymen along the siege line as they rushed forward with their scaling ladders. Their swords and battleaxes slung on their backs, reflected the campfires and the moon in tiny glints of light that shown through the dark void between his campfires and the city walls. Hannibal couldn't see the arrows from the ramparts raining down on them as they ran, but he knew they were there from the tell-tale screams of the men that they hit.

He felt familiar desires surging inside of him. He gripped the hilt of his father's *xiphos* sword and fought the urge to ride forward on his elephant, tell the men to raise their shields and get as close to the wall as possible to confound the enemy's aim, and to direct the action himself. He found his attention fixated on the source of the screams as he drew shallow, rapid breaths.

Calm yourself...

"How long do you think these walls have stood, Maharbal?" he asked. "Two centuries? Three?"

"Longer, perhaps," Maharbal answered.

Hannibal drew a deep, long breath before looking side-to-side down the length of the wall.

"For all the years they kept this city safe," he said, "no one will remember the names of those that built them. But they *will* remember who tore them down."

"I believe they will, General."

Hannibal's battering ram buckled the city's western-most gate. Behind him, soldiers who had been shot, crushed or stabbed while manning the siege engines lay dying or writhing, struggling with their horrible injuries. Hannibal would ensure that the survivors returned home with a share of the booty, but he knew that a part of them was lost forever.

All of this would be worth it. The World Without Rome would be worth it.

A great crack reverberated in the night air. The bolt to the western-most gate broke, and the battering ram withdrew. The enemy continued raining missiles down on it from the walls. Still, the battering ram's crew cheered in victory as the breach opened. The defenders on the wall would now have to collapse on the compromised gate to cover the opening, which would allow Hannibal's men to scale the walls on ladders with far less resistance than otherwise. While the infantry went over the walls, his faster and heavier forces would exploit the breach.

"Three volleys!" Hannibal shouted down to them, and his command echoed down the line.

A line of bowmen and skirmishers ran toward the breach. Hannibal raised up his standard—a purple banner adorned with a ram's head—and a soldier on the elephant behind him blew a single horn blast. Several war elephants trumpeted, and though Hannibal was nearly certain they were reacting to the sound of the horn regardless of the context, he wondered for a moment if they knew they were about to ride into combat. They were, after all, exceedingly intelligent animals.

On the other side of the gate, Hannibal knew, the city's defenders were formed into that most ancient of Greek formations, the phalanx, to repel the Carthaginian attack. Hannibal watched his skirmishers shower them with arrows, stones, and javelins, then let the enemy sweat for a few minutes. He drove Surus forward, triggering the avalanche that would fall upon the defenders. The once-feared line formation of hoplite heavy infantry was now as outdated as the war chariot, yet the Greeks still favored it. Hannibal felt he had shattered it a thousand times, and this time was no different.

Rocks and arrows flew from the ramparts and fell like rain, hitting his shield and his elephant's armor with loud pings. Annoyed but mostly unharmed, the elephant trumpeted once more. The front rank of enemy hoplites in their Corinthian helmets held up their long spears, trembling, as Hannibal stabbed down at them with his pike.

In this situation, the true value of the war elephants was in shocking and overwhelming the enemy. They drove the phalanx back so that the real killing could begin, for behind Hannibal was Maharbal and twelve thousand Numidian horseman—the finest light cavalry in the world and the best mercenaries money could buy. They rode bareback on their horses with nothing but a rope to steer, screaming like madmen. Lightly armed with spears, javelins, and short swords, they would throw the enemy into disarray before Hannibal's heavy African infantry came to seal the victory.

By sunrise, what was left of the city's defenders had melted away, gone or dead in the streets. From atop his elephant, Hannibal surveyed the devastation his men had wrought. Fires raged all over the city and would likely live until they ran out of material to devour. He contemplated the debates that would soon begin far from here, in the palace in Carthage and the Senate in Rome, over what to do next, but their control was a grand illusion that brought a knowing smile to Hannibal's lips. His will alone drove events. All others were merely reacting to what was set in motion long ago when he swore an oath to destroy Rome—an oath that the blood of his father had consecrated and sealed. Hannibal alone was master of his own fate.

Part I: Hannibal's War

SCIPIO

Rome

The roar of over a hundred thousand spectators around the track in the *Vallis Murcia* was absolutely deafening in a race so close. Approaching the penultimate turn, the noise filled Scipio with fire. The rumbling beneath his feet, the burn of reigns in his hands, and the sounds of the crowd, made him lean forward in his chariot, grit his teeth, and urge his horses on. Scipio *needed* to win. He'd known victory here only once before, and he'd craved it every sleepless night since. Nothing could compare. It made him feel more alive, more seen, and more loved than anything else ever had. Like Atlas temporarily relieved of his burden, even if only for a few fleeting minutes, the crushing weight of the world had slipped away. He was almost there again.

The drivers in red and white had fallen back little by little with each lap, and the race had turned into a contest between Scipio in green and his closest opponent in blue. Scipio had the inside of the track, but he was nearly half a horse-length behind Blue. As they went into the turn, their blinders prevented Scipio's team of horses from panicking as the wheels of the two chariots ground up against one another and made a horrible screech. Blue was trying to force Scipio off the track. It was a common tactic, one for which he prepared. He would feign defeat, as he'd practiced a hundred times.

Scipio slowed his horses down as they came out of the turn, did his best to ignore the thickening dust, and watched for Blue's reaction. His horses were now beside Blue's wheels, but Blue remained focused on the strait before him. They neared the midway point, and Scipio slowed more than he had planned and practiced, falling farther behind. It was a bigger chance, and what others might call a rash decision, but this kind of recklessness was often what Fortune demanded. There was more than enough room for Blue to move over to the inside, but Blue's neck seemed incapable of moving his head to see it.

There it was... the turn, coming up fast. Scipio drove his horses forward, determined to regain the position he had surrendered before the turn. He wouldn't go down without a fight.

Just when he began to creep back up, Blue swerved to the inside of the track to block Scipio's path. Finally! Scipio drove his horses to the outside and urged them on, harder than ever before. Though he was now behind, Scipio had the advantage he had sought - more track. He stepped to his right to put more weight on that side, then pulled the team to the left.

He could feel the right wheel come up almost right away, and panic seized him. Its dark hand reached into his chest, clutched his heart in its cruel grip, and squeezed. He was going to overturn, crash, and they'd pull his mangled dead body off in minutes so that the next race could start...

But his heart beat free with a thud in his chest when the wheel met the earth once more.

Scipio urged his horses on again, finally getting Blue's attention as he pulled alongside him. Blue turned his head and looked him square in the face. Scipio couldn't resist a toothy smile and a wink before he pulled his horses hard to the left, grinding his wheels against Blue's. The maneuver spooked Blue's horses right off the track. His right wheel hit the median and spun off the chariot.

Crossing the finish, Scipio raised his fist in triumph to a booming roar. It was only after the earsplitting song of the crowd died down that he looked to see what had become of his vanquished opponent. The Blue driver was bruised in body and spirit, but alive and walking. One look at his hard countenance and Scipio recognized the bitterness of defeat. He had felt it himself many times before, and he learned a valuable lesson from it each time.

Only his closest friend, Claudius Pulcher, was there to greet him with his ubiquitous grin after the laurel ceremony.

"You're an idiot," Claudius told him, putting his arm around his friend's broad shoulders. "You know, most people have drivers to do this for them."

"Listen to them, Claudius," Scipio told him, gesturing to the crowd. "The glory I win here is mine and mine alone."

They found space to sit on the Palatine Hill side of the track, where the wealthier spectators could always be found. Claudius's slaves brought them water, and Scipio dumped a cup of it over his bowed head. He took a cloth the servant offered, wiped the grime from his face, then grasped the comet-shaped talisman that he wore around his neck. It was a tired, worn piece of metal, dull and full of scratches; hardly the sort of charm found around the neck of a young nobleman. Scipio kissed it and let it dangle on its silver chair.

"You've worn that thing in every one of your races," Claudius said, pointing to his chest. "Six of which you lost."

"So?"

"So, if it works, shouldn't you win every time?"

Scipio shrugged dismissively.

"I don't believe in any of that."

"Why wear it at all, then?"

"It was a gift," Scipio told him, before gulping down his water and holding out his cup for another. "From my brother."

"You have a brother?" Claudius asked. "Why have you never told me this?"

"*Had*," Scipio corrected him. "Lucius."

"What happened to him?"

"He was killed," Scipio replied and looked back over his shoulder toward the Forum, where Lucius had died. "Not far from here, actually. We were very young."

Over the yammering of the crowd around them, a group of girls giggled as clear as if it were the only sound on the entire hill. He looked to his right, past Claudius, and spotted three young women casting flirtatious eyes in their direction. They were rich, judging by their jewelry and the colorful Greek-style *himations* they wore. Scipio had no doubt who they were admiring. Claudius had a striking face that most often bore an expression somewhere between easy confidence and smug self-satisfaction. He also had a head full of wavy golden locks—a rare asset in a blue-blooded Roman patrician. It made most women and even some men blush and stammer the first time they spoke to him.

Scipio waved the girls over and held his cup out to them, but they played coy, hiding their faces in their little circle. One of them peeked around her friend and Scipio smiled at her.

"You like girls too much," Claudius told him, ignoring the

women. "Take it from me—they're more trouble than they're worth."

"Just having a bit of fun, Claudius. Since when are you averse to that?"

"You know I'm not," Claudius said, taking a sip of his wine. "Just... watch yourself."

"That's enough, girls," a shrill voice told the women. Scipio heard a matronly woman say as she cast a stern, disapproving look in Scipio's direction before herding the maidens away.

"Supper at my house tomorrow," Claudius said, ignoring the scene.

"Having a party? What's the occasion?"

"We might as well enjoy ourselves while we can," Claudius answered, emptying his cup of wine with one large swig. "We'll all be marching through ankle-deep mud in Hispania soon... Or perhaps you missed the few thousand refugees from Saguntum in town."

Scipio kept his eyes on the track, pretending not to care.

"I'm well aware of the situation in Hispania," he said. "My house has been filled with men speaking of little else but Saguntum and Carthage all summer."

"And what does your illustrious father, our Consul, think of it all?"

"Nothing he cares to share with me," he replied.

Scipio's father, Cornelius, was one of two Consuls—the pinnacle of magisterial power in the Republic. One of the main duties of the Consuls was leading Rome's armies. If the notoriously aggressive Carthaginian general Hannibal Barca followed through on his threat to attack Saguntum, Rome's only ally in far-off Hispania, his father would lead Rome's legions and allies against the might of the Carthaginian Empire.

"Anyway, don't assume anything," Scipio told him. "Senator Fabius's delegation hasn't yet returned from Carthage. War might still be averted."

"Listen to you! Taking an interest in politics at last!" Claudius teased, eliciting a scoff. "Perhaps you'll follow your father to war."

"I have no intention of going anywhere," Scipio replied. "Look around you. Rome is filled with the best games, food, wine, women... And I will not leave it because someone expects me to go fight, least of all my father."

"Anyway, you'll come tomorrow?" Claudius asked.

"I'm dining with Senator Paullus."

"Sen—You're still sniffing around his daughter, aren't you?"

"Aemilia Tertia," Scipio snapped.

"*Ae-mil-ia*," Claudius teased.

Scipio answered with an elbow to his friend's ribs.

"Why don't you just have her already and move on to the next one like you always do?" Claudius asked.

"It's not like that."

"How, then?"

"I like her," he said.

"She's fiery... smart, opinionated..."

Thinking of her brought a smile to his face, but it also troubled him. Just when Scipio had learned to be happy, he met a woman and glimpsed a life he never knew he wanted.

"Ave, Calvus Cornelius!" someone called out from behind them.

Scipio and Claudius quickly stood to greet Scipio's beloved uncle.

"Congratulations on your race, nephew," Calvus said as he approached them, stepping around the spectators. "At least you won something today."

"Whatever do you mean?" Scipio asked and took a sip of his wine, though he well knew that his uncle was referencing the day's elections.

"The results of the elections for the quaestors are in," Calvus told him. "You lost."

"Really?" Scipio said and drank more wine, feigning some sort of consideration of the news while silently celebrating it.

"Really," Calvus answered.

Though his uncle bore a smile, Scipio could tell he was anything but pleased. His chubby face and scalp were reddened by the sun beating down on him during his trek here from his home on the Palatine. Beads of sweat were forming on his nearly bald head faster than the servant that accompanied him could dab it away.

"Well, I suppose I should have made a speech or something," Scipio mused.

"Probably," Calvus agreed.

"Perhaps if my revered father had been here today, he might have seen that his son can be successful at something."

"And whom does the success here serve?"

"Those wise enough to bet on me, of course."

"Snark doesn't suit you, nephew," Calvus scolded him.

"May I offer you some wine, Senator?" Claudius asked as his servant offered a cup to Calvus.

"Thank you, no," Calvus said, then turned to Scipio. "Your father wishes to see you at home—*now*."

"Of course, he does."

Scipio and Calvus bid farewell to Claudius and made their way up the gentle slope of Palatine Hill through the cheering spectators, some of whom recognized and congratulated Scipio on his victory as he passed.

As they neared some of the city's grandest temples, they crossed a busy ancient road of packed dirt called the Salt Path, where a small crowd gathered around a man reciting one of the epic poems commemorating a battle of antiquity, the anniversary of which today's games celebrated. Scipio recognized the poem from his youth. It was about three soldiers, led by "Horatius the One-Eyed," who held off the entire army of an invading Etruscan king at a bridge across the Tiber—the *Pons Sublicius*.

Scipio remembered well sitting on his bed with his sister and brother as their father had recited this very poem, his hands in the air and eyes wide as he described the villainous last King of Rome marching on the new Republic that had banished him. His brother had his face buried in his sister's chest as she'd held him, the story nearly too frightening for him to hear; but Scipio had hung on every word as his father described the courage of the soldiers who had stepped forward and volunteered to hold the bridge, ready to lay down their lives to save the Republic from tyranny. Hearing it now, he remembered how the child he'd felt about being from a prominent Roman family and swelling with pride whenever he heard a tale filled with impossible courage in the face of adversity.

Now he saw it as so much maudlin tripe-filled heroic acts that no one ever actually saw for themselves because they never happened in the first place. Regardless, he still knew one passage by heart.

But the Consul's brow was sad,
And the Consul's speech was low,
And darkly looked he at the wall,
And darkly at the foe.
'Their van will be upon us
Before the bridge goes down;
And if they once might win the bridge,
What hope to save the town?'

Then out spake brave Horatius,
The Captain of the Gate:
'To every man upon this earth
Death cometh soon or late.
And how can man die better
Than facing fearful odds
For the ashes of his fathers,
And the temples of his gods?

And for the tender mother
Who dandled him to rest,
And for the wife who nurses
His baby at her breast?'

***

"A pampered, spoiled patrician brat!" Cornelius loudly admonished his son. "That is what they see. Is that what you are?"

"Father, I..."

"Because that is not what I raised!" Cornelius boomed and began pacing, rubbing his forehead.

Cornelius's *tablinum*, a private office where he received his clients, doubled as a library and had been one of Scipio's favorite places when he was a child. He cherished the memories of reading scrolls with his tutors by the lamplight so much that the place had an aura of the sacred. It had seemed cavernous to him back then, perhaps because of what it contained... how vast and wonderous the words on all these scrolls made the world seem. Now he saw the tablinum for what it was—an ordinary dinky

14

room overcrowded with junk. The walls even seemed to close in as he sat. It was his father's favorite room in which to reprimand him.

Scipio saw his mother, Pamponia, glance pensively in the room as she passed. *She must have heard Cornelius's tone*, Scipio thought, *and decided not to involve herself.*

"You're twenty-one, Publius," his father said.

"Twenty-two," Scipio quietly corrected him, but Cornelius didn't seem to notice or care.

"And you still behave like a child!" his father went on. "All you do is play these... these... ridiculous games! Chariot racing now, is it? Competing with slaves! Getting drunk with your friends and chasing girls... Is that all you choose to do with everything this family and this city have given you?"

He wasn't wrong, Scipio thought, but he was also only half right. A father was everything to a boy—mentor, teacher, patron. Cornelius had been away for so much of Scipio's life that Calvus had filled that role whenever he could. Still, Scipio had craved his father's attention and approval through adolescence; but yearning turned to resentment and anger. He found the approval he needed in the roar of the crowd and love in the warm arms of his feminine conquests. When those failed to fill the void, there was always wine. Now his father seemed determined to pull him away from all those things that gave the slightest bit of comfort in some vain attempt to mold Scipio into his own likeness.

"I did what you asked," Scipio said. "I stood for office."

"And didn't make a single speech!"

Scipio stood with his hand over his chest, leaning toward his father, and said, "You know I never wanted anything to do with politics. Yet, you made me run."

"Because you owe it to—"

"I owe nothing!" Scipio said, raising his voice to his father for perhaps the second or third time in his memory. "Not to you, or Rome, or anyone!"

Cornelius drew a sharp breath of air. His eyes bulged from their sockets and his gaunt cheeks seemed to sink even more deeply. It tickled Scipio to see his father's entire bald head turn red.

"Selfish child!" Cornelius snarled. "This family has served the Republic for over two hundred years! I've spent *my life* in public service. But you... When have you ever served anyone other than yourself?"

Scipio plopped back down in his chair and cradled his cheek in his hand with his right elbow propped on his thigh. He decided against proffering any response and prepared to let his father go on for as long as he wanted, but, to his surprise, the next voice he heard belonged to one of the six burly lictors assigned to Cornelius for his year as Consul of the Republic.

"Excuse my interruption, Consul," he said, holding out the message. "Urgent."

Cornelius snatched the message from him. As he read it, his complexion turned from red to pale with frightening speed. Something serious was going on.

"Get the Magister," Cornelius told the lictor. "Have him call the Senate to session as soon as possible."

"Yes, Consul," the lictor answered and hurried away.

"We'll finish this later," Cornelius told Scipio as he started for the door.

"Father," Scipio called, standing up. "What is it?"

"Saguntum has been destroyed," he said. "We're going to

war."

VARRO

The austere main chamber of the *Curia Hostilia*, where the Roman Senate regularly met, was not where Gaius Terentius Varro preferred to speak. Rather, he loved the raised platform of the Rostra outside. It was there that his passionate loyalists among the common people of Rome would flock to hear his fiery diatribes. He loved to hear them hoot and holler when he denounced the "Hellenist" elites and urban intellectuals intent on turning Rome into an effeminate Greek city-state. They roared with laughter when he mimicked and mocked politicians, and they chanted his name when he promised to restore Rome to its former greatness.

As much as he basked in the ardor and approval of his fans, his popularity among the poorer plebeians wouldn't get him the ultimate prize—to be Consul. For that, he needed the approval of his colleagues in the Senate, which just happened to be the group of people he hated the most. Each year, the Senate approved the list of candidates for Consul to keep elites like themselves in power. Power kept turning over from one man to another, each looking, acting, and sounding as boring as the last.

Varro knew why they wanted to keep him from being a Consul. Oh, they had let him be Tribune of the Plebs—a position that dealt exclusively with the rights of the common people; and they'd allowed him to run for and occupy other offices whose lack of power and excess of responsibilities precluded his interest. But Consul? Never... and he knew well the reason why. They knew that he would outshine them all. He would be such an amazing leader that the people would demand he stay in office much longer than one year. He would so transform the position that anyone that followed him would be a pale shadow of Gaius Terentius Varro. Despite their opposition, the office *would* be his... As soon as he accumulated enough power to take it for himself.

The purpose of the Senate meeting was to decide on war with Carthage, and whether they could and should wage it. Varro was personally indifferent to the matter, but he knew he had to be in favor of it. Fighting was associated with manliness and virility, and though he'd never personally fought in one, he wanted to be associated with war wherever he could. But Varro's primary purpose was the same at every Senate session, and that was to accumulate power the same way he accumulated wealth. This included many tactics, the most crucial of which was making those who opposed him pay a high price for doing so. Today, he planned to take full advantage of the crisis with Carthage to defame the man that was currently highest on a long list of enemies: Cornelius. It was Cornelius and his allies that stood in the way of his ambitions by smearing him as a demagogue and a charlatan. It was Cornelius's reputation as a statesman and soldier that gave his voice weight, and so it was Cornelius he had to tear down and destroy.

Varro stood among his fellow senators and made sure to keep his eyes fixed on Cornelius, who was sitting in one of two chairs facing the assembled senators. The other was occupied by Tiberius Sempronius Longus, Cornelius's Co-Consul.

"Carthage attacks from the South while the Boii attack from the north," Varro said to his fellow senators. "You see how our enemies circle us like wolves? For wolves do not hunt the strongest of the herd. No! They hunt the feeble, the sick, and the weak! This is how they see Rome, thanks to our gutless Consuls!"

The room erupted in murmuring as the old Senate Magister banged his stick on the floor in a plead for order. Varro remained fixated on Cornelius's gaunt face. The Consul was aloof as always, not speaking until the chamber was quiet once more.

"Though I'm loath to contradict Senator Varro's assertion that I'm a weak weakling making Rome weak… " Cornelius began, eliciting laughter from many.

Varro shrugged, doing his best to appear as if Cornelius's mocking tone didn't faze him in the slightest. Inside, however, he was seething with rage. This was why, of all his enemies, he hated Cornelius most. Varro wanted Cornelius to shout back, insult him, attack him—*anything* but make a mockery of him. Laughter at his expense felt like thousands of barbs on the end of whips, scourging him to death.

"I believe we must fight," Cornelius said. "But I also believe we must fight as few as possible. That is why my colleague and I ask for more time for diplomacy. This is Hannibal's war. He alone is the aggressor. We may yet succeed in convincing Queen Adonica and her Ephors to disavow him, permitting us to narrow the conflict to Hispania."

"Ha! Now they ask for more diplomacy! Senators, this is not a matter to be settled by words! It is because of their words that our interests suffer," Varro said with a finger pointed at Cornelius and Sempronius. "It is because of these Consuls that the world no longer fears or respects us! Perhaps Cornelius is simply tired and lacks the fortitude that his office requires."

Many Senators in the *populares* faction laughed, and Varro took his seat feeling immensely satisfied. He was able to strike at Cornelius's virility and intelligence in one well-delivered line. *You see, Cornelius? You're the laughingstock, not Varro!*

There were no formal alliances in the senate; only loosely aligned groups that voted together on issues, or out of loyalty to an esteemed colleague. The political battle lines lately settled around the abstract but acutely felt issue of Rome's culture and identity. Varro drew most of his support from the *populares*, who were populists and conservatives opposed to the creeping influence of Greek and Etruscan philosophies and cultures.

"It is not a matter of will, but of resources," Cornelius said. "Legate Manlius Vulso is already heavily engaged with the Boii tribe in Cisalpine Gaul, and we've already committed to sending two more legions to relieve him at Mutina. We must raise at least eight more legions to fight Carthage in Hispania and Africa. We may have no choice but to fight Hannibal, but the conflict with the Boii is a self-inflicted wound. It was the Censor, Flaminius, that sponsored the bill to confiscate... "

Varro turned his attention to the leather *calceii* shoes on his feet. He lost interest the moment Cornelius went after Gaius Flaminius, a *populares*-aligned Senator who had been a Consul five years ago, and who was now a Censor.

Cornelius was saying something about how Flaminius bought votes by illegally taking land from the Samnites that the Boii tribe claimed and giving it to his supporters... or something like that. Varro didn't care. Neither, he thought, did the common people. They didn't understand any of these mundane details of law and diplomacy. The people wanted a story, one in which they were the heroes. Half of them thought that Cornelius was better than they were because he knew about these matters. The other half—Varro's half—knew that Cornelius only thought himself better because of his so-called learnedness.

Flaminius did a terrible job defending himself, so another member of the *populares* faction who was seated beside Varro,

Marcus Cato, rushed to change the subject by complaining about the allies not levying enough troops to support Rome's campaigns.

"Why must Rome shoulder so much of the burden for the defense of Italy?" Cato was saying. "Capua, in particular, has for too long ignored our requests for... "

Varro yawned and stared up at the ceiling of the chamber, forgetting for a moment to at least appear as if he were paying attention. He stared vacantly at Cato as he droned on.

He liked Cato... at least most of the time, even if he thought he was something of a phony. At twenty-seven, Cato was the youngest Senator, but he had already proven to be a talented soldier and an even better politician. When speaking to the public, he was a firebrand in Varro's mold. Inside these walls, however, he did his best to fit in with the elites he claimed to hate.

When Cato was finished and it was Cornelius's turn to speak, Varro's attention returned to the discussion.

"Perhaps the allies would be more willing to help if we extended full citizenship to them," Cornelius said. "The *lex Fabia* would do precisely this, and extend Latin rights to the tribes of Cisalpine Gau—"

That was enough! The idea of expanding the right of Roman citizenship to those people was so revolting that Varro felt as if Cornelius had forced something exceedingly bitter into his mouth.

He leaped to his feet and clutched at his toga.

"Disgrace!" he cried, pointing a short, pudgy finger at Cornelius. "You would pollute our citizenship with foreign blood and make Rome the capital of a polyglot empire! You would replace true Romans with barbarians beholden to you and your perverse vision of Rome's future!"

The room erupted in cheers and jeers, both of which Varro loved.

Citizenship was a prized status, and even those states open to immigration were often wary of giving it out too quickly to newcomers. The Latin states were, for the most part, peoples in Central and Southern Italy that Rome had subdued and integrated into its web of alliances. The elites in those societies were often granted or bought citizenship, but granting citizenship to all the free people in every Latin ally would more than double the number of Roman citizens. Most would likely not vote with the *populares*, whose nativist outlook had driven their opposition to expanding citizenship for decades. It would be a disaster for the *populares* and, by extension, for Varro.

The old Magister banged his walking stick on the floor once more. He had to be over ninety. Varro rolled his eyes. The old man was supposed to enforce the Senate's arcane procedural rules, which, for reasons no one seemed to know, were never written down. For this reason, the duty always fell upon the one who'd been in the Senate the longest, even if the man was as ancient as the pyramids. The more difficult it was to quiet the chamber after Varro spoke, the happier Varro was.

He was still waiting for the clamor to end when he heard Cato speak into his ear.

"A little less provocative," he said. "Remember, this is about the war. They want unity."

"Right, right..." Varro said, nodding in agreement, though he disagreed strongly. Unity did not serve his purposes, and so was useless. He simply couldn't afford to antagonize Cato until his own base of support in the Senate was firmer.

Cato pat him on the shoulder, and Varro sat down to let him speak.

"The *lex Fabia* is well-intentioned but misconceived," Cato said as the noise died down to a level over which he could speak. "It proposes to expand citizenship in the mistaken belief that it would mollify our allies, when all it would do is destroy what it means to be Roman."

Varro knew that Cato was playing his part. He was the moderate to Varro's extremist. In reality, both of them could probably be considered extreme by anyone familiar with the bounds of Roman political discourse; nevertheless, playing this game helped make what Cato said appear reasonable. It moved the conversation in their favor.

Cato continued, "Rome may have begun as a nation of immigrants, but it cannot remain one; lest we lose what makes us unique among the peoples of the world. Instead, let us take up the most excellently crafted bill introduced by our colleague, Gaius Oppius, Tribune of the Plebs."

Clever boy, Varro thought. The *lex Oppia* was a law that the *populares* had been trying to pass for a long time. It was meant to reassert the "proper roles" of men and women in society through restrictions on women's wealth, clothing, modes of travel, and right to divorce. It was a highly divisive topic, and therefore one that Varro loved with all his heart. So far, Cornelius and his faction, whom Cato had brilliantly branded "Hellenists," had resisted it; however, tying it to funding for the war took advantage of the political climate emphasizing so-called "unity." Still, he didn't want Cato to get all the credit for the *lex Oppia* gaining traction.

"The *lex Oppia*?" Sempronius sneered as Cato sat back down.

"Isn't this the bill where we take every drachma from every woman in Rome and make them all dress like farm slaves?"

"No one expects them to dress as farm slaves," Cato retorted, as several Senators chuckled at the imagery. "It would simply—"

"The *lex Oppia* wouldn't come close to financing this war if it lasts beyond a single campaign season," Sempronius said. "It would have no effect other than forcing women to transfer their wealth to their husbands or sons, not to mention making them shut-ins in their own country. Come now, Marcus! Surely we're past all this nonsense."

"It would restore the natural authority of men over their families," Cato insisted. "The way it had always been before our laws were changed to accommodate the petty indulgences of women."

"Hear! Hear!" Varro cried. "What is Rome coming to, when a woman does whatever she wants, without regard for the wishes of her father or husband? We all know how intemperate they are. Why should we—"

"What's the matter, Varro?" Sempronius interrupted. "Can't hold onto your wife, so you need to hold onto all her money instead?"

The Senate erupted in laughter, and Sempronius officially made it onto Varro's enemies list.

"I must remind this assembly that we have not yet voted on war with Carthage," Cornelius said. "Which I feel we must do before deciding how to finance it. Now... If there are no more remarks regarding—"

"With your permission, Consul," Varro heard the unmistakably gravelly voice of Aemilius Paullus say.

Varro groaned and flopped his head back with his eyes closed. Paullus was a reliably cautious voice, but it would be difficult for Varro to attack him as cowardly. He had fought in more campaigns than anyone in this room and was now one of the most respected elder statesmen in Rome. He had that magical quality of gravitas that orators the world over craved. Varro used to envy him for that, but he now knew that gravitas was nothing next to raw passion.

"In my life, I've fought in many of Rome's wars," Paullus said. "I see here many of those who fought alongside me, and so are unlikely to share in this... enthusiasm to begin another. We would be remiss to think that, if we decide to fight, we will win quickly or cheaply."

"But we would, Paullus," Varro assured him. "If I were leading Rome's armies."

"Take care of what you say, Senator Varro," Paullus replied. "War is a violent teacher. We must think long and hard before we commit ourselves to one. Passions run high at the start, and they often cause things to happen the wrong way around. Action comes first, and it is only when we've begun to suffer that we really begin to think."

The silence that fell like a heavy blanket over the chamber as Paullus finished and sat down was sobering, even for Varro. Glancing around, he could see that the other Senators either agreed with or were at least deferential to him. Varro once thought this was power, but then he realized it was only the shadow of power. True power lay not in credibility, prestige, or persuasiveness, but in fear. If Paullus had true power and wanted to stop the war from happening, everyone in that chamber, including Varro, would vote against it for fear of paying a terrible price for crossing him. What stopped them from contradicting him now was their sense of shame—that Paullus was a better man than they were. What gave Varro his advantage was that he had never known shame at all.

He stood up and looked around him.

"Who are we to abandon our allies?" Varro asked them. "What will the world see and think if we allow Saguntum to fall without so much as a Roman sword drawn in anger? Senators! I urge you now to vote for Rome, for honor, and for war!"

The room erupted in cheers, and Varro basked in them. He didn't allow his eyes to linger long on those who weren't cheering, but he would remember who they were. Like the rest of Rome, they needed to know the price they would pay for defying Gaius Terentius Varro.

SCIPIO

"Perfect," the servant told Scipio as he set the last fold in the toga.

The tailor had custom made it from the finest Egyptian cotton. The dye used to make the dark red border, indicating Scipio's status as a patrician noble, was imported from Tyre. It was made of the finest material the Mediterranean world had to offer. Scipio wished he could see himself in it as Aemilia and Paullus would, but the highly polished piece of silver he used to see his reflection wasn't large enough.

When he was finished preparing for his dinner at Senator Paullus' home on the other side of Palatine Hill, Scipio walked onto the mosaic tiles of the atrium floor toward the vestibule at the front of the house. The sounds of men speaking in his father's *tablinum* caught his attention.

Cornelius was a Consul preparing the opening campaign of a

major war. Any other Roman father in his position would have had his son with him at every opportunity, Scipio thought, to be a part of it and learn from firsthand. Hearing the voices from his father's study reminded Scipio of a time, not so many years ago, when he truly wanted to be at his father's side. It was what drew him toward the *tablinum* now, to catch a snippet of the conversation he was missing.

He didn't need to see his father's visitor to recognize him by voice. Senator Fabius Maximus Verrucosus had a distinct way of speaking that was far slower and more deliberate than other orators. A conservative critic of the new "Hellenist" urbanism, he was not politically aligned with his father; yet Fabius loomed so large as a victorious general and elder statesman that he seemed to transcend politics, and so was not governed by its laws.

"What did you think of their new queen?" he heard his father ask. "Adonica, is it?"

"Young," Fabius said. "But shrewd. Still... I saw the fear in her eyes."

"Her Ephors?"

Fabius grunted in reply.

"She isn't the problem," he said. "Two theaters, both outside Italy. Our soldiers may be under arms for years, away their farms, while their families accrue debts. Eventually, the smaller farmers will sell their land and slaves will work it. They move to the city, and when they can find no work and find themselves on the public dole..."

Scipio didn't linger long outside the door for fear of letting his father ruin his night.

When he stepped back into the atrium, he found his mother between him and the vestibule. Scipio was not close with his mother, nor did he desire to be. Pamponia had many of the qualities he sought to avoid in women. In public, she was the consummate aristocratic Roman woman—a socialite and excellent conversationalist, completely supportive of and subordinate to her husband. In private, however, she was frequently a nervous wreck, especially when his father was away. Her inability to do much of anything but remain in bed for long periods of time was one of his bitterest memories of youth.

"Tell me you won't go to fight this war," she pleaded.

In truth, he hadn't thought much of it. Now that the games were over, Aemilia had been the only thing on his mind. Though he had no desire to go and fight like Claudius did, he wouldn't tell his mother. He long ago made the decision to never allow her to influence his decisions. Her judgment was too clouded by myriad fears he did not share. Merely answering her would give her the impression that she had some influence over how he lived his life, so he said nothing as he stepped past her to leave.

"Your father loves you, Publius," she said.

He could count the number of people on one hand that called him "Publius" instead of his cognomen, Scipio. His mother was one, and it annoyed him.

"Don't patronize me, mother," he snapped. "I gave up trying to win his affection long ago."

"It's not his fault," she said.

"Well, I suppose it's mine, then," Scipio replied. "I could even live with that, if he'd only ever tell me why he's always hated me."

His mother looked at him with desperate sadness on her face, lips quivering as if on the verge of tears, but Scipio felt a cold mixture of pity and contempt.

She put her hand on Scipio's cheek and looked in his eyes.

"You were always such a sweet, shy little boy," she said. "Until... "

She trailed off, as if mentioning the death of his brother would force her to relive it.

"Believe me, mother," he said, taking her hand from his face. "I'm well aware of my failure to fill the void Lucius left in this family."

"I didn't say that," she objected. "What do you want from me, Publius?"

"To be left alone," he said. "You managed that well enough when I was young. Can you not now do the same?"

She looked at him in shocked silence for a moment, then her face hardened as she opened her mouth. Scipio braced himself for some biting reply, but a familiar voice called to him from the entrance of the house.

"*Ave*, Publius Cornelius *Juvenior*!"

Scipio didn't need to turn to know who it was. Only one person called him "Junior." He got his eye-rolling out of the way before turning around with a forced smile.

"*Ave*, Quintus Metellus," Scipio greeted his brother-in-law.

"My condolences on your election," Metellus said, approaching them. "Your sister and I are heartbroken, of course. Ah, Pamponia... You look splendid, as always."

He kissed his mother-in-law on the cheek.

"Thank you, Metellus," she said quietly.

"But why is my sister not here with you to heap derision on me?" Scipio asked. "Is she not well?"

"My dear brother-in-law, you have us wrong," Metellus told him. "In fact, we are saddened by these little follies of yours; if not for your sake, since you so clearly enjoy making a mockery of

29

your name and inheritance, then for the sake of your father, to whom your family and country owe so much."

He paused as if waiting for a reply, but Scipio decided not to give him the satisfaction of one.

"Cornelia is not here because I've come as Military Tribune, not as a son-in-law," Metellus said. "Several of us will be here to discuss the campaign against Carthage. You... are aware of the war with Carthage."

He nodded, holding his gaze. "I am."

"Metellus," Cornelius called from the tablinum. "Come. The others will be here soon."

"Yes, Consul," Metellus answered.

Scipio saw his father cast a scowl his way before disappearing inside. Standing next to Metellus must have made him seem even more mediocre to his father than usual. If Scipio had to draw the person that he imagined his father would have wanted for a son, it would be something like Metellus—tall, fit, and rugged-looking. In a uniform, he looked more like a marble statue of a demigod than a real person.

"Will you be joining us?" Metellus asked.

You damn well know I'm not.

"Sadly, I have a previous engagement," Scipio replied.

"Well... I wouldn't want to keep you. Better fortune, *Juvenior*."

Metellus turned toward the *tablinum* with a spring in his step.

***

Aemilia was talking, but Scipio was in his own head. *She has to say yes*, he thought. *Didn't she? No... she wants to say yes. She must want to say yes. Her lips are moving. Gods, I love her lips... What is she saying?*

"... I mean, it's bad enough that the divorce laws are still so unequal," Amelia was saying, though her points were barely registering with him. "But basically, confiscating the wealth of every free Roman woman? Can you imagine it? How can they call us citizens and even consider something so absolutely backward?"

"Um-hmm."

They were lounging in the *triclinium*, the formal dining area in Paullus's small but elegant home on Palatine Hill. Still waiting for the master of the house, they were drinking water and wine under the watchful eyes of the servants who, no doubt, would give Paullus a full report, especially if the young people got too comfortable with one another.

He went through the logic of it again in his mind. They were both upper-class patricians. Their fathers were political allies, even if not particularly friendly. She was only a few years younger than he. They had known each other for three years now... *She's going to say yes*, he thought. *Of course, she is going to say yes!*

The thoughts swirled around and repeated, but they did nothing to soothe him.

"... And this Varro character," she said. "Where did he even come from, anyway? Did you know he's the low-born son of a butcher?"

Scipio shook his head, trying to seem interested as his nervousness rose to a crescendo. He would soon be physically sick if he didn't ask.

"One day, no one's heard of him," she continued, "the next he's a Tribune of the Plebs, and now a Senator?"

"Let's get married."

She stopped abruptly and looked at him, frozen. He could

look at her face for hours, just gazing at her brown eyes, counting the freckles around her nose and cheeks that showed so much better when she stayed too long in the sun.

Finally, she dropped her head, and Scipio's heart sank in his chest.

"Scipio... " she began but hesitated.

"Am I that bad?" he asked. "Would I not make a good husband?"

She looked up at him again, and now he wondered if he had mistaken pity for love.

"You're the son of a Consul," she said. "You could have any woman in the city."

"I don't care about who I am in this city," Scipio told her. "If you would go with me, I'd leave Rome far behind us. We could start somewhere else, just you and me."

"Don't you see? That's part of the problem."

"What is?"

She took his hand comfortingly.

"I love you, Scipio," she said. "I do. But I love my family, and I love Rome. I could never leave them, not for anything... and it worries me that you could. Don't you have any attachments to this place, other than to me?"

He sat back, withdrawing his hand, but she reached out and took it again, looking him in the eyes.

"Scipio... " she called gently through the fog of his pain. "I know you feel like you've let people down—people important to you, and I know how much that must hurt. I know you'll do anything to avoid feeling that way again. But to love someone, to *really* love them, you must take the chance that you might disappoint them, that you'll hurt them, and that they'll hurt you."

He was trying to listen, if for no other reason than to rebut whatever reasons she had for rejecting him, but as she spoke, the reality that she had turned him down and that there was nothing he could do about it began to set it. His face burned and his lips quivered. He brought a hand to his brow and covered his eyes. He couldn't look at her, not now. He was far too ashamed.

"Do you—" she began, but another voice interrupted.

"My apologies," Paullus said, entering the room from the atrium. Scipio immediately leaped to his feet, gathering himself.

"Senator... " he greeted him with a slight bow, trying to avoid eye contact for the moment.

Aemilia greeted him in a much more leisurely manner, getting up and kissing her father on the cheek before he took his place on his *kline*—a couch large enough for a diner to recline and enjoy their meal. They made small talk as they ate, but he could barely look at her. The conversation inevitably turned to the topic on everyone's lips that day, the war with Carthage.

"Your father must have taught you much about war," Paullus said.

"Scipio is closer to his uncle, father," Aemilia interjected. It must have been, Scipio thought, her way of reminding him that it was a sensitive subject.

"The Consuls are levying another two legions each," Paullus said. "And an equal number of allies. Will you go with your father?"

"I don't know yet," Scipio replied.

Aemilia put a hand over her mouth, as if the idea that he might go came as a shock to her.

"Excuse me," she said and went off toward the private bedrooms.

It was an awkward situation. He'd never really been alone with Paullus, and now he was in the middle of a heavy conversation with him without Aemilia present. He tried to think of something—anything—to speak with him about. All he could really think about, however, was Aemilia.

"Don't look so down," Paullus told him between slurps of his fish stew. "You've lost a battle, not the war."

Scipio looked up at him, mouth agape.

"May I ask what—"

"My servants told me before I came in," he admitted.

"Of course," Scipio muttered.

"I thought you might ask soon enough," Paullus said, putting his stew down and wiping the remains from his goatee. "I'll be forthright, Scipio. I didn't forbid her from accepting your proposal, but I counseled against it."

"May I ask why?"

"Because you don't want it," Paullus told him.

Scipio was incredulous. Who was this old man to tell him what he wanted?

"You may believe you love Aemilia," Paullus went on. "You may believe you want to marry her, but you don't."

"Senator," Scipio began to confer respect before questioning him, "how do you... ?"

"Family," he said. "Responsibility."

They were just words, said with no context whatsoever; yet, Scipio found himself frowning at them. They were bitter... almost disagreeable.

"I... I... " Scipio stammered, but he didn't know how to respond.

"You're not ready," Paullus told him softly.

"Apologies," Aemilia said, returning to her *kline* with a female servant in tow. "What were the two of you talking about?"

"I was just extolling the virtue of duty to young Scipio," Paullus said with a wink.

"Oh gods, Scipio," she said. "I'm shocked you're still awake."

"No, we were, um... " Scipio said, before clearing his throat. He needed to buy some time to think. "We were just getting started. Please continue, Senator."

Paullus began talking about the first war with Carthage, about his decision to run for the office of Military Tribune and take command of soldiers headed to Sicily.

Scipio nodded along, though he wasn't really listening.

Family. Responsibility.

Why hadn't he associated those with wanting to be with Aemilia? He did love her, he knew; yet, the thought of having to take care of her, of their children, that they would depend upon him... It repelled him.

When he turned his attention to what Paullus was saying, Scipio saw a scar on the old man's right forearm. It was a slash, probably, from some enemy weapon long ago... or perhaps an arrow had grazed him. In any case, it made him wonder what Paullus thought of it all.

"What was it like?" Scipio asked. "War, I mean."

Paullus leaned on his pillow, looking contemplative.

"It's different for every man, I think," he said. "I saw some become monsters, others become martyrs, and still other something like heroes of old. But what I remember most was coming home. Nothing after that could be as it was before."

"What had changed?" Scipio prompted him.

Paullus took a drink of wine, and Scipio could almost see him coming back to the present in his mind. Finally, the old man put the cup down and looked up.

"I did," he said.

***

The planning session for the campaign to Hispania continued late into the night. Scipio returned home to find his mother had retired to her bedchamber while his father hosted his legates and tribunes, all of whom sounded half drunk.

Rather than suffer the humiliation of being left out of discussions, Scipio called a servant out to the *peristylium*, the house's colonnaded open-air garden. When all its oil lamps were lit, it made a decent nighttime range for both archery and javelins. Scipio favored the later for relieving the anger and frustration of having his proposal rejected. Paullus's words were also rattling around in his mind. *You're not ready... Family... Responsibility...* He needed to do something before trying to sleep.

He threw all five javelins at human-shaped cloth targets mounted on hay bales and missed with all five. As the servant retrieved them, Scipio heard the crunch of a sandal on the gravel that surfaced the garden's pathways.

"Who taught you to throw a javelin like that?" Calvus asked, stepping into the light.

"The way I've been throwing, I wouldn't be too proud of your instruction, Uncle."

"How was dinner with Senator Paullus and his lovely daughter?"

Scipio hurled a javelin at the target with an angry grunt. Calvus watched as it soared over the hay and hit the roof before dropping, taking some red tiles down in the process. It was a loud enough racket that the drunken laughter in the house died down a moment, but it soon resumed.

"That good, eh?" his uncle chided.

Scipio frowned at him before taking a second javelin.

"If I were a farmer's son," he said, "I could have whoever I wanted for a wife and no one would look twice. All her and the father would care about is that I have a hovel, a few crops, and a... pig, or something."

Calvus chuckled as Scipio threw the javelin, hitting the hay bale low and to the right.

"But you're not," Calvus reminded him. "You're a Cornelii, one of the great and ancient—"

"Great and ancient patrician houses of the Roman Republic," Scipio said, finishing his sentence. "Thank you, Uncle. I'd nearly forgotten. Want to tell me again how my great grandfather saved the city from the Etruscans?"

Scipio practiced his stance, shifting his weight back and forth between his back and front leg.

"What did he say?" his uncle asked.

"Nothing I haven't heard before from you and father," Scipio said.

"Well, perhaps that's because I spoke to him."

Scipio turned, nearly dropping his javelin.

"What?"

"He came to me," Calvus said.

"May I ask what it is that you said to him?"

Calvus stepped closer, and Scipio fought the urge to retreat. Calvus was the only man in his family he trusted. No matter what, he still needed his uncle.

"I know you better than anyone," Calvus told him. "I see how you react when you hear the word 'family.' It's as if the rock of Sisyphus just landed on you to carry for all time. You honestly believe you're ready to marry?"

Scipio might have been angry, but he was beginning to believe that Calvus was right. Even if she'd accepted, at some point in the future, perhaps not very long from now, the weight of being a *pater familias*—the head of a family, responsible for its success and failure, its life and death—would have crushed him.

"In the old days, we might not have cared," Calvus told him. "We'd have married you off to someone your family chose. But times are different."

Someone inside laughed especially hard, reminding Scipio that his father was in there, drinking and talking with his brother-in-law and other officers, plotting a war.

"We'll begin raising additional legions in the morning," Calvus told him.

"I thought you might," Scipio murmured, bringing his mind back to his javelin. He turned back toward his target and adjusted his grip.

"Join us for the Hispania campaign."

Scipio scoffed and shook his head without bothering to turn around.

"Does *he* want me to go?" he asked as he set his stance and threw again, grazing a target in the upper right corner.

"*I* want you to go," Calvus told him.

Scipio took the next javelin and held it upright like a walking stick. He hung his head in thought.

"No Carthaginian ever crossed me," he said, picked his head

up again and turning around. "No. I don't give a damn about the war."

"Don't give a damn about the war," Calvus told him. "Give a damn about me... and the others that have to fight it. Like it or not, you're an elite; and we can't ask other people to pay for Rome's wars unless we fight alongside them. And anyway, you're quite the talented soldier when you choose to be."

"Talented?" Scipio asked, holding out his hand to his sloppy javelin throws. "I think the Republic will survive without me."

"Perhaps," Calvus said. "You know, those lays you disdain, the ones about the Tarquin wars... "

"Where the hero kills a thousand enemies with a stroke of his sword? What of them?"

"You used to like them."

"I was a child," Scipio replied. "I didn't know how full of—"

"Our stories don't tell us about the past as much as they tell us about ourselves; our ideals, our hopes, our fears. If you behaved more like you shared in all of that, it might well sway Paullus's opinion of you... and his daughter's."

Scipio looked back at him in cautious hope. He still doubted he could do anything to affect his situation and change his fate, but Calvus seemed to believe he could.

"Look at it this way, then," Calvus said, glancing over his shoulder at the house. "Coming with us will annoy the hell out of your father."

Scipio smiled, turned, and hurled his javelin, hitting the target near dead center. Calvus laughed.

"You could throw like that every time, if you wanted to," he said.

"Sure," Scipio answered coyly with a shrug. "But then you'd

be disappointed when I miss, instead of happy when I don't."

Calvus ruffled Scipio's hair, beaming at him with pride the young man had never seen from his father. It was then, just for a fleeting moment in the lamplight, that he saw the flash of a white toga and what he thought was the back of his father's bald head disappearing into the house.

HANNIBAL

Hispania

Hannibal was already awake when his infant son began crying. The night air was comfortably cool. Late summer in Hispania had been brutally humid only weeks before, but now a soft midnight breeze wafted in from the ocean. He'd been sitting on a stool in his tent, watching his wife, Kara, enjoy the kind of peaceful sleep he couldn't enjoy. Her skin seemed to glow in the pale moonlight coming through the open flap.

If anything in this world is sacred, he thought, *this is.*

His son stirred in his crib, and she began to wake. He watched her pick up their baby and sit on the bed to feed him. Their son had just begun to suckle when she looked for him.

"Kara," he called to her, and she squinted in the moonlight at him.

"You should be resting," she said.

"I'm thinking too much."

"About what?"

He had promised to share everything with her—the joys, the victories, the suffering, and sorrow... She had held him to that vow, but things were beginning to change. Their life together had been romantic and adventurous. He took pains to never make her feel like she was something apart in his life, but he knew he had to begin pulling away from her now. Otherwise, he might never leave, and he had to.

She turned her head to look out at the night sky, revealing the long scar on her right cheek. It was the first thing Hannibal had noticed about her. She was a slave then. Now, she was the most powerful woman in the Iberian Peninsula. Kara was Celtiberian—the result of centuries of Celtic migrants from the north and native Iberians living together, blending their families and cultures until new and distinct tribes came into being. Her features were different than those from Africa, with whom he'd grown up. The Celtiberians women had all looked similar to him— pale and ragged. But the scar made her stand out from the other brothel slaves that were brought before him when he conquered the southern city of Gad. She was a survivor, and he recognized her as such right away. Fierce, strong, and willful; they had a connection that transcended their differences in language and culture, and it ignited a burning passion.

"The ships aren't coming, Kara," he told her.

"I don't understand," she said as he sat beside her.

How could he explain it to her? He barely understood it himself. Politics... He'd grown to hate that word. King Gisco had given him free rein in Hispania, but that was when Carthage had little to lose. Now his young daughter sat on the throne, and she was unwilling to risk the new empire she'd inherited. She wanted Hannibal in Hispania, to fill her coffers with silver from its mines, tribute from her wealthy new subjects, taxes from its ports, and proceeds from selling conquered tribesmen for slaves. Queen Adonica wanted Rome to come to Hannibal, and for Hannibal to defeat it in Hispania. She only saw what could be lost, and so was preoccupied with how to keep it. It blinded her, in Hannibal's view, to what could be won by fighting this war in Italy.

He scratched his bearded chin and said, "There are many who think we cannot defeat Rome."

"But not you," she said.

"I must show them they are wrong," he said, taking her free hand in his. "If I stay here and Rome sends an army, even if I destroy it, they will send another, and another, and another after that. I must take the fight to *them*, my love."

It was only in the last year he'd taught her to read a map and she'd learned where Italy was, and Hispania, for that matter.

"How?" she asked. "Without ships... "

"I will go over land," he told her, noting the confusion in her furrowed brow and open mouth. She must have heard Hannibal and his officers discuss it a dozen times. The coast of Gaul was full of Greek cities allied to Rome, and they would fight. It would give Rome time to muster its full resources and not only overwhelm Hannibal, but to invade Africa as well.

"Over land?" she gasped.

"There's more," he said. "Kara, I need you to stay in Hispania," he said.

Now her face turned from confusion to something closer to anger. He moved to the bed, but she scooted away from him.

"Haven't I always fought beside you, Hannibal?" she asked as little Hamilcar fussed. She stood to burp him. "You would abandon us here while... "

"I would never abandon you," he assured her. "But our son cannot make this journey."

That seemed to calm her a bit. Hannibal cradled one of their baby's chubby feet in his hand.

"I'll leave an army to garrison Hispania, under your

command," he said. "You'll have about thirty thousand men."

"What? Why?"

Hannibal reached over, pulled her back onto the bed so that she sat next to him with Hamilcar in her arms, and held her close.

"Some of the tribes are going to revolt when they see me take half my army out of Hispania," he said. "I need this place, Kara. The money for my soldiers no longer comes from Carthage. It comes from here. From New Carthage, the mines, the taxes... "

"Hannibal, I always knew that this was something you needed to do," she said. "You say if you do not destroy Rome, it will enslave the entire world. I know what it is to be a slave. I saw the ones who kept me in chains every day."

"What are you saying?"

"I love you," she said. "You are my life... my life, Hannibal. I'll support you, whatever you need to do. It's just... hard to hate something I've never seen and know almost nothing about. It makes it harder still to understand why you'd ever think of leaving us."

"I will come back to you," he said solemnly. "And if I don't... our son will still know me through you and the world I leave behind, free of the tyranny of Rome."

She got up and placed their sleeping son back in his cradle.

"How am I supposed to rule Hispania without you?" she asked him as they returned to bed.

"You know how," he said. "You've watched. You've learned. Keep the tribes divided against one another and dependent on you to protect them. You're smarter than you know, Kara; smarter than me. You can do this. I know you can."

It came down to trust, and he knew that his wife trusted him with as little reservation as she could tolerate. Her expression gradually softened into something like stoic acceptance. She turned and laid on her side with her back to him.

"I will do as you want," she said.

He turned her over on her back.

"I know you will," he said, rolling on top of her to make love. "I just hope my brothers say the same thing when I tell them tomorrow."

HASDRUBAL

The goat had made a good sacrifice. Hasdrubal had chosen it himself at a market in New Carthage, taken it with him, and cared for it for the entire campaign. Offering it to Baal and Tanit had been difficult, but he very much wanted to honor and please the gods. He needed no sign acknowledging their pleasure with his undertaking in return. He was certain they knew his heart, and they would reward his piety when they saw fit. After burning the fat, organs, and inedible parts on the alter, he gave the rest of the goat to the soldiers that had helped in the ceremony.

Aside from the fact that Hasdrubal was four inches taller and a bit broader than Hannibal, the two brothers could pass as twins. They shared the same dark complexion, curly hair, wide nose, and sharp deep-set brown eyes. Since they grew out their beards on campaign, they looked even more like each other, and their late father as well. Then there was their younger brother, Mago, who looked so different from both Hannibal and Hasdrubal that they often wondered if he shared the same father with them.

Hasdrubal caught his nine-year-old son, Mathos, a split second before he could enter his Mago's tent. Even among the sprawl of the enormous camp, Mago's dwelling was easy to spot.

It occupied prime real estate on the perimeter, equidistant from a latrine and a cooking area. It also had a purple ram's head banner posted outside. It was ostentatious, sloppy, and most unmilitary—perfectly suited to its owner.

"Where are you going, Mathos?" he asked, placing himself in front of his son.

"Uncle Hannibal wants to see you and Uncle Mago," his son told him.

"Where is he?"

Mathos pointed toward the command tent, which was perched on a hill with a view of what was left of Saguntum and its harbor. To Hasdrubal, it was a beautiful sight. The partially caved-in red-tiled rooves, the columns left without anything above them to support... the smoldering ruins that looked so much like he imagined Rome would look after this army razed it. Beyond it, the clear blue waters of the western Mediterranean— the sea that Carthage again would claim as its own.

Hasdrubal stroked his beard, thinking of how to explain away his brother's licentious behavior to his son. For all Mago's faults, he loved his nephew.

"I think your uncle is... sleeping," he said. "Why don't you go find us some water while I go wake him?"

"Father, it's late in the day," Mathos pointed out. "I don't think he would be—"

"Just get the water and wait here," his father told him. "Understood?"

His son nodded and left. Hasdrubal found Mago inside, busy at his favorite pastime—fornication. He was flat on his back on his bedroll while one of the many prostitutes that orbited the camp was on top of him and grinding away, moaning loudly.

"Good morning, brother!" Mago called to him cheerfully as the prostitute rode on, heedless of the intrusion.

"Hannibal needs to speak with us," Hasdrubal told him, taking a tunic from the tent floor and throwing it at his brother.

"What... now?"

"Now."

The prostitute rolled off him and collected her clothes as Mago groaned in annoyance. Hasdrubal left the tent and the prostitute soon followed a few minutes later, he assumed with her fee.

Soon after, Mago emerged in high spirits, shaking out his wavy locks of brown hair. He carried a cup with him, as he nearly always did. Before Hasdrubal could admonish him for his excessive lustiness, Mago called to his approaching nephew.

"Good morning, Mathos!"

"It's much past noon, uncle," Mathos pointed out, pouring water into his uncle's outstretched cup.

Mago sipped it and looked up in the sky, squinting against the beaming sunlight.

"It is," he agreed, and ruffled Mathos's hair. "Why am I drinking this, then? Why don't you see if you can find us some wine?"

"Leave my boy alone, Mago," Hasdrubal grumbled as he led them toward the command tent.

"Why?" Mago asked innocently, putting his arm around Mathos's lanky shoulders. "He has a lot to learn from me. Isn't that right, Mathos?"

"All he can learn from you is how to squander the gifts the gods have given him," Hasdrubal returned gruffly.

"Some gifts I use very well," Mago responded. "Or didn't you see back there?"

"I told you that this is a sacred mission. You besmirch it and our father's name with your petty indulgences."

Mago laughed off the admonishment and they walked on a moment in silence. Two war elephants passed them, going in the opposite direction. Hasdrubal loved to watch his son's eyes when he was near them, to see the awe and wonder that he used to feel as a boy when he saw these magnificent animals. When they were past, though, Mathos seemed pensive.

"Father?"

"Yes?"

"Is sleep an indulgence?"

Mago chuckled, eliciting a familiar glare from his older brother.

"As much as your uncle Mago sleeps, it is," he answered, which only made Mago laugh that much harder.

***

Hannibal's camp was a hive of soldiers, blacksmiths, carpenters, engineers, and cooks busy doing all the tasks that kept an army of over sixty thousand in the field and ready to fight. Thousands of merchants, slave traders, and prostitutes following it wherever it went around Hispania. Just outside the command tent, Hasdrubal found a dozen Carthaginian and Iberian officers gathered around a large rectangular table in the shade of an orange tree. He could sense the tension immediately in the serious expressions everyone wore. Hannibal and Kara were standing at the head of the table, directly opposite from where Mago took up his position.

"Hello, everyone," Mago greeted them. "Nice to see your smiling faces as always."

Hasdrubal heard a crunch as Mago bit into an apple. *Where the hell did he get an apple?* It was one of the dozens of things Mago did each day that perplexed him.

Hasdrubal looked at the map on the table and saw that it depicted the east coast of Hispania to New Carthage, the Pyrenees mountains, coastal and central Gaul, the Alps, and the Po River Valley in the region known as Cisalpine Gaul. It was much different than the entire map of Italy that included Sicily and Sardinia, which they'd been using to plan their invasion by sea.

"Thinking of summering in Gaul, are we?" Mago asked the assembly, his mouth full of fruit. "I wouldn't recommend it. Hairy, smelly beasts. And the men... "

"We're leaving Saguntum," Hannibal announced.

"May I ask why?" Mago asked.

"Adonica has denied my request for ships."

Hasdrubal fumed with anger. The ungrateful royal family had never understood this. He prayed the gods would reveal their plan to them, but they had not yet seen fit to do it.

"Excellent!" Mago said, holding his arms out as if expecting all to join his celebration. "Back to New Carthage, then?"

Mago's flippant attitude toward the venture added to Hasdrubal's annoyance; it was blasphemous.

"No, Mago," Hannibal replied. "We're going to Italy."

Yes, we are. Hannibal's words were reassuring. They took the sting out the news about not having the ships. Even if he didn't know Hannibal's plan, it was enough to know his resolve was intact despite the setback. Almost as satisfying was watching Mago's countenance fall.

"We're going to swim there, are we?" Mago sneered.

"We go by land," Hannibal said.

The alarmed murmuring began at once, and Hasdrubal's mood turned from annoyance and anger to elation. It was as audacious as it was brilliant, a plan only the gods could have inspired.

He heard Mago slam his goblet down on the table and turned to see his younger brother glaring at Hannibal.

"You smug, arrogant—"

"You watch your tongue!" Hasdrubal bellowed, but Mago remained unfazed.

Out of the corner of his eye, Hasdrubal saw Mathos take a step back. He turned to his son, who met his gaze with fear in his eyes. The water pitcher shook a little in his hands. He consciously softened his expression, trying to let the anger leave him. It was Mago's smile and a wink at his nephew, however, that elicited a small grin from Mathos. The gesture and its effect diminished Hasdrubal's anger with his brother, but the general tension around the table remained.

Hannibal's cavalry commander, Maharbal, finally spoke.

"General... Rome will send an army here," he said, pointing back toward the ruins of Saguntum. "We can beat them here."

Maharbal was the highest officer in the army outside the Barca brothers, in charge of both the Carthaginian cavalry and the far more numerous Numidian mercenary horsemen. It was a formidable task. In Carthage, it was said the Numidians were the closest things to centaurs left in the world, and that they were put on a horse as soon as they could walk. Naturally, then, the Numidians had balked at having a Carthaginian command them. It took the better part of four years and twice as many battles for Maharbal to win their respect, but he had emerged one of the finest cavalry officers in Carthaginian history.

"We can't destroy Rome from Hispania," Hannibal told them.

"General," Maharbal began, pointing to the map. "We've discussed this. The coast of Gaul is full of Greek cities allied with Rome. The delay alone would—"

"Not the coast," Hannibal interrupted, putting his finger on Saguntum and tracing the route as he spoke. "We move fast through Hispania into central Gaul, resupply here, at Vocantia, before we cross the Rhone... and go straight over the Alps."

He put his knuckles down on the Alps and looked up with a grin and gleam in his eye. Hasdrubal looked up in pure joy.

"It's brilliant," he said intensely, taking Hannibal by the arms and looking squarely at him. "You're the chosen one, brother."

He nodded to Kara, who was standing by her husband with her head held high and an expression that conveyed both pride and nervous anticipation.

"That's over seven hundred miles," Maharbal said, as if Hannibal didn't realize the distance, or needed it to be said aloud. "No one has ever taken an army this size through the Alps; and to make it that far before the snows close the passes, it's... impossible."

Hannibal pointed at him, as if Maharbal had confirmed the plan's soundness.

"The Romans think this as well," he said. "And that's exactly why it will work."

Hasdrubal looked around at the faces and saw apprehension. Men whispered to one another, looked at the map, and rubbed their chins. He was ready to pounce on any doubts or dissension. It seemed they were content to keep whatever negative feelings they had to themselves, all except Mago, who laughed bitterly.

"Will the gods change the weather, brother?" he asked. "Or

maybe they'll just... part the mountains for you."

"Why do you talk to him this way?" Kara asked Mago.

"Four years," Mago said, seething. "Four years we've been fighting in Hispania. For what?"

"You'd have nothing if it weren't for Hannibal!" Kara barked.

"Nothing? Kara, I would have a soft bed, a woman in it, some decent wine... If it weren't for Hannibal, I'd have *everything*!"

"I've heard enough of your whining and sacrilege," Hasdrubal said, stepping closer and looming over Mago. "Let him go home, Hannibal. We'd be better off without him."

"Yes," Mago agreed. "And let me take Mathos as well, because a boy shouldn't be growing up in a camp full of filthy mercenaries!"

"Everything we've done has been for this," Hannibal told him, pointing to the map. "Can't you feel it? If we don't do this, and do it now, all this will have been for nothing. This is our chance. This... this is destiny."

"Destiny?" Mago spat. "Freezing and starving to death on some mountain in Gaul? We've spent years rebuilding the Empire, and now you're going to jeopardize all that for this... this sick obsession with Rome!"

"Do the oaths we took before the gods mean nothing to you?" Hasdrubal asked Mago. "Oaths sealed with the blood of your own father!"

"The oath I took when I was *five*?" Mago shot back. "That oath, brother?"

"General... " Maharbal said calmly. "Please reconsider this. There is no way... "

Hannibal turned his head and snapped, "We will *find* a way!"

A silence swept the room, and everywhere within earshot of

the tent. Hannibal's eyes went from Maharbal to each of the other officers around the table, one by one.

"We will either find a way, or we will make one!"

He punctuated the vow by pounding the Alps with a clenched fist, as if beating their image would flatten the mountains.

"Is that understood?" he asked them.

"Yes, General!" Maharbal and the other officers answered dutifully.

Mago scoffed and began backing away from Hasdrubal. He pointed an accusatory finger at Hannibal.

"You're insane," he said.

Hasdrubal grabbed him by the arm, but Mago angrily shook off his grip and stormed off.

"I'll talk to him," Hannibal told Hasdrubal. "I need you to do something."

"Yes, brother."

"Take Maharbal and anyone else you need. Clear the way for us through Gaul as much as possible. Bribe the rulers in Massilia. We can't afford having them tell the Romans we're in Gaul. Whatever the price they ask, pay it. And we'll need reinforcements, as many Gauls as you can get."

"They'll flock to you," Hasdrubal promised.

"Most important," Hannibal told him. "There are no bridges across the Rhone. Find a way across that won't take us too far north."

"I will."

Hannibal took his brother's face in his hands and pressed his forehead to his.

"Baal and Tanit protect you," he said.

"And you, brother," Hasdrubal returned.

Hannibal repeated the ritual with Mathos, adding, "Take care of your father."

"I will, uncle," Mathos assured him.

MAGO

Mago returned to his tent and sat, waiting for his anger to pass, but he was restless. Soon he was up and out, roaming the camp with no destination in mind, drinking from his wineskin. Eventually, he found himself near Hasdrubal's tent, though he wasn't sure why his legs had carried him there instead of to one of the brothels he frequented. He wanted his brother to come out, he supposed, so he could smack him right in his self-righteous face.

It was Mathos, however, that emerged with luggage to load onto a cart bound for Gaul. His nephew had somehow remained a kind-hearted and loving boy despite all the cruelty and violence he'd seen. Mago didn't want to wait for his brother to beat that decency out of him and replace it with some mindless religious fervor.

"Mathos... " he called to the boy, and his nephew came over with a cheerful smile.

"I shall miss you, Uncle," Mathos said. "Or... Will you come with us to Gaul?"

Mago squatted to be at eye-level with the boy but ending up a bit lower. He looked up at him, squinting in the sun.

"You have hair the color of wheat," Mago told him. "Like your mother."

It always seemed to please Mathos to hear of his mother,

who died during his delivery.

"Was she very beautiful, like my father says?" he asked.

"She was," Mago answered, nodding. "It was the one thing your father and I agreed on."

They shared a chuckle.

"Listen," Mago said. "You should ask your father to send you back to Carthage for your education. I don't think he'd refuse if you were the one to ask."

His nephew furrowed his brow.

"Why would I do that?" he asked. "I go wherever father goes."

Mago looked into the boy's naïve and trusting eyes, trying to formulate an answer he would understand.

"Eventually, a man must stop following his father and find his own path. Do you understand?"

"Why?"

"Because... because... " Mago struggled, sighed, and shook his head. More sober, he might have had the patience to formulate a response, but presently, it was useless.

"Just... Take care of yourself," Mago finally said. "We'll talk again in Gaul, yes?"

Mathos nodded, and Mago brought his forehead to his nephew's.

"Baal and Tanit protect you, Uncle," Mathos said.

"And you," Mago said, turning to go refill his wineskin.
***

"Imagine my dilemma, Mago... " Mago heard his approaching brother say.

"Gods, Hannibal... "

Mago filled his cup from his wineskin. He was sitting on a rock planted in the ground near a cliff overlooking the ocean, about two hundred yards from the edge of the camp. He enjoyed sitting here alone, watching and listening to the waves crash against the rocks below. Evidently, Hannibal knew that as well.

"One of my best commanders happens to be my brother."

"Where is he, then?"

"I'm speaking of you."

"Well, I learned from the best, didn't I?" Mago replied, raising his cup in a mocking toast. "To you, brother."

"The problem is you're only worth a damn when you're sober, which is for precisely one-quarter of every day."

"I'm working on cutting that down to an eighth."

Hannibal snatched the wineskin from him. Mago was surprised to see him take a large swig of it himself.

"Bit out of character for you," he said. "Kara must not be entirely happy with this little plan or yours, I take it."

"You don't think it will work."

"I know it won't work," Mago replied.

"Tell me why, then."

Mago took a breath. *Why bother?* he thought. Once Hannibal was set on something, nothing had been known to change his mind. If he managed to talk sense into Hannibal and rethink this march to oblivion, he'd just be delaying the inevitable. Hannibal was going to Italy. Now, in the spring, five years from now... It didn't matter. He knew it was futile, but if nothing else, perhaps challenging the plan would cause Hannibal to reconsider every part of it, challenge his assumptions, and make some adjustments.

"How many men?" Mago asked.

"Total about forty thousand," Hannibal replied. "We'll have to subdue the tribes north of the Ebro River to protect our supply lines, leave another thirty-thousand here; and we'll hire another few thousand Gauls."

"It's simple," Mago said. "We can't keep forty thousand men fed for an entire campaign season without ships and supplies from Carthage. Resupplying from here, assuming the northern tribes don't kill all the men we leave behind, will take months."

"We'll make allies in Italy," Hannibal said, eliciting a bitter laugh from his younger brother. "The Romans treat them like dogs. They've only to see that Rome can be beaten, and they'll defect."

"Oh... Now we're liberators, are we?"

"We are whatever we need to be to divide Rome from its allies," Hannibal said.

"Right. Perhaps those Gauls we recruit can scream 'we come in peace' on our way down from the mountains."

"They'll have a simple choice," Hannibal said testily. "Be with us or against us."

"Hannibal destroys your city now, or Rome destroys it later. That choice?" Mago looked off in the direction of Saguntum. "Didn't turn out so well for those poor wretches, did it?" he quipped.

Hannibal followed his gaze to the ruins. To Mago's astonishment and horror, he then proceeded to pour the remaining contents of the wineskin onto the ground.

"Politics may decide the war as much as fighting, and you have a good mind for it," Hannibal said, tossing the empty wineskin back to his brother. "That is why I need you sober."

"And what on earth makes you think I'm coming with you?"

Mago demanded. "I'm not one of your true believers."

"You'll go, Mago," Hannibal said confidently, stepping closer to him. "You'll go because you're my brother, and I need you."

He clapped Mago on his shoulder before making his way toward camp.

"You can only draw water from that well so many times, Hannibal."

"I know," Hannibal called back a moment before a war elephant trumpeted loudly.

"Or perhaps I'll just stay here and look after the elephants," Mago mused loudly.

"They're going!" Hannibal yelled.

"Through the Alps?"

"Yes!

"Bu—Well, I hope they taste good!" he shouted at his brothers back.

He cursed his entire family under his breath before hurling his empty cup toward the sea.

Aemilia

"What on earth... ?" Aemilia uttered as she and her friend, Servillia, approached the Forum.

The two women had gone to the port city of Ostia together before the two Consular armies sailed for Hispania and Sicily. Aemilia hadn't intended to go, but she'd received a letter from Scipio asking to see her. Thankfully, her friend Servillia needed to see off her betrothed, whom she'd only just met a few days before, and was able to go with her.

The commotion they found in the Forum upon their return

was, like nearly all public gatherings, a mostly male affair. Women were allowed, but most were too busy running households and raising children to attend public spectacles. Aemilia's and Servillia's servants went ahead of them, making a path for the two noblewomen through the mass of people as much as they could, while several of the mostly low-born plebeian men gave them suspicious or outright hostile glares. On the Rostrum stood the Pontifex Maximus himself, resplendent in gray ceremonial robes. He looked more like a bystander, however, than the high priest of the state. He stood aside looking dignified, but his silence spoke volumes. He was powerless.

Marcus Cato was standing in front of him, grimacing, holding out his hands to the mob. He was the one who Aemilia thought was in control, if anyone was.

"Over here!" Servillia said, pulling her by the hand toward the temple of Saturn.

They climbed the first steps to a landing crowded with people shouting epithets, curses, and shrill denouncements at the Rostrum.

Whore! Kill her! Cut her throat! Slut! Justice demands it!

"It's a Vestal," Servillia said.

With her servant's help, Aemilia pushed her way up higher. She stood on her tiptoes, but she could only see the bowed head of a woman kneeling on the Rostrum in front of Cato. She would not have been able to discern if it were a man or woman had the women not worn the gleaming white robes of the Vestal Virgins. Her hood obscured her face.

"What did she do?" Aemilia asked Servillia.

"It could only be one of two things," Servillia said as Cato tried to quieten the crowd.

"Romans! Romans!" he shouted, and the demands for the blood of the young woman before them subsided for the moment.

Aemilia could see, however, that their appetite for violence hadn't diminished. Their scowls and snarls remained on their faces. None of them, Aemilia thought, knew this girl personally. How was it that their hatred could burn so bright?

"This woman took an oath to tend the sacred flame of Vesta—a task vital to the security and future of our Republic! Yet she chose to betray Rome, and the gods of Rome, for a few fleeting moments of carnal pleasure!"

The crowd erupted in anger once more, and Aemilia was fearful for the girl. Cato was pouring hatred into the crowd like mud into a pigsty, and the mob was wallowing in it.

"This is pathetic," Servillia leaned over and said to Aemilia.

"Why are they doing this?" Aemilia asked.

"Are the gods punishing us for her crimes, and the crimes of the Vestal Virgin Floronia?" Cato asked, and the crowd answered predictably with howls for her blood. "Certainly! But what made these two Vestals forget their place? For Vesta is the goddess of the home and hearth, and we fail to honor her when we allow women to behave as men! To waste the wealth of the nation on luxuries from the East; to speak at our assemblies; to petition the courts in defiance of their husbands and fathers! We must look at ourselves, at what is happening to our Roman culture and traditions! We've allowed foreign ways to pollute our ways and degrade our race! This, friends, is what has angered the gods!"

As the crowd erupted, spewing more venom at the Vestal, Aemilia stepped closer, trying in vain to get a better look.

"They're going to bury her alive," Servillia said quietly. Aemilia knew that was the penalty, but it hadn't actually been done in over a century.

"Her crimes," Cato went on, "should remind us all that a moment of weakness, a single moment of losing our Roman austerity and giving in to the licentious, effeminate ways of the East..."

As he was speaking, the kneeling Vestal picked her head up, apparently determined to hang it in shame no longer. It was then that Aemilia recognized the porcelain cheek, fair brow, and graceful neckline she had known so well throughout her childhood. They belonged to her cousin, Opimia.

Aemilia felt frozen in place. She turned her head as her eyes darted in every direction, searching the crowd for Opimia's father or her own... anyone with the influence to speak to the crowd and talk them down, but they were nowhere to be found.

"Aemilia," Servillia called to her, seeming far away. "Aemilia!"

She stopped scanning the crowd and turned her head to see Servillia's face close to her own. It had to be, just to be heard over the murderous roars of the mob.

"She's my cousin," Aemilia told her.

"Gods... " Servillia gasped and wrapped her arm around her friend's shoulders.

On the stage, Opimia stared past the crowd to the temple of Vesta beyond, where her Vestal sisters watched in horror. Her expression betrayed neither fear nor remorse. Aemilia remembered Opimia before she had left for the College of the Vestals—the virgin priestesses that kept the sacred hearth fire of the city alight. Should it ever go out, tradition held, the city would fall. Opimia had been the pride of the family for having been selected for such duty. She'd been just a girl then, but while she was only a few years older now, it was no girl Aemilia saw on stage. It was a woman, and a brave one, that refused to give the crowd the satisfaction of believing their condemnations were earned. She would meet her fate with her head held high, proud and unafraid, if doomed.

"Let's go," Servillia said into her ear. "We don't want to see this, Aemilia. Come on."

"No... " Aemilia replied, eyes fixed on her cousin.

"What?"

"I have to stop this."

She followed her servant, who made a way through the angry, screaming Romans between her and the Rostrum. She hadn't made it half the distance when Servillia's slave caught up to her.

"Are you out of your mind?" Servillia demanded, but Aemilia ignored her and tried to continue. Servillia grabbed her wrist and held her back.

"Let me go!" Aemilia cried, trying to break free from her grip.

"Listen to them!" Servillia implored her friend. "You think you can reason with this? They'll just kill us as well."

"This is madness!" Aemilia cried, pointing to the Rostrum. "Cato has whipped up this mob just as the Consuls and half the other magistrates have left the city. There's no one here to stop them because they've all gone to war!"

"There's nothing you can do, Aemilia!" she told her. "Understand me? *Nothing*."

Aemilia noticed then that she'd been trembling, though for how long she had no idea. As Cato went on about the degenerate state of society, she found herself bursting into tears. Servillia held her friend close as their slaves looked around them nervously. It felt as if the crowd could close in at any moment and swallow them whole.

"Come... " Servillia said, wiping the tears from Aemilia's face.

She looked back once more as they made their way toward Palatine Hill, but her cousin was no longer in sight. On the walk home, her grief soon turned into anger. She'd wanted so badly to bound up the Rostrum and unleash a diatribe that she was somehow sure would silence and shame both Cato and this vulgar crowd, but as the anger faded enough for rational thought to return, she realized Servillia was right. Nothing she could have said or done would have changed Opimia's fate. She had to make her father see what kind of danger Cato and his ilk, under the banner of populism, posed to the rule of law; and if he wouldn't listen, she would find people who would. She was too late to save her cousin, but she would do everything in her power to ensure something like this never happened to anyone else.

SCIPIO

Scipio was seasick, as were so many other soldiers sitting in the bellies of his father's ships. He was riding with his fellow *equites*, which meant a slightly more comfortable and roomier ship. It also meant their horses went with them. In the open air was one thing, but trapped in the confines of the lower deck, the smell of even well-kept horses and their manure made his nausea much worse. The flies were constantly heard, sometimes seen, frequently felt, and rarely killed. The sweaty, nauseated men swatted at them listlessly.

Just days before, Aemilia was one of the thousands that had come to say goodbye to the men in Cornelius's Consular army, which altogether numbered around sixteen thousand, half-

Roman and half-allied. In the months between marshaling and now, Scipio had seen her for only a few precious hours. In a way, it was a relief. The sting of her rejection was still fresh in his mind, and the training had focused his attention on something other than her. Seeing her at Ostia, however, brought all the feelings rushing back.

"How long will you be gone?" she'd asked.

"A year," he'd answered. "Perhaps a little longer. You'll probably be married by the time I return."

"Me?" she'd laughed. "Your father's probably going to marry you to some tribal chieftain's daughter to seal an alliance."

Her teasing had made him smile, but it hadn't assuaged his melancholy. She'd put both hands on his chest plate and looked him in the eyes.

"It's not this armor that separates us," she'd told him.

Those words echoed in his ears as they boarded the ships. He hadn't needed to ask her what she meant. Now he tried to think of the sound of her voice, to summon it up from memory... Anything to get his mind off his nausea.

"Gods, why have we stopped?" Scipio moaned, looking out the hole for the oar handle at the Corsican coast. It hadn't moved in some time.

He envied Claudius, who was sleeping fitfully next to him. His snoring was horrendous, causing the other *equites* to wake him up every so often so they could at least try to sleep themselves.

"Claudius... " he called, but his friend snored on. He shook him and called louder, "Claudius!"

"Huh?" he groaned, his head jerking upright.

"How can you sleep?" Scipio asked.

Claudius sat up groggily and yawned.

"How're your stomachs holding up, boys?" Scipio heard a man ask loudly from the stairs leading to the main deck.

He looked over to see the voice belonged to a friend he'd known since they were in Grammaticus together, learning advanced mathematics, poetry, and rhetoric. Lars Herminius Aquilinus was one of the few fellow patricians that Scipio could stand. Most noblemen played the dutiful Roman, but Lars actually was the part. Scipio had never met anyone else that could be both ambitious and unselfish. Somehow, Lars seemed to pull it off.

"Scipio! Claudius!" Lars called to them as he made his way between the seasick men.

They stood to greet him. Lars was their *Decurion*—a junior officer in charge of a ten-strong cavalry troop.

"Sit, sit... " he said, planting himself down next to them.

"What are you doing down here with the rank and file, sir?" Claudius asked.

"Ha! You think I'm a snob, is that it?" Lars asked. "Don't make me have you flogged, soldier."

"We're still not moving," Claudius said, looking out the oar hole. "Maybe the augers are keeping us."

The augers were priests that divined the will of the gods through the actions of birds. Consuls were either augers themselves or remained in constant consultation with them on campaign.

"My father would never let a priest hold him back," Scipio assured him.

"He sounds like my father," Claudius said.

The reference to his friend's long-dead parent piqued Scipio's interest and momentarily distracted him from his nausea.

"You never talk about him," he said.

"Because I barely knew him," Claudius said with a yawn, sitting back and closing his eyes.

"Doesn't your family talk about him?" Lars asked.

"Whispers," he replied before opening his eyes and staring blankly into space. "Except my mother, who tells me only what a failure he was and how he brought shame on the family name."

"Sounds... harsh," Lars offered.

Claudius laughed bitterly and said, "You don't know the half of it. Here... she gave me this at Ostia."

He produced a dagger from a sheath on his belt and handed it to Scipio. The polished steel blade shone brightly even in the dark confines of the ship. It was exquisitely crafted, probably sharper than the swords they carried. A fine weapon. He heard Lars whistle, obviously impressed.

"A little odd for a mother's gift," Scipio said, handing it to Lars for inspection. "But nicely made."

"Read the inscription on the blade," Claudius told him, handing his friend the hilt.

Lars held it up, trying to get more light, and Scipio saw the words on the blade. The inscription was in an older Greek dialect than that which was presently spoken, but Scipio could discern the meaning. *Η ΤΑΝ Η ΕΠΙ ΤΑΣ.*

"Return with your shield... or on it? Is that right?"

"Something the women of Sparta used to say to their husbands and sons going off to war," Claudius explained. "They used their shields as stretchers for the wounded and dead, apparently."

"Whoa... " Lars gasped, his eyebrows raised, creasing his forehead. "Tough old bird, isn't she?"

"That's my mother," Claudius sighed, returning the dagger to its place. "She'll redeem my name even if it kills me. So here I am."

"Here we are," Scipio rejoined, looking around their dank, humid space.

Scipio had been vaguely aware of the issue. Claudius's father had been a Consul in the first war with Carthage. Several men in his family had served under him, and they all said vaguely positive things about him. Still, a battle had been lost, and Claudius's father had shouldered the blame for it. Fair or not, it was the way of things.

"Foolish of me, isn't it?" Claudius asked.

"No," Scipio finally said. "At least, no more foolish than being here to impress a girl."

Claudius and Lars laughed, and Scipio smiled as he heard himself describe his own absurd situation, but he quickly turned serious again.

"Or my own father, for that matter," he said.

Claudius smiled wryly and patted Scipio on the back.

"Speaking of which... " Lars said, standing up. "The Consul sent me here for you... both of you."

***

For his part, Scipio was surprised to find himself aboard the flagship on one of the first days of the campaign along with Lars, his father, uncle, brother-in-law, and Claudius. Even more surprising was the sight of a disheveled civilian lounging on deck drinking wine. Lars, Claudius, and Scipio saluted Cornelius, who quickly pulled Scipio and Claudius aside.

"I have a rather... delicate mission," Cornelius told them. "I need men who I trust can be discreet, and who can speak Greek fluently. You two fit the bill. Are you ready to do your duty?"

"Yes, sir," they both answered.

Cornelius indicated the shabby civilian and said, "This pirate..."

"Smuggler, sir," the man interjected. "Call me Tybal."

"Tybal... claims that a large Carthaginian army is in Gaul. If that's true, we're headed in the wrong direction."

"How does he know this?" Claudius asked.

"Hannibal's own brother was in Massilia," Tybal explained. "Stirring up Greek veterans and the beards to join up with him."

"Beards?" Lars asked.

"Gauls," Tybal replied. "Hundreds of them. Maybe thousands by now."

"What was this man's name?" Scipio challenged.

"Hasdrubal," Tybal answered immediately. "Nice enough guy. Had his little boy with him."

"It could still be deception," Scipio suggested. "A Carthaginian trick to have us chase our tails around Gaul."

"Decep—I'm an honest man, sir!" Tybal objected, taking a swig of his wine.

"You're here selling us information," Calvus said. "Is Carthaginian gold less valuable to you than ours?"

Tybal mulled it over a long moment, as if the thought of playing both sides had never occurred to him. Finally, he shrugged.

"Fair enough," he conceded breezily, his feigned indignation gone.

Cornelius looked at Lars.

"Map," he ordered.

Lars immediately unrolled a map of Hispania, southern Gaul, Corsica, and the northwestern Italian coast.

"Your mission is to locate the main body of Hannibal's army, if it's in Gaul, and its route of march. Get some sense of their size and disposition. If you can, find out about this business of recruiting Gauls into their army. Now, Massilia... " He pointed to the city, located on the coast, east of where the Rhone River joined the sea. "... is an ally of Rome."

"Then why didn't they send word about a massive Carthaginian army coming its way?" Scipio asked.

"Precisely," Cornelius told him, nodding.

The nod from his father, though slight, seemed unforced. Scipio found himself flushed with pride and energy, ready to carry out this mission no matter the odds, and he chastised himself for being foolish. It was just a nod. It didn't change anything between them.

"You'll need to go covertly, as Greek merchants," Cornelius said.

"How much time do we have?" Scipio asked.

"Two days," Cornelius answered. "I'll keep the fleet beyond the horizon until the second night, then bring it in toward the city. You'll have to meet us as far out at sea as you can."

"If he's there, we'll find him," Scipio said confidently.

"Look near sources of fresh water," Cornelius advised them. "Rivers and springs. Armies on the march are thirsty beasts. Hannibal will likely have elephants with him as well. The noise and the dust they kick up should make them easy to spot, so don't get closer than necessary."

Cornelius stepped back and looked at his son and Claudius.

"Now, both of you," he said. "Good luck."

It was the sort of briefing any commander would have given his scouts for a reconnaissance mission. Go here, collect this information, come back by this time and report. But this was anything but a standard mission to Scipio. His father had charged him with gathering information that could drastically affect the war and, by extension, Cornelius's reputation for military prowess. He thought he'd given up caring about his father's lack of affection or respect. He knew this mission wouldn't undo more than a decade of enmity between them, but still, if he did this well, maybe the next decade could be different.

***

They waited until dark, then changed out of their uniforms and into simple tunics before setting off in Tybal's small ship. Luckily, it was a clear night with no rain or wind with which to contend. Under a blanket of stars, they rowed toward what seemed to be a crack in the looming cliff wall.

"We're going in there?" Scipio asked Tybal.

"That's a *calanque*," Tybal told him "Too narrow for ships like yours. But for us... " He completed the thought with a smile that showed several gaps in his line of teeth.

When they got closer, Scipio could see their destination more clearly by the light of the moon and stars. It was a narrow inlet with steep walls of white—probably limestone, he thought.

As they rowed past the rocks that marked the entrance to the inlet, the walls seemed to grow narrower, threatening to crush them like an intruding insect. Scipio looked back to the Roman fleet as waves made the boat rise and fall. He gulped, wishing in that moment for the security of being with thousands of his fellow soldiers on warships rather than bobbing up and down as Tybal barely steered them clear of treacherous rocks. Finally, they set the anchor, took their bags, and waded ashore.

In the dark, they began the treacherous trek to the top, from where they hoped to slip into Massilia unnoticed. Looking up in the darkness at the imposing climb ahead, Scipio took his comet pendant out from under his tunic, kissed it, and put it back. Although not vertical, the rocky incline was steep and treacherous. They made their way up slowly, using their hands to pull and steady themselves when necessary. Tybal led, claiming to have done this several times before, followed by Scipio and then Claudius.

Nearly halfway up, Scipio heard some rocks tumble behind him. He looked back to see Claudius holding onto a rock and trying to get his footing.

"Claudius... " he called to him.

Claudius nodded to him, panting.

They had barely resumed the ascent when Scipio heard more rocks tumbling, but louder. He looked back again to see Claudius tumbling down, desperately trying to grasp something to arrest his fall. He watched, horrified, as his tumbled off a rock and out of his sight.

Scipio scrambled down faster than he knew he should. Near the place where he'd seen Claudius tumbling down, he lost his footing. He grasped wildly for anything to hold on to, but the vegetation slipped through his fingers. He saw something bigger out of the corner of his right eye and flung himself at it with all the energy he could muster, hoping it was solid. He hit a young tree hard, banging his right shoulder against it, but he managed to hug it and arrest his fall. He took a breath before he looked around to his left for Claudius. He was nowhere in sight.

"Scipio... "

He looked down see Claudius at his feet, hanging on to the rock on which he was standing, with both hands. Scipio hooked his arm around the tree and dropped to his knees just as Claudius let go with his left hand. He reached out for Claudius's the moment his friend's grip on the rock gave way and caught his right wrist. All thoughts of anything but holding onto it soon faded to nothing.

"Pull!" he called.

Claudius reached up, grabbed the ledge, and pulled.

Scipio felt his left forearm beginning to shake as it strained against the tree. Claudius scrambled to get a foot on the ledge, but he missed. He tried again and missed a second time. Scipio's grip on his friend's wrist began to give.

He didn't know which god to thank afterward, but somehow, Scipio was able to tighten his grips on both the strap and Claudius, and then pull both with all his strength. Claudius got his foot onto the ledge, pulled himself up, and grabbed another tree. Afterward, they laid on their backs, both exhausted and panting.

"Thank you, brother," Claudius said eventually.

It was the first time Claudius had called him "brother." In the midst of everything, such a simple thing nearly brought Scipio to tears; but he sniffed them back, smiled, and patted Claudius's hand.

The pain came over him all at once. His chest, arms, and shoulders were on fire, and he was almost certain he wouldn't be able to move.

"Where's our pirate?" Claudius asked.

Wincing, Scipio shook his head. When he rested his hand on his own chest, the familiar feeling of the comet talisman sitting between his pectorals was not there. He felt around his chest for it, then felt for the leather strap around his neck to no avail. He cursed and rummaged around in the dark.

"What?" Claudius asked.

"My talisman... " he said, shoving aside stones and grass, looking desperately. "Help me!"

"I'm sure it must be... "

"Just look for it!" Scipio snapped.

The two men fumbled in the dark, crawling on all fours.

"I'll get you a new one," Claudius told him.

"I don't want a new one, Claudius! I—"

A glint in the moonlight caught his eye. He scampered over to it, cleared away the dirt and leaves... and there it was, the leather strap still present but broken. He breathed a deep sigh of relief as he picked it up.

Scipio sat against a tree, exhausted, just before a rope came down near them. Tybal lowered himself down on it.

"You two done resting, then?" he asked.

***

Massilia was a Greek colony, but it was also the gateway to Gaul. As Scipio walked through it for the first time, much of what he saw was familiar. Temples to recognizable gods and shops selling all manner of goods lined an agora that was smaller than the Forum but similar in design and purpose. Walking a cobblestone road, he heard a wind instrument similar to a horn but softer playing a melody in low notes. Hearing it reminded him that this was not Greece, where he had visited and would have felt more comfortable. The smell of food being cooked and served in taverns was also unfamiliar and unappetizing to him. In fact, it was rather nauseating. Most of the Celts in the city to trade or work were easily discernable from the Greeks. They had unkempt beards and hair and wore clothing made of animal skins, sackcloth, and furs, though some had adopted the clothing and grooming styles of the Greek colonists.

They began their search where they expected to find soldiers for hire—a tavern Tybal knew well across from a brothel that Scipio suspected the smuggler also knew well. The tavern keeper, a burly Celt, recognized Tybal when they walked inside.

"Tybal, you old pirate!"

"Smuggler," Tybal corrected him, flashing a gummy smile at Scipio and Claudius.

"Wine's all the way from Greece today," the keeper told them as they took seats at a table.

The tavern had a smattering of patrons, half of whom appeared to be locals while the other half were seeming to be foreign traders. Tybal held up three fingers and the tavern keeper left to fill the order.

"He knows you?" Claudius asked.

"If I'm not at sea, I'm here or across the way," he said. "Just let me do the talking. You do the paying."

When the tavern keeper returned with their wine, Tybal engaged him immediately.

"Little light in here today," he said, looking around the empty tables.

The keeper grunted in agreement.

"Some fool from Carthage has been hiring up every able-bodied man in town," he said. "All he's going to do is get my best customers killed. Except you, of course."

"Going to war, are they?"

"Something like that," the keeper replied, turning to go.

"Is he still around?"

"He might be," the keeper said coyly, glancing at Scipio and Claudius. "Who's asking?"

"Not me," Tybal answered. "You know me better than to take me for a fighter. But my young friends here... They're up for some pillaging and raping in Italy if there's some to be had."

Tybal and the keeper shared a chuckle, and Tybal kicked Scipio lightly under the table, implicitly ordering him to laugh as well. Claudius followed their lead.

"Where are you from, friend?" the keeper asked Scipio.

"Greece," he told him. "We probably came in with that wine you're holding."

"Wine merchants."

"Olive oil, actually," Scipio said. "We just bought a ride on the same ship."

The bartender grunted and looked around.

"Where's you're uh... olive oil, then?"

"We just offloaded it," Claudius explained.

"For a handsome price, too," Scipio added, flashing his coin purse discreetly.

The keeper seemed unimpressed.

"Seems like you have all the coin you need," he said. "What do you want with the Carthaginian?"

"Olive oil is good business," Claudius replied. "But war... that's the biggest business of all, isn't it?"

"Well... he might be around," he said. "I'm not sure."

Tybal nudged Scipio in the ribs and jerked his head at his purse. Reluctantly, Scipio laid some coins out. The keeper looked away and cleared his throat. Again, Tybal nudged him, motioning more urgently to the purse. Annoyed, Scipio put more money on the table before the keeper finally picked it up.

Holding up one of the coins, he said, "That's what's called a referral fee."

He motioned to a tall Gaul eating a portion of meat at a table near the back, the drippings of which were falling into and remaining suspended in the thick hair of his beard.

"Dext will take you to him."

AEMILIA

Aemilia and her father sat in the circular *Comitium*, a circular open-air venue with five levels of seats. It was situated between Senate House and the Rostra, where Varro was scheduled to speak in defense of a fellow populist Senator, Quintus Barbatus. Barbatus had been accused of accepting bribes for state contracts for building ships in Rome's navy, was tried, convicted, and fined. It was up to the Censors—two magistrates that kept the official census regulated issues of public morality—to remove him from the Senate.

It was not a law for speakers on the Rostra to face the *Comitium* and the Senate when they were making a speech, but it made sense to speak in that direction. The *Comitium* was where the popular assemblies met to vote on laws. It was simply a custom that recognized the authority of the assemblies and the Senate. On a day like today, only the wealthier Romans were able to send servants to reserve seats for them in the *Comitium*, while the rest of the people attending the speech would have to stand outside in the Forum and only see the backside of the speaker on the Rostra.

Varro stepped onto the platform and, with one glance at the

Comitium and Senate, turned his back on the very body to which he belonged. It was a flagrant and deliberate act to subvert tradition and thumb his nose at the elite, Aemilia thought. His throngs of supporters cheered and howled in delight, while those in the *Comitium* rolled their eyes and wore amused grins.

"I thought the Censors had the power to remove a Senator for corruption," Aemilia said.

"They do," Paullus answered her in a low voice. "After Quintus was convicted of corruption and fraud, Papus ordered his removal from the Senate."

There were always two Censors—one patrician and the other plebeian. Paullus was referring to his cousin, Aemilius Papus, who was currently the patrician Censor. Like the two Consuls, each had veto power over the other's decisions.

"What's the issue, then?" she asked.

"Varro and Cato don't want to lose the seat. They're pressuring Gaius Flaminius to veto his removal."

Flaminius was the plebeian Censor and a populist politician. Many considered him Varro's forbearer in style, but Aemilia always thought of Varro as a unique aberration. She often wondered how his supporters saw him—as a giant of a man, simply because he was tall? As a font of wisdom, simply because he was wealthy? She looked at him and saw a bizarre-looking man in his sixties with a constant scowl, pugnacious, vulgar, and fat, with eyebrows that looked like two gigantic furry caterpillars.

"How could he do that?" she asked indignantly but keeping her voice low. "The man was convicted in court!"

"It's a desperate attempt to keep as many votes as they can in the Senate," Paullus answered.

She looked to the end of the Rostra, where the guests of the speaker sat to show their support for him. Cato was there, seated among other *populares*, a satisfied smirk on his face. She watched him whisper and laugh with his friends as Varro started. Finally, she could take no more and looked away.

Her father patted her hand, which she found patronizing, but it was easy an easy thing for her to forgive. She knew that her father loved and respected her. He just didn't want her to worry about politics as much as she did. He believed she could never have much control over it, after all was said and done, and worrying about something you have no power over was useless. He had taught her that women could wield incredible power, but always behind the scenes. It was unseemly for a woman to be openly assertive—yet another social convention at which Aemilia bristled.

As she listened to the speech, however, Aemilia began to doubt her own desire to participate in this game. The day was heavily overcast, working to Varro's favor. Everyone could see him without squinting and shading their eyes as he strutted about and spoke.

"This so-called 'evidence' at my colleagues' trial was nothing but hearsay and forgeries!" Varro was saying, earning nearly an equal number of cheers and jeers. "The entire thing was rigged, start to finish. The inquest itself was led by a Cornelii of some sort... Was he related to Consul Cornelius? He would have to be... Cornelius is a foolish, foolish man. Very stupid. Perhaps stupidity is a trait of the whole clan. I don't know."

He paused while his supporters laughed and shouted curses at Cornelius, though neither he nor any of his immediate family was there to hear it.

"And now, fellow citizens," Varro went on, "many, many people have told me that the jury was bribed to deliver the verdict. Bribery! I could hardly believe it myself, but these people made a very, very credible case; and they were very honorable, honest people who told me this. If you heard what they told me, believe me, you'd be as furious as I am. Believe me... "

The crowd erupted with furious shouting. Some shook their fists or made obscene gestures at the wealthy Romans watching from inside.

"What is he talking about?" Aemilia asked her father. "Who said that?"

"No one," Paullus answered.

She looked at her father, trying to discern how he felt about Varro's popularity. He had told her not to worry, but that was him being protective. He seemed to want to laugh at what he heard coming from Varro's mouth.

"My friends!" he said a few times, trying to calm the crowd and continue. "My friends! May there be no doubt there is corruption in this place. May there be no doubt that there is fraud in this place! But it is not my friend, Quintus Barbatus, that has committed it. No, no, no... He is a great man, a very, very smart man, and he is fighting for you, the forgotten, hardworking people of Rome! You do your work, you honor the gods, you fight their wars, and I can tell you... I know, and many people even in the Senate agree with me, that these urban elites who conspire against Senator Barbatus don't care about your struggle. And this so-called judge, this Cornelii magistrate... This so-called *learned* man was biased beyond belief! Beyond anything I have ever seen, or anyone has seen, ever in the annuls of Roman law!"

The truth was, Aemilia thought, no one really knew or cared about Senator Quintus what's-his-name. The crowd wanted Varro to do what he did best—portray the common Romans as victims in a heroic battle to "take back" their Republic. Cato had pushed this idea, smearing the opposition with the "Hellenist" label. Varro may have been the one to truly turn this ginned-up conflict between commoners and elites into popular support for himself, but Cato was the one who truly deserved the blame.

"This is not about one seat in the Senate," Varro went on. "This is about democracy itself! You all see, those of you who come to my speeches, how big the crowds are. Massive! Unbelievable massive! I was told my speech last month was the most attended even in all the years of the city. Huge! Just huge... These sneering elites ask why that is. They know. They know why it is! They just don't have the fortitude to admit it! You see them, strutting through the Forum... "

Varro walked with his nose in the air, mimicking the supposed pride and snobbery of the elite, getting laughs from supporters and others.

"*Oh... The commoners are getting together. They're figuring things out. They're thinking for themselves!*" he said as he strutted, satirizing an upper-class accent. "*We have to stop this immediately!*"

The crowd roared with laughter as Varro shook his head in feigned disgust.

"They want Senator Barbatus gone for the same reason they want me gone," Varro told them. "So that they can spit on our traditions, spit on our values... So that they can spit on our dignity as natural-born Romans and do it all with impunity!"

It made little sense. It didn't have to. The crowd was enthralled, hanging on his every word. Even those that jeered at the beginning seemed to nod along toward the end. After thirty minutes of Varro's rambling diatribe, the only man whose opinion mattered, Gaius Flaminius, came to the Rostra. Aemilia watched in disbelief as he vetoed the order to remove a man from the Senate who was convicted in court of receiving hundreds of bribes and misallocating massive amounts of state funds to enrich himself and his clients.

***

"I think I'm going to be sick," Aemilia told her father on their walk home.

"What?"

"That speech... or whatever that was," she said. "Tell me the last time a senator, or any official, was convicted of a crime—*any* crime, let alone using his office for personal gain—and was not removed from office."

Her father chuckled, which she found incredibly condescending.

"It's just politics, my dear," he told her.

"Don't you see?" she asked. "Varro just showed that laws don't matter, that the courts don't matter. The truth doesn't even matter to that... *mob.*"

"That mob is the people of Rome," he told her.

"All that matters to them is spectacle, and if Varro makes a better spectacle than his opponents, he wins. No matter what, he can whip up these ignoramuses he calls his supporters, and he can say that the sky is red and that everything else is a lie, and he'll be believed, even when he is the biggest liar of them all!"

"Aemilia, I know it looks dangerous," her father said. "When we get home, we'll read and talk about the history of Athens. You'll see that people like him come along once in a while in democracies. They have their little victories here and there, but their hubris is always their downfall."

"And what if his hubris catches up to him when it's too late?" she countered.

"Too late for what?"

"For all of us!" she shouted. "For Rome! How are you so sure Varro won't take us all down with him?"

"Because I've lived a long time," he said calmly, which only heightened her anger. "And I've seen this all before. The people aren't as foolish as you think."

He wasn't hearing her. It was a problem with her father, and one of the only ones that really bothered her. He was steadfast in his beliefs about the unchanging nature of ethics, politics, virtue, and everything else in the moral universe. It was as if, in his mind, societies were all headed in the same direction, toward greater inclusivity and tolerance, and Rome was leading the way. Most of the time, she found his faith in his country touching and even inspiring, but sometimes she felt it blinded him to the darkness that was so obviously present in men and, by extension, the Republic. Even Opimia's death had not woken him to the danger that populism posed.

"Fabius Maximus hosts a dinner party each year at the close of the Plebeian Games," Paullus said, referring to the games honoring Jupiter due to start in two days' time. "Perhaps you'd like to accompany me to it."

"Of course, I will," she said.

"I only mention it because Varro will be there, with his spouse," he said. "Maybe you want to see him up close, even ask him some questions."

It piqued her interest. She would never be allowed to argue with Varro in public, but she relished the chance to challenge him.

81

"Will Cato be there?" she asked.

"I may be able to arrange it, if you wish."

"Oh, I do."

He stopped walking, and she turned to face him.

"If this is about Opimia... "

"It isn't about her," she promised.

She was being truthful, she thought as they resumed walking. It wasn't about Opimia. This was about Cato.

SCIPIO

For a few drachmas, the Gallic mercenary called Dext was able to secure Scipio, Claudius, and himself a ride up the Rhone River on a ship carrying goods destined for villages and towns in central Gaul. Scipio and Claudius worried they would run out of daylight before reaching the Carthaginian camp. They walked at a fast clip with Dext from the point where the boat dropped them on the western bank over hills and fields that seemed to stretch out for endless miles.

It was mid-afternoon when they came over a rise to a sprawling mass of tents, men, and animals. As they approached, unpleasant smells grew stronger—manure, fish drying in the sun, and the body odor of a horde of unwashed men. It was an ominous sight. If Hannibal's brother, or whoever was in charge, suspected that he and Claudius weren't who they claimed to be, their fate would be much worse than being turned away as recruits. Torture and crucifixion were certainties. The Roman prisoners that survived captivity in the last war had told stories of nails pulled, near-drownings, being squeezed into sarcophagi with countless insects, and worse. The Carthaginians had imported the cruelties of the Eastern despots to the western

Mediterranean, and they had honed terror into a fine all-purpose weapon.

"Vernon!" Dext called to a tall blonde Gaul when they were deep inside the camp. "I've brought some Greek lambs for the slaughter!"

Dext evidently found his own metaphor uproariously funny and broke into hearty laughter. He slapped Claudius on the back with such force he stumbled forward and almost fell on his face before leaving them with Vernon.

"Alexandros," Scipio introduced himself.

"Ikaros," Claudius followed.

Like most educated Romans, Claudius and Scipio spoke both Latin and Greek very well. Their tutors and slaves had also taught them some other languages—in Scipio's case, Gallic and Punic—but they were not at the same level of proficiency. Greek wasn't a universal language, but it was nearly so among the educated elites in every country throughout the Mediterranean World. Scipio and Claudius didn't expect to find any such men in this camp, and they expected to use their limited Gallic, but, to their surprise, Vernon opened his mouth and spoke excellent Greek.

"Where are you from and how did you find us?" he asked them.

"Corinth," Claudius answered. "We just unloaded our olive oil in Massilia and heard you were looking for warriors."

Claudius's Greek was slightly better than Scipio's. If Vernon was sufficiently fluent to detect and recognize dialects and accents, Claudius was their best chance at getting by him.

"Warriors, yes," Vernon said, eyeing them. "Merchants, no. You have weapons? Armor?"

"We were hoping you'd have some for us," Claudius

answered.

Vernon frowned and grunted, arms folded in front of him, sizing them both up. The Gaul spat on the ground. Watching him, Scipio's main worry switched from torture and death to seeing his father's frown when he returned to the ship, not to mention his brother-in-law's smug face.

"Can you read and write?" Vernon finally asked them.

"Yes," Scipio answered, his tone a bit more eager than he'd intended.

"Greek, Punic, and Latin," Claudius added.

Vernon squinted and shook a finger at them as a broad smile came across his lips. Scipio was certain they'd gone too far. The Gaul was smelling a trap. It seemed he might bark for guards to come, take them away, and go to work on them to get the real story of why they had come. It made Scipio want to reach for his dagger, but he refrained.

"I knew it," Vernon said. "Educated bunch, the Greeks!"

Scipio and Claudius laughed politely. Vernon seemed to relax, dropping his arms to his sides.

"The General will probably want you all to himself, then," he told them. "Believe it or not, literacy is a rare commodity here. Come on, I'll put you near him."

They followed him into the camp, looking around as they walked. It was clearly much less organized and sanitary than its Roman counterparts. There was no uniform spacing between tents, no markings distinguishing this area from that, and no clear delineation of units. They ended up at a spot near what was apparently the command tent, which was marked with a purple banner bearing a ram's head logo and guarded by a single sentry near the entrance. Scipio recognized it as the symbol of the Punic god Baal. Whosever tent it was, he was at least Carthaginian.

They unloaded their packs and waited for anyone to come out, trying to get the first clear and up-close look at their enemy.

***

It wasn't a general, but a boy about ten years of age that eventually emerged from the command tent with his attention fixed on a piece of rope about three feet long. Manipulating the rope in both hands, the boy passed the tent's single guard, seemingly heedless of him and everything else around. He passed Scipio and Claudius, relieved himself at the latrine area, and turned back again.

"Boy," Scipio called.

Mathos snapped his head around and Scipio waved him over.

"What are you doing?"

"A sliding hitch knot," Mathos replied.

"Why?" he asked

"My father said we'll need to tie lots of knots in the mountains," said the boy.

"Which mountains?"

Mathos shrugged and sat down next to them, continuing to work on his knot.

"Where are you from?" the boy asked.

"Greece," Claudius replied.

"You have many mountains there?"

"Of course," Scipio said. "Mount Olympus, for one."

"Hmm? What's special about that one?"

"The gods live there," Scipio replied, as if it were obvious.

"Baal and Tanit live in Greece?" Mathos asked.

Scipio looked to Claudius for help, but he just shrugged.

"I'm Alexandros," Scipio told him. "This is Ikaros."

"Mathos."

"I think I know this, Mathos," Scipio told him, holding out his hand.

Mathos gave him the rope and Scipio tied a knot, channeling everything Uncle Calvus had taught him on their sea voyage to Alexandria. It was the only journey he'd made by ship before this campaign.

"This one?" he offered when he was done.

"No," Mathos said. "This end is supposed to be a loop, and it's supposed to slide here."

Scipio untied it and began again.

"Little young for the army, aren't you?" Claudius asked.

"I'm a general's aid," Mathos answered proudly. "For my father."

"Really?" Claudius said. "What's his name?"

"Hasdrubal... the Great."

The corners of Scipio's mouth tried to turn up, but he fought them down. He couldn't believe his luck. They'd been brought right to the tent of Hannibal's brother!

"That's it!" Mathos said excitedly just as Scipio finished the knot.

"Watch," Scipio told him, untying the knot and starting again.

They practiced it a few times until Mathos was satisfied he could do it.

"I shall see you're rewarded," Mathos promised, rising to his feet.

"No need."

The boy smiled and bowed.

"I should like to visit Greece someday," he told them.

"I hope you do," Scipio replied, returning his smile.

Mathos nodded and went back into the command tent, practicing the knot as he walked.

"Gods!" Scipio whispered.

"Easy," Claudius said.

"Everything we need may be right in that tent!"

Claudius laid back on his pack.

"It's getting dark," he said. "Try to rest."

Scipio laid back as well, but as physically exhausted as he was, he was far too excited to settle down. He wanted to run into that tent, grab everything he could, and run like the Furies themselves were on his back.

HASDRUBAL

Hasdrubal was far to the north of his camp, at the only suitable place he'd found to cross the men, animals, and carts of Hannibal's army to the other side of the Rhone River. The Volcae tribe diverted a massive amount of water upstream to feed their irrigation systems. As a result, the Rhone there was wide but flowed slowly and was only waist-deep in the middle.

Hasdrubal had wanted Vernon to come with him, but the wily Gaul had taken the opportunity to put one of his relatives on the payroll. Vernon's cousin, Owen, claimed to know the lay of the land well from hunting and trapping as a boy.

"You're sure this is the only place to cross?" Maharbal had asked when they first laid eyes on it.

"The only other place is another day's march north into lands of the Alverni," Owen had answered. "They have a bridge, but it would take forever to cross it."

"Why?"

"It's just wide and strong enough for one man on one horse at a time."

To verify his claim, Hasdrubal had sent scouts north days ago, but they returned with no different news.

"The Volcae are friendly with Rome," Owen warned as they approached the crossing point. "And their Queen, Cynbela, she's... difficult."

"Queen... " Hasdrubal scoffed. "Why don't they just step aside?"

"It's close to their settlements in the area," Owen explained.

"She also seems to know Hannibal can't take the army farther north," Maharbal said. "Why else demand such a steep toll?"

"This is the only place we can cross the river," Owen told them. "The only place the width and depth are suitable. She knows it."

"We must strike a bargain," Maharbal said. "Or else fight."

"The gods will provide," he assured them.

They crossed the river on rafts under armed guard. The Volcae were already building defenses on the embankment, preparing to contest Hannibal's crossing. As soon as their feet hit dry land, the guards whisked them away to the hall of their queen. By Carthaginian standards, it was a primitive structure. It was little more than a large stable built of wood with a thatched roof and surrounded by a stone wall.

Cynbela was as much a performer as a ruler. Deep horns bellowed before she made her entrance into the hall, and her court roared at the sight of her. The men banged their weapons against their shields and pumped their fists in the air as she walked past them. It seemed that the Volcae were ready to fight then and there, but Hasdrubal reminded himself that it may all be an act. Nevertheless, their spirit impressed him.

"You have asked our price," the husky and dower Cynbela said, sitting in her splendid chair and flanked by her two brawny adult sons. "It is Vocantia."

Vocantia was a fortified town on the other side of the Rhone, centered on a freshwater spring. Other than Massilia, it was the only town in Gaul that Hasdrubal had seen with stone walls. Taking it would require a siege that would last, he estimated, about a month—far too long for Hannibal to pause his march. In addition, Hasdrubal had already arranged to purchase food and supplies from the town elders to resupply Hannibal's army when it arrived. Betraying them would earn them a reputation for treachery.

Hasdrubal studied her face and posture. He was experienced at dealing with tribal chieftains from countless sessions such as this in Hispania. She was tough and stubborn, much like Hannibal. She would likely be a strong adversary if it did come to a fight. Hasdrubal glanced at her sons, who sneered disdainfully at the seated visitors from Carthage. He had hoped they might be a moderating influence on their mother, but they seemed to be itching for a fight.

"Queen Cynbela, we can pay you in gold," Hasdrubal told her. "We can pay you in slaves. We can even pay you in arms. But we cannot take Vocantia for you."

"Why you cannot?" she demanded in her broken Greek, lifting her chin and tilting her head back.

"Because we have already made a deal with Vocantia for supplies," he explained.

"You made a pact with them," she said.

"Yes, a pact."

"Did you not make a pact for peace with Rome?"

"That's... different," Hasdrubal stumbled, shaking his head. *She's clever.* "We're wasting time. Hannibal will be here in days, if not hours. We need to get across this river before—"

Cynbela brought her hand crashing down on the table, surprising her guests as well as her own warriors, who jumped at the sound.

"Volcae are not a great army," she said. "But we are strong, proud..."

"Fighting will do neither of us any good," Hasdrubal said. "And we have a common enemy in Rome. We can—"

"The Volcae have no quarrel with Rome! Rome does not come here, bring its army here, to our land, and make demands. *You* do!"

Hasdrubal waited a moment, but he could see her anger would not abate.

"Your majesty," he said calmly. "Please listen to me. Hannibal will not take a fortified town. We don't have time to—"

"You listen, Carthage!" she interrupted. "Volcae are here three hundred years. No one crosses unless we allow! We know Hannibal. We are not afraid of Hannibal! Let him bring his army, his giant beasts, and I swear by Belenus, we will strike them down if he dares challenge Cynbela!"

Her warriors erupted in cheers and waved their weapons in the air. Hasdrubal and Maharbal exchanged an anxious look. They would wait for the hooting and hollering to die down, then resume the negotiation, but the hope they had to settle this issue before Hannibal arrived was diminishing rapidly. Crossing a river with an opposing force on the other side was a dangerous proposition for any army. Fighting the Volcae would be a waste of time and resources, and possibly a strategic disaster. Cynbela could delay them just long enough for the Romans to discovered Hannibal's plan, and intercept them before they ever made it Italy. Their entire war plan could be compromised right here on the Rhone.

SCIPIO

It was well after nightfall when Scipio heard horses approaching. He watched from the corner of his eye as Hasdrubal and Maharbal dismounted in front of the tent. Mathos immediately came out to greet them, and Scipio casually glanced over to see Hasdrubal briefly hug his son before the boy led the horses away.

"Find Vernon," he heard Hasdrubal order Maharbal. "Tell him we're back."

Maharbal disappeared into the darkness of the camp as Hasdrubal disappeared into his tent.

"That's him," Claudius whispered. "Hasdrubal."

"It must be," Scipio whispered back. "But where has he been?"

Claudius shrugged. "Do you think he knows where Hannibal is?"

"Maybe," Scipio answered, checking around to make sure no one was eavesdropping. "We have to think about leaving soon."

"We'll need those horses," Clausius said. "I'll see if I can find them. This camp is such a mess."

Claudius went in the direction Mathos had gone while Scipio watched Hasdrubal's tent. The guard soon let two other men inside. Scipio crept through the darkness to reposition himself at the rear of the tent to eavesdrop.

"Any progress with Cynbela?" he heard a muffled voice inside ask in Punic.

"None," another answered. "Where's Hannibal?"

Scipio brought his ear closer to the tent's fabric. More voices... some feet shuffling... He couldn't hear anything clearly enough. He caught words and phrases, but mostly undiscernible murmurs.

"If this map is accurate... "

"...but we're out of time with the army so close," he heard the voice say. "We'll still need scouts to look for any fording places north and south of the Volcae we missed."

"... need half a day's start at least... "

"They can... that... We'll get some scouts to leave tonight."

"It might take some time to... "

Scipio felt a hand on his shoulder and his heart jumped into his throat. He grabbed the hand and reached for his dagger, but Claudius stopped him and placed a finger to his lips. Together they crept back to their assigned sleeping space.

"Horses?" Scipio inquired.

"In a pen on the other side of camp."

"I heard them talking about a map."

The flaps on the tent opened and three men exited, still talking about scouts and supplies. A single soldier stood guard at the entrance.

"Come on," Scipio whispered, heading back to the rear of the tent.

"Are you crazy?" Claudius asked as Scipio laid on the ground parallel to the tent.

"We need that map," Scipio told him.

"We have enough information. Hannibal is here somewhere. Let's just get some horses and find him."

"I need half a minute, in and out."

"Let's just go," Claudius pleaded.

"I need this, Claudius," Scipio insisted. "You need this win just as much as I."

Claudius sighed again, but he nodded in acquiescence.

"Just keep an eye on the guard," Scipio told him.

Claudius lifted the tent's rear flap enough for Scipio to crawl inside, then took up position to watch the guard.

Inside, Scipio got to his feet and looked around in the dim light. There were two cots, an oil lamp, clothes, and weapons. They were traveling light. The map Hasdrubal and the others were studying earlier was flat on top of one of the cots. He brought the lamp close to see that they had marked a crossing point on the Rhone and identified possible entry points into the Alps. After studying it briefly, he rolled it up as quietly as he could.

It was then that Mathos entered the tent, rope in his hand, still practicing his knots and just as oblivious as he'd been earlier. The boy looked up and stopped dead his tracks just a few away. He saw the map in Scipio's hand and tensely backed away a step.

"Easy, Mathos," Scipio whispered to him.

Mathos turned and Scipio lunged, grabbing the boy by the arm, and dropping the map. He pulled him back much harder than he'd intended, and the boy stumbled and fell. He let out a cry for help just before his head hit the table with a loud thud. Mathos fell to the ground, limp.

Scipio immediately dropped down to tend to Mathos. He was so focused on the boy that the rest of his surroundings, including the map, faded away. He turned Mathos's listless body over. Then it happened. He saw it for just for one moment, but he was certain he saw it. It wasn't the face of the boy he'd met hours earlier, but another from a long time ago and a place far removed from that tent in Gaul. For one fleeting moment, it was his brother, Lucius, that looked back at him with glassy, lifeless eyes. Then he was gone, and Mathos was there again.

He stared at that face, not knowing what he'd expected to happen. Would Lucius's face return, or would Mathos blink and come alive in his arms? He didn't even take notice of the Carthaginian guard entering the tent with his sword drawn. Before he could take a step, one of Claudius's hands came around the soldier from behind and covered his mouth just before the other slashed his throat open. The Carthaginian stumbled, grasping at his gushing neck, and knocked over the oil lamp before falling to the ground.

"Scipio, let's go!" Claudius called, grabbing Scipio by the arm. "Leave him!"

The oil from the lamp spilled on the table and cot, and the flames quickly spread.

Claudius kept pulling him away, but Scipio remained frozen and staring at Mathos's corpse. Only Claudius pushing the body away and tearing at his tunic shocked him from the trance.

When they got to the horse pen, they could see the three men from the tent with several scouts on horseback. They barely escaped being noticed when the commotion from inside the camp lured their enemy's attention away long enough for the two Romans to slip into the pen.

"What's that?" they heard one of them ask.

"Fire!" another yelled.

The three of them quickly grabbed pails of water and sped off on foot in the direction of the billowing flames. Gauls were running in every direction. Some were shouting orders, but no one seemed to be listening. Men were gathering up their possessions and getting them away from the destruction. The scouts watched the spectacle, mesmerized, as Scipio and Claudius quietly guided two horses out through the gate. They mounted quickly and dashed off, but the horses' whinnying caught the scouts' attention. As they rode hard westward into the darkness, they heard the scouts calling angrily to them, and knew they were being chased.

The scouts quickly got Scipio's attention when they fired an arrow that grazed his right arm. He looked back to see the scouts loading two more arrows at full gallop. Scipio leaned forward on the horse, pictured the scout pulling the drawstring in order to time his turn, and veered to the left. The arrow barely missed this time, whizzing by his head. When he looked back, the scouts had fallen farther behind. Soon after, the scouts broke off the pursuit and headed back to camp.

HASDRUBAL

Inside the camp, Hasdrubal found his tent fully ablaze. The fire had already spread to tents and equipment located nearby.

"What happened?" he asked Maharbal and Vernon. "Where's my guard?"

He looked around, confused and angry, as Gauls ran everywhere to put out fires anyway they could. It was then that he realized Mathos hadn't been with him since he returned to camp. The realization seeped to hit him squarely in his solar plexus, nearly doubling him over. He grabbed Maharbal by the tunic, pulling him close.

"Where's Mathos?" he asked, on the verge of panic. "Where's my son?"

"I'll find him!" Maharbal answered. "Just get this under control before the whole camp burns to the ground!"

Hasdrubal's head was spinning as Maharbal ran off into the camp. The fire, the tents, Vernon running with water—all of it began to blur as the dread set it. He could hear his own breathing, but the chaos around him seemed muffled, like a thing happing far away.

"Mathos!" he called, coughing from the smoke. "Mathos!"

***

In the early morning hours, Hasdrubal knelt by the charred remains of his son. Maharbal had given orders to repair whatever equipment could be salvaged from where the fire had eaten a hole in the heart of the encampment, but he did not oversee the work. He stuck close to his friend instead, constantly checking to see if there were any changes in his posture or mood. He laid a hand gently on Hasdrubal's shoulder.

"I mourn with you, General," Maharbal told him.

Hasdrubal didn't respond.

"Maharbal," Vernon called, and then motioned him over.

"All of the men are accounted for," he reported.

"Good... "

"Except two," Vernon continued. "Greeks. I met them myself yesterday. Two horses are also missing. Scouts chased what they thought were two horse thieves, but they lost them."

"Gods... "

"What should we do?" Vernon asked.

"We commend Mathos to the gods," Hasdrubal said.

He scooped up the charred corpse and turned to them, blood in his eyes, seething with anger and grief.

SCIPIO

Time was running out, but the sense of urgency with which Scipio had entered Hasdrubal's encampment the day before was gone. He let Claudius sleep during the morning hours and took a turn himself, but neither felt rested. They decided it was too dangerous to go farther west to look for Hannibal and his army and began meandering to the north and east.

He knew that he should have been paying attention, but Scipio preoccupied himself with going through the events of the previous night. He thought himself an incredible fool to think about winning glory in war as he did on the racetrack. Why hadn't he just listened to Claudius? They'd still be where they are now, he imagined, but Mathos would still be alive. Scipio would be joking and laughing with Claudius as they rode west in search of Hannibal, and they would return to his father with something useful. *He would still be alive but for your weakness.* Mathos would be alive. Lucius would be alive...

"If we keep going this way, we'll hit the Rhone," Claudius said. "It turns west at some point, I think."

Scipio was riding in a stupor, letting his horse guide itself. They were on a winding path leading up, they hoped, to the top of a ridgeline where they could get a better view of the surrounding countryside. All day he'd had the comet pendant in his left hand, rubbing it constantly between his thumb and forefinger.

"Who knew an entire army would be so difficult to find?"

Claudius asked. "Or that Gaul was so big. Well, I suppose I should have known that one. Didn't you, Scipio? Scipio?"

"What?"

"Why don't we stop and get some rest?" Claudius suggested.

"At the top," said Scipio.

The summit provided a wide view of the countryside. Luckily for them, it was a clear day. The scene before them was surrealistically serene—green grass and vibrant patches of yellow and purple flowers, a neat patchwork of farmland and country homes with thatched rooves on gently rolling hills, and birds singing in the trees.

"I didn't realize Gaul was so beautiful," Scipio murmured.

"See anything?" Claudius asked.

Scipio finished scanning and replied, "Earth and sky."

They dismounted and sat, letting the horses graze beside them. Claudius took a swig of water from his animal-skin bladder, then prodded his sulking friend until Scipio took a few gulps himself.

"I killed that boy, Claudius," he whispered.

"It wasn't your fault."

"Yes, it was," he said. "I wanted to give that map to my father, like a gift. I keep thinking that things between us can be different, if only... "

"If only what?"

"I don't know," Scipio said, closing the comet into his fist.

"I thought you didn't give a fig about what your father thinks of you."

"I don't," Scipio said, but he knew the moment the words left his mouth that it might not be true. "I just... wanted to show him

98

I could do something. That I'm worth something." He paused and sighed, wiping away his tears. "None of that seems important anymore."

"Look, people die in war," Claudius said. "Children included. Thousands of them, sometimes. It's just the way of things."

"But what sort of coward kills a child?" Scipio returned.

"Well... I know plenty of high-born Romans," Claudius said. "I can tell you that ninety-nine in a hundred would have let me fall the other night rather than risk themselves."

Scipio looked at him, trying to gauge his sincerity.

"I should think they're brave enough to do what I did," Scipio said.

"Perhaps," Claudius replied, before adding, "but they're not stupid."

It took a moment for Scipio to even realize it was a joke, and it barely elicited a smile.

"I used to think about my father a lot," Claudius said. "I studied the Battle of Drapena, going over it again and again, trying to figure out where he went wrong and why he lost, but then I realized something. Losing a battle wasn't his mistake. Letting that failure define him, that was his mistake."

Scipio knew he was right, but he still felt miserable. Looking at the talisman in his hand, he thought of the few moments that he'd allowed to define his own life. He felt a strange urge to cast this thing that hung around his neck away, lose it forever in the forests of Gaul and never think of it again. It felt heavy as lead in his hand, and he was sure that he could bear the weight no longer. Yet he couldn't bring himself to do it. He couldn't remember life before Lucius had given it to him. It had always been there. If anything in the world were truly his, it was this talisman of the tailed star. He put it back around his neck and tucked it away safely beneath his tunic.

Claudius stood up and dusted himself off.

"For Rome?"

"For Rome," Scipio echoed meekly and took Claudius's outstretched hand to pull himself up.

As they mounted their horses, they looked around for their next place to scout.

"My father said to look near water," Scipio said, looking northeast. "I should think... "

There was something, Scipio thought, but he wasn't sure. He shielded his eyes from the sun with his hand and squinted

"What?" Claudius asked.

"There," he said, pointing his other hand. "Above the trees... What do you see?"

***

From their vantage point in the wood line, Scipio and Claudius could see only a small part of the massive army at any one time. The column would emerge from the other side of the walled town it was passing, come into their view, and then disappear into the forest. They dared not get any closer, but it was unnecessary in any case. What they could see was enough to know it was Hannibal. The huge animals were proof positive.

"Ever seen one?" Claudius asked.

Scipio shook his head, staring at the elephants in amazement. He could see how they dwarfed the horses and men that rode them. He delighted in their long snouts and the amazing sounds they made, like nothing he'd ever seen or heard before. The pictures in Rome hadn't done them any justice. To see them move, carrying soldiers on their enormous gray bodies, seemed like witnessing a Titan come back to life.

"How much must they eat?" he wondered aloud.

"How much must they shit?" Claudius countered.

This time, Claudius succeeded in getting at least a little laugh from his friend. Seeing the elephants reminded Scipio that there was wonder in the world. Eventually, the childlike awe faded and his frown returned.

"We have to get back Massilia," Scipio said. "My father needs to know this."

Claudius gave an exhausted moan as they mounted their horses.

"There might be an inn down there in that town," he said hopefully, pointing to Vacantia. "Your father will wait another day if—"

"No time," Scipio said. "We may have to ride through the night as it is and hope we don't get ambushed."

"Hmph... You're right, of course," Claudius grumbled. "I just hope we don't fall asleep on the horses... Or that the horses fall asleep on us. Maybe we'll find some lonely farm girls with space in their beds."

"Not likely," Scipio told him.

"Why not?"

"You snore."

Claudius laughed and said, "They wouldn't turn us out for that. Not after they see Castor and Pollux."

"You named your balls?"

"Haven't you?"

He shrugged. "Maybe."

They rode on for a long moment, until Claudius's staring

finally wore him down.

"Romulus and Remus."

"Sure," Claudius replied. "But which is which?"

HANNIBAL

The dirt road to Vocantia was dry and dusty. The Carthaginians and mercenaries in Hannibal's army covered their mouths and noses with a cloth to keep the dust from their lungs as best they could. A few more miles and they would be at the Rhone.

Hannibal joined his quartermaster, Gisgo, in watching the army walk by. They had traveled fast and far the last few days, and they wanted to see the general condition of the men and animals, carts and wagons. The march to this point had been Gisgo's success as much as Hannibal's. As skilled at logistics as Hannibal was at tactics, Gisgo had an uncanny ability to calculate how fast his army and their components could move over various types of terrain during different seasons. He knew how much food they could expect to consume, how much of it they could forage, how much they needed to bring with them, how much water they needed at each stage of their movement, how many beasts of burden would probably go lame, and how many days it would take to fix the broken carts and wagons those animals pulled. Those skills allowed Hannibal to plan his campaigns to minimize the ill effects of terrain and weather, and they made Gisgo the least replaceable officer on his staff.

A small party approached them from the town on horses. One carried a banner with a picture of a trident puncturing the ground and water flowing from the three holes, which Hannibal guessed was the town seal.

"Welcome to Vocantia!" one of the men called out in Punic.

The day before, Hannibal's scouts had met a Gaul at Vocantia that called himself "Owen" and claimed to work for Hasdrubal. He showed them the area, including the fording site Hasdrubal had decided they should use.

"Are you Owen?" Hannibal asked the Gaul.

"I am, General," he replied with a polite nod. "These men are elders of the Vocantii tribe. They came to bid you welcome, bestow blessings of their gods for a successful war on the Romans, and offer what food and supplies they can spare."

Hannibal bowed slightly in gratitude and was met with bows in reply.

"Tell them we're grateful and we'll pay for the supplies," Hannibal told him.

After Owen had finished translating, he pulled Hannibal and Gisgo aside.

"About your crossing point on the Rhone... "

"The campsite you showed us is close to it, yes?" Hannibal asked.

"Very close," Owen said. "The people there are called the Volcae. Hasdrubal and Maharbal have been up there several times, trying to negotiate passage with their queen, but it's been difficult."

"What does she want?" Gisgo asked.

"Vocantia," Owen replied quietly.

Hannibal looked over Owen's shoulder at the town. He'd brought no siege equipment with him. It would have slowed him too much, and besides, his plan was first to defeat Rome in the field. Only after her armies were destroyed could he lay siege to Rome itself. There would be plenty of time and materials with which to build siege engines then.

"The tribes here are constantly bickering over land," Owen explained. "Perhaps—"

"No," Hannibal said. "I didn't come here to fight Gauls, especially not ones with walls like that."

"Yes, General," Owen replied.

"Hasdrubal is going back to negotiate with Cynbela tomorrow," Owen told them.

"Where is he now?"

"A day's march south with about five thousand Gauls."

"Send scouts," Hannibal told Gisgo. "Tell him to break his camp and join mine at the river."

"Yes, General," Gisgo replied, whirling around and heading off to find his messengers.

"You go to the Volcae tomorrow," Hannibal told Owen. "Tell this Cynbela you speak for me."

"What shall I tell her?"

"Tell her the toll will be paid in gold or steel," he said. "The choice is hers... But I will cross."

"Yes, General," he said. "If I may... I'm very proud to be here with you on this mission."

It was just the sort of attitude Hannibal had hoped to find among the Gauls. He rewarded Owen with a clap on the shoulder and a grateful nod.

HASDRUBAL

The scouts asked to speak with Hasdrubal as soon as they arrived at his camp in the early evening. The sentries took them instead to Maharbal, who stood at the edge of a solemn

104

ceremony. They watched quietly as Hasdrubal laid his son's charred body, wrapped in linen, on a woodpile in front of a stone altar.

Hasdrubal remembered as clearly as if it had been ten minutes ago how he'd once wrapped his infant son in a swaddling cloth not unlike the shroud now covering him. He remembered holding him close to his chest and whispering prayers to the gods to forever keep his family safe. His weeping prompted the men around him to cast their eyes down in a show of respect. Hasdrubal kissed his son's forehead and remained for a time, bawling over his body.

Eventually, he stepped back, wiping the tears away. Maharbal handed him a torch, which he tossed onto the pyre. Flames soon engulfed Mathos's remains. Hasdrubal stood before the burning body as if mesmerized by the sight of it. He held out his hands with palms up in supplication, offering prayers to Baal and Tanit.

Maharbal stood beside him, making a futile attempt to share his grief.

"I would fall on my sword to see my wife and son again," Hasdrubal told him.

Hasdrubal always needed a purpose, a duty. He'd found that once in his family. Over a decade ago, when Hannibal had been raising funds and troops for a campaign to expand Carthage's holdings in Hispania, Hasdrubal had no intention of joining him. Then his wife had died in childbirth, and he came to believe her death was divine punishment for breaking his oath to destroy Rome. His sister, a priestess of Tanit, confirmed his suspicions. Having to look after his son had seen him through that dark part of his life. Now Mathos was gone as well.

Hasdrubal stepped closer to the flames and dropped to his

knees, tilted back, and tore open the front of his tunic. He looked up at the stars and held his arms out straight, as if offering his breast up to a god that was ready to plunge a dagger into it.

"Great Baal," he prayed. "I have nothing. I am nothing. I am not a husband. I am not a... "

Hasdrubal choked up, but he gathered himself and went on.

"I am not a father. You have tested me, and I have kept to your holy path. With all my heart, I give to you the rest of my life. My every thought, my every deed, will be in your service. I will conquer in your name. Your followers will be countless, their devotion boundless. I will only ever ask one thing in return... "

His face burned hot with rage, and his voice dropped to a near whisper.

"Just one thing," he said between clenched teeth as his fingers curled in to form fists like iron hammers. "Let me have vengeance. *Let me have vengeance.*"

SCIPIO

Tybal was true to his word. They'd found him in the brothel in the middle of the night, drunk and sleeping like a baby. He took the two Romans out the same way they had come in, and they sailed out to meet Cornelius's fleet shortly after the sunrise.

"Look at these two!" Calvus said, helping Scipio and Claudius onto the deck from the rope ladder. "Two days in Gaul and they look like they've been across the River Styx!"

Below them, Tybal's tiny ship bobbed in the waves. Scipio suspected that Tybal was still somewhat inebriated when Calvus tossed a purse full of coins down to him, but the smuggler was sober enough to catch it a flash his signature gummy smile.

"What did you find?" Cornelius asked them as soon as they

were on board.

"Hannibal is here," Scipio reported. "North, about two day's march."

"And the Gauls?" Calvus asked.

"About three or four thousand, I'd say," Claudius said.

"He's headed for the Alps," Scipio said. "Tens of thousands of men."

"And elephants," Claudius added.

Scipio expected some sort of reaction to the news from his father, but Cornelius didn't seem surprised. It was a successful mission, but Scipio didn't yet know what, if anything, had changed between him and his father.

"Metellus," Cornelius called.

"Sir?" Metellus answered promptly.

"Send word to the Senate," Cornelius told him. "Tell them Hannibal is marching for Italy, and I shall stop him."

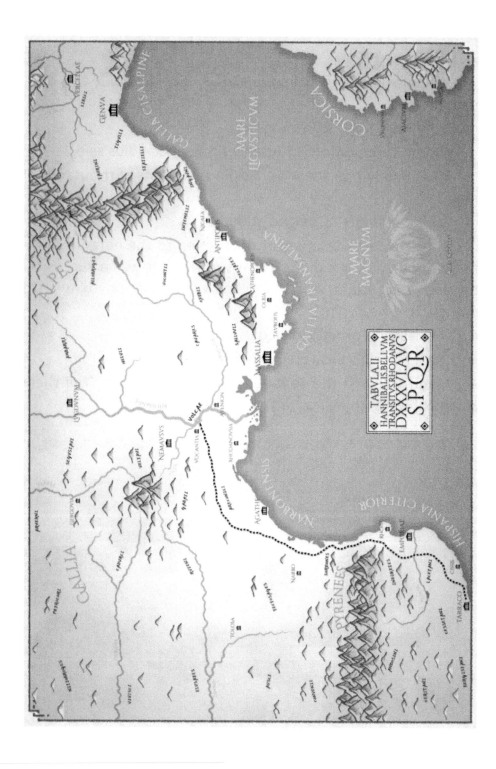

Part II: The Crossing

CORNELIUS

Cornelius knew that Massilia was an oligarchy where a few hundred of its wealthiest citizens made laws, appointed judges, and elected magistrates from among themselves to serve fixed terms as town officers. He also knew that its security forces consisting of militia numbering a few thousand, and that these were led by three "generals." He expected them to muster the militia to either resist the Romans, if they thought that Rome knew of Massilia's duplicity; or to greet the Roman allies with an honor guard. If the former, Cornelius expected the officers to flee the city at the sight of his warships. He was surprised when a Centurion boarded his ship and informed him that the leaders of the town were in custody. He found them where the pier met the earth, kneeling on the packed brown dirt with their hands tied behind their backs under the watchful eyes of their Roman captors as Cornelius approached with Calvus and Metellus. They looked as if the soldiers had dragged them out of bed, blinking against the early morning sun and glancing at one another. Most of them didn't even pick their heads up to look at Cornelius as he approached.

A small crowd had also gathered, though not nearly sizable enough to cause Cornelius much concern. He guessed that these were the town officers' family members, friends, clients, and patrons. His suspicions were confirmed when, as he approached, a man's voice called from the crowd.

"Consul!" it called. Cornelius looked up, but he couldn't

determine who it was. "My son had no choice in this! The others threatened him! He... "

The man was drowned out at the end by a cacophony of appeals, threats, and attempted bribes. People in the crowd reached out their hands and tried to move past the soldiers to get closer to Cornelius, but the legionaries stood their ground. Marcius, a Military Tribune on Cornelius's staff, stood beside the prisoners.

"Consul," Marcius greeted him with a salute, then gestured toward the prisoners. "These are the officers of the city of... "

When Cornelius opened his mouth, the front ranks of the crowd fell silent, and the rest quickly followed suit.

"Crucify them," Cornelius ordered.

The verdict seemed to stun the small crowd, but it soon erupted into sorrowful and rage-filled cries. Again, they tried to surge forward, but they were no match for the line of legionaries.

Cornelius followed his staff through the city's agora on their way to the house of one of the condemned. It was small by patrician Roman standards, but it would do as a temporary command post. In any case, he didn't plan on staying long. Hannibal was making a run for the Alps, and he had a long way to go to catch up.

Cornelius ordered his men to set up in the atrium, which was soon crawling with soldiers bringing in tables to hold the maps, tablets, and everything else Cornelius and his senior officers needed for their work. After leaving orders for the infantry to assemble and begin their march north, he gathered his staff in the formal dining room. The table there now held a map of Gaul.

"Vocantia," Calvus said, putting an elephant figurine on the map by the town. "That was where Scipio and Claudius spotted

Hannibal—three days march north from here. Hannibal's camp is no doubt somewhere closer to the Rhone by now."

"No bridges across the Rhone can accommodate his army," Metellus said.

"If the map is accurate," Cornelius reminded him.

"If there was a bridge that big, we would know of it," Calvus assured him. "No... He'll have to ford it somewhere."

"We've questioned several locals," Marcius offered, stepping forward. "We believe the only place he can cross is here."

Marcius traced an arc with his finger where the Rhone forked. Cornelius immediately recognized the name of the tribe whose lands were on the other side of the Rhone from Hannibal's camp.

"Volcae," Cornelius said with a grin. "Friends to Rome. The gods favor us... I hope."

"Friends or not," Calvus replied, "Hannibal has enough men with him to conquer all of Gaul."

"I think those estimates are suspect," Metellus interjected. "Scipio is... inexperienced, and prone to nervous exaggeration."

"Regardless," Calvus said, "They'll have more than we do, and if the numbers are correct, Hannibal may have two men for every one of ours."

"Mercenaries," Metellus said with a dismissive wave of his hand. "How many will fight, once they see the legions assembled? Consul, I recommend we seek a decisive battle on the western side of the Rhone, trapping him with his back at the river."

"No," Cornelius said. "I don't need a decisive battle. The man intends to take the fight to us, in Italy. We hit him here, in Gaul; he'll be delayed and bloodied. We'll finish them off in Italy, after the Alps take their toll. Better yet, we inflict so much pain on Hannibal that he goes crawling back to Hispania with his tail between his legs."

The staff officers chuckled, but the mood was anything but light. Cornelius did his best to seem confident of his plan, but finding Hannibal unexpectedly in Gaul had rattled him more than he'd have cared to admit. Only later, when he was alone with his brother, did he feel free to give voice to the fear, uncertainty, and doubt that had been with him for days.

"The man made it nearly all the way across Gaul before we even realized he was out of Hispania," he said as a household slave poured them both cups of both mixed with water. "He's already three-quarters of the way to Italy, and we're nowhere near him."

"It raises the question," Calvus said. "Are our enemies getting faster, or are we slowing down?"

"Both, I think," Cornelius answered, and he shared a laugh with his brother. "Can we catch him?"

"We need to send the cavalry up ahead and get some eyes on him," he said.

Cornelius grunted his agreement, staring at the two small wooden horse heads on the map by Massilia that each stood for three hundred Roman *equites*. It was the first time he had looked at those little figurines and thought not of the tactical value of the force it represented, but that his son was among them.

"You were right, by the way," he said, raising his cup to Calvus. "Publius did well."

"He did," Calvus replied. "But I don't think his performance as a soldier was ever among your issues with him."

Cornelius drank some more. He was tired, more tired than he ever remembered being so early in a campaign.

"I gave Cornelia her first doll, just before we left for Sicily," he said. "Publius was this tall..."

He held his hand less than two feet from the floor and saw Calvus smiling.

"He could barely walk," Cornelius went on. "Lucius was still in his mother's womb. It was... difficult to leave them."

"I'm sure it was," his brother said. "As I'm sure it was difficult for them.

"But I could never have imagined it would have been harder to come home," Cornelius told him. "Publius had grown into this... timid little mouse. He seemed afraid of me... like I was a stranger. He wouldn't even look me in the eye, Calvus. But when I wasn't looking at him, I could feel him watching me... Judging me. Hating me. But Lucius was *so different* from him."

He felt his mood lighten and heard his own voice lift at the mention of his younger son.

"The light in his eyes, it... it was like nothing I've seen, before or since," Cornelius continued. "He would run to me when I came in the house. *'Fast as Mercury!'* he would say. Remember?"

They shared another laugh, but Cornelius's smile quickly faded from his face.

"Then he was gone," he said.

He remembered seeing his eldest son standing in the atrium, with eyes downcast and his white tunic and his shins streaked with red stains so dark that Cornelius initially mistook their color for black. He barely remembered the name of the man who stood next to him—the slave he had latter freed for his loyalty and bravery through the revolt, for going out into the chaos of the Forum and sifting through the carnage to find his boys and bring them home... But it was the limp body he carried in his arms, his face turned toward the slave's chest like a suckling infant, that he could never forget.

"The wrong son died that day, Calvus," he said. "It should have been him."

"Did you tell Publius you feel this way?"

"Of course not!" Cornelius snapped, raising his cup to his lips.

"Do you think you needed to?"

Cornelius hadn't devoted a single thought to that question before Calvus had now made him confront it, but he already knew the answer. It was in how Scipio had talked to him, the way he looked at him, the way he held himself in his presence—like a wounded puppy one moment, with sneering contempt and haughty pride the next.

"Get him," he told Calvus.

***

By the time Scipio arrived, it was nearly time for the evening meal. Cornelius had been waiting with Calvus and Metellus for the food to be brought in, but the slaves had not yet taken the map from the table. It gave him something to look at instead of Scipio, who walked in sharply and greeted him with a salute.

"I'm promoting you and Claudius Pulcher to *Decurion*," Cornelius told him without looking up. "And giving you both commands of cavalry troops."

He expected some sort of reply, but his son seemed intent on making this even more awkward than it already was.

"You had a difficult mission," Cornelius said, again pretending to study the map. "And you handled it very well."

Metellus stood and stepped close to Scipio, looking down at his shorter brother-in-law.

"Do you think you're ready to handle this kind of responsibility, *Juvenior*?" Metellus asked.

"Yes, sir," Scipio answered firmly.

"I do not," Metellus returned. "And I doubt you'll prove me wrong this time, now that Claudius Pulcher isn't there to help you."

"Enough," Cornelius found himself saying with sternness that surprised him and drew looks from both his brother and son-in-law.

Metellus took a step back. Cornelius decided to let his son-in-law fume in place, then he cleared his throat and leaned over the table.

"We'll be marching the legions north on the eastern side of the Rhone to catch Hannibal as he crosses," he said, tracing his route on the map. "I'm sending the cavalry up both sides simultaneously to reconnoiter the enemy camp and their crossing point, and to monitor their movements until I arrive with the legions."

"Yes, sir."

"Cavalry from Legion Five will be on the western side," he said. "On the eastern side, you will go first, out in front of everyone, with the rest of the cavalry from Legion Three spread out behind you. Sweep the route. If any of Hannibal's men have crossed the Rhone, I need to know. This, here; this is the land of the Volcae. They're friendly to Rome and trading partners, but you are to avoid contact with them, lest an incident between us occur. The last thing we want is to have to fight Gauls on top of Carthaginians."

He nodded. "Yes, sir."

Cornelius looked up and Scipio saluted, turned on his heel smartly, and went to leave. Metellus grabbed his brother-in-law by the arm and looked down at him.

"Try not to muck this one up," he growled.

Scipio shook Metellus's grip and left.

Cornelius looked over at Calvus, looking for some reassurance.

"He'll be fine," Calvus told him, lifting his wine to his lips. "Probably," he added before taking a gulp.

MAGO

Mago had been inconsolable since news of his nephew's death reached the camp. He wanted a drink more than anything—more than going home, more than a woman, more than a decent plate of food. Yet, he refrained for one reason: he wanted to be sober the next time he saw Hasdrubal. For an entire day, he sat brooding in the darkness of his tent, thinking of all the times he'd told Hasdrubal to send Mathos back to Carthage. Now it was too late... he was gone.

If one looked hard enough, Mago believed, they could find a character in a story that could describe their own life. For him, it was Cassandra, Princess of Troy. Like her, Mago felt he had the power to foresee the future, and that it was more curse than gift; for like Cassandra, he was frequently correct but seldom believed beforehand. It made him wonder why his warnings fell on deaf ears, and he tried to find the answers in that story. Perhaps, he thought, people like Priam and Hector, or Hannibal and Hasdrubal, held some beliefs so strongly that they would blindly sacrifice everything else rather than face the truth. Still, it was his lot in life to try and make them understand those things that, to Mago, were obvious. Maybe if they read the *Iliad*, Mago thought, his brothers would see themselves in the Greek king, Agamemnon, who had to sacrifice no less than his own daughter

116

before he even set sail for Troy. Perhaps they would see then that the true costs of war can never be foreseen but reveal themselves little by little as the struggle unfolds, and the only thing we can know about them is that they will be horrific. *Yes, they might see that... Then again, probably not.*

When Hasdrubal finally arrived in camp, Mago emerged with a ferocity that surprised everyone—even himself. He walked directly up to Hasdrubal, who towered over him, reached back, and punched him in the jaw hard enough to knock the big man down. Hasdrubal sprang to his feet and tackled Mago, got on top of him and began pummeling his younger brother; but Mago managed to throw him off, and they grappled, cursing one another amid their grunts and yelps of pain. The soldiers nearby stood watching, mouths agape. Eventually, Maharbal intervened, and others followed. With considerable effort, they managed to forcefully separate them. Both brothers' tunics were torn, and Mago's lip was split. The metallic taste of blood filled his mouth, but he barely noticed.

"You see what your damned war has cost us?" Mago bawled as two brawny Celtiberians held him back. "He was a child!"

"He was *my* child, Mago!" Hasdrubal yelled back.

"You had no right! No right to drag him here! He's dead because of you, you shit!"

"The gods willed this, not me!"

"I piss on your gods!" Mago cried.

The blasphemy seemed to stun Hasdrubal into silence, but its effect was fleeting. His face soon hardened into a snarl and he yelled back at his brother.

"Why don't you just say it?" Hasdrubal cried.

"What?"

"You hated our father!"

Mago shook the Celtiberians off him. Hasdrubal also broke free and pointed a finger at his younger brother just as Hannibal stepped inside the ring of soldiers that had formed around them.

"You hated him!" Hasdrubal thundered. "You've always hated—"

"Yes!" Mago shouted back. "I hated him! Hated him for leaving us like he did, like a *coward*!"

"Mago... " Hannibal started, but Mago was apoplectic.

"I hated him for dooming us to this," Mago said, indicating the camp around them with a wave of the hand. "For tying us down with his failures! You both blame Rome for what he did, but *he* decided to fall on his sword. *He* made us take those oaths. Just as *you* started this war," he said, pointing to Hannibal, then shifting his attention to Hasdrubal and said, "And *you* kept Mathos here. But go on, both of you. Blame Rome for all of it... just like father."

Hasdrubal spat in Mago's direction and stormed away. Mago returned the gesture and promptly returned to his tent, where he could finally allow himself some wine.

***

It had only been a day since he'd learned that Mathos was dead, but in that time, he had neglected to do things he would have normally done at the end of a march. He knew that his clothes and body stank, even if he didn't notice the smell until after returning to his tent from outside. Spilled wine and a spot in the corner where he had urinated a few times also contributed to the wretched condition of his quarters. The only thing he'd bothered to set up was his bedroll, which was where he was when Hannibal entered. Mago saw his brother scrunch his nose and kick an empty amphora out of his way as he approached.

"I'm in no mood for a lecture, Hannibal," Mago said from his bedroll.

Hannibal cleared a space and sat on the floor next to him.

"Did you not hear me?" Mago asked. Irritated, he picked his head up to glower at his older brother.

"If I could, Mago, I'd give you as long you needed to mourn him," Hannibal said. "But I can't."

Mago groaned and put his head back down.

"The Romans landed at Massilia," Hannibal told him. "I need you with me."

"Hannibal needs no one but Hannibal," Mago grumbled.

"You know that's not true."

"Massilia is at least three days march," Mago said. "We'll all be dead in the Alps before the Roman catch up."

"We may have to fight our way across the Rhone," Hannibal told him. "I need you to come with me."

Mago was silent and still for a long moment, hoping Hannibal would go away. After a while, it was clear that he wasn't. Finally, Mago picked his head up and squinted at his oldest brother.

"You're serious, aren't you?" he asked.

Hannibal didn't need to answer. No one mattered in his world—not really. Only Rome did. It made Mago wonder what Hannibal would do with the rest of his life, once Rome was no more; but most of the time, he doubted Carthage would win the war. The greater mystery Mago supposed, was what Hannibal would do when faced with failure. He could only hope, for the sake of Hannibal's wife and newborn son, that Hannibal would choose differently than their father.

HANNIBAL

It seemed that the entire Volcae tribe, from young boys to old women, were emplacing obstacles on the eastern bank of the Rhone directly across from Hannibal's camp. He planned to give them a final opportunity to back down and let his army pass through unhindered, but he was nearly certain that they wanted to fight. While Hannibal reconnoitered the Volcae defenses, Gisgo organized the men into work parties to make enough rafts for the men, baggage, and animals.

From a hilltop, Hannibal gazed across the river and saw the Volcae emplacing an *abatis*—rows of offset sharpened logs in the embankment meant to impede his men when they charged up the embankment at the enemy. In his mind's eye, he saw the ranks of Volcae that would soon stand there, weapons in hand, ready to cut down his soldiers. The river was wide enough that enemy archers and skirmishers wouldn't be a factor until Hannibal's men were more than halfway across. Still, those trying to cross would have to be shielded on all sides except the rear. That meant at least ten men per raft—two with shields to the front, four with shields to the sides, two rowers, and two with shields proving top cover. It would be a slow-moving craft, but it was the only way to make an opposed river crossing with what he had on hand. Those that made it across would then have to deal with the emplaced obstacles and more arrows, then fight their way uphill. It would be difficult and tiring, keeping their shields up while climbing. The battle scenario that played out in his head was both costly and time-consuming. After the crossing, he would probably not be able to move quickly again for several days as they regrouped and treated the wounded; all the while, the Romans would be closing in from the south.

No... it would not do.

He needed to fight and win this battle fast and decisively. He needed to take control of this entire zone to get his men across in a single day. Fighting their way up the embankment wasn't an option he'd consider. They needed to arrive on top of the enemy defenses, or at least level with them. Given a few days, they may be able to make larger rafts to carry small siege towers. Yes... he could picture it. They would get his men across, and the Volcae would lose their main advantage of being able to fire at the crossers from above. Even flaming arrows would not pose that much of a danger, provided they crossed quickly. Impale the towers on the *abatis*, drop the gates right on top of the embankment, and Hannibal's men could emerge level with their enemy. The rafts would need to be monstrously wide to be stable. It would take a minimum of two weeks, even with the labor force he had at hand, to design and build enough of the beasts. The Romans would arrive long before that, and Hannibal would have to fight an even larger force defending the other side.

"They'll take three of ours for every one of theirs," he heard a voice from behind him say, and he turned to see Mago taking a swig from his wineskin.

Hannibal laughed.

"What are you so happy about?" Mago asked.

"Glad to see you're back in the fight," he answered him. "Even if you are a pessimist."

"Well... I have to balance out your sunny disposition, don't I?"

Hannibal led his mounted reconnaissance party, consisting of Mago and two of his guards, north. They stayed in the tree line, out of the enemy's line of sight, as they rode parallel to the riverbank. The land soon became wooded and steep. After a few miles, the Rhone split into western and eastern tributaries, and Hannibal could no longer see the Volcae villages across the river.

Leaving the guards and horses behind, Hannibal and Mago made their way through the forest to the river's edge. Once there, Hannibal began shedding his clothes.

"Have you lost your—?" Mago began, but his objection was cut short.

"Come on," Hannibal chided him. "It can't be that cold. Besides, you can use a bath."

There was no way to adjust to the cold water. They waded in as quickly as possible and had to swim before they were midway to the median. The current carried them a little farther south than Hannibal had expected. When they found their footing again, they were in the mud near the bifurcation point. The cool air hit their skin and set them shivering when they emerged and made their way into the tree line.

"What are we doing here?" Mago panted.

"Seeing what lays beyond," Hannibal told him, chuckling when his brother predictably rolled his eyes.

Descending the tributary's eastern bank, they broke through the undergrowth. Leafless branches mercilessly scratched their exposed skin. Finally, they could see the eastern tributary. On the far side was a steep embankment, which Hannibal guessed was part of the Volcae irrigation scheme. He quickened the pace and led his brother north along the bank, trying to use the exercise to warm their wet bodies.

"How far do you think we floated down?" Hannibal asked.

"Maybe a quarter of a mile," Mago guessed, his teeth chattering.

"Pay closer attention this time," Hannibal told him, and heard

Mago groan as they waded into the water.

"I bet they bathe their beasts and dump their shit in this river," Mago said as they swam.

The water was shallower on this side of the bifurcation. There was no swimming, but they were still tired and breathing heavily when they reached the other side. Hannibal held his finger to his bluish lips and Mago nodded. After crawling on his belly up to the top and peeking over, Hannibal laughed with joy.

"What?" Mago whispered from below.

"Come see for yourself."

Mago crawled up, and both men looked out over a field of wheat stalks cut to within six inches of the ground. Far afield stood a few cottages, where they could see some adults working as children played.

"I don't see anything," Mago said with a shake of his head.

"Just as I'd hoped," Hannibal answered. "Do you think you could find your way back here?"

Mago looked around and said, "Probably."

"How about in the dark?"

"I don't know. Maybe."

"You'll have tomorrow and the next day to prepare."

"Then what happens?"

"You're going to lead five thousand men here."

SCIPIO

Before he even met the soldiers that he was to command, Scipio sought out his old schoolmate, Lars Herminius. Lars had been his *Decurion* for two campaign seasons, and Scipio considered him one of the better officers in the cavalry.

He found him in the belly of the ship on which they had both arrived, just as he was taking his horse out of its stall to disembark.

"I only have a few minutes," Lars told him. "Walk with me."

His weapons and armor secured on the horse's back, Lars took the animal by the bit and guided him toward the ramp to the upper deck.

"I'm guessing you didn't ask for this promotion," Lars said.

"What makes you say that?"

"Because I know you," he replied as they walked up the ramp onto the sunlit deck. "And you look like you're walking to your execution instead of meeting your men."

Scipio was taken aback. He hadn't thought of how he must have looked, but Lars was right—it did feel like a punishment of some sort.

"Come on," Lars said. "Just lay it all out, right now, before they see you. What are you afraid of?"

"Aside from getting myself killed?" Scipio asked facetiously.

"I've seen you risk your life for some cheers and a laurel at the track," Lars replied. "Come on. What is it?"

He was ashamed of what he would say, but he knew there was no point in speaking with Lars if he was not going to be candid.

"Before, it was just me," Scipio said. "I mean, if I messed up, I might get myself killed, but it was just me. That was fine. Now someone else might die because of me."

"Men die following orders," Lars told him. "You can't protect them and do your job at the same time, so don't try."

They walked the horse onto the pier, and Scipio realized they wouldn't have much more time together. Both their troops were waiting for their *Decurions*.

"I don't have to take care of them?" Scipio asked.

"I didn't say that," Lars replied. "I said you can't *protect* them. You take care of them by making sure they're ready to fight. That'll give them the best shot of getting home alive."

Lars stopped his horse and turned to Scipio.

"Look, soldiers are simple creatures, Scipio. They need food, sleep, and discipline. That's all. Take care of them and they'll take care of you. That's what I say, anyway. And for the love of the gods, Scipio, pick your head up! You think your men want to see you like this? Especially for the first time. They can't be confident if you're not. Where's that cocky ass that thought it'd be fun to race chariots with the slaves?"

Scipio allowed himself a small smile.

"Having some luck on your side always helps as well," Lars said. "You see this?"

He showed Scipio a bronze bracelet on his right. When Lars turned it over, Scipio could see it was shaped like a phallus wrapped around his wrist.

"Do you have one?" Lars asked.

"Right between my legs," Scipio answered.

"Seriously... I've known you since we were children," Lars told him. "You're bright. You're capable. That puts you head and shoulders above most junior officers."

Scipio took a deep breath and tried to exhale the gloominess, knowing that Lars was right—his men had to see him confident.

"It makes sense," Scipio told him. "Thank you, Lars."

Lars smiled and lightly punched Scipio's shoulder.

"Good luck, *Decurio*," he said, and walked toward his waiting men.

***

Scipio took command of a ten-strong troop that had two established leaders, Appius and Plinius. They would now serve as his deputies and lead four men each. Plinius was the senior of the two and older, around thirty. He looked and sounded perpetually grumpy, which made Scipio wonder if it was an act to keep the men in line or his natural disposition. Appius was about the same age as Scipio and carried himself with the ease, confidence, and swagger of a patrician.

They rode north out of Massilia as several ships headed to the mouth of the Rhone, carrying other Roman cavalry on a mission to scout the Carthaginian army. At dusk, they set up camp on the southern slope of a hill near the crest. They were still far from the enemy, but Scipio did not want to risk their cooking fire being spotted. As soon as their armor was off and their horses watered, the porridge began cooking and the men slowly gathered into a group separate from Scipio and his deputies.

From the sounds of their laughter, Scipio would have guessed they were out drinking wine instead of living the rugged life of soldiers in the field. They laughed at each other's lack of knowledge of the world, bragged about how far they could throw a spear and how well they rode their horse, and called each other out for supposedly lying about how long they lasted in bed. Scipio listened, enjoying their conversation every bit as much as they did, but chose not to participate in order to maintain some aloofness.

One of the soldiers looked like a man sitting in a circle of boys, towering over his laughing comrades as he spoke.

"Now, wait a minute... " he said.

Scipio had trouble remembering some of their names, having met them all at once, but this one was easy to remember. Over six feet tall and over two hundred lean pounds, Magilus was by far the biggest soldier out of the three hundred cavalrymen in their legion.

"Wait a minute... " he repeated while the laughter died down. "I don't know Maxentius's wife, but I do know Maxentius, and I don't think she started sleeping with half the men in his village as soon as he left home."

"Thank you, Magilus," Maxentius replied.

"No... she was already sleeping with them well before he left!" Magilus delivered the punchline with gusto, making others roar with laughter.

"*Decurio...* " Plinius called to Scipio, using the title for his new rank. From the cooking fire, he held up a bowl and spoon. "Officers eat first," he said.

He ate while the men lined up by order of rank and time in service, from most senior to most junior. Gaius, a slim young soldier from a poor neighborhood of Rome called Suburra, was last. The boy received about half of what the others had gotten. It was the first time something given out based on rank seemed unjust to Scipio. Why should any one of them receive less or more food, when they all shared the work? As an officer, Scipio did far less physical labor than a low-ranking soldier like Gaius, but he got double the food. The porridge that had tasted so good after a hard day now sat in his stomach uncomfortably.

"What are we doing in Gaul, anyway?" Maxentius asked as they stood in a loose circle and ate the flavorless mush.

Gaius looked up from his bowl at Scipio.

"We're not in Hispania?" he asked. "I thought we were going to Hispania?"

"We haven't even left Italy yet," Magilus told him. "We're headed south, toward the Alps."

"The Alps are in the north," Maxentius said, then looked at Scipio and asked, "Aren't they?"

"We're in Gaul," Appius told them, abruptly ending the discussion.

"Why?" Magilus asked.

"Hannibal is here," Scipio told them, but was met with blank stares.

"Who's Hannibal?" Gaius asked.

The question took Scipio by surprise. Regardless of the extent of their knowledge of geography, he thought they would at least know who they were being sent to fight.

"I know this one," Maxentius said, holding up his index finger. "He's a Carthaginian."

"Just be glad we aren't farther north," Plinius told them.

"Why?" Appius asked. "What's farther north?"

"Druids," he answered, his gravelly voice low, as if speaking the name too loud would summon them. "They're sorcerers... priests of the local gods."

The men quieted, and none seemed to blink as they listened to Plinius.

"You've seen them?" Appius asked him.

"Not me, no," Plinius said. "Thank the gods. A few years ago, we were up this way, a little farther north on the other side of the Rhone, fighting the Voconti. A few of them refused to surrender and headed north. We would have left them alone, but word got back to our general that a druid was up there, stirring up the northern tribes, pitting them against us. He sent a maniple to get the druid and bring him to us. They never returned."

"You never saw them again?" Appius asked.

"We found some parts," Plinius said. "The locals told us the druids prized Roman blood, especially nobility. Used it in their magic, they said. Anyway, we withdrew before the winter set in. I don't think any legion has gone that far north since then."

Plinius took his empty bowl and spoon back to his sleeping area, leaving the men to steal anxious glances at each other. Scipio was worried that their fears would get the better of them, but the penalty for desertion was death, and he doubted that any would take that chance because of a scary story.

Overall, his impression was that the soldiers in his care were jovial and, for the most part, likable. Their ignorance of the world was shocking but also endearing. There was something childlike about them, a naivete and innocence that made them seem in need of protection from the harsh realities of life, despite having the bodies of men.

As darkness fell, Scipio and Plinius made a watch list. The rest of the men squatted and knelt in a circle, hooting and hollering occasionally, and other times groaning.

"What are they doing?" Scipio asked.

"Hmph... Gambling, probably," Plinius suggested. "Even though I told them not to. New officer comes in, they'll try to get away with things."

Scipio turned his head as several of them wailed in agony while others cheered after a dice roll.

"You men!" Plinius called. "I told you before! No gambling!"

Scipio could hear the groans of disappointment as the circle broke up.

"Just as well," said Magilus. "Gaius always takes all our money anyway. Lucky turd... "

The men laughed as Gaius put the dice back in his bag.

"Why not?" Scipio asked Plinius. "I don't see the harm."

"Nothing good can come of it, sir," Plinius answered him. "Gambling leads to losing. Losing leads to fighting."

"It's their only entertainment around here," Scipio said.

"Sir... "

"You all can gamble, if you want," Scipio announced before Plinius could voice any further objection. If they harbored some ill-feelings about the meal, he could make it up to them now.

The men all looked over at him in disbelief.

"New policy," Scipio said. "Within reason, of course."

They gave cheers to him, and Scipio chuckled at their delight. Plinius, however, did not seem pleased.

"Sir, maybe we can talk about—"

"You see how happy they are," Scipio said. "It's good for morale."

"Yes, sir."

Before he could turn to leave, Plinius took him by the arm.

"Change is fine," he said. "Just make sure that your changes are good for our mission, good for the men... Not just good for yourself, sir."

Scipio nodded to his deputy. With that, his deputy turned and shuffled off to his sleeping area. It seemed to be good enough for Plinius, at least for now.

In The Shadow of the Furies

AEMILIA

Aemilia knew that this was one of the most politically important times of the year, but she'd never participated in it this deeply. After the harvests, country people came into Rome for the Plebeian Games, several holidays, and *Mercatus*—the fall market. Candidates for every office take full advantage of the event that clogged the Forum stump for support. Courts convened to hear civil cases, assemblies gathered to hear arguments for and against proposed laws, and the Senate met to hear motions and vote on issues ranging from war and peace to city sanitation.

Over the course of countless dinner parties hosted in the fine houses of Palatine Hill, Senators of all factions would meet, argue, make deals, and hash things out before anyone sat in the great chamber. This evening's party was in the home of her family friend, the most respected of all Romans, Senator Fabius Maximus Verrucosus.

It was not Fabius that Aemilia wished to see, however. This was her first chance to see Marcus Cato up close and confront him about what he had done to her cousin. After much pleading, Paullus had used his considerable influence to arrange for them to sit at their hosts' table with Cato; unfortunately, it also meant sitting with Varro.

Their host and his matronly wife, Lucretia, greeted Aemilia and her father in an atrium adorned with some of the most beautiful frescos Aemilia had ever seen. The scenes from their city's ancient past were instantly recognizable. There was the hero Aeneus fleeing Troy with a small band of survivors as the city burned; on an adjoining wall, a she-wolf suckling the twins Romulus and Remus; across from it, Brutus was leading the rebellion that overthrew the last King of Rome. Their subjects seemed ready to jump off the walls and join the party.

More impressive was how the guests, including her father, treated Fabius. Though they were at opposite ends of the Roman political spectrum, both Paullus and Marcus Cato were extremely deferential to the man. Even the notoriously irreverent Varro seemed a little humbled when standing in front of Fabius.

With seven diners, the three *klines* around Fabius's table were nearly full. They could each comfortably fit three diners reclining on their sides or stomachs with their heads toward the table in the center, but Varro's circumference was nearly equal to two normal-sized diners. Luckily, Fabius placed Cato on his own *kline* next to him and Lucretia. They were directly across from Aemilia and Paullus. On the third *kline* were Varro and his surprisingly attractive wife, Valeria.

At these sorts of gatherings, women were largely expected to sit, eat, look pretty, and leave the men to do all the talking. Aemilia restrained herself from speaking at first, being content to listen and observe. Above all, she wanted Cato to speak and reveal himself to her, as unvarnished and unguarded as possible.

Unfortunately, Varro was taking up all the space in the conversation. The servants had barely begun to bring out a course of lettuce and boiled eggs when Varro began attacking his political enemies.

"I, for one, wouldn't give a fig for Cornelius's chances of catching Hannibal in Gaul," Varro said. "At every turn, the Carthaginians have outsmarted our Consuls. We need someone as daring and intelligent as Hannibal to defeat him, not some... Greek-loving phonies."

"You admire Hannibal?" Fabius asked.

"We're much alike," Varro said with a nod. "Tough, demanding. We're men of action, not muddle-headed pondering and words. We see what we want, and we take it."

As if to illustrate his point, Varro seized a peeled boiled egg from a plate and popped it whole in his mouth. *Pig*, Aemilia thought to herself as she watched the folds of fat on Varro's neck jiggle with every chomp of his jaw.

"I hardly think that fair," Paullus said. "No one knew Hannibal was even *in* Gaul before Cornelius's scouts discovered him."

"He should have known," Varro shot back. "You would have, Fabius."

It was one of Varro's favorite rhetorical tricks, and it played on men's pride. It fostered a sense that this was "us" against... whomever Varro was attacking that day.

"How can you miss something as big as an army moving toward you? And with elephants? How could you... Cornelius should be ashamed! Massilia didn't warn us because they have no respect for us. They know our Consuls are stupid and weak. It's pathetic! They're laughing at us! Just like the rest of the world."

"Nevertheless," Fabius said, "the Senate must now define a clear path forward."

It wasn't the first time Aemilia had noticed Fabius's slow and deliberate way of speaking. Her father had told her that a stutter was the reason. "Fabius the Tongue-Tied" many Senators called him—behind his back, of course.

"We should recall Sempronius immediately," Varro blurted out. "We must defend the lands that we work, which feed our children and our army. Italy first!"

"The people to whom you deliver your... speeches have no

concept of strategy," Paullus said, clearly hesitant to dignify Varro's diatribes by calling them speeches. "They don't know the value of having troops in striking distance of Africa, or even of taking Hispania. We do."

"Are you calling your fellow citizens stupid, Paullus?" Varro asked. "Do their opinions not matter as much as yours?"

"You speak of people that can locate neither Rome nor Carthage on a map," Paullus replied. "Are you saying their ignorance is as good as my expertise?"

"Just what is wrong with an Italy first strategy, anyway?" Varro challenged him.

"Tell me, Senator," Paullus replied. "Why does it always seem you're advocating precisely the policies that Carthage would want us to adopt? Like shrinking back into Italy and leaving Sicily undefended?"

Varro was beet red and ready to erupt, and Aemilia braced herself for a lengthy diatribe against elites and their "lies" about him. To her surprise, however, Varro's retaliation ended with the glare that he gave to her father. Perhaps, she thought, it was Varro's ingrained respect for Paullus's reputation, but she knew that Varro never showed respect of his own accord. *Why now, then?*

She noticed Valeria's hand resting on Varro's arm. Aemilia didn't know when she'd moved it there, but it might well have been what calmed the raging storm of her pugnacious husband's indignation. *Interesting...*

Finally, Cato spoke up.

"I, for one, believe we should prepare for a long war," he said, clearing his throat. "It's why I've taken the liberty of drafting a number of resolutions to put before the Senate and popular assemblies in the coming weeks seeing to the welfare of the people's morale and piety, as well as to raise much-needed funds for the war effort."

"And what might these resolutions propose?" Fabius asked.

"Policies that every true Roman can support," Cato said. "For one, I propose an indefinite ban on foreign cults and religious practices."

"And how, exactly, would that help win the war?" Fabius asked, eyebrows raised.

"Many ways, Fabius," Cato told him. "I'm surprised one as learned in both religion and politics as yourself should need to ask."

Aemilia rolled her eyes as she brought her wine to her lips. Looking over the brim of the cup, she saw Valeria looking back at her with a slight smile and knew that she must have seen the gesture. *It seems she feels the same*, Aemilia thought.

Cato launched into a lengthy discourse about the importance of honoring Roman gods as protectors and guardians of the state, and how immigrants and expatriates living in the city were perverting the hearts of Romans by enticing them to worship gods with no place in the Roman pantheon. As it went on, Aemilia could feel the wine she was melting away the veneer of passive feminine acceptance that every patrician Roman female was taught since childhood. She had a complete rebuttal to every point in her head, but she was still holding her tongue. Men could be emotional in their rhetoric; women could not.

"Hear! Hear!" Varro agreed enthusiastically, raising his cup to Cato. "These foreigners come to Rome, and they just take advantage of us in every way!"

"Of course, all things Greek would be at the top of this of

things to ban," Paullus said to Cato. "How can you ban foreign religious practices, after all, when Greek culture is infused with Greek religion. Am I correct, Cato?"

"Precisely," Cato answered. "Romans are of a proud agrarian tradition, Paullus. The Samnites from which I and most Romans descend passed down to us a rigorous way of life that every day we are losing. These petty distractions the urban intelligentsia are so enamored of—poetry, philosophy, plays, histories... " he spat each subject out of his mouth with disdain. "How do they benefit the average Roman? Plato and Aristotle do not put food in our mouths. They do not keep our enemies at bay or honor our gods. Greeks! Heads addled by useless ponderings, bodies softened by urban living and self-indulgence. We will surpass them in greatness, Paullus, but only by remaining quintessentially *Roman*—pious, pure of mind and spirit... as a free people must be."

Aemilia glared at him, seeing him up on the Rostra as the crowd screamed for her cousin's death. This rant against intellectuals was even more reason to hate him. Cato wanted all of Rome to be as mindless as the mobs he manipulated with his venomous rhetoric. She wanted to launch across the table, grab him by his toga, and scream into his self-righteous face.

"Forcing people to think and behave in a single fashion is not freedom," she said, a slight trembling in her voice as she pushed down her fury. "It is slavery. *That* is what you and your policies offer, whatever patriotic rhetoric you dress it in."

The entire room seemed to stop breathing for a moment. A woman rarely challenged a man in this sort of setting. Aemilia was more outspoken than most, but there was still etiquette to consider. Not addressing him as 'Senator' was bad enough, but her tone had conveyed a direct mocking of him. She realized that it was rude of her, but she was barely in control of herself.

Cato glowered at her as if she had directly attacked his honor. Perhaps it was even the first time a woman had spoken up to him. Even Varro, comfortable with verbal brawls as he was, shifted his rotund frame in the *kline* awkwardly when he saw Cato's expression.

"How *dare* you say... " Cato began with venom in his voice, but he stopped midsentence as some sort of realization seemed to dawn across his face.

"Ah, yes," he said. "Opimia was a cousin of yours, wasn't she? You're upset. Any woman would be. But your anger with me is misguided."

"Just another misguided, hysterical woman," Aemilia said in a tone that dripped with sarcasm.

"Aemilia... " Paullus began, and she knew how close she was to being silenced—a step Paullus had never taken with her.

"It's fine," Cato told Paullus, swiping the air with his hand. "There were several witnesses to the infidelity of both Vestal Virgins Opimia and Floronia, and their guilt had already been decided by the *Pontifex Maximus*. I was merely speaking about the root causes of their transgressions."

"Grandstanding to a mob," Aemilia shot back.

Cato put his wine cup down hard on the table, grimacing.

"I implored them to have mercy on the girl!" he said, raising his voice. "They wanted her buried alive. I got them to let her end her own life, restoring whatever honor she had left."

"How merciful," Aemilia said, picking up her wine and rolling her eyes.

She then heard the slight but unmistakable sound of a woman's laugh from Valeria's direction, and she looked over to

137

see her putting her finger to her lips and clearing her throat. The smile on her lips this time, however, was unmistakable.

"The women were not to blame," Cato said, his voice tense with anger. "This was my message. This absurd Platonic notion of women's equality to men has been creeping into our laws and culture for far too long, and it is time to set things right. Our republic once respected a man's right to do as he wishes within his own household. This is nature's law. Greeks once knew this well enough that they tried Socrates and sentenced him to death for setting children against their fathers."

"You believe his fate was deserved?" Fabius asked.

"Richly," Cato answered.

"I suppose you'd say the same of anyone with independent thoughts," Aemilia said.

Cato immediately turned, an ugly snarl on his face, and snapped at her.

"He subverted the teachings of his students' fathers, and he refused to honor his gods! Few crimes ever recorded have been so heinous!"

"He taught his students how to think, Senator," she countered. "Not what to think."

"That is a lie Socrates's followers so skillfully advanced to save themselves from the same fate," Cato said. "Now, the Greek-loving intellectuals among us subvert our own society with the same twisted thinking to corrupt the building block of Roman society—the family."

"Is that what the *lex Oppia* does?" Aemilia asked. "Protect families?"

"Precisely," Cato replied. "At the beginning of the Republic, a man had absolute authority over his fam—"

"Beginning of the Republic?" Aemilia interrupted and scoffed. "Three and a half centuries ago, when a man could beat his wife to death for the criminal act of drinking wine? That's where your laws intend to take us?"

Cato began speaking over her before Aemilia even finished.

"It does no such thing," he was saying. "Of course, we would never take away—"

Aemilia returned the favor by speaking over Cato, raising her voice to match his tone.

"I think you know very well it would bring us to within a breath of—"

She noticed that Cato began raising his voice as her points irked him, and she refused to be silent.

"P-P-Perhaps... " Fabius loudly interrupted them both, raising his hands as if to separate them. "Perhaps we c-could discuss the c-c-Consular elections."

Aemilia and Cato signaled their acquiescence to the wishes of their host by falling silent, though the air between them simmered with hatred and contempt.

Cato had reacted more severely than Aemilia had anticipated. She now knew that he had a temper when it came to his opinions being mocked, especially when it was by a woman.

"Senator Varro," Aemilia said, "I'm surprised you're not standing for Consul this year."

"Many have expressed that thought," he answered, nodding to her in appreciation. "In fact, many, many, very intelligent and distinguished people have asked me why I haven't yet held the office. Smart people ask me that all the time... very smart people. Now you may count yourself among them."

"How thrilling," she said flatly. "Might I know any others that have asked the same?"

Varro answered by stuffing some dates into his mouth. For whatever reason, he seemed to let the small slight go, which Aemilia knew was something he was not wont to do. She looked up to see that Valeria's eyes were narrow and her gaze was fixed on her. Aemilia felt like a bird on a sill that just noticed a cat about to pounce on it, but instead of bearing her claws, Valeria calmly put her cup down on the table as her husband gorged himself.

"My husband consorts in many social circles," she said to Aemilia. "And hears a great many things from a great many people. We cannot always remember who said what to whom, can we?"

It was a pathetic answer, but it provided Aemilia with an excuse to get her first good look at the woman who was, she estimated, at least twenty years younger than her oafish spouse and much too pretty for him. Her hair was perfectly done up with bejeweled golden pins, and her pink and blue Greek-style *himation* complemented her slim figure.

"You have a sharped-tongued daughter, Paullus," Cato said.

"It is the companion of a sharp intellect," Aemilia said.

"And where is a woman to apply such an intellect?" Cato asked. "At the loom, perhaps?"

"Politics," she said.

Cato laughed as if it were an obvious joke, but no one laughed along.

"You might as well say you're interested in flying like a bird," he said. "Women are wholly unsuited to the world of politics and law."

It was tempting to jump back into a heated exchange with Cato, but she heard Fabius draw a heavy breath and decided on a different course.

"What do *you* think, Valeria?" Aemilia asked.

She half expected the woman to blush and stammer since she was suddenly the center of attention for reasons other than her charm and sex appeal, but Valeria didn't seem fazed in the slightest.

"I believe women are incredibly powerful already," she said. "In all the households of Italy, the *Domina* reigns supreme. Doesn't she? We may allow the men to think they are in charge, but everyone knows who the true master of the home is. Don't we?"

The men at the table laughed politely, though Aemilia was less than amused.

"And are we to simply content ourselves with housework?" Aemilia asked her.

"Politics is ugly, dear," Valeria replied. "As you can see here. Necessary, perhaps, but dirty. Good women are too virtuous to sully themselves with it."

Cato raised his wine to her, and Aemilia saw something in the way Valeria returned his look. It may have been nothing, she told herself; though Cato seemed at least intrigued by the woman, if not slightly infatuated. She would have to check her gossip sources. Affairs were always useful information. For a married woman, it could be critically important to keep it secret.

"Again," Fabius said, "I believe we should discuss proper candidates for Consul."

"Ah! An important topic," Varro said. "Very, very important..."

Aemilia drew a breath to object, but she felt her father's hand on her shoulder. She knew the expression well. *Drop the subject.*

No matter how much it means, drop it. She could live with that if it meant living to fight another day, for her father had taught her that politics was not always about having loud and boisterous arguments in the Senate or in front of the popular assemblies. Things were done in subtler ways in quieter places.

As Varro effusively praised himself and his supposed accomplishments in business, Aemilia noticed Valeria was looking at her. She tried not to look back, watching her out of the corner of her eye while seeming to politely listen to Varro; but Aemilia was positive that Valeria was staring. She had come to take the measure of Cato and Varro. Valeria, it seemed, was now taking measure of her.

Scipio

Scipio led his troops north for a day along the eastern side of the Rhone river. Based on the map his father had shown him, he estimated they would reach the Volcae tribe's lands the following day. If he could find a vantage point, he hoped to see the Carthaginian camp across the river and their preparations for crossing. If not, he could simply ride back without incident, having swept the route for the infantry without encountering any enemies or obstacles. Either way, it seemed likely that he would be able to do what his father wanted and that no one would be hurt. At this point, that was all that he wanted.

From the top of the hill where they would set camp, they could see the river to their left and the land in front of them becoming flatter. There saw no villages, but the curling black smoke on the horizon suggested hearth fires.

As the sun set, the men set up their sleeping areas and Scipio found himself looking west across the water, trying to see a

Roman patrol moving parallel to him on the other side of the river. All he saw were trees. It bothered him that there were no other Roman units in sight, but his hunger soon overrode all his other concerns. As bland as he knew it would be, smelling the food begin to cook made his mouth water and his stomach grumble.

"Porridge..." young Gaius grumbled as it cooked in an iron pot of a small fire. "I can't wait to get back on regular rations."

"I can smell the bacon cooking all ready," Magilus said, patting his stomach.

"That was the reason I joined up in the first place," Gaius said.

"What was?" Scipio asked him.

"Three good meals a day, sir," Gaius answered, taking a bite of his bread ration.

Scipio chuckled, but he quickly saw that Gaius was serious.

"You really joined the army to feed yourself?"

"Yes, sir," Gaius answered. "Campaigns fatten me up. Full-time soldier, full-time eater."

"Aren't you an *equite*?" Scipio asked, referring to the class of Romans that could afford to buy and outfit his own warhorse.

"No, sir," he answered.

"When there's a cavalry shortage, the state takes some infantrymen and buys them horses," Appius explained. "Plinius was one of those, too. Isn't that right, Plinius?"

"Officers eat first," Plinius said, holding up a bowl to Scipio. "Come on, sir."

Scipio stepped up and took a bowl. Plinius filled it with porridge up to near the top as the others lined up behind him. Gaius, he saw, was at the back.

"Gaius," Scipio called. "That's your name, correct?"

"Yes, sir."

Scipio motioned him over and handed him the bowl. Gaius looked confused.

"Eat up," Scipio told him, taking Gaius's place at the back of the line.

"Officers eat first, sir," Appius said. "That's the way."

"New orders," Scipio said firmly. "Officers eat last."

Appius glanced at Plinius, as if he expected him to countermand Scipio's order, but Plinius just shrugged and continued serving. Appius stepped to the back of the line and took a place in front of Scipio. The eating order was now completely reversed—the lowest soldiers ate first, and highest last. By the time Plinius had served the others and himself, Scipio took the meager scrapings and tried not to seem disappointed, no matter how much his stomach objected.

The temperature dropped quickly, and the men gathered around the fire to begin their gambling. Scipio wrapped himself in his heavy cloak and thought of Aemilia as he rested his head on his bag. He could only picture her waiting for him to return, as unrealistic as that was. Suitors were probably lined up at her father's house, he knew. Still, it gave him a little comfort to think of her lying next to him in the warm Italian sun tickling his nose with a blade of grass and laughing...

The next sound he heard was a soldier's voice urgently calling him.

"*Decurio!*" it said.

Scipio felt as if he had just closed his eyes... Something was happening. Why was Appius standing over him?

"*Decurio!*" Appius yelled and shook Scipio back into a frantic reality.

There were noises close by—clanging, scuffing, grunting. It sounded like a fight, and Scipio instinctively reached for his sword. Appius stepped back as he drew it.

"Come quickly!" Appius said, motioning him to follow.

When they got to the spot, the first thing Scipio saw was Plinius, sword in hand, scowling. At his feet, three men had the giant Magilus pinned to the ground on his stomach while they locked his arms behind his back. Scipio didn't see Gaius until Appius ran over to him. The young soldier was propped against a tree with his hand over the side of his stomach, grimacing. A dark stain was spreading from the spot, and another soldier was trying to staunch the bleeding with a wadded tunic.

"He's a cheat!" Magilus was yelling. "His dice are loaded! He was cheating! He stole from all of us!"

Plinius showed Scipio a dagger still wet with blood.

"The wages of gambling," he said.

Scipio's eyes darted around the camp, secretly hoping to see something that might magically rectify the situation.

"How is he?" Scipio asked, looking at Gaius.

"I've seen men suffer worse and live," Plinius replied, "and I've seen them die from less."

"Get him some water!" Appius ordered, prompting a soldier to spring into action.

Scipio looked around again for that magic solution as a thousand thoughts raced in his head, flying through his consciousness like leaves in a windstorm.

"The penalty for killing a fellow soldier is death," Plinius said, snapping him back into the moment.

"He cheated us all!" Magilus protested from the ground. "He's the one needs killing!"

"Shut your mouth!" Plinius bellowed.

"He might pull through," Scipio said, looking at Gaius sipping some water. "We'll just... try to stop the bleeding."

"And him?" Plinius asked, pointing to Magilus with his sword.

Scipio hesitated. There were no good options. Plinius must have sensed his indecisiveness and stepped in.

"Stand him up," Plinius told the soldiers, who struggled to maintain the control of Magilus as they brought him to his feet.

Plinius brought his lips close to Scipio's ear.

"Do it quick, sir," he said in a low voice. "And be done with it."

"And lose two men instead of one?"

"Out here, we enforce discipline," Plinius told him. "It's the only thing that keeps—"

Before he could finish, Magilus broke free with a loud cry, grabbing the sword from one of the men who had held him just a moment ago. Both soldiers stumbled back and scrambled away. Magilus lunged in Gaius's direction, and Scipio found himself bounding directly into his path with his sword held at the ready. The challenge seemed to freeze Magilus in his tracks. He blinked hard and stepped right, but Scipio mirrored his movement, keeping himself between the two.

Magilus dropped the sword, mounted a horse, and bolted away. Plinius hurled a javelin in his direction. It missed, and Magilus disappeared into the darkness.

"I'll get him," Appius promised, grabbing his helmet.

"Stand down!" Scipio told him before Appius could get to his horse.

"What are we doing, then?" Appius asked him.

Scipio took his comet charm from under his tunic and rubbed it as he looked around. His gaze rested on Gaius, who looked back up at him with desperate eyes.

"Seal the wound," he told Appius.

Appius rested the top half of his sword in the fire.

"We can't let him die," Scipio said to Plinius.

"We have a mission, sir," Plinius said. "Don't go trying to fix one mistake by making others."

Scipio cursed loud enough to turn the other soldiers' heads. Everyone was standing by the light of the still-glowing fire and waiting for an order—his order.

"We need help," he heard one of his soldiers quietly say to another.

Help... But no one was around. No one, that was, except...

"We can take him down to the Volcae," Scipio said.

"Gauls?" Plinius said with raised eyebrows, "Sir, no... "

"He needs a bed and a roof over his head if he's going to have a shot at making it through this," Scipio said. "The Volcae have all that down there. Maybe even medicine of some sort."

"We were supposed to be avoiding the Gauls," Plinius said. "Those are orders. What if something happens down there and things turn sour?"

"It's a risk," Scipio acknowledged. "But one he's worth taking, right?"

Plinius looked over as Appius brought the glowing sword to the wound. Scipio winced as Gaius's bit down on a piece of leather to muffle his shrieks. The hot metal sealed the wound and cooked the skin around it, producing a foul odor.

"Pack and mount up," Scipio told them. "We head down at

first light."

***

The rain began before dawn, and soon it was apparent that there would be no true sunrise. Scipio's troop began riding north toward what they hoped was the Volcae village as the gray sky grew lighter. They descended from their camp into a forest littered with slick red and orange leaves along the eastern side of the Rhone. Gaius was riding on the back of Appius's horse, bandaged, slumped, and barely conscious. Like his men, Scipio wrapped his dark burgundy cloak around him to keep as dry and warm as possible, but the exposed skin on his hands and face was numb from the cold.

As the day wore on, they rode northeast into the woods on a well-tread trail not yet thick with mud. They stopped several times, always on high ground, trying to see the Volcae settlements or other cavalry troops. Appius used the breaks to tend to Gaius, soaking his wound with vinegar and applying whatever healing herbs he could find before they moved on.

Scipio could feel Plinius's eyes on him the whole way. He hadn't said a word since they'd left camp, which he estimated was about eight hours ago. It left Scipio alone with his head full of self-recrimination. He wanted to blame Magilus for this predicament, but he knew that he had only himself to blame.

"What is that?" he heard Plinius ask.

He looked to his right to see Plinius motioning to his hands. Scipio looked down at them to find that he was holding his comet talisman, rubbing it between his index finger and thumb.

"It's nothing," Scipio answered, put the talisman back around his neck, and tucked it under his tunic.

He looked back over his shoulder in the direction of Appius

and Gaius.

"This is my fault," he said to Plinius.

Plinius grunted by way of reply, though not in a tone that Scipio couldn't determine was agreement or dissent with the statement.

"You think so as well?" he asked.

"I've known a lot of officers," Plinius said. "The good ones don't look to blame people when things go wrong, not even themselves. They just... see what needs doing, take charge, and get it done."

"What if you can't make up for what you've done?"

"You do what everyone else does. You learn from your mistakes, and you move on."

They rode in silence a while before Plinius asked him, "What have you've learned from this, if anything? That you shouldn't let the men gamble?"

"My uncle always taught me that a leader needs to make his own decisions," Scipio said. "But he also taught me that it was more important to be respected than popular. I was stupid not to heed that advice."

"Arrogant as well," Plinius added. "Ah, well... You wanted the men to like you. I think you can be forgiven for that."

A few moments later, Scipio heard Plinius chuckling to himself.

"Magilus could have cut you in half last night, by the way," Plinius said. "You know that, don't you? What were you thinking, stepping to him like that?"

"I wasn't thinking," Scipio admitted.

Plinius grunted again, this time in a way clearly denoting approval. Scipio even saw a smile curl the corner of his mouth.

"I think there's hope for you yet, young *Decurion*," Plinius said, and his expression reminded Scipio of how his Uncle Calvus often looked at him when he got something right for the first time—hitting a target with his bow, delivering a spear just right from the back of his horse, or even solving a math problem his Greek tutor had given him. He remembered once longing to see it in his father's expression, but that was long ago.

"Whoa... " they heard the lead soldier, Maxentius, stop his horse. He called Scipio forward using hand signals.

"What is it?" Scipio asked him quietly as he approached, peering around them. He held the reins in one hand and his spear in the other, ready to thrust it into Magilus's chest should he appear.

Maxentius pointed uphill into the woods to their right. It was difficult to see at first, but when it moved, he could see a horse among the trees looking back at him. The reigns on its head identified it as a Roman cavalry steed.

"Good eyes," Scipio said to Maxentius.

Scipio dismounted and took a few cautious steps toward the horse, holding his spear and shield high. The animal regarded him with seeming indifference as Scipio approached, scanning the forest floor and trees in front of him for any sign of his fugitive soldier. He took the horse by the bit and pet its forehead and face down to its muzzle. It was then he noticed something that didn't quite blend with the foliage. Something white... Feathers, attached to a very straight stick. An arrow... stuck in the ground, perhaps? Then there was another, and another...

It was Magilus, flat on his back. His lifeless eyes stared at the sky as rain ran down his lifeless face. The big man had fled without his armor, not that it would have stopped the direct hits, of which there were several. Scipio looked up at the ridgeline as he guided the horse back to the trail, but he didn't see any sign of archers.

"Magilus," he told Plinius quietly, handing him the horse's reigns.

A snap. It had sounded like a small tree branch on the ground broken under foot. The rain created a steady level of noise from which it was difficult to discern footsteps on wet leaves, but this was clear and distinct.

Scipio held his spear at the ready and waited, calming his horse as it tried to move.

"Romans?" someone called to them, but the direction from which it came was unclear.

Scipio could hear and see his own breath in the cold air as he scanned the woods ahead of them. The man he spotted blended in so well with his surroundings that he was nearly invisible. He wore a fur on his back, with the top half of a bear's head for a hood. The roof of the bear's mouth and snout extending out from his forehead like a visor. Beneath it, he was wearing a tunic, a dark belt, and something Scipio had heard about but never seen before—a garment went around each leg individually. The man's white nose and reddish beard showed under the bear's mouth. The hood obscured the rest of his face in shadow.

"Are you Romans?" the Gaul asked Scipio in Latin.

"We're not here to fight," Scipio answered.

The man took a few steps forward, keeping his gaze steadfastly fixed on Scipio and his men.

"That's not what I asked," he said.

"We are Romans," Scipio acknowledged.

"Why are you here?" the Gaul asked.

"Give the word, sir," Plinius said quietly, indicating the men were ready to attack.

"They're supposed to be friendly," Scipio whispered back.

"You want to bet your life on that?" Plinius asked. "There's only one of him."

"One man didn't do that to Magilus," Scipio said.

"Whatever you're thinking of doing," the man said, "think carefully."

Scipio put his spear and shield on the ground, then showed his hands to the Gaul.

"We mean you no harm," Scipio told him. "We've come to ask for your help."

The answer didn't seem to satisfy the Gaul. He whistled a few notes, and a dozen Gauls materialized from the forest ahead of them, their bows drawn.

"This is our land," the man with the bearskin said, approaching Scipio. "Volcae land. You need our permission to pass. So, I'll ask again, Roman. Why are you here?"

"We have a wounded man," Scipio said, motioning to Gaius. "We need medicine and shelter for him. We can pay you... a little, at least."

"That's all?"

"That's all," Scipio told him.

"I said this was *our* land, Roman," the man replied. "What kind of hosts would we be if we didn't drink together?"

It took a moment for the words to register with Scipio, particularly since the man's tone hadn't been inviting. He breathed a sigh of relief when the man began to laugh and the other Gauls placed their arrows back in their quivers. A bearskin-wearing Gaul with a peculiar sense of humor was the last thing he expected to find here.

"Call me Ros," the man said.

They buried Magilus where they found him and followed Ros through the wet autumn forest. He seemed friendly enough and spoke better Latin than some of his less-educated soldiers, but Romans had an innate distrust of people from the north, given their long history of raiding Italy. Scipio wouldn't have trusted them under other circumstances, but half a day had already gone by since Gaius had been stabbed. Without treatment, the wound would almost certainly turn bad and be the death of him.

They walked north along the river a few miles until they arrived at a tiny village consisting of a handful of thatched-roof cottages made from mud brinks and dung like their bucolic Italian counterparts. Ros's barracks was a similar rustic structure, but it had the luxury of stone hearths at either end. They put Gaius in a cot close to a fire and tried to feed him, but after a few sips he vomited into a bedpan.

Scipio hovered near Gaius as his men ate. He was too anxious to have an appetite, having already lost one man and now on the verge of losing another.

"You're lucky we have space," Ros told him. "Most of the soldiers are up north with the Queen."

Plinius felt Gaius's forehead for a few moments, then huddled with Ros and Scipio.

"Too warm," he told them. "The wound may already be turning."

"What did you use to treat it?" Ros asked.

"Wine and vinegar," Plinius answered. "Some rosemary."

Ros gently peeled back the bandage and examined the wound.

"It's too severe for those," he said, then took a sniff. "But it's not ripe. We need moldy bread or honey to pack the wound."

Scipio was impressed. Ros was clearly a smart soldier, one that knew how to heal as well as kill.

"Do you have any of that?" Scipio asked him.

"Not here," he said. "The druids have some things that work well, but you never know what they'll ask for in return."

Druids... He'd heard nothing about them before Plinius's told his tale the night before last. He was skeptical that such a large element could be massacred without Scipio having heard of it, but he hadn't intended on finding out if any of the story was true.

He looked at Gaius a moment. The boy was young. All of them were, including Scipio, but Gaius had a babyface. His light hair and fair complexion made him seem younger still. If there was a chance that the druids could save him, then going to them for help was a risk worth taking.

"How far are they?" he asked Ros.

"Not far."

"Will you take me to them?"

Ros nodded, and Plinius pulled Scipio aside.

"Druids are sorcerers," Plinius whispered. "I didn't tell you half of what I've heard about them. They're known to flay men alive to please their gods."

"He needs something stronger than we have."

Plinius glanced past him at Gaius laying helpless on the cot.

"He may already be beyond help," said Plinius.

"If I'm not back by dark, continue our mission," Scipio told him, and then left with Ros.

HASDRUBAL

Under the same gray sky, Hasdrubal emerged from his tent, fully dressed and ready to ride. He walked in the drizzling rain to the pen and found his horse, a brown colt he'd named Bucephalas. He'd owned him nearly a year, but this morning the animal seemed spooked by him, and he pulled away as Hasdrubal took him by the bit.

"Easy now," Hasdrubal said to him, leading him more forcefully to the gate. "What's wrong with you?"

Bucephalas whinnied and tried to rear up, but Hasdrubal pulled him down forcefully. He looked into its black eyes, trying to discern what was behind them. Could he feel Mathos's absence? Had he the wherewithal to notice that the boy who cared for him so well had perished in the flames he saw the other night? Regardless, what did an animal know of pain? If it could feel a fraction of what Hasdrubal felt, he would be hopelessly broken. Perhaps he missed the boy that fed and brushed him, but the anguish of losing Mathos was Hasdrubal's alone to endure. But perhaps, Hasdrubal thought, it was something else. The Numidians believed that horse and rider shared a bond so intimate that they knew each other's hearts, and what filled Hasdrubal's heart was darkness and wrath.

Perhaps sensing that his owner was about to lose his temper, Bucephalas relented at last. Hasdrubal rode him to the edge of the camp, where he found Maharbal riding in the opposite direction. In the direction from which the cavalry commander had come, Hasdrubal could see a dozen cavalry troops of ten to twenty riders each assembling for their daily patrol. He knew what their mission would be, given the situation—screen south, skirmish with Roman cavalry to keep them at bay, and keep tabs on the legions marching north, but the legions couldn't march in this weather; at least, not in Gaul.

"Where are you going?" Maharbal asked him.

"Who's your best troop leader?" Hasdrubal asked, ignoring his question and looking at the troops assembling to leave on patrol.

Maharbal hesitated.

"You're going to make me ask twice, Maharbal?"

"No, General," Maharbal said, then pointed to one of the assembling units of horsemen. "Sikarbaal."

Hasdrubal set off toward the troop without another word. He could feel Maharbal's eyes on him the entire ride over. He tried to ignore it, and fought the urge to turn and bark at Maharbal to mind his own business... But the cavalry *was* his business. Maharbal was their commander, and though it was Hasdrubal's prerogative to do as he pleased, he knew he was intruding in Maharbal's space.

"Sikarbaal," he called once he was close enough from the unit to hear him.

The young Carthaginian cavalry officer understandably looked both surprised and alarmed when he saw Hasdrubal approach.

"Yes, General," he answered.

"Did you see any yesterday?" Hasdrubal asked him.

"Any what, sir?"

"Romans. Did you see any of them?"

"No, sir," Sikarbaal answered.

"We will today," Hasdrubal told him. "Follow me."

SCIPIO

"Who is this Druid?" Scipio asked. "Did I say that right?"

The bear's head hood only allowed him to see part of Ros's face at any given time, making it difficult to read his expressions. Though he decided to trust the Gaul for now, Scipio kept his armor on and carried his sword. His arms and horse would at least give him a fighting chance of escaping any ambush he might be walking into.

They had been riding, albeit at a slow pace, for almost an hour; having followed a trail north out of the village and then going off it, heading north away from the river. The rain was getting heavier and the skies darker as the day wore on. Scipio had been holding the comet talisman in his hand since the two men left Ros's barracks, but he was careful to keep it concealed in his closed fist. He didn't know what significance it carried to the Gauls in this region, if any. Perhaps they thought it an evil omen, and they would withdraw their help.

"Druids," Ros replied. "Three of them. They're a sort of priestess, sorceress, oracle... "

"They do all that?"

"We're not as rich as you, Roman. They have to do it all."

They rode in silence with Plinius's story rattling around in Scipio's mind. It hit him then, that he was in a strange land, with strange people, going to meet strange priests that served strange gods. It spiked his anxiety, and he fought the urge to turn back then and there, but the image of young Gaius dying steeled him to press on. Still, he had to give voice to his fears.

"They're not going to cut my balls off or anything like that, are they?" he laughed awkwardly.

"No, no... " Ros assured him. "Not both of them."

Scipio leaned forward to see his face under the bear's head and saw Ros's smile.

"Funny," he muttered.

"They will want payment," Ros told him. "It just may not be what you expect."

"How's that?"

"It's hard to predict what they'll want," he said. "And whatever they offer, accept it."

"Where did you learn Latin?"

"Rome."

"You've been there?"

"Lived there for a while," Ros replied. "You've very lucky being born there, you know."

"I've spent most of my life wishing I hadn't been born there," Scipio told him.

"Why?"

"I have my reasons," Scipio replied. "Anyway, I thought most Gauls hated us."

"Many tribes believe you threaten our way of life," Ros told him. "They're right, but they won't admit why."

"Which is?"

"Because your ways are appealing, but we're too proud to abandon the ways of our fathers. Take up the Roman ways, the elders say, and soon we will be their slaves; or worse, we'll *become* them. We'll forget our gods and worship theirs, and all the tribes will disappear until everything is Rome."

It was the first time Scipio had ever heard a foreigner express this kind of sentiment, and it surprised him. His Greek tutors had taught him that all peoples wanted to govern themselves and would not long abide a foreign ruler. They chaffed and rebelled, and they only settled when they became an equal part of the empire that had conquered them. Even then, if they weren't assimilated to ways of the conqueror, they rebelled as soon as circumstances permitted. It was for this reason that empires rose, splintered, and fell. Rome was just another power, bringing all Italy under its authority while constantly dealing with rebellions.

This Gaul was saying that Rome possessed another kind of power, separate and distinct from its military might. Aemilia always told him that Rome was unique among the nations, but he had always thought of her words as simple patriotism. Perhaps, he now thought, there was something more... something that people like her and Ros saw that he could not yet perceive.

He barely had time to reflect before Ros announced that they were coming upon the druids' home. As they came over a rise, Scipio saw a large structure in an otherwise vacant valley full of bright green grass. The structure was circular, though he could only see the front. Its main feature was an enormous conical roof made of what appeared to be straw and sticks, from the center of which poured gray smoke. The roof came down so close to the ground that it looked like the entire building *was* the roof.

They tied their horses to the closest trees and walked down. Scipio placed his talisman back around his neck as they approached the house. The door, which looked a hundred years old, had a small peephole through which shown a single speck of light. Ros knocked and spoke a few words in a language that sounded like Gallic, but which Scipio had never heard. The light shining through dimmed as someone on the other side inspected them.

The door opened, revealing a single petite figure in a hooded gray robe that draped down to the packed earth floor. She and Ros exchanged words in the strange tongue. Scipio thought hers was the voice of a young girl. When she turned her head toward him and he could see her face clearly, he estimated that she was around twelve or thirteen. She looked at Scipio with considerable skepticism, inspecting him from his helmet to the *caligae* on his feet. She reached a slender hand toward him and placed it on the chest plate over his heart. She drew a short, quick breath, as if something had startled her; then she looked up into his eyes before abruptly withdrawing her hand and disappearing into the cabin, closing the door in their faces.

Scipio turned to Ros, hoping for some explanation, but the Gaul just shrugged.

"I guess we wait here," he said.

They heard muffled voices from inside for several minutes before the door creaked open and the girl stepped aside to let them in.

The interior was as spartan and primitive as the exterior, with no windows or separate rooms. The only sources of light were the fire in the middle and oil lamps suspended from the straw ceiling. There were no beds or obvious places to sleep; only tables holding what looked like cooking utensils along with clay jars, bowls, and pots. Drying herbs, fruits, flowers, and thin tree branches with green leaves hung on wooden racks. At a spinning wheel by the fire sat a tiny hunched figure in a robe identical to that which the young girl wore. Strands of long gray-white hair spilled out the front, but her face was hidden from them. She didn't move from her seat when Scipio and Ros entered, seeming content to continue spinning her thread.

"Don't be frightened," said a deep and sultry woman's voice in Greek, prompting both men to whirl around. "If you come as friends, you shall leave the same."

"We do," Scipio answered.

The figure that emerged from the shadows was clearly an adult woman. The rope tied around her waist made her robe seem more like a dress hugging her feminine curves. In each hand, she carried a cup of wine, which she held out to them. Scipio hesitated, but Ros's words came back to him as he saw the Gaul take the cup with a grateful head bow. *Whatever they offer, accept it...* He did. It was much stronger than he was accustomed to drinking, with no water added to dilute it, and flavored with some sort of spice.

The woman pushed her hood back, revealing a beautiful face of porcelain skin and green eyes, topped with a head of bright red curls that flowed down to her large breasts. She was like no creature Scipio had seen before. She was as if the statue of some goddess come to life. He found himself drawn to her, but also alarmed and edgy.

"I am called Veroandi," she said, taking their empty cups and placing them on a table.

"Scipio."

She stepped closer to him—so close that her bosom was nearly touching his chest plate.

"You are a son of Rome?" she asked.

"I am," he replied, doing his best to conceal his trepidation.

She touched the hilt of his sword hanging in its sheath at his side with a single elegant finger and asked, "Who do you come here to fight?"

"Carthage," he answered.

From the other end of the room, they heard the scrape of metal against metal—sharp, sudden, and short. Scipio's heart seemed to leap into his throat, and he instinctively placed a hand on the hilt of his sword and whirled in the direction of the sound. The old woman was there, still at her spinning wheel, holding a spun thread in one hand and a pair of shears in the other. He breathed a sigh of relief and found himself chuckling at his own jumpiness.

Veroandi said a word in the Gallic-like language; not to him, to someone past him... behind him. He turned to see the youth that had greeted them at the door draw back from him, the dagger in her hand shining in the light briefly before it disappeared into her robe. It occurred to him that if he had drawn his weapon in haste, he might be bleeding to death on the ground.

"My apologies," he said. "I must confess to hearing odd stories of druids."

"No doubt," Veroandi said, lifting one eyebrow slightly in amusement. "What may we do for you, Scipio?"

"One of my men is hurt," Scipio told Veroandi. "We need something to keep his wound from turning."

Veroandi motioned to the young girl, who began picking out a variety of herbs from the racks.

"I have silver... " he began, reaching for his coin purse, but she stayed his hand.

"We don't need your coin," she told him.

"How shall I pay you, then?"

Veroandi placed her thumb on Scipio's cheek and her index finger on his forehead. It was if she were inspecting an animal for purchase. When her eyes met his again, it was such an intense stare that Scipio thought she might press her lips against his at any moment. Stepping back, she spoke some words to the old woman, who stood up and shuffled toward them, holding the thread out in front of her in both hands like an offering.

"What are they saying?" Scipio whispered to Ros.

"I don't know," the Gaul answered.

"Isn't that Gallic?"

"It's a... kind of Gallic."

"A dialect?"

"They speak it in lands far to the north," Ros told him.

"Briton?" Scipio asked, his curiosity piqued

"No, no... " Ros told him. "Farther than that."

The answer shocked him. In Rome, there were those who were not convinced Briton existed, and anything north of it was certainly beyond the world known to him. Unlike the Carthaginians, the Romans were not seafarers and had only secondhand contact with distant people. They learned to be skeptical of sailor stories, especially when those sailors were also merchants enticing you to buy their wares. Strange yarns of a mystical place called Briton could really sell some tin.

"Briton's real, then?" Scipio asked.

"I hope it is," Ros laughed. "I've been there twice."

Again, Scipio was surprised, but the druids did not afford him any time to process his new knowledge of geography.

"The sybil says that you wear something over your heart," Veroandi said to him, stepping close to again.

She reached over and tugged at the leather strap around his neck. He pulled the talisman from under his tunic. The battered silver and copper comet came out and clinked against his chest plate, just above the spot over which the young girl had held her hand when she'd greeted them at the door. Now it was the old woman who spoke in her craggy voice.

"She wants to know why you carry this," Veroandi told him.

"I was born in the year of the tailed star."

Veroandi looked at him a bit askance just as the old woman said something sharp and quick.

"No," Veroandi said. "You are too old."

Scipio was taken aback. How could they possibly dispute something like this?

"You have a younger sibling?" she asked.

"I did," Scipio replied. "My brother."

"Two years younger."

"Yes... " Scipio said, amazed at the accuracy of their guess.

"It was he who was born under the star," she told him. "Not you."

Scipio wanted to object, to tell them they didn't know what they were talking about. None of these women knew him or Lucius, or anything about them. But did they know the stars that well? *Perhaps...* His searched his memory to remember when his brother gave him the talisman... . Or *did* he give it to him? He had no memory of accepting it from him, or of Lucius presenting it.

Her work done, the slender young girl stepped close to him and took the talisman into her palm. An image flickered in Scipio's mind, hazy at first, but there. He didn't know if it was memory or something he was conjuring up to fool himself. Nevertheless, he saw it clearly, walking through the Forum in the heat of summer toward the site of the gladiator games. Lucius was plodding along beside him, taking his time and looking about with his nose in the air, trying to walk with the dignity and pride that came with being part of a family of such renown. He'd just had his hair cut, and his face was losing its childish roundness— things that made him look a tad older than his five years. He had the tailed star with him. It was as if the talisman were walking in front of him to herald the boy from which greatness was expected, but its true purpose was much simpler—it fastened the leather belt around his brother's waist. It was the same herald that Scipio later found, battered and alone, among the blood-soaked stones not far from his brother's corpse.

"It... was his belt buckle," Scipio mumbled, only semi-aware that he was speaking aloud.

The young girl withdrew her hand slowly, gently, with eyes diverted. She stepped back and took the old woman's arm, helping her forward.

"Roman... " Ros called.

The sound of the Gaul's voice brought Scipio fully back to the present. He looked to Veroandi, who was standing by the fire with a laurel branch in her hand.

"My soldier is badly hurt," he told her. "Please... I must—"

"Your soldier will live," she assured him, and though he had no rational reason to believe or trust her, he nevertheless did.

Veroandi held the laurel branch out over Scipio's head. The old woman recited what sounded like a prayer before she pointed a bony finger at his talisman.

"You must give us this," Veroandi told him.

His head still reeling from the memories that the druids forced him to revisit, Scipio stepped back, clutching the pendant as if to guard it from an aggressive usurper.

The old woman stepped closer and looked up at him, and Scipio saw her clearly for the first time. The lines of age were

165

clearly present, but the softness of her wrinkled face spoke to a quality that he had so seldom seen in anyone. There was a kindness in her eyes, a peacefulness... the serenity of one who was unburdened by fear, anger, and pain. She seemed beyond them all. It dulled the acute anxiety that had struck him when they had asked for the one thing he could never remember being without. Still, he wanted to keep it around his neck. He held it in his right hand, seeing every scratch and dent in the light of the fire.

He felt the urge to refuse, turn, walk out the door and ride his horse all the way back to Rome. *What's to stop me?* he thought. *Only being branded a deserter, the shame of cowardice... all for a piece of metal.*

"Your man is waiting," Ros reminded him, instantly conjuring the image of Gaius laying in the cot by the fire, his skin cold and clammy, wet with perspiration, his dead body still clutching his blanket. Why hadn't he given a trinket to these women in exchange for his life?

Scipio snatched the talisman from his neck and held it out to the old woman, who quickly took it and used her spun thread to tie it to the laurel branch Veroandi had held. The young girl then helped the old woman to a seat by the fire. Veroandi motioned for Scipio to sit on a stool across from her.

Without a word of warning, the old druid threw the laurel and pendant in the fire. It seemed to make a sharp, high-pitched sound when it hit the flames. He tried to reach into the fire and grab it, but his arms would not obey his commands. They seemed frozen in place, as did the rest of his body. The sudden paralysis, however, was not the terrifying experience it should have been. He cared only about watching the laurel and pendant burning in the fire, and he stopped trying to move. Perfectly still with eyes wide open, his focus on it was soon lost, and the talisman was just a blur in a blur.

High-pitched, confused, desperate cries filled his ears. His focus returned, and the soft light returned to the form of dancing orange flames. His ears filled with the cries of terror and confusion, the clang of metal striking metal amid the grunts and screams of fighting men; the fire grew so intense that he tried to draw back from it, but the flames crept closer to his face. He shut his eyes tight and covered his ears with his hands, but the sounds of swords clashing and the screams of dying men grew louder still until he felt his head would explode.

Stop! He thought he could hear himself yell, though he knew his lips were closed. *Stop! STOP! STOP!*

Silence... He did not even hear himself breathing. A slight ringing in his ears was all that was left. He uncovered his ears and opened his eyes to see before him only a void. The round house, the druids, Ros... everything was gone. No apparent sound or light.

I am dead, he thought. *They poisoned me...*

A tiny speck of light, twinkling like a star in an otherwise pitch-black sky, barely perceptible. Still, it was there—something instead of nothing, holding his undivided attention and growing slowly. A flame flickering and challenged by winds he neither saw nor felt, but never extinguished. It floated there, and he tried to reach out and take it in his hands to protect it, this invaluable fragile light in a sea of darkness.

Other flames sprang into existence, one at a time, beginning as far from him as this one had, and all moving toward the one. Some flickered and died on the journey, but many made it to him and joined until they were a shining sun.

The flames of the hearth fire came into focus, and Scipio saw the face of the old druid behind them. He blinked and glanced around him. The druids, Ros, the racks of herbs and tables with vases and bowls... Everything was restored. The old women spoke to him in words he could not understand before the young girl helped her back to her place at the spinning wheel, where she resumed her work. He stood and rubbed his face, trying to clear his head of whatever had affected him. He looked into the fire, trying to see the talisman, but there was no evidence of it having been there at all. *Could it have burned so quickly?* he wondered.

"What did she say?" he asked Veroandi.

"The sybil offered a prophecy," she told him.

"About me?" he asked.

She didn't answer right away, and Scipio immediately suspected the prophecy was a bad one. Perhaps he'd die in the war; or worse, be captured and enslaved.

"Speak," he said before remembering where he was and adding, "Please... Did she see the future?"

"You saw the future," she answered.

"I... I saw... " he stammered, trying to formulate a coherent statement that made any sense of what he'd just experienced.

"You saw a choice you will have to make," she explained. "And it will come sooner than you think. Beyond that is for you to determine, son of Rome."

Veroandi took a breath.

"You will stand when all others sit," she said.

She paused. He waited, so long that he thought that may have been all the old woman needed to say, but then she continued.

"You will carry a torch through the darkest of nights," she

said. "Four letters before you, and an army of ghosts behind."

It was the kind of prophecy that oracles often gave, Scipio thought—vague and subject to misinterpretation. Still, only fools ignored these little warnings from the gods.

Veroandi held the door open for them, letting what little light shown through the clouds come into the round house.

"Farewell, son of Rome," she said, holding out a jar of ointment with her other hand.

***

They rode for several minutes in a misty rain before Ros broke the silence.

"Well?" he asked.

"Well, what?" Scipio replied.

"Were we not just in the same house? Did you not hear what...?"

"Why did you let me stay there for that long?"

"Stay where?" Ros asked

"At the fire."

"You were only there a few moments."

"I fell asleep," he said. "I... had a dream."

When Ros didn't answer, Scipio turned to see him.

"Are you feeling alright?" Ros asked him with a puzzled expression.

"I fell asleep."

"You had no time," Ros said. "You sat down a few moments, the old woman said something, and you got up."

Not enough time? Scipio thought. *What could they possibly have done?* It made no sense.

"You had a vision," Ros said, pointing at him. "That druid said so. You saw the future, she said."

"I saw no such thing," Scipio snapped. "Eating certain mushrooms can cause people to feel strangely and see things that others do not. Those... crazy witches must have put something in the wine."

"I think they said you'll be a great leader," Ros said.

"I am no leader!" Scipio told him, stopping and turning his horse to him. "I'm barely a soldier. The only enemy I've killed was a..." he nearly choked up before he could get the words out again, as the memory of Mathos hitting the table came back to him.

"He was just a boy," Scipio continued, "in the wrong place at the wrong time. This is my third day as an officer, and I've already lost a man, and I may lose another before we even see a battlefield. Does any of that sound like a great leader to you?"

He turned his horse and began riding on again.

"Chances are that I'll die in a ditch in Gaul and the world will be none the lesser for it," Scipio went on. "Because I just... can't do it."

"Can't do what?"

"Any of it!" Scipio answered. "I couldn't take care of my brother; I can't care for my soldiers, and I'll never be able to take care of a family. I only ever take care of myself."

He rode ahead a little, not wanting to ride beside the Gaul and continue the wretched conversation.

"You won't even allow the possibility that the druids saw something in you that even you don't see yet?" Ros asked him. "You didn't know Briton was real until I told you I'd been there. Perhaps you know yourself no better than you know these lands."

Scipio ruminated on Ros's words for several minutes before grunting in concession, which drew an amused laugh out of Ros.

He remained skeptical, nonetheless. Even if the druid witches had some insight to give, the past was full of examples where oracles could mislead or be misinterpreted with disastrous consequences for those who put their trust in them; and this was a country of strange gods.

HASDRUBAL

Hasdrubal had Sikarbaal and his twenty-strong cavalry troop swim the river early in the morning, before the rains began to swell the waters; and then turned south. When they spotted the first Volcae settlement, they road east to give it a wide berth. They climbed for what seemed like hours, though time was difficult to tell with no sun in the sky.

The rain continued into the darkest and coldest night Hasdrubal could remember. He could hear the men grumbling. He guessed that they wanted to turn around soon, or at least set up a camp. The rain had soaked their clothing, which, unlike the cloaks of their Roman counterparts, were not treated with water-repelling animal oils. He could see the suffering in the anxious and miserable expressions on their faces, and he disdained them for it. Hasdrubal didn't feel the rain and cold in the same way. Physically, it may have had the same effect on his body; but his spirit was undiminished. He was just as sharp and focused at the end of the day, soaking wet with a rumbling stomach, as he was at the start.

"General," Sikarbaal called as he rode up alongside him. "Perhaps we should look for a more suitable campsite to rest."

Hasdrubal kept his focus in front of him, scanning as far as he could. They were nearing the top of the ridgeline, from which he hoped to have a better vantage point to spot campfires.

"General... " he heard Sikarbaal called again after a few moments had passed.

"When you're out like this," Hasdrubal replied, "soldiers only care about their food and their sleep. It's up to you to make sure the mission is done before they get either. Understand?"

"Yes, General," Sikarbaal answered. "But... It's just, our mission is screening. We've screened... Haven't we?"

Hasdrubal turned his head, and his expression was evidently enough to make the aggressive young cavalry officer beat a hasty retreat.

At the top of the ridge, it was just as Hasdrubal had hoped. He could see a valley clear of trees and the rolling hills on the other side. His eyes looked from under his hood, right to left, up further, left to right, up a little further, right to left... *There*. One tiny, barely perceptible flicker of light near the crest of the hill— a light he would stomp into the ground, extinguishing it and its memory forever.

He dismounted and tied his horse to a tree limb. Sikarbaal followed suit.

"We go on foot," Hasdrubal told the young officer. "No armor. Nothing that can rattle, drop, break, or make any sound at all. Leave two men here with the horses. All the rest follow me. Four take bows, the rest only swords."

He waited as the men removed what little armor they had. Their clothes were dark, but their hoods wouldn't cover their faces and the light from the fire would reflect off their skin; and they would need every second they could get. Hasdrubal wrapped his face in dark cloth, leaving only his eyes uncovered. The others followed his example.

They set off at a jog through the gloom toward the distant

fire. The feeling of being soaked and freezing dissipated as they silently closed in on the enemy in the darkness, and soon the flames were the only things on which he could focus his vision and attention.

"Let me have vengeance," he whispered to Baal.

At the foot of the hill, Hasdrubal halted them. He grabbed Sikarbaal and brought his face close to his. The young officer's eyes were wide, his breath quick. The look was a familiar one to Hasdrubal—the terror and thrill impending combat induced in men.

"Swordsmen in a line," Hasdrubal whispered. "Archers spaced between them. Stay together. Understood?"

"Yes, General," Sikarbaal whispered back.

Hasdrubal looked straight up the hill at the Romans' campfire. When the men were in position, he let Sikarbaal give the hand signal to begin the advance. The clouds and rain made for a stealthy approach. Each step fell on wet foliage. Hasdrubal's jaw was clenched tight, and the knuckles on the hand that held his sword behind him were white. He saw all the soldiers around the fire in their signature dark red cloaks. He didn't bother to count them. There could be two, twelve, twenty, two hundred... His only focus was on the back of the Roman in front of him. Nothing else existed as they approached step by step through the blackness.

Not even the enemy's horses whinnying at the last moment gave them away. Hasdrubal put his sword right through a red cloak and its wearer. Arrows flew over bright orange flames as the victim's comrades sprang to defend themselves. Hasdrubal saw a flash of steel to his right, coming for him. He lunged backward and held up his sword, but the Roman fell dead at his feet as Sikarbaal withdrew his sword from his back. It was over in less than a minute.

Hasdrubal looked around in the light of the fire as Sikarbaal's men delivered the wounded Romans their coup de grâces. Less than ten Romans—the smallest element of cavalry they could have encountered. Still, the rush of killing was satisfying. He looked up, closing his eyes to the rain, and whispered a prayer of thanks to Baal.

"We should leave," he heard Sikarbaal say.

He looked about to see Sikarbaal and his men gathered by the fire, looking wretched. Hasdrubal guessed that, for most, it had been their first taste of close combat. It could be difficult, but still... Why weren't they happier? They were all alive and, as far as Hasdrubal could see, unharmed. Yet instead of celebrating, they just stood there, wiping the blood from their hands and shivering like mad. Their mouths hung open, and their eyes were wide.

Have they no taste for blood? thought Hasdrubal. He felt like leaving them in disgust, but he had a better idea. He would teach them to appreciate victory, and to give due homage to the gods that provided it.

"We're not done yet," Hasdrubal said darkly.

CATO

Marcus Cato nearly choked on the wine. He and Varro had just reclined on the gaudy *klines* that fit perfectly in Varro's garish home, and he was not expecting such an announcement without any preface. It was as sudden, rash, and inappropriate as anything Varro has ever said.

"Say that again, please," Cato asked of him.

174

"I will stand for Consul," Varro told him.

"That's... what I thought you said," Cato replied, and took a large swig of wine.

"You're my most loyal friend, Marcus," he said as the slaves brought olives and bread. "I wanted you to be the first to know."

Varro munched some olives and spat the pits into the palm of one of the slave's hands, then wiped his pudgy fingers on the slave's fine uniform.

It was ill-mannered, grotesque, and unnecessarily humiliating... quintessential Varro. The man was ostentatious in every detail. Even his servants were over-done and garish. Most slaves in Rome wore simple tunics, but Varro's wore lavish gold-trimmed affairs, fine leather sandals, and even makeup. *Makeup!* Truly bizarre was how Varro interacted with them.

Cato was here to get his host to pledge his support for the candidates the conservatives in the Senate would nominate in the coming election, not to hear Varro pitch himself for office. The issue Cato struggled with was not whether he liked Varro (he didn't), but how useful the man could be. They were close to getting enough votes in the popular assemblies to get the *lex Oppia* passed, and finally denying the Hellenists of an important source of funding—wealthy Roman women such as Busa of Canusium. Most of his colleagues, even other populists, didn't take Varro seriously. They thought of him as a liar and blowhard, and not a very bright one at that. Cato believed they were largely correct in their assessments, but they were unimaginative in their reaction to a man so clearly popular with the people. They would need his supporters to beat the Hellenists. Varro as a Consul, however, was absurd on the face of it; but Cato had to tread carefully.

"Aren't you going to say anything?" Varro prompted him.

"Oh... yes, yes... " he sputtered, a little nauseous at the notion of Varro having power to himself. "Well, I... I think it... would be... *interesting...* "

"Just say what it is you think, Marcus," he said, shoving another bunch of olives in his mouth.

"More wine, please," Cato said, holding his cup up to the slave. "Hold the water."

He drank again, hoping Bacchus would bring him some wine-inspired words.

"At this point, I think it would be... *premature,*" Cato said.

"How so?"

"Where to begin?" Cato replied. "Republican politics is about building consensus, not establishing the kind of dominance that you're used to in your... commercial affairs."

Varro audibly sighed, tucked his chin, and looked up from under his ridiculously bushy eyebrows. *Bored already,* Cato thought. He wondered how a man with such a short attention span ever got anything done.

"Their reputations buy Cornelius and his sort influence," Cato went on, trying to simplify things for a simpler mind. "Whereas we have only sheer numbers in our favor. We're winning more elections, which means more appointments to the Senate."

"Thanks to me!" Varro boasted.

"Thanks, in part, to you, but we need more time."

"Time?" Varro bellowed. "Time? To do what?"

"To build your support among the upper classes," Cato explained. "For you to be Consul, you would need support from the *equites* and patricians, and their extensive networks of clients, of course."

"I don't care if they respect me," Varro grumbled. "They've never treated me or my family fairly. Just look at the way they humiliated my father in election after election, simply because he didn't serve in the legions."

"Yes, but—"

"The worst part of it," Varro continued, "is their hypocrisy. They're hypocritical, very, very hypocritical. They don't accept people like you and me because we're *real* Romans. Yet they want to give citizenship to anyone who wants it. Come one, come all! Filthy Greeks, Phoenicians, Jews, Gauls... "

Cato reached for his wine again, looking at the downcast faces on his slaves. Slaves, Cato knew, came from everywhere. Some were people sentenced to slavery for serious crimes, but most were imported from the very countries Varro was now insulting. The opinions of slaves didn't matter, of course, but they were not deaf.

"The best people from those countries don't leave home, Marcus. We're getting their worst, their losers, their criminals. It's not fair, Marcus. It's very, very unfair. It's not our country anymore, Marcus. We need to take it back from these elites that wouldn't know a true Roman if he hit them right in their big bent noses! Common, everyday *Romans* made Rome great—not the elite, not filthy immigrants... "

"I agree," Cato said, cutting short a diatribe that could go on, he estimated, into the next morning. "But the Consuls are expected to unify Romans, and much of what you say, inciteful as it may be, is considered very... incendiary."

"Of course, it is!" Varro said, taking a gulp of his wine greedily. He used his slave's tunic to wipe his mouth. "It *has* to be."

"Be that as it may, it is also a touch divisive."

"The people love it," Varro assured him, a smug grin now on his lips. "It gets them excited and talking about me, about what *I'm* saying. The elites think they have some monopoly on truth, like those moldy philosophers they read. Facts are bought and sold, Marcus. They're a commodity, like everything else in this world. If you offer the people a better truth to what the other guy is selling, they'll buy yours."

"Perhaps," Marcus said. "Although some consider it demagoguery. Not I, mind you... "

"Who?" Varro demanded with a ferocity that made Cato flinch and nearly drop his wine. "Who says this? That's very unfair, Marcus; very, very unfair. It's them, the people who are saying those things. *They're* the demagogues!"

"Nevertheless, it is another obstacle."

"Marcus, will you support me or not?"

"I shall speak to Fabius," Cato told him, and Varro sighed dramatically. "If he believes you have a chance, I'll support you."

"Fa-Fa-Fabius... " Varro said, imitating the stutter of Fabius's youth.

Cato smiled politely.

"May I inform Fabius that you will, regardless of his decision, support the candidates that—"

"Yes, yes, Marcus," Varro answered. "Of course."

He swatted the air with his chubby hand.

"Fabius will be pleased," Cato said.

"You've already chosen him, haven't you?" Varro asked, drinking wine until it spilled from the corners of his lips.

"These processes are complicated," Cato said carefully. "I'll be happy to include you in the discussions, of course."

"Who is he?" Varro asked.

Cato was unsure if it was a request or a demand.

"Gaius Flaminius is currently the favorite among the plebeians."

"Flam—he had to *buy* his last election!" Varro said.

"That's what Cornelius says, but—"

"He says it because that's what it was, Marcus," he said before stuffing a piece of bread in his mouth. "Cornelius is a snob, but he isn't stupid. My appetite is lost."

Cato cleared his throat.

"You must understand something," he told Varro. "The Senate isn't just split between elites and populists. The populists are split as well. Men like Fabius Maximus—they're the old guard. They expect our obedience and your loyalty, above all."

"You give them just that, Marcus!" Varro said, shooting food particles from his mouth onto the rest of the food on the table between them.

"I listen to them," Cato explained. "I pay them due respect, but most of all I respect the influence they still have. I believe you would benefit from doing so, as well."

"Of course, of course," Varro said, suddenly striking a conciliatory tone before licking each of his fingers. "You and I are self-made men, Marcus. That's why I'm disappointed in your deference to Fa-Fa-Fabius and his backroom deals."

"The Senate must approve the list of acceptable candidates for Consul," Cato said. "This is the way it has always been."

"Well, maybe your lot shouldn't have that power," Varro blurted out. "If someone with my kind of support cannot be a Consul, the system is hopelessly corrupt, Marcus. Hopelessly corrupt. All of them... They're all the same... entrenched, corrupt elites."

"Of course, they are," Cato agreed, nodding quickly. "But building a coalition means convincing them to support you *despite* the fact that they can't stand you."

"Perhaps I should just make them fear me."

Cato had let several remarks such as that slide, unsure of whether Varro was serious. Varro never directly announced his intention of taking more power for himself than was granted a Consul, but his frustration with the checks and balances of the Roman Constitution was palpable every time the subject arose.

"The Hellenists will use all their dirty tricks to defeat you; that is, unless they benefit enough from your power."

Varro grunted. It was as close as he came to conceding a point.

"I have nothing they can't get for themselves," he grumbled.

Cato hesitated. The solution to Varro's quandary was so blindingly obvious to him that it escaped his lips despite his reservations about putting the notion in the man's head.

"Then you must take something from them," he said. "Something they hold dear, and hold it hostage."

Varro dismissed the slaves, and Cato watched for a while as Varro ate the rest of the meal in brooding silence. Eventually, it soon became obvious that he wished to be alone, and Cato excused himself.

Each time he left Varro, Cato was astounded at his sheer ignorance and buffoonery. Still, Varro could be a useful fool with the right guidance. He'd built a passionate base of support—larger and more loyal than others appreciated, and Varro was shameless—a quality the usefulness of which many underappreciated, but not Cato. When the time came, all of that would hopefully propel Cato and his allies to unmatched political power, and Rome would never be the same.

SCIPIO

The ointment from the druids seemed to have effect. By morning, Gaius was well enough to sit up and ride his horse, but Scipio ordered him to rest until the next day and then ride south to the legions.

Ros alone came out to see the Romans off.

"Don't bother looking for Hannibal's men on this side of the river," he told Scipio as they led his horse from the stable. "The Carthaginians haven't crossed anywhere south of Cynbela's camp. She's had ambushes set up for days, and we've had no contact."

"I'll pass that on," Scipio said with a nod of thanks. "Look, I've seen Hannibal's army. It's massive. I mean forty, maybe fifty thousand men. If he attacks in the next few days, the legions will be too far south to be of any help to you."

"What are you saying?" Ros asked.

"If I were you, I would let them pass."

"The Volcae will fight, whatever the numbers," he said. "We may lose; we may die, but we will fight."

"You cannot win. Not without us."

"Sometimes we fight for greed, sometimes for fear," Ros replied. "Other times for honor, to show you won't have demands put on you in your own land."

"Even if it costs you your lives?"

"Only the gods live forever, Roman."

It was an attitude that mirrored heroes in those histories that

Scipio thought were bogus. Seeing it here, among the very people who were often the villains in those epic poems, he was reminded of the words he heard from the mistral on a day that seemed a lifetime ago: "*To every man upon this earth, Death cometh soon or late. And how can a man die better than facing fearful odds for the ashes of his fathers and the temples of his gods?*"

Scipio leaned over and reached out his hand.

"Good luck, Ros of the Volcae."

"And to you, Scipio," Ros replied, gripping his hand. "I hope we meet again."

***

As he led his troops northeast to continue his scouting mission, Scipio thought how lucky he was to have run into friendly Gauls. Now having encountered many more of them than he'd ever met before the war, it seemed to Scipio that the differences distinguishing one nation from another mattered far less than he'd been taught to believe. He thought to visit Gaul after the war was over, to see Ros with the big and joyfully tumultuous family he imagined he would have by then, sit by a fire with him, and swap stories as old friends.

Less than an hour into the ride, on a road still muddy from the previous day's rain, they stopped two Roman cavalrymen from another troop who were riding south hard. Scipio could see in their expressions something between shock and horror, but there was no sign that they'd been in combat.

"Where are you going?" Scipio asked them.

"To find the legions, sir," one of them answered.

"Is Hannibal moving?"

"I don't know... Maybe."

"What news are you relaying in such a hurry, then?"

"You have to see it for yourself, sir," one of the soldiers said.

His companion pointed north and said, "Top of the next hill, sir. About a mile up, you'll see it. Our *Decurion* is there."

The men continued their ride south and Scipio turned to Plinius for an explanation, but his deputy only offered a shrug and shook his head.

From the foot of the hill, they could see a Roman cavalry troop stopped near the top. When they got closer, Scipio saw Claudius on foot. His normally coiffed hair was a mop of blonde curls, and the usually clean-shaven face the girls all loved was scruffy and dirty, but to Scipio he never looked better.

"Claudius!" he called, ridding over to him quickly and then dismounting.

"Scipio... " Claudius greeted, though his tone was more subdued.

It when he embraced his friend that Scipio saw bodies behind him. He stepped back from Claudius and took in the drizzly display. Eight dismembered corpses of Roman *equites* were there. They had been slaughtered like sacrificial animals; their organs burnt in the fire. It turned his stomach, and the sounds of men retching nearby indicated he wasn't the only one.

"We think they sacrificed them to their gods," Claudius said.

It was then that Scipio saw it, still wrapped around the wrist of an arm hacked off the body and left by the fire like trash. He didn't want to get closer, to see it for himself and confirm what he feared. He just stared at it, telling himself it wasn't him.

"Scipio... " he heard Claudius say, but he found himself pulled toward the arm, forced to crouch and pick it up, looking at the bronze bracelet it wore. He already knew what it was and who it had belonged to before he saw.

"Lars... " he said.

He looked up to see Claudius standing there, but his presence was no longer comforting.

Lars, who had so much ahead of him, whose men had loved him, whose parents cherished him, and who had studied next to him in *Grammaticus*... Who took the time to talk to him just two days ago, and gave him the slightest bit of confidence in himself... Lars was dead. He'd been gutted and dismembered, like some fish pulled from the river, and left to rot along with seven others. The carnage before Scipio filled him with such anger that every other feeling seemed distant and insignificant. That this happened—that *people* had done this—was the only thing that mattered at all. The excessiveness and theatricality of it were so far beyond anything he had seen or heard that the crucifixions in Massilia seemed merciful in hindsight.

"They practiced human sacrifice to their gods in the old days," Claudius told him. "Still, I... never heard of anything like this."

"No," Scipio said with a sneer. "This was not for any gods. This was for us."

The fury rose in him like an incoming tide. The images in his mind of Carthaginians ripping these men apart in sadistic glee filled him with rage. They were filthy, vile little animals without respect for anything other than filling their bloodlust, tearing at the flesh of their victims... without honor, without dignity, without remorse.

He mounted his horse.

"Scipio!" Claudius called twice. "Where are you going?"

"Hunting," Scipio snarled, and he led his troops toward the swollen river.

HANNIBAL

There was never enough time on campaign to do everything that was needed. Hannibal had been watching Mago prepare for that night's operation for almost two days while attending to his other duties, but now that it was imminent, it seemed rushed. He was trying to see to the preparation of the rafts that his men would use the next day when Maharbal approached him with a young cavalry officer at his side.

"Have you seen your brother this morning?" he asked Hannibal.

"Mago's up north," Hannibal replied.

"Hasdrubal."

"In his tent," Hannibal said. "I gave orders he was not to be disturbed."

"He rode out yesterday on patrol."

"He did?" Hannibal asked hopefully. He'd been worried that his brother would sink into despair at a time and place that he had no capacity to help him. Just leaving his tent and doing something a mundane screening patrol was a positive sign. "Where is he?"

Maharbal introduced the young officer, Sikarbaal, who related the entire story of the previous night's carnage, omitting no detail that he could recollect, and gave the names of the men he had taken with him as additional witnesses. The young officer was clearly shaken. It must have taken courage, Hannibal believed, just to talk with Maharbal about what Hasdrubal had ordered him and his men to do.

"General," Sikarbaal said, his eyes downcast. "I want to fight. I know killing the enemy is what we do, but this was... "

"I understand," Hannibal told him. "You did the right thing by telling us about it. We'll take care of it. Go and rest."

Sikarbaal bowed slightly, eyes still downcast, and stepped away.

"Where is Hasdrubal now?" Hannibal asked Maharbal.

"His tent."

Hannibal brooded a while in silence.

"We've fought many campaigns together, Hannibal," Maharbal said. "What Sikarbaal described was unlike anything I've ever seen. Are you going to allow it?"

"No," Hannibal answered firmly. "We can't win people to our side if we gain a reputation for savagery."

"Then you must speak with him."

Hannibal took a breath and looked out over the river to the Volcae staring back at him.

"Hasdrubal won't understand," he finally said. "The Romans are the enemy. They always have been and always will be until we end them. He'll ask what difference it makes what we do to them."

"It's not about the damned Romans," Maharbal replied. "This is about us, about who we are. General... "

He grabbed his commander by the arm, which he had never done.

"He must be stopped," Maharbal said, making sure Hannibal was looking him in the face as he said it. "Immediately."

Hannibal was angry, more with Hasdrubal but now also with Maharbal for trying to force his hand. He pulled back from Maharbal and stood up a little straighter.

"Pull all the cavalry back in," Hannibal ordered. "The last thing we need is more skirmishes in Gaul when we're supposed to be moving through here as fast as possible."

"Yes, General."

Hannibal turned his back and said, "I'll deal with my brother," before walking toward his tent.

***

At dusk, Hannibal summoned Hasdrubal to the command tent. When he saw his tall brother approaching, Hannibal ordered the lamps lit. Maharbal and Gisgo were there also, along with the four soldiers Hannibal used as his personal guards on the battlefield. As he approached Hannibal, Hasdrubal saw all of them assembled. He also saw the spear-toting guards, and Hannibal thought his brother surely knew then that something was about to happen. Ignoring the others, he addressed Hannibal directly.

"What is it?" he asked.

Hannibal stepped closer to him with arms crossed.

"I need you to raise another army in Hispania," he said.

He may as well have slapped Hasdrubal straight across his face. His brother looked shocked and confused, looking from Hannibal to the dour expressions on the faces of the other generals, none of whom seemed to react to the news.

"What are you talking about?"

"The tribes on the Ebro are likely to rebel," Hannibal explained. "Kara may not be able to hold them down with what I left her."

"The Romans could launch an attack on New Carthage," Maharbal added. "Even with—"

"That's not what this is about," Hasdrubal interrupted him. He then pointed at Maharbal and said, "They told you about the

Romans we killed."

Hannibal stared intensely at his brother, containing his own anger. Hasdrubal had never felt so distant from him. It was if they had been attached to one another their entire lives and a canyon had opened between them in the span of just a few days.

"Every man here knows my commitment to this war," Hasdrubal said, raising his voice. "The gods know my commitment to it. How dare you—any of you—take it from me?"

"We all know what's in your heart, brother," Hannibal said.

"Haven't I been there for you longer than anyone?" Hasdrubal asked. "Haven't I proven myself time and again?"

"You have," Hannibal answered with a nod.

Hasdrubal's face twisted into a snarl as it turned red. Since they were adolescents, he had used the height he had on his older brother to intimidate him only a few times, but never as an adult. He did so now, stepping closer and looking down at him. Hannibal heard his guards step in closer, their spears at the ready.

"I came here for *you*," Hasdrubal bawled, pointing to Hannibal's chest. "For *you*, Hannibal! My son's ashes are scattered in Gaul for *you*! I have nothing left. Nothing! And you would deny me vengeance against those that took everything from me?"

Hannibal dropped his hands to his side, wanting to embrace and comfort his brother far more than he wanted to banish him; but he stood his ground. Maharbal was right. He had to act, and he had to do it now.

"Brother..." Hannibal said softly.

Tears of sorrow and rage flowed from Hasdrubal's eyes. After a moment, he sniffed back the tear, scoffed, and shook his head.

"I was wrong," he said. "The gods didn't choose you. You haven't the *stomach* to do what needs to be done."

"What needs to be done?" Hannibal repeated the words.

"Yes!" he thundered and looked around at their generals. "You stand here judging me? All of you are here because you know what Rome is! You know what they are! And it will not end when you burn the city. Rome is *Romans*. While any one of them is still alive, anywhere in the world, Rome still stands!"

"Brother," Hannibal said in a low voice, getting Hasdrubal to look away from the others and back down at him. "Of everyone, you've been the most loyal, the most devoted. That's why you're going to Hispania instead of hanging on a cross."

Hannibal stepped away, leaving his seething brother standing in place, and stood beside the other generals.

"Pick five men to go with you," he said to Hasdrubal. "And be out of my camp by midday tomorrow."

Hasdrubal looked around at them all.

"I curse you," he spat, drawing some gasps and looks of shock. Curses were deadly serious things, especially coming from a priest of Baal like Hasdrubal. The soldiers were apt to believe a curse placed on their officers might well doom the army.

"The gods curse you," Hasdrubal said before storming away.

It was, Hannibal thought, the worst decision he'd ever made. It was easy to make, but the consequences were devastating. He'd grown close to Maharbal and Gisgo over the years, but no one was closer to him than his brothers. Sending one of them away like this was akin to severing his own hand.

Thankfully, he didn't have time to contemplate the situation with Hasdrubal. He had to get an army across the river and well on their way to the Alps before the Romans could catch them.

The rain had slowed the enemy's march, no doubt, but they were still coming. Hannibal tried to clear his head of his brother's wrathful words by diverting his attention to the map he had sketched of the area. It included the layout of enemy defenses, as far as he could discern them, and the position of his camp. Above them, a tiny wooden horseman represented Mago leading a column of troops north through the darkness.

MAGO

Mathematics was never Mago's forte, but he knew enough that getting five thousand men to march ten miles in the dark and cross two river tributaries before dawn was a daunting task. The only advantages he identified were his unfettered access to the western side of the Rhone and his enormous pool of manpower. His plan used them both.

No matter how much he opposed prosecuting this war, he found this small part of fighting it engrossing and a welcome distraction from his grief over losing his nephew. He had done this march back and forth three times by day and night. He knew the way by heart. Still, he shared in whatever sense of adventure that he thought the other soldiers must have felt. Moving in the dark, without torches to light the way, as quietly as possible with *five thousand* men and beasts, armor clanking and horses clopping along, looking to him to lead the way.

The night grew darker and colder as they marched. The column, which was just a huge moving line of men and animals, began to "snake." Parts of it would slow down and contract, then suddenly expand and speed up. For those in the middle or end, it was physically and mentally exhausting to stop, wait, then run to catch up, only to stop again.

Mago had put them all in a specific order or march. His archers were first. He used them to secure the crossing zone, placing them on either side of it facing north and south. If anyone spied them, the archers would have a good chance of stopping them from telling anyone what they saw. After they were in place came the part Mago had been dreading, and for which he had his subordinate leaders rehearse several times. They split the force into ten parts and assigned each a lane number. Yellow flags on the western sides of large trees on both sides of the tributary delineated each lane. The system was simple enough for the soldiers to use even if they got disoriented, by counting the number of flags to the right or left to make sure they were still in their assigned lane. It was the best he could do to ensure they avoided collisions and crossed as quietly and efficiently as possible.

Even with this measure in place, Mago anticipated a decent amount of chaos during the night. Marking and numbering the lanes, however, proved extremely useful; and the rafts the men had built held up better than he'd expected. The men were quiet enough that Mago could hear owls hooting and the occasional bat flapping its wings. When the crossing began, he could hear them whispering to one another and the sounds of the paddles moving the water, but it was much quieter than he'd expected. Very few rafts tipped over. In the median between the two tributaries, their leaders immediately directed them across to the western bank of the eastern tributary, where they found their lane numbers again. This was the noisiest part—men making their way through the trees, breaking branches, and cursing whenever they stumbled on logs. When they were about half done, Mago made his own way across and through the woods. He stood on the riverbank as the men crossed the second tributary. On the other side was the enemy riverbank.

He kept the men and horses as quiet as possible, but it was becoming difficult. As the sky began to lighten, he grew concerned about the people in the cottages far across the fields. They were likely still asleep, but with his men still crossing the eastern tributary, he couldn't take the chance that they would rise, see an army assembling in their fields, and spoil the operation by warning the Volcae warriors. He sent cavalry to the cottages to make sure their occupants stayed indoors until they were well on their way south. As they finished crossing, the men brought their rafts onto the bank and formed up in their units.

Mago was tired but exhilarated. He would have considered it a success if he'd been able to get half his men over before dawn, but the sun found him with nearly all of them on the Volcae side of the river. He gave the order to move south.

HANNIBAL

Hannibal took in the strange sight of a large Gaul with a long yellow beard bearing a double-headed battle-ax, dressed in animal skins, standing like a blonde giant in the middle of a raft while two smaller Gauls rowed on either side. Lusitanian archers kept a watchful eye as he approached the bank. So did Hannibal's personal guards, who stood between their general and the mysterious envoy with shields and spears ready.

"I am Ronan, son of Cynbela!" the Gaul bellowed.

"Hannibal Barca."

Ronan reached behind his boots, and Hannibal heard the archer draw their bows. The big Gaul hoisted severed head of Owen, who Hannibal had sent to deliver his ultimatum to Queen Cynbela.

"This is what happens to anyone that dares threaten the Volcae in our land," he declared, tossing it at the guards. They parted and let it fall at Hannibal's feet. Without looking down at it, Hannibal glanced across the river at the *abatis* and the Volcae warriors standing on the bank above.

"We've negotiated in good faith," he told the Gaul Ronan. "We offered a fair price. All we've received in return have been exorbitant demands and threats. Still, I will give you this last chance, despite your foul slaying of my emissary. Let us pass, and we will still pay you—"

"You will pay in blood, Carthaginian!" Ronan roared.

Hannibal took a beat, hoping to ease the tension a bit.

"You will lose this battle, Ronan, son of Cynbela," he said. "You must know this. Rome may act the friend now, but they care only for themselves. Eventually, they will enslave you just as they will enslave the rest of the world."

Ronan sneered and pointed at Hannibal.

"You have brought an army here!" he yelled. "Not Rome! You make demands, not Rome! This, here, now... is between *us*!"

Again, Hannibal took a beat.

"You're right," he finally said to the surprise of everyone within earshot. "We have no right to demand anything of you... Except that we can, and we are. This is a world of men, not rights. The strong do what they can. The weak do what they must. Now stand aside."

Ronan nudged the rowers, who pushed the raft away from the bank and returned as they had come.

"Get the first rafts ready," Hannibal told Gisgo when Ronan was about halfway across.

Looking up in the sky to judge the position of the sun, he

found himself looking too often for Mago's signal. He stroked his beard and scratched his face, silently willing Mago on.

It wasn't until about an hour later that Mago evidently reached the point where the terrain would no longer conceal his movement. Per their plan, he used dried palm fronds to start the fires and make the smoke signal. Only then did Hannibal give the order for the "turtle" rafts to go in. Dozens of them carried men holding shields on all sides, with two oars popping out the sides to move them along. Almost immediately, the archers on the opposite bank began to fire, and Hannibal's men began shouting cheers of encouragement to their comrades on the water. Some even waded into the river up to their waist, hurling insults at the Volcae and challenging the archers to fire at them. The arrows fell well short of the targets until the turtle rafts were about midway across.

He couldn't see Cynbela, but Hannibal knew she would be watching. It would not be long, he thought, before she recognized that something was wrong. As the rafts came within range of her archers, they slowed down. Some of them turned up or down river while others stopped and drifted, then advanced again slowly. A few even started heading back. Hannibal could hear the Volcae shouting taunts of their own. They even cheered, likely believing they had stopped the first wave from even reaching the eastern bank.

A horn blast silenced their celebration. Hannibal saw the Volcae turning as the first volley of arrows caught them completely unprepared. A commotion broke out in their ranks, with men yelling and pushing. Others let out blood-curdling screams, no doubt grasping at missiles lodged in their arms, legs, backs, and stomach. Mago's men nearly got another volley off before he saw a single Volcae warrior raise his shield. Hannibal delivered the opposite of what he thought the Volcae expected. Instead of a fight from the high ground against attackers to their front, the Volcae found themselves making a desperate attempt to reform their lines to fight an enemy at their rear as even more arrows rained down on them.

Now he saw Cynbela, who made her presence on the battlefield known with a bright blue cloak. She was mounted on a large white horse and rode to where the infantry was now rushing to line up. A roar came up from her men when they saw her fearlessly riding by under fire, rallying the shocked warriors. Meanwhile, with only a few archers firing down at them, Hannibal's men began reaching the east bank of the river, climbing up the embankment to the *abatis*.

"Cross in force," Hannibal told Gisgo, who relayed the order down the line.

The Volcae archers soon found themselves on another front line, as the crossing Carthaginian infantry found their way to them from behind. They would soon be at the backs of Cynbela's infantry. This was the point where Hannibal had hoped Cynbela would yield and lead her men off the field. It was not to be. Instead, she personally led the frontal attack on Mago's line. Hannibal watched in admiration as the Volcae warriors followed her to the man.

Hannibal had fought many Gauls and knew their tactics well. They used small shields and large weapons, took wild swings, and screamed like madmen to unnerve their enemies, crashing their weapons with terrifying force. Most of the time, it was quite effective. When the units they faced failed to break under the initial shock of their attack, however, Gauls found it difficult to regroup and repeat attack with the same ferocity. They also found it difficult to retreat once they were engaged without exposing their backs to enemy spears. Mago's more disciplined African infantry would tear them to pieces.

Hannibal heard the terrible crunch of colliding shields and clashing swords as Numidian cavalry slammed into the Volcae left flank. The enemy infantry managed to turn and fight more fiercely than Hannibal had anticipated. They nearly repelled the attack, but they failed to reform their lines, and the Volcae found themselves fighting on three sides.

For the Volcae, nearly all was lost. To minimize the chances of the Gauls fighting to the death, Hannibal left them an escape route to the southwest. They took the offer. The crossing secure, the Hannibal ordered his cavalry to remain in place rather than give chase to finish off the Volcae.

The looting of the settlements at the crossing point commenced just after Hannibal's crossing. They may have lost their queen and their homes, Ronan told the survivors later that night, but the honor of the Volcae remained intact, and that was far more valuable than farmland and huts.

Scipio

"I think it's done," Claudius told Scipio, dismounting his horse.

The day before, they swam the cold waters of the Rhone to the western side. It was dangerous, but Scipio was determined to find any Carthaginians he could before they crossed the river. He suspected that the Carthaginians would have foragers and cavalry out while they prepared, but once the crossing began, the chances of finding a small unit separated from Hannibal's main army would be low.

Still, they saw no one that first day, nor the morning of the second. By noon, they had ridden so far north that they spotted

Hannibal's main force as it crossed the river. On the other side, they could see smoke rising, which they guessed was the Volcae villages burning.

Claudius set up on a hilltop about a mile away from where Scipio had set up his own observation post much closer to the Carthaginian rear. While he couldn't monitor the crossing like Claudius could, he chose the spot to intercept any units splitting away from the main body. He had become a predator watching a herd, waiting for some small element to come out on some mundane mission.

Claudius came to him in the afternoon.

"The Numidians are massing," Claudius told him. "I think they're getting ready to cross."

"They're going to protect the rear as they do," Plinius said.

"How do you know?" Claudius asked.

"It's what I'd do, if my main threat from the rear were cavalry," he explained. "The infantry is still nearly a two-day march south. We're the only ones this far north, aren't we?"

"Look," Scipio told them, pointing down at a small unit emerging from the line on horseback. "I count six."

"Where are they going?" Plinius asked.

Scipio mounted his horse without answering.

"Mount up!" he told his men.

"You know this is against orders," Claudius warned his friend, holding Scipio's horse by its bit. "*Avoid contact.* That's what they told us."

"Let go, Claudius."

Claudius did as he asked and stepped aside.

***

Whoever they were and wherever they were going, the Carthaginians evidently did not expect to encounter any enemies. Scipio followed at a distance for about two miles before he was satisfied that no other Carthaginian units were around.

Scipio's troop approached from the rear at full gallop. The enemy didn't turn their heads until the last moment, when it was far too late to react. In front, Scipio drove his spear through the rearmost Carthaginian, flew by the others and drew his sword as he turned his horse back around. The ambush was sudden and violent, and most of the Carthaginians were already dead or mortally wounded by the time he got back to the melee.

There was a big Carthaginian among them, fighting a Roman *equite* sword-to-sword with fierce intensity. The sound of steel hitting steel rang in the air as Scipio rode at him. He didn't get there in time to prevent the big Carthaginian from slashing his soldier's throat.

In rage, Scipio slashed wildly with his sword, but the Carthaginian dodged. The man leaned a little too far and fell off his horse, hit the ground hard and lost his sword. Scipio dismounted as the man scrambled to his feet. Plinius charged the man with his spear, but his horse reared up. The delay gave the Carthaginian enough time to dodge the spear thrust, step back, and pick his sword up.

The big Carthaginian pivoted to face Scipio, who attacked with a loud cry. The man managed to parry, and they locked swords. Fighting on instinct as much as muscle memory, Scipio swung his left arm and caught his enemy's face with the side of his small round shield. Stunned, the big man stumbled back and barely managed to stave off another attack. Before he could fully recover, he tripped on his own feet and fell backward onto the dirt road, banging his head.

Scipio stepped on his wrist and prepared to drive his sword through the man's throat when Plinius's voice stopped him.

"He's a general!" he said, pointing to the banner one of the slain Carthaginians had been carrying. Scipio glanced around to see that the five other Carthaginians were dead. Thankfully, he'd only lost a single man. Still, when he saw his men taking the slumped body out of his stirrups and laying it on the dusty ground, he felt a pang of regret. He didn't even know the boy's name, and he'd led him to his death.

Scipio heard something from the Carthaginian between laughing and weeping. He looked down at the bearded face, who spat blood into the dust. Hurt and helpless, the giant now seemed pathetic and small.

"Drop it," Scipio commanded in Greek, stepping on the man's wrist harder.

The Carthaginian struggled, tears streaming from his eyes and blood running from his nose and lips, as he struggled to free his hand. He finally relented and released his grip. Scipio kicked the sword away and stepped back. The man rolled onto his side and got to his knees. As he looked up, Scipio saw more hatred in the man's dark brown eyes than he had ever seen before.

"Do it!" the Carthaginian screamed in Greek.

The Romans formed a circle around the man, waiting for their leader to take the general's head as a trophy. Scipio had wanted to do exactly what the Carthaginians had done to Lars and the other *equites*, or worse. Staring into the teary eyes of his enemy, the rage he'd felt only moments before escaped him, and he felt only pity.

The man brought his bearded throat to within inches of Scipio's sword.

"Do it!" he repeated in Greek. "Kill me as you killed my son!"

"What did you say?" Scipio asked.

"You Romans murdered my son!" he cried. "Murdered him in cold blood! He was ten! Go on! Let me join him in the underworld!"

Hasdrubal... Scipio had only seen him once in the dark, but this was him. Of that, he had no doubt. He took another step back, shaking his head and lowering his sword to his side.

"Do it!" Plinius urged him.

"Kill him, sir!" cried another one of his men, but his mind was back in that tent, holding Mathos's limp body, seeing Lucius's face.

"Kill him!" they urged him.

"No, no, no... " Scipio muttered.

Plinius kicked Hasdrubal in the kidneys, sending him to the dirt.

"Don't!" Scipio ordered.

"After what they've done?" Plinius snarled.

"Let him go."

His men were aghast, but their reactions didn't immediately register with Scipio as they sounded their protests. Plinius stepped closer to him to speak into Scipio's ear.

"We should take him back," he said.

"I said let him go!" Scipio barked.

As the men backed off, the seeming act of mercy had no effect on Hasdrubal's hostility. Again, he spat blood and glared at Scipio with undiminished hatred.

"Get on your horse and ride," Plinius told him.

He got up and looked around, and Scipio wondered for a

moment if he would resume fighting despite the odds of seven men to one. The Romans parted enough for him to walk out of the circle. Without another word, the snarling Carthaginian mounted his horse, nursing the side where Plinius had kicked him, and rode west.

***

On the long ride back, Scipio devoted a lot of thought to what he would tell his father. He needed to have a story deflecting blame from himself... But would Plinius contradict him? All Plinius knew was that his new commander was the Consul's son, the nephew of one legate on his father's staff and the brother-in-law of another. Plinius would assume that contradicting Scipio, his commanding officer, would be a waste of time and might be punishable. Scipio decided he would tell his father that Magilus and Gaius quarreled over a private matter, that Magilus had died in the fight but Gaius survived; that the Carthaginians had ambushed them, and that they had merely been defending themselves. Plinius wouldn't object, no matter how many lies Scipio told to protect himself. There was nothing that he could do now to change what had happened. Why make things harder for himself?

This was his plan, and it soothed his anxieties about his debriefing until they arrived at the horse pen in Cornelius's camp the next day. When the time drew near, the thought of telling all those lies, especially in front of Plinius, sickened him as much as the gory sight of his slain friend on that hilltop.

"You'll be reporting alone, sir?" Plinius asked in a tone that made his unhappiness clear. Scipio thought he was probably angry that the rich and privileged got away with everything. It was unfair; as unfair as having officers eat first, but it was the way things were... That was, until Scipio had decided to change it.

"Sir?" Plinius prompted.

"Bring everyone," Scipio replied.

In the command tent, Scipio reported to his father, uncle, and brother-in-law that Hannibal's crossing was likely finished. He then relayed every detail of his patrol to them, acknowledging where he had disobeyed his orders and allowing gambling. Plinius and the rest of his troops stood silent as Cornelius sat in his chair listening, expressionless. Afterward, Metellus dressed them down.

"We should have you all lashed!" Metellus shouted as he paced in front of them. "Do you know how many Roman soldiers—*your brothers*—might have been saved if we knew what Hasdrubal Barca knows? Hundreds? Thousands? All you men will be on half rations for one week and forfeit—"

"I'll take the lashings," Scipio told him.

Metellus stopped abruptly and stepped to Scipio.

"What did you say?" Metellus snarled, his face inches from Scipio's.

"I'll take the lashings... sir," Scipio answered his brother-in-law.

Lashings were serious. They were not to be just accepted like a cut in pay, reduced rations, or extra duties. Plinius, Appius, and their soldiers stole furtive glances in their commander's direction while remaining at attention. Metellus took a step back and looked back to his father-in-law.

"The men did nothing wrong," Scipio told him. "They were my decisions, my orders. The consequences should be mine alone."

Cornelius dismissed Scipio's soldiers without punishment, keeping only his son in the tent with his staff officers. He stepped to the side of the table and looked at the map.

"Now, there's essentially nothing between Hannibal and the Alps," he said.

"We're still a full day's march away," Calvus said. "He's gone."

"Metellus," Cornelius called.

"Yes, Consul."

"Turn the legions around," he told him. "We're returning to Massilia."

"I shall give the order, Consul," he said.

Metellus saluted, gave Scipio one last sneer, and left.

Cornelius stepped over to his son, looking at him squarely.

"Why?" he asked. "Why did you attack them, against my orders?"

"I wanted to pay them back for what they did to Lars Herminius and his men."

"That offense may have gotten you lashing of the tongue," Cornelius said. "Letting Hasdrubal go is what's going to get you the lashing with a whip."

Cornelius waited for a long moment, but Scipio refused to say anything.

"Marcius... "

"Yes, Consul," Marcius answered.

"*Decurio* Scipio is hereby stripped of rank and will be flogged for violating standing orders to detain captured enemies. Set up a post and see the punishment done. The other *equites* will watch in formation."

"Yes, sir."

Scipio saluted his father as Marcius took him by the arm.

He hadn't known what to expect, but relief wasn't it. The crushing weight of his father's expectations was finally off him and things could go back to the way they were. There was no pressure now to be the perfect son, the perfect soldier, to win and keep his father's affections. He could be himself again; but cathartic it was not, and he wondered why. This was, he thought, what he wanted—no expectations, no responsibility, no one to disappoint... Except his men. Had he let them down? He asked himself why he should care. They would get another officer or elect one, and things would go on for them. Still, he felt he had abandoned them.

"Count yourself lucky," Calvus told his nephew as they walked. "I would have given you the lashing. I advocated for you, Nephew, and the moment you get into a position with the least authority, you violate your orders and come back with two less men. If you won't tell your father why, at least tell me."

"I killed that man's son," Scipio told him.

"What?"

Calvus pulled him back and stepped in front of him, stopping Scipio and Marcius in their tracks.

"On the mission in Gaul," Scipio said. "It was... my mistake."

"And you tried to alleviate your guilt by releasing him?"

Scipio didn't answer. He couldn't. He didn't know why he'd made that decision, only that it felt the least wrong thing to do. He heard his uncle sigh and put a comforting hand on his shoulder.

"Ah, well... " he said, stepping beside him so they could resume walking. "You took responsibility. That, at least, you did well, but you need to learn to take orders and keep control of yourself."

"I will," Scipio promised.

"I know," Calvus said. "Few things make a soldier learn faster than a flogging."

Part III: Inveniam Viam

HANNIBAL

Wind howled through the pass, blowing the stinging rain directly into the faces of the men crawling their way toward what the locals called "Cat Mountain." Hannibal was near the front with the light infantry and skirmishers, trying to set a pace that would hopefully get them through the mountains before winter set in. They were not far beyond the foothills and already dealing with mountain roads barely wide enough to accommodate the elephants. Many featured steep inclines to one side and sheer drop-offs to the other. He lost his first scouts the second night in the mountains. Two foraging parties went missing the following day. They were presumed dead, either by falling or at the hands of local highland tribes. Now, their "guides" from the foothill tribes had disappeared. The mountains were devouring men.

Each night, Hannibal made it a point to watch the men march before he chose a site for their camp. Gisgo would often watch alongside him. As quartermaster, Gisgo kept a close eye on the needs of the soldiers. If the men looked tired, they would pick a place where they could stay at least a day, else they would make a hasty site for one night. Today he saw shoulders slumped, weary eyes on the ground or barely able to look up at his, and wrappings around boots to pad the soles. It had been a hard day of ascending, and the men were moving slow.

When they reached a plateau, the scouts spotted specks of flickering light hundreds of feet up the side of Cat Mountain—campfires. Hannibal halted the entire column. Soon, he realized that getting the men back on their feet would likely be impossible for a while, and he let the last hour or so of daylight go to waste. He counted six fires on the mountainside, and as the sky grew darker, the flames became more visible.

They were being watched.

Hannibal pulled Vernon from the formation and pointed out the fires.

"What can you tell me about the Gauls here?" he asked him.

"They're called Allobroges," Vernon answered, looking up at the fires. "Highlanders. Sometimes, they come down to trade. Mostly, they stay up here. Farmers, shepherds… "

"Thieves," Hannibal added.

Vernon nodded and said, "A lot of travelers don't make it through here. This road is theirs. They built it."

"Have the men light extra campfires," he instructed Gisgo. "If they're estimating our strength, I want them to overestimate it."

Maharbal and his cavalry scouts returned with more bad news.

"They led us to a ravine," he reported, referring to their missing guides.

"They're probably up on that mountain," Hannibal said. "How far to the ravine?"

"The entrance is about two miles ahead," Maharbal answered, squatting to take a rock in his hand. He used it to cut in the nearly frozen earth, depicting the terrain in front of them.

"About a hundred-foot drop," he said, eliciting an impressed whistle from Gisgo. "One road through it, on our left."

"Wide enough for the elephants and carts?" Gisgo asked.

"Wide enough," Maharbal answered. "And open, for now."

He laid a few rocks on either side of the gash he'd made.

"Steep incline on both sides, up to ridges," he said, pointing to the rocks, then ahead of them. "They start up there, to the right of the campfires."

Hannibal cursed his luck. The Gauls had led them into a trap. He knew that admonishing himself over it was useless, but it was difficult not to. He studied the little map of the terrain that Maharbal made, looking for a way to maneuver on the Allobrogian tribesmen.

"Can you get to the road from the ridge above?"

"In some places, yes," Maharbal replied. "But it's steep."

"There's no way around?"

"Not that we could see. Too steep in either direction for the carts and elephants. If we want to keep moving forward—"

"It's not a matter of wanting," Hannibal said, standing up. "So, this road is the only way through. Yes?"

"Yes, General," Maharbal answered with a nod.

"Take me to it."

By the time they arrived, it was nearly dark. Hannibal, Gisgo, and Vernon surveyed the road and the ridge overlooking it with Maharbal and a small cavalry detachment. They could now see that there were more than a dozen campfires on the eastern ridge.

"They're already set up to attack the column," Hannibal said, looking up. "They know we have to take this road."

"Yet they leave it open," Maharbal said. "If they were going to attack, wouldn't they block it?"

"If I were them, I would. I'd let just enough of us through that we could kill and rob them, then block the road with boulders so the rest couldn't come to their aid."

"That's risky," Vernon said. "Their villages are on the other side, to the east. If they attack and fail... "

"They *will* attack," Hannibal said.

Hannibal looked up again. A campfire had gone out, and another was dying.

"Where are they going?" he wondered aloud.

"Home," Vernon said. "They know we're settling in for the night. They'll probably leave a few men to watch our camp, just in case we move before dawn."

As it grew darker, Hannibal tried to recall everything he had seen of the terrain in front of him. The ravine with its sheer drop to the rocks below, the road through the pass, the ridge running on the west side of Cat Mountain, overlooking the road. In a single long, narrow, slow-moving column with no room to maneuver, his army would be at its most vulnerable. Going around was too far, and going up was too steep; they would go through, at least until something blocked their way. The terrain was a sword that cut both ways. The Allobroges could not come down from the ridge without risking plunging to their deaths. Like the Carthaginians, they were limited to using the road. They would have to attack and steal as much as they could and flee using the same thoroughfare, and they would have to come at his army head-on. Taking those ridges while the Allobrogians slept was the only way to guarantee they could not block the road.

"Can we pay them off?" Hannibal asked Vernon.

"With this terrain," Vernon replied, "I wouldn't trust them to take the bribe and not attack all the same."

Once on the other side, Hannibal could hold the Allobroges' villages at risk, but only if his army made it through relatively intact. If they managed to block the road, he'd be forced to retreat and look for another way around, likely getting lost in the maze of mountains.

When they returned to their hasty camp, Hannibal's first visit was to his light infantry—the skirmishers. He knew that their morale was low. Most were raw recruits from Hispania and the Balearic Islands. They were markedly less valuable than his mercenary Numidian cavalry, his war elephants, his heavy African infantry, his Celtiberians, his archers, or even his pack animals; and they were aware of their place in the pecking order of the army. It was the skirmishers who went ahead to check the trails, forage for supplies, and flush out enemies lying in wait. Since reaching the mountains, they had been taking causalities every day.

"Adalram!" he called when he saw their commander.

"Yes, General!"

"Get your officers," Hannibal ordered, getting in line to get a bowl of the same porridge the skirmishers ate.

With a small bowl for himself, he stood by a campfire to eat, looking at the scruffy young faces around him. Some murmured and whispered to each other. Others simply stared at him in awe.

"How was the climb for you?" he asked them in Punic, hoping they had learned enough to know what he was asking.

"Very hard, General," one answered.

"The rocks," another added. "Some places, one step in the wrong place left or right... "

The others nodded and murmured in agreement.

"It's harder than you thought?" he asked.

"It's *higher* than I thought," one of them said, and the others laughed.

"Perhaps you thought we would sprout wings and fly to Italy," Hannibal said.

Their laughter warmed the night air. Hannibal chatted with them for a while before the light infantry commander, Adalram, tapped him on the shoulder. Behind him were ten men, most of whom Hannibal didn't recognize, even though he made it a point to meet all the junior leaders before they left Hispania. Evidently, there had been a lot of attrition. Hannibal brought them around the fire. There was a growing crowd straining to hear him speak.

"You saw all those fires up there today, on the high ground?" he asked them, pointing to where the fires had once been.

He received some nods and words of acknowledgment. Either they had seen the fires or were too embarrassed to admit that they hadn't.

"There's a tribe here called the Allobroges," Hannibal explained. "About two miles up is a ravine, and there's no way around. When we go through it tomorrow, we'll be vulnerable. They'll raid the column and take what they can. Gold, supplies, food, weapons... Anything they can get their hands on."

He looked around to see they were paying close attention. It was their food and baggage the locals were planning to steal, after all.

"They call this Cat Mountain," Hannibal went on. The name got a few chuckles. "Can anyone guess why?" he asked.

He was answered with silence and blank stares.

"Ever see a cat with its back up?" he asked.

He saw nods and heard grunts. They got it.

Hannibal slurped the last of the tasteless porridge and turned the bowl upside down, then inverted his spoon and placed it next to it.

"The cat's back, and the cat's head," he told them, shaking the bowl and then the spoon. "In between is the neck... the ravine we have to go through. If the Allobroges are up on the cat's back, what do you think they'll do to us way down in the ravine?"

He saw furrowed brows and slack jaws.

"They'll hit us with rocks, arrows... everything," he explained. "Take what they can, block the road with boulders and run."

He saw nods and concerned faces. They got it.

"We must take that high ground tonight," he told them. "We can't use any light, either. I need skirmishers and few cavalry up there to hold it and give the rest of the army cover to go through tomorrow."

"We have to go now, General?" one of them asked.

"Watch your lazy tongue, boy!" Adalram snapped.

"It's fine, Adalram," Hannibal said, before turning back to the men. "I know you're tired. We all are. The others will have to march to the mouth of the ravine so that we can cross at first light; but yes, we must go now."

"We?" he heard a voice asked.

"I'm going with you," Hannibal told them.

That seemed to surprise them more than anything he had said to that point. They looked more serious now than annoyed that they would have to do more work tonight. Perhaps, Hannibal thought, his going with them impressed upon them how important this really was.

"They've left for the night," Hannibal told them. "They don't think we have it in us to climb up there and take that ground from them while they're at home, braiding their wives' beards."

It was the first time he'd heard his men's hearty laughter in any large group since they had begun their ascent.

213

"But when they come back tomorrow, we'll have a surprise for them," Hannibal said with a grin. "Won't we?"

The men nodded and rumbled.

"*Won't we?!*" he yelled, and the men cheered in reply.

He smiled as they patted him on the back and head, touching their commander for good luck. For one night, morale among the skirmishers was high.

As the campfires burned and the Allobroges assigned to monitor Hannibal's movements settled in for a cold night on the mountain, Gisgo got the army in a single column formation and moved them two anguishing miles through the darkness to the mouth of the ravine. Less than a hundred remained to tend the hundreds of fires they left burning at their original camp to give the impression that they were still there.

Hannibal could not see Gisgo's column from where he was, and it worried him. Aside from runners that might not have made it back down the mountain alive, there was no way to communicate with the main body of his army. He would never have normally put himself so far from the center of his forces, but taking the high ground and providing cover for them would, in his estimation, be decisive.

As the climb and night wore on, the cloud broke. The moon and the stars improved visibility, albeit a little. The men scarcely noticed, their heads scanning the dark forest floor in front of them for rocks and fallen branches. Even the horses seemed exhausted and resistant to move forward as they neared the top of the ridge. When the earth finally leveled out, it came as a needed relief for their weary legs. From there to the end of the ravine they moved more easily, and they reached their objective a few hours before daylight.

After leaving orders to be woken as soon as it was light enough for the army to move or at first sight of the enemy, Hannibal wrapped his cloak around himself, sat under a sturdy oak tree, and closed his eyes.

***

"General! General!"

He opened his eyes to see the sun was nearly up. They had let him sleep too long.

"The army is moving," Adalram reported.

Hannibal stood up, opening his cloak. The cold morning air made his body shiver and his teeth chatter.

"The Allobroges?" he asked, following Adalram to where they could watch the army move.

"No sign of them yet," Adalram said. "But look... "

He pointed south and swept his finger east, beyond where the ravine ended. There were cottages and small plots of farmland enough to constitute a small village. Distant smoke from the other side of a hill suggested more villages.

Gisgo's column was crawling along the road as the soldiers peered from their elephants, carts, and horses down to the rocks below on their right. The elephants were nervous, rumbling and trumpeting as their riders and handlers drove them forward.

Hannibal tried not to look beyond getting out of this place, but he couldn't help but think of the higher Alps that awaited them. Soon there would be nothing but pines; then, they would be above the tree line. It would be increasingly dangerous, physically taxing, and slow. The last thing he needed was to have to fight Gauls along with the weather and terrain.

"General!" Adalram called. Hannibal looked up to see him pointing in the direction of the village. "Horsemen!"

There were about a thousand Allobroges, Hannibal estimated, making their way from their village in the valley to the south end of the ravine on foot and horse. The rush of nervous anticipation before battle overtook the fatigue of the night climb.

He put his hand on Adalram's shoulder and locked eyes with him to ensure he had his full attention.

"Infantry on the left, cavalry to the right, skirmishers in the middle," he said.

"Yes, General!"

Adalram hurried away to form the battle lines as the raiders approached. Hannibal watched as the enemy split themselves into two groups, half heading toward the ridge he and Adalram held and half toward the road along which Gisgo's column rumbled along. The men moving toward the ridge began shouting to one another, pointing to Hannibal's skirmishers peering down at them. They then halted, leaving Hannibal waiting to see what they would do. He heard a horn sound, and the party of Allobroges that had been headed toward the ravine stopped.

Hannibal still felt the initiative was with him, as it was the Allobroges that were reacting to his moves, and not the other way around; but until the column was through, he had done about all he could do. He watched as the two parties of raiders rejoined, no doubt to decide what to do.

"Go home... " Hannibal found himself urging them, though he suspected they would not. Down there, moving through the ravine on the road—*their* road—was more weapons, gold, animals, and food than these highlanders could resist trying to steal. His best hope was that they demand a "tax" for the road's use.

It was not to be. The raiders spread out again into two parties, as before. The first advanced toward the ridge but stopped well short of Hannibal's position. He was trying to discern what they were doing there when a horn blast echoed through the ravine, and the enemy horsemen charged straight at the front of the Gisgo's column.

"Archers, draw!" Adalram ordered.

The skirmishers didn't wait for the command, firing as soon as they estimated the enemy was within range. The slingers' rocks and archers' arrows came down on the charging enemy hard but not all at once, giving them a chance to raise their shields. Hannibal cursed his luck as he saw the horsemen charge through the missiles and collide with the front of the column. He then realized what the other Allobrogians were doing. They were blocking him from riding down from the ridge and flanking their raiders. He was stuck up there with his men, firing down to no avail.

The raiders cut through the first few men easily. If only he'd had the African infantry at the front... or, better yet, the elephants. He had arranged for everyone else to go in front of them so that they could ensure the road ahead was wide and stable enough for his elephants. The great beasts were lumbering in the back when they could have been spooking the enemy horses in front.

Disaster struck. A mule panicked and stopped, too spooked by the sound of clashing weapons and the cries of men to move forward. It tried to turn and, due to its harness, backed up and sent its cart into the rock face, blocking the road. African infantry tried to rush forward but could not get through. An Allobroges raider took the mule by the bit and tried to force it forward, but the animal strained back and shook its head violently. An archer climbed to the top of the supplies on the cart and fired at the raiders. He hit the mule and it bolted, taking himself, the cart, and two men to the rocks below.

Hannibal gripped his father's sword tighter and struck a tree with his other hand as he watched the scene unfold. He knew well that indecision could be catastrophic in battle, but he only had bad choices. He didn't have the men with him to drive off the Allobroges blocking his decent to the south, and it was far too steep to charge down to the road below. Watching the infantry trying to engage the raiders, he couldn't decide if intervening was worth the risk of causing greater chaos and risk losing more men and animals when they fell from the road.

He could wait no longer.

"Cavalry on me!" he called, mounting his horse.

He could see the fear in his men's eyes as they formed a line at the precipice of the steep slope, parallel to the road below. He drew his father's sword, closed his eyes a moment, and took a breath. This could very well be his end, and he wanted his father's spirit with him now.

"Don't rush down," he told the others. "Now... Forward!"

The horses whinnied and scrambled for footing as their riders drove them forward and down. It proved to be the most terrifying thing that Hannibal had ever done on horseback, charging down what seemed a cliff's face toward the shields of an enemy on a narrow road, the other side of which was a hundred-foot drop. The rider on his right was going too fast.

"Easy!" he called to him.

The rider struggled to pull the crying horse back, but it was too late. They went down hard and rolled like a boulder into one of the raiders, taking them all over the side. Two men and their animals tumbled into the ravine bellowing horrible cries, but it cleared just enough of the road for a few African infantry to get through and hold the enemy at bay as Hannibal's cavalry hit the Allobroges and pushed them toward oblivion.

Hannibal hacked the arm from a tribesman thrusting a spear at one of his soldiers. A Numidian cavalryman used his javelin as a spear, thrusting it at a raider and spooking his horse. It backed up, lost its footing, and fell with its rider. Apparently, they needed only to hear the screams of a few of their comrades before the rest of the Allobroges retreated in the direction from which they came. The skirmishers adjusted their fire on the Gauls at the foot of the ridge, forcing them back.

"Come through!" Hannibal ordered the African infantry. "Secure the road! Move!"

The infantry easily pushed the remaining raiders back off the road and formed up like a wall, shielding the end of the road as it let out into the valley. The Allobroges didn't challenge them. As the column began to exit the road, the remaining enemy retreated to their villages.

An observer that witnessed the engagement without knowledge of the context in which it took place might have thought the Carthaginians had won, but Hannibal counted it a loss. When his army moved out of the ravine, he realized he had lost over a hundred men and animals in a matter of minutes.

He had made tactical errors, but it was the Allobroges who made the strategic blunder of attacking a force they were ultimately unable to either defeat or turn back. Now Hannibal was at their doorstep, and the villagers had little to keep them out. He would have been content to pass this place without incident. Now he would teach the Allobroges a sharp lesson.

SCIPIO

Scipio had been flogged by a centurion that knew a surprising amount about the subject. Before he was brought out to be beaten with a rod in front of the three hundred other Roman cavalrymen assigned to his legion, the man came to him and described exactly what was to happen. Scipio was lucky, he explained, that it wasn't the lash. He would take a few hits in the stomach, his bottom, and, most painful of all, on the soles of his feet. The centurion knew exactly where and how hard he could strike with his rod so that it inflicted a good deal of pain while avoiding breaking bones and damaging organs. Recognizing he had a special guest in the Consul's son, the centurion gave him the courtesy of a piece of leather to bite down on and kept a cheerful attitude until it was time to wield the baton.

Thankfully, his father decided to hold off on administering the punishment until they returned to Massilia, which spared him from having to ride a horse with a severely bruised backside. Afterward, he was taken below deck on a *quinquereme* and laid face-down on a table meant for surgical amputations while the ships were loaded. He'd been there an entire day and night, barely able to move to drink water and relieve himself, listening to the waves lap against the hull and soldiers walking around above deck, before Calvus came to see him.

"How are you feeling?" Calvus asked, inspecting the bruises on his back.

"Tenderized."

Calvus laughed and said, "They went easy on you." He pressed down on a welt, making Scipio wince. "Still sensitive?"

He was rewarded with a nasty look from his nephew.

"No broken bones, at least," Calvus said. "The centurion was good."

"Father will probably promote him."

"Has he come to see you, your father?"

"He's consistent in making me his last priority," Scipio answered bitterly.

"Well... he's very busy."

"So are you, Uncle," Scipio retorted.

Calvus paused, and the look in his eyes worried Scipio that more punishment was coming.

"What is it?" he asked.

"I'm not going with you to Cisalpine Gaul," Calvus told him.

"What?"

"I'm going on to Hispania," Calvus said. "As we originally planned."

"Why?"

"To threaten the crown jewel of Carthage's empire," Calvus replied. "We need to establish a proper foothold and choke Hannibal's supply lines."

"We're splitting the army?"

"Not quite," Calvus explained. "Your father will be taking command of the legions we sent against the Boii, and we're dividing the cavalry. So, you have a choice to make. Hispania with me, or Cisalpine Gaul with your father."

More than anything, he wanted to go home. All he'd encountered in this campaign was horror, pain, and anger. If going home wasn't an option, he wanted to stay with Calvus. Not only did he love him better than his father, but Italy was the more dangerous place to be. They'd failed to stop Hannibal in Gaul, so most of the fighting would likely be in Italy; and his father would want to engage the Carthaginians as soon as they came through the Alps. Going to Hispania would likely mean fighting ill-motivated mercenaries and locals, trying to win alliances with Celtiberian tribes more than great victories, but he would be stuck there for the winter, if not the rest of the war. That meant years might pass before he would see Aemilia again. She would marry someone else—of that, he was certain. He needed to see her soon if he was to have any hope of winning her over.

"I'll go with father," he said.

"Are you sure?"

"I'm sure."

"I just thought after this... " Calvus said, motioning to his back.

"I'll live," Scipio quipped. "Besides, I want to annoy him as long as possible."

His uncle laughed, but Scipio saw the apprehension on his face.

"This wouldn't have anything to do with a certain senator's daughter, would it?" he asked.

"It has everything to do with her," Scipio told him.

Calvus looked at him with pride and then slapped him on the back, sending a wave of pain through Scipio's body.

"Oh, Gods!" Scipio winced.

"Oh... sorry," Calvus said, though he was laughing.

It made Scipio laugh at his own predicament, even if it hurt all over to do so. Calvus seemed to find humor in that as well, and he laughed harder still. At last, he wiped the tears of laughter from his eyes and tussled his nephew's hair.

"Well then... " Calvus said. "Fight well, *Decurio*."

Scipio felt himself choking up as Calvus kissed his forehead and turned to leave.

"I was stripped of rank," Scipio reminded him.

Calvus turned back to him and asked, "Didn't anyone tell you? Your men voted you back into command."

"I'm sure they did," Scipio replied wryly.

It took a while for the fact that Calvus wasn't teasing him to sink in. When it did, he felt much more shock and confusion than pride or gratitude.

"We get lots wrong, the two of us," Calvus said. "But it seems we get some things right now and again."

CATO

Cato hunched over on his seat and rested his forearms on his thighs while beads of sweat came from every pore of his naked body. He had been through this ordeal hundreds of times now, each of which seemed more torturous than the last. He was almost certain every other man that shared the experience with him dreaded it just as much as he did, if not more; but they always lounged in that cursed room that smelled like Pluto's ass and smiled at each other, professing their love for this twisted custom. This, after all, was the final portion of an elaborate urban ritual of Roman life—the bath.

Of course, he would almost never come here of his own volition. He was always coerced by one fop or another wanting to seal a political alliance, buy some influence, or pitch some business scheme. On this occasion, however, it was Cato that had issued the invitation to his childhood friend, Lucius Valerius Flaccus. At the end of a long morning, they were standing in the *laconicum*, the hot room of the East Baths, sweating out the impurities that pervaded the city air and clung to their skin, and waiting for a special guest to arrive.

"At some point, Marcus, everyone needs help from someone," Flaccus told Cato. "It is why we're here, is it not?"

Cato picked his head up and looked through the steam-filled air at Flaccus, who was lying on his back and taking up the entire length of a concrete bench. With one leg dangling off, one hand resting on his stomach and his other forearm resting on his forehead, he looked like a sculpture of a man in agony; but the smirk on his face belied his posture.

"A man should rise or fall on his own merits," Cato told him.

"How dare you insult me?" Flaccus jibbed. "You know damned well I have nothing approaching merit. Patronage is the Roman way. Merit means nothing if it isn't recognized. If it were not for my own vicious little clan, you'd be the most meritorious pig farmer in Tusculum."

Cato forced a little smile. Regardless of how true Flaccus's words were, hearing them stung.

"I would welcome the support of you and yours, Lucius, as always," Cato replied, sitting upright.

"So... which office are we running for now?" Flaccus asked.

"What makes you think it's an office?"

"Because I know you, Marcus," he said. "Better than you know yourself. Even as a child, you were recklessly ambitious. It's why my father loved you so."

"And you?"

Flaccus opened a single eye and turned his head in Cato's direction.

"You're asking if I hated you just because you bested me in contests of sports or martial skills?" he asked.

Flaccus sat upright on the bench with some effort, grunting

between chuckles, and Cato noticed his friend was getting fat. He had always been lazy and disinclined to exercise, but he'd also been thin. Perhaps age was catching up with him.

"No," Flaccus continued, and held his arms out grandly with his chin up. "I am Lucius Valerius Flaccus. I need no successes to be successful."

"Your grandfather would have slapped you across the face if he could hear you now," a deep voice echoed in the dark room.

The two men looked in the direction from which it came, and a familiar figure seemed to materialize out of the steam. Fabius was sixty-eight, and his skin was already sagging where it had once held the muscles snuggly on his lean frame.

Cato stood out of respect and bowed his head slightly, welcoming the elder statesman, but he remained standing before Fabius for another reason. Still several years short of thirty, Cato's stout, muscular body and smooth skin contrasted sharply with Fabius. Naked before each other, the superiority Fabius possessed in his senator's toga was lost, however temporarily. The message was clear—Fabius was the past, Cato the future.

The old man seemed to get it quickly, for he snorted and took a seat across from Flaccus.

"What *are* you up to, Cato?" he asked.

"Up to?" Cato echoed innocently.

Fabius rested his head on a pillar and looked down his long nose at him.

"It's no secret that Flaccus's family has been a great source of support for you," Fabius said. "You've never asked anything of me, so I can only surmise that your invitation means you need something money can't buy."

"Isn't it obvious?" Flaccus asked Fabius, reclining on his side this time and letting his stomach hang over the ledge of the bench. "He wants to be a Plebian Aedile."

"Why do you think I want that?" Cato asked him.

"Because it's next, Marcus," Flaccus replied. "There's an invisible ladder in Rome for the low-born, each rung of which is a public office; and you're climbing it at the speed of Jupiter's thunderbolt. Your talent and my money have gotten you this far, but you're getting to the point where you'll need more powerful friends."

"This is about more than my personal ambition, Lucius," Cato replied, still standing between the old man and his old friend. "It's about the greatness of Rome."

Cato heard Fabius snicker and turned to see the old man bent over with his head in his hands, slicking back his gray hair.

"Something funny, Senator?"

"Hmph... As many times as I've heard it, it still amuses me to hear someone conflate Rome's interests, Rome's greatness, Rome's pride and shame, with his own."

Cato retook his seat and probed the old man's brown eyes. Fabius was the elder statesman of the conservative side of the senate, and Paullus was his liberal counterpart. For decades, nearly every political decision of any consequence was the result of discussions between those two alone; but they were aging, and their power was waning.

"I invited you here, Senator, to inform you that Varro intends to stand for Consul," he said.

Flaccus burst out laughing as if the very idea were absurd, but Fabius did not seem to think the same. The old man sat up, the amused look replaced with a more solemn visage.

"What of his support for our list of candidates?" Fabius asked. "Will he support the conservative side of the Senate?"

Cato coyly shrugged and took his seat again.

"We didn't meet in the Illyrian War," he finally said.

"Of course not," Cato said. "I was a rank-and-file cavalryman. You were a Consul."

"Yet your name reached my ears more than once," Fabius said. "You'll have the chance to serve Rome again in the legions. This war will go on longer than anyone thinks—long past the tenures of our present Consuls."

"Perhaps," Cato allowed.

"Your military talents would be wasted as an Aedile," Fabius told him. "As prestigious as the post may be, we do not need men like you to be efficient administrators right now. We need them to be leaders. Stand for Military Tribune, Marcus."

Cato was outwardly even-tempered, if not a little disappointed. Flaccus had unwittingly played his part well—better than he would have, Cato thought, had he conspired with Cato before Fabius arrived. Flaccus believed, Cato knew, that he knew Cato better than anyone; but Cato only ever showed Flaccus what he wanted him to see. It was how he controlled what Flaccus thought of him, and it kept his family's money flowing to Cato's campaigns.

"I don't like your politics, Cato," Fabius told Cato. "But Varro's politics I positively loath. I find his nativism especially odious. The bill he sponsored to restrict citizenship to free-born men born to free-born Romans so offended my sensibilities that I nearly wrote you off merely for your association with him."

"Like it or not, Fabius, there are many Romans who agree with his sentiments about foreign peoples," Cato said.

"And that is unfortunate," Fabius replied. "But merely exploiting the ignorant bigotry of the masses weakens Rome even as it strengthens Varro."

"I'll allow that his tactics are unconventional," Cato said. "But the people appreciate him. Varro believes in Rome for Romans."

"Varro believes in nothing but his own grandiosity," Fabius retorted. "He should not—*must not* be a Consul... especially now. If we cannot agree on that, we have nothing further to discuss."

"Whether I agree with you or not is moot," said Cato. "You can't keep him off the ballot forever. He'll convince his followers that the Senate is subverting the will of the people, and he'll have a point."

Fabius seemed to dwell on Cato's words a long time, not saying anything. Finally, Cato could take no more.

"It's too hot in here," he said, and stood up. "My balls are sagging nearly to the floor. I'm going to the *palaestra*. Perhaps we could finish our discussion there."

Cato dressed and headed out to the *palaestra*—an exercise yard adjacent to the bath. Luckily, it was empty except for a couple of youths wrestling at one end. He got himself a cup of cold water, found a shady spot, and sat on the grass, enjoying the crisp fall air. He silently vowed to himself to never again use the bathhouses. There were entirely too many naked people in there sharing the same filthy water, then sitting around and sweating. It was disgusting and indulgent. So very... *Greek*.

He waited there a long time before Flaccus and Fabius came strolling out in their togas. Cato hated the toga as well. It felt like wearing a curtain. It was one more petty indulgence, imported from Greece, that was ruining the Roman spirit.

"I'm tired of losing to the liberals, Fabius," Cato said, squinting from the sun as he looked up at them. "If Varro can build the support we need to push through the laws we favor and keep Rome Roman, I'll support him."

"Varro cannot be allowed to command soldiers," Fabius said. "In temperament, experience, and judgment, Varro is entirely unsuited to lead even a dog."

"That is for the people to decide, Fabius," Cato retorted. "Not you."

"Stand up," Fabius ordered.

A pang of fear shot through Cato's chest for a moment as the voice transported him to an army camp somewhere far from Rome, where an officer held the power of life and death over his soldiers and his commands were to be obeyed at all personal cost. He stood up quickly, not fully realizing he was under no formal obligation to obey the old man's dictates.

"What do you want, Cato?"

That was the question Cato had been waiting for the entire afternoon. Arguably the most powerful and respected man in Rome was asking him what he wanted. The Varro gambit had worked better than he had hoped.

"Help me get Paullus's faction to withdraw their opposition to the lex Oppia going to the Comitia."

Fabius took a half step back, and his eyes narrowed. It was as if, thought Cato, the old man suddenly realized he was in a negotiation.

"Why do you want this law so badly?" he asked.

"Because, Senator, I was not born with the advantage of a patrician's family name and fortune," Cato replied, indicating Flaccus, who bowed slightly in thanks for the recognition. "But I have something nearly every man lacks, and it isn't ambition, nor intelligence, nor virtue."

"Don't keep up is suspense, Marcus," Flaccus said. "What is it you have that the rest of us are so sorely in want of?"

The corner of Cato's mouth turned up in a smile for the first time that day as he looked at his old friend and answered with a single word.

"Vision."

HANNIBAL

Morale in Hannibal's army improved after sacking the Allobroges' villages. They had gained momentum from picking the enemy's livestock and grain stores clean. They would need it to make it through the next leg of the journey. In addition, they had taken hundreds of able-bodied enemies as slaves to lighten the load on the soldiers and animals. It may have been excessive, but Hannibal had wanted to deter the other Alpine tribes from planning similar raids.

The men sang songs as they marched through a wide pass, but their jovial mood passed quickly. Before them loomed a wall of gray and white mountains that they were headed straight toward. It extended east and west as far as the eye could see and disappeared into clouds. Like an enormous blanket, the high Alps smothered the cheerful banter and songs; and they were left marching in silent dread.

The climbing was less treacherous than tiring as they began their ascent. Each time they thought they were done going up for a while, they found the way inclining again. It was as if the Alps were conscious of their intrusion and determined to make it as painful and exhausting as possible for them to continue going deeper into them. The scouts failed to find any reasonably level avenue that did not take them too far east or west. They had to stay marching dead south as much as the terrain would allow.

Gisgo was already fretting about the roads. Up in the higher climbs, he warned, it would be snow and ice that would start to slow them down and wear on them if they failed to find ways through at lower altitudes.

"Is this how you pictured it?" Mago asked his brother as the army passed before them.

"Something like it," Hannibal replied.

Hannibal normally stayed near the front to make it easier for the returning scouts to find him, but now they were moving the men into position to bed down for the night. They looked somber but healthy, without any serious limping or struggling to breathe; but they were clearly wary of the truly high Alps in front of them. The air would be cold and more difficult to breathe, further slowing the march. They were already getting their first flurries of snow.

"You always had a flare for the dramatic," Mago said, then blew into his hands and rubbed them together as the elephants approached. "I have to admit... people will be talking about this for a long time."

"What do you think they'll be saying about us?" Hannibal asked.

Mago grinned and replied, "... and they were never seen again."

It made Hannibal laugh hard enough that the soldiers passing by turned their heads in wonder.

"Is that father's sword?" Mago said, tapping the scabbard at Hannibal's side.

"Sometimes I carry it."

"When?"

"Times like this."

Mago took a drink from his wineskin. He offered it to Hannibal, who shook his head.

"If I fall," Hannibal told him, putting his hand on the hilt of his sword, "I want you to take it. A Barca should hold it over Rome."

"Hannibal, if you fall... this, whatever all *this* is... It will be over."

Mago probably wasn't joking, Hannibal knew, but he chose to pretend his brother was as committed as he was to destroying Rome.

Hannibal closed his eyes. The warm Sicilian breeze that came to him when he thought of the day his father died was a world and a lifetime away, but he could feel it as sure as the blustery wind. It might have been a pleasant mental escape, if it weren't for the images that came with it.

"Do you remember what father told us that day in Sicily?" he asked Mago.

"I remember he made you hold that damned thing while he fell on it," Mago answered. Even now, the spite in his voice was crystal clear.

"To seal our pact," Hannibal said. "That is what the gods demand—sacrifice."

"It was what father wanted, Hannibal," Mago countered. "Not the gods."

"Our oath to destroy Rome is *sacred*," Hannibal said. "Nothing less than the blood of our father made it so."

"Father didn't draw us together on some holy quest, Hannibal," Mago returned. "He cursed us to hate and kill people we don't even know, simply so he could feel better about his losing a war to them. If I were you, I'd drop that thing into the deepest crevice I could find."

Hannibal could almost always tell when Mago was being snarky and when he meant what he said, and he meant what he'd just said. He just didn't know how that notion could live inside Mago. Toss their father's legacy away? Abandon their duty? These were alien concepts.

"You know the difference between us and the Romans?" Mago asked.

Hannibal heard him, but he was distracted by Vernon and Gisgo walking alongside the column, making their way towards him. Several middle-aged highland tribesmen followed them, all dressed in furs, which indicated high status.

"Hannibal?" Mago called.

"Hmm? What was that?" Hannibal asked Mago, though he was still distracted by the approaching Gauls.

"Beware of Gauls bearing gifts," Mago said, motioning to the tribesmen, and left him.

Hannibal leered as the tribesmen bowed to him.

"General Hannibal," Vernon translated as one of them spoke. "These men are elders of the Salluvi Tribe, whose lands lie south and east of here. They heard tales of the great force that smashed the Allobroges at Cat Mountain, and they wish to thank you for liberating the region of that wicked and oppressive people."

He thought himself a decent reader of men, even when he didn't speak the same language; but Hannibal couldn't tell if this was true atonement for their countrymen's attacks, a pragmatic reversal of policy, or outright deception. He studied their leathery bearded faces, trying to discern what lay behind this supposed contrition. They were excellent liars, these highlanders, and he had to presume they were lying now. They could not have been truly happy that he'd sacked their cousins' villages. The question was whether they were cowed or outraged.

"In thanks for your generous acts," Vernon went on, "they wish to offer you guides to cross the southern mountains ranges."

Hannibal grinned behind his make-shift scarf, though he had heard the doubt in Vernon's voice even as he translated.

"Tell them that I accept," he told Vernon, and the Gaul raised his eyebrows in reply. "I only require a small token of their good faith."

Vernon translated, and the elders discussed it amongst themselves. Hannibal saw them glance nervously at him, as if Hannibal was the one that could not be trusted. If this was an act, it was a good one. Finally, they gave their answer.

"They wish to know what the general—"

"Tell them that I require fifty women between the ages of fifteen and thirty, and an equal number of men between fifteen and forty."

Child-bearing women and fighting-age men made excellent hostages. No matter who they were, they would be valuable.

After Vernon translated, the Salluvi tribesmen discussed Hannibal's offer in hushed voices. An argument, or at least a heated discussion, broke out between them. If there was some resistance to giving him that many hostages, it was understandable. Hannibal avoided making eye contact, trying to appear disinterested in their response in hopes of removing any impression he may budge on the demand. Finally, an answer came. It was one of the rare moments in his life that Hannibal felt unsure of what would happen next.

"They have agreed, General," Vernon told him.

Hannibal turned and left as the tribesman again prostrated themselves. When Hannibal faced the mountains again, they didn't seem as high, the snows as cold, or the path ahead as arduous as they had only moments before. It was irrational, perhaps, but he gave his instincts the benefit of the doubt. They were better predictors of human behavior than his intellect.

"General... " Vernon began when he caught up to him, but Hannibal knew what he was going to say and stopped him.

"Save your breath," he said. "We're fumbling around in the dark out here. In this terrain, six armies could be converging on us right now and we'd know nothing about it until they were on top of us. Maybe hostages will make them think twice about fighting."

AEMILIA

Aemilia had been dreading Varro's big political season party since her father had told her she would be escorting him to it. Despite his many tirades denouncing them, it was apparent to her that Varro loved hosting Rome's elite; at least, he loved to be *seen* hosting them. His speeches about them were not lies in the sense that he believed what he said about them, to a degree, but what he yearned for most of all was to be *acknowledged* as one of them.

She could feel all of Varro's contradictory attitudes—his loathing and envy of the Roman elite—from the moment his slave welcomed her and her father at Varro's door wearing a bright red tunic. Nearly all household servants in Rome, including Aemilia's, wore drab garments, but not Varro's. His had to be as loud as the man himself.

"A rather large celebration for such a minor holiday," Paullus observed when Varro greeted him.

The many guests that had arrived ahead of them were mingling, drinking, and no doubt gossiping.

"I'm happy you could attend, Paullus," Varro said and embraced him, turning Aemilia's stomach. She held back her sneer as he turned his head to her and said, "And you as well, Aemilia."

She bowed her head demurely to her host, as was expected.

"You have a... remarkable home," she told him.

"Why the extravagance?" Paullus asked. "Do you plan to announce your candidacy for the Consulship?"

"Why do you ask?"

"I seem to remember a party you threw not so many years ago, not unlike this one, where you announced your candidacy for Tribune of the Plebs," Paullus replied.

"An office more noble, in my opinion, than the Consulship," Varro said. "Needless to say, I can do much better than the two men we call Consul today."

"May we expect a similar announcement this evening?"

"We'll see," Varro answered. "We'll see what happens. Enjoy yourselves."

The house was ostentatious by even the wealthiest of Roman standards. Everything from its furniture to its gardens and fountains were larger and gaudier than anything Aemilia seen in a private home. The large fountain in the atrium depicted dolphins playing in the water, but the figurines were too large and lacked detail in their faces and fins. It was like everything else in a house where the mosaics and paintings, delicate fountains, fine furniture, and open courtyards of most patrician homes were absent. Crude imitations stood in their place that were larger and probably more expensive, but utterly tasteless.

Towering above the tacky mess was a statue of Varro that he obviously had commissioned for himself, though he claimed it was a gift. His head was recognizable, but it was atop a body utterly unlike that of Varro. It was as lean and muscular as the idealized male physiques only gods possessed. It was draped in a toga and holding his hands and arms outstretched and slightly downward, as if calling to the masses to rise up. The statue even bore a *corona civica*, one of the highest military decorations in the Rome and something she was certain that Varro had never earned. If he did claim to have earned it, he would be censured, fined, and banned from public office. Having his statue wear it, however, was another matter. While it suggested that Varro had won the honor, it did not cross the line of outright claiming such. It was the object of widespread derision among the many who knew the truth. Among his supporters, however, such mockery was just more proof of the vast conspiracy of nefarious elites against their champion.

It wasn't long after Varro left them that Cato and Flaminius found them. Aemilia still couldn't look Cato in the eyes without burning with disgust and hatred. She wondered sometimes if she ever could. Despite what had been said at Fabius's home, she still blamed Cato for the death of her cousin. He seemed smugger and more self-satisfied every time she saw him after that day on the stage, and she fantasized about picking up the nearest object and smashing it into his thin, cruel lips.

Flaminius was unusually well-groomed. The frugal senator rarely visited the barber, let alone spent his money on a skilled one. He must have been trying to impress the other guests.

After the customary greetings, Cato went straight to the

point.

"Senator Fabius would like a word with you, if you have a moment," he said, and glanced at Aemilia before adding, "in private."

Her father disappeared and Aemilia returned to mingling, but it bothered her to be cut out of an important discussion. There were other places where men conducted business and women couldn't go, such as the baths. It wasn't enough that the men excluded the women from voting and holding office. They excluded them from even hearing what they were discussing at times. The decisions they made impacted the lives of women as much as they impacted those of men, and Rome was supposed to be long past the days when women were thought of as slaves to their fathers and husbands. Progress had been made. *Progress*, which, by definition, was good. Why did it always seem that there were those, like Cato, who wanted to go backward?

She found herself brooding next to one of the house's many garish fountains. Though it was ugly, she found the sound of the splashing water soothing. She closed her eyes, and her thoughts drifted to Scipio. She wondered where he was, what he was feeling, what he was thinking... But she couldn't summon a picture of him in his uniform, even though that was what he'd been wearing the last time she'd seen him at Ostia. Instead, she could only picture him riding around a track on his chariot, in an endless circle, chasing something she couldn't fathom.

"You have a good instinct for politics and people," a deep male voice told her. She opened her eyes to see Senator Fabius approaching. "I see much of your father in you," he said, "and your mother."

"Is that what you pulled my father away to discuss?"

"I won't apologize for that," he said, sitting beside her. "Sometimes, it is better to work things out in private."

"And sometimes people want to know the questions before they are presented with the answers," she replied. "But thank you for the compliment, Senator. Though I think you flatter my powers of perception. For all my wits, I cannot understand the appeal of a man like Varro."

"The appeal is simple," Fabius told her. "He offers simple explanations to complex problems, usually blaming elites for everything. In uncertain times, many people tend toward more... extreme solutions. Sometimes that is populism."

"What is this thing called 'populism,' anyway, but a celebration of ignorance and mediocrity?" she asked.

"An astute observation," he said. "To some extent, elites always organize their societies in ways that benefit them. When they go too far, populism can bring back balance between freedom and equality."

"It just amazes me that my own countrymen, who were raised to value the same things I do, think so differently about everything," she said.

"For them, it's not about thinking," he said. "It's about feeling. How does a politician make them feel about their country and themselves? As elites we often make them feel inferior, slow-witted, lazy. Varro tells them that it is the elites who are the inferior ones, and that they are salt-of-the-earth true Romans. If you were one of them, which would you prefer to be true?"

That Fabius had taken an interest in her was clear, though his reasons were not. Aemilia hoped that he was telling the truth when he said that her mind was impressive; however, she knew an older man's interest in a younger woman was rarely for the woman's benefit. Even if his interest wasn't sexual, he could be trying to use her to leverage her father for something.

"What did you speak about with my father?" she asked him.

Fabius swallowed his wine and regarded her a moment.

"We discussed who would be acceptable candidates for Consul," he said.

"Was Varro one?"

"You should discuss this with your father," he said. "You're an intelligent girl and wise enough to realize you don't know everything. You would do well to remember that when you speak with him."

"Is that what you came to me to speak about?"

"Not quite," he said, and cleared his throat. "This *lex Oppia* that Cato and the other populists are pushing... "

"What about it?"

"It must be opposed."

"My father and many others are—"

Fabius waved his hand for her to stop.

"I think it's time you made your voice heard, Aemilia," he said. "You should tell the people why you oppose it. You should tell them why women oppose it, and why men should oppose it as well. Speak up, and do it soon."

From his tone and demeanor, she got the distinct impression that he was withholding much from her, though she couldn't imagine what.

"What makes you think I can make any difference?" she asked him. "I'm one woman."

Fabius grinned as if that phrase amused him, patted her on the hand and stood up with some effort.

"People underestimated me my whole life because I was different," he told her. "I've done my best not to imitate them. It was something to see, the way you challenged Cato the other day in my home. You may not have been able to tell, but you rattled him worse than anyone has been able. Whether he cared to admit it or not, you frighten him."

It was invigorating. She felt as if Minerva herself had come from Olympus to be the gods' champion in the Senate against Cato. If that were the case, however, she would have some gifts from them to help her on her quest. She doubted Fabius had any helmets that could turn her invisible or sandals to allow her fly, but maybe he had some advice.

"How would I even take on a Senator, let alone a bloc of them?" she asked.

"Well," he said. "If the scales are always against you, add more weight to your side."

"How?"

"I don't know," Fabius said. "But I hope you find a way."

***

When he was gone, she took her time returning to the party, pondering what he had said as she strolled the garish halls of Varro's oversized monument to his own wealth. She needed to rally women against the law, but she needed a pretense to get them together. Of the several possibilities she considered, the holiday of Bona Dea stood out, but it was in a matter of days. It would take considerable effort, but... Why was she even worried? Her father and the other liberals in the Senate would never allow it to go to the *Comitium*.

As she approached Varro's *tablinium*, she could hear a woman's voice. It could only be his wife, Valeria, she thought.

Varro had two sons, she believed, but no daughter. She stopped, looked around to be certain no one was watching her, and pressed her back flat against the wall. She crept closer to the open door, anticipating getting a good piece of gossip. She could only catch a word here and there.

"... Hieronymous... Lilybeaum... "

It was too hard to resist having a peek. She peeked through the crack between the door and wall. Inside, a slave waited with his back to the door. Seated at a table messy with scrolls, another slave was writing something with expensive writing instruments—a quill and ink—while Valeria paced behind him.

"Did you get it all?" Valeria asked.

"Yes, *Domina*," he answered.

"Send it immediately."

Aemilia quickly turned and walked in the direction of the *triclinium*, hoping that if Valeria or her slave saw her that they would believe she had just walked by on her way back to the party.

"Aemilia," she heard Valeria call her from behind, and she nearly froze in place. She summoned a somewhat overly pleasant smile before turning around.

"Lady Varro," she greeted Valeria in a light, breezy tone.

"Hear anything interesting?" Valeria asked.

"Anything?" Aemilia asked and cleared her throat.

"At the party," Valeria finally said, and Aemilia tried not to seem too relieved. She thought Valeria probably sensed something was off.

"Just, um... boring... political talk," she stammered. "You know... "

"Mmm... Well, I'm going on a little trip to visit cousins in Sicily soon," Valeria said, linking arms with Aemilia and leading her back to the party.

"Oh, what fun!" Aemilia replied, inwardly rolling her eyes at herself for such a childish reply.

"But I was thinking, before I go, perhaps we should have some girl time, you and I."

"Well, I suppose that... " Aemilia stammered as they reached the *triclinium*.

"Good, it's settled then," Valeria said, squeezing her hand. "Saturday, yes? Wonderful!"

Before Aemilia could think of a reason to excuse herself from it, Valeria was already talking with another group of people. It was annoying having to come back here. She only hoped Varro himself was not here when she returned. And what was 'girl time', anyway?

***

Resting at home that evening, her father told Aemilia the bottom line of his mysterious meeting in the middle of the party.

"Varro will not be Consul," he said. "That is what is important. He's far too... erratic."

"Cato wanted Varro to be a Consul?"

"Wants," his father told her as a slave helped him remove his toga. "But we've reached an arrangement... of sorts."

Paullus yawned and sat down on a couch.

"Our faction will not support the *lex Oppia*," he told her.

Thinking about her earlier conversation with Fabius, she began to put it together. Somehow, her father and Senators like him had decided to use the *lex Oppia* as a bargaining chip. They were gambling that it did not have enough support to pass in the *Comitia* and become law.

"But we will not oppose it," he told her. "It was part of the deal to reign in Varro."

He might as well have stuck her heart with a dagger. The disappointment and hurt were visceral. He had betrayed her. For the first time in her life, her father was not on her side, and it was crushing. All the education and encouragement he had provided her meant nothing. In the end, he cared nothing for who she was and what she stood for.

"Aemilia... "

"How could you?" she gasped, tears welling in her eyes.

"Varro is too popular with the common people," he explained. "We cannot afford to take the chance that—"

"If women could vote, he'd never stand a chance!" she said, wiping the fallen tears away.

"Aemilia, you know that isn't possible," he said. "Not now, anyway."

"When then?" she asked.

He reached out to her, but she pulled away.

"Good night, father," she said stiffly, and retired to her chambers without the kiss she had given his cheek nearly every night of her life.

VARRO

Varro looked over the Senate in smug satisfaction as his colleagues' impassioned voices filled the chamber air. The clamor was more soothing than any music to his ears because he had caused all of this division and loathing. They all danced to his tune. Few remained impassive whenever he spoke. Year after year, he learned to provoke reactions from the elites as strongly as he inspired fervent support from the masses. Many thought he wanted the elites to accept him as one of their own. He did not. He wanted to be acknowledged as first among them, above all of them, because he knew that he was different from them. He was better.

Elites had to be trained like dogs through tutoring, priesthoods, and military service; all of which he hated. He had been a mediocre student, and his military training showed him to be a subpar soldier. The one area in which he excelled was rhetoric, and he devoted most of his youth to honing his skills. Having little respect for the more popular speakers of his time, he found inspiration in one that had lived and died two centuries before—Cleon of Athens.

In Cleon, Varro had found a kindred spirit. Most Greek writers despised him, but Varro thought that evidenced the man's greatness. The Athenian elite had heaped scorn on him, calling him "demagogue" and worse, but still he rose to the pinnacle of power in his country despite his low birth. Like Varro, Cleon did not possess so-called "virtues," such as courage, resiliency, justice, temperance, magnanimity, modesty, prudence... What did that matter? He may not have been "ethical" by the conventional definitions, but he was successful and effective in business and politics. His name lived on, and his words traveled through time and across the sea to Varro, while others more "ethical" and "brave" died on battlefields, were honored for a moment and then forgotten. Cleon had been successful precisely because he made his own ethics and allowed himself to break even those. Varro intended to do just the same.

He held up his hand in a call for silence in the Senate chamber. Regardless of his authority, the hoarse old Magister would never calm this raucous long enough for him to continue speaking.

"And I say... " he shouted until the noise was low enough for his voice to rise above. "And I say it is high time King Hiero and the rest of our so-called allies in Sicily to pull their weight! What have they offered since this war began? Nothing! No troops, no money, no support of any kind! Yet, if they were the ones attacked, we would be expected to come to their aid. We would, too! That is why the rest of the world takes advantage of us! They are laughing at us!"

He scowled, though he could barely contain his joy as the Senate erupted again in shouting and arguing.

To his dismay, Paullus stood up. Cornelius was the man Varro hated most, and Paullus was the man he hated second-most, but for different reasons. He had everything Varro envied but was always denied—respect and deference. When Paullus stood up, he did not even need to shout as Varro did. People simply listened, as if Paullus was the voice of reason and wisdom. For what? Varro was far wealthier than the entire Paullus clan. Shouldn't his acumen in amassing that wealth earn him the same reverence as that sad old man? Were his years spent toiling in the world of business not as valuable as Paullus's years marching around in the army?

"Colleagues, I would remind you all that our alliance with Sicily is bilateral," Paullus said. "Sicily bears no such responsibility unless Rome is the one that is attacked, not a third party such as Saguntum."

Many in the chamber clamored in agreement and voices rose to confirm that this was, in fact, the case.

"When we go to war, our allies must follow!" Varro asserted, and the populist bloc cheered him for it.

"Perhaps they should," Paullus acknowledged. "But they are

under no obligation to do so."

"Then we are under no obligation to defend Sicily!"

No cheers this time, to Varro's dismay. Instead, he felt his cheeks and forehead flush red as the sounds of laughter and disbelief reached his ears.

"We are under precisely that obligation, should they be attacked," Paullus told him, amazed at Varro's lack of understanding. "It is how alliances work, Senator."

"I was not speaking literally," Varro deflected. "And no matter. Hannibal and his barbarians approach from the north. Cornelius, the fool, sends his brother to Hispania. For what? Are they cowards, or simply lost?"

This time, the laughter was with him once more. Cornelius's decision to send Calvus with most of his troops to Hispania had been a point of some disagreement in the Senate. Varro did not understand why, nor did he care to learn. The fact Cornelius had done something with which half the Senate disagreed was all he needed to know.

Since the war began, the number of Varro's opponents still in the Senate had been considerably reduced. Many of them were now staff officers or commanders for Cornelius or Sempronius.

Marcus Cato stood up next.

"I urge you all to vote in favor of recalling our army from Sicily, and redeploying them in Cisalpine Gaul," he said. "Hannibal must be dealt with first, and Cornelius is in no position to do so with the legions and allies we sent against the Boii. We need Sempronius and his legions here, not idle in Lilybeaum."

Though Varro hated it when someone else was the focus of attention, he appreciated Cato's way with words. Cato could explain things in ways that senators could accept. He was like a puppet with snootier diction than the master holding his strings.

The vote went their way. Sempronius would be recalled, leaving Sicily undefended.

***

Varro left the Senate flush with victory and feeling invincible. He would have given an impromptu speech in the forum if it were not for his prior engagement with Livius, a gifted writer and political orator, at the baths. On his way, he had two slaves make a hole in the crowd to pass through the Forum—a place so congested and busy that he often walked through completely unrecognized. It irked him that such a place existed.

That day, though, he *was* recognized. As he stopped to sample some fruit, he felt the stare of someone as if it were burning him. He turned to see, between the passersby, Paullus's young daughter, Aemilia. She was standing there, without attendant slaves or being carried in a *lectica* as befit a woman of her class. She was just staring at him. The passion he'd seen in her eyes at the party was not there, nor was any readily discernable emotion. She just looked on with an aloof curiosity, the way a man does when he sees an odd animal in the wild. *No*, he thought. *It was not curiosity. It was something else... accusation.* Yes, that was it; those were *accusatory* evil eyes. He didn't acknowledge her, and she returned the favor; but her eyes seem to see straight through all parts of his carefully constructed veneer down to his naked being, making him stand in shame for all the world to see: a worthless, greedy, emasculated old fool, without dignity, unworthy of love...

That woman! Who was she to make him feel that way? Her—a woman! A dirty, impure, tainted... *She* was the shameful one! Who knew what nefarious, perverted acts she'd committed in her own life?

"Dominus? Dominus?"

He had no idea how long his slave had been calling him. He turned his head away from Aemilia just a moment, and she was gone when he looked back.

With his ubiquitous scowl, he picked up his chin, puffed up his chest, and continued through the crowd to the bath. It might be a year early, but he had a campaign to plan.

AEMILIA

Visiting Varro's home for the second time in days, Aemilia was surprised to find herself in a tasteful dining room much smaller than the main one used to host lavish dinner parties. It was devoid of ostentatious displays of wealth, a fact that led her to conclude that it was probably decorated to Valeria's taste.

She wasn't certain why Valeria had invited her, but she never assumed good intentions when it came to anyone connected with Varro. At best, Valeria might believe Aemilia could be useful to her in some way. At worst, that she was a threat to Valeria or her husband.

"So... what shall we talk about?" Valeria asked as her servants poured the wine and served the first course of olives and artichokes. "Men? Gods, no... "

Aemilia laughed and covered her mouth to ensure no wine came out.

"Come... don't be shy," Valeria said, lounging on her *kline*.

"Thank you for having me here, Lady Varro," Aemilia said, raising her wine in salutation.

"The pleasure is mine," she said. "And please... call me Valeria. It's hard, making friends with women. I don't have any sisters, and my mother left when I was young."

"I didn't know," Aemilia said.

"She ran as far from my father as she could," Valeria went on. "I don't blame her. He was an ass, but it meant leaving me as well."

She took a drink of wine.

Aemilia had no choice but to accept the invitation. Norms and politics demanded it. Still, as dangerous as she thought Valeria might be, she was intriguing. How did a woman that seemed so intelligent and cordial tolerate—nay, *support*—the pig she called a husband?

"Sorry," Valeria said, putting the goblet down on the table. "I'm boring you with my family's drama. Shall we have some almonds? I have them sent up from Tyre and hide them for myself."

Valeria called a servant over and asked her to bring her almonds in flawless Greek.

"Why hide them?" Aemilia asked.

"If you were married to a tasteless boor, would you share them?"

They shared a laugh at Varro's expense. The almonds were delicious, as Valeria claimed. By the time the main course of chicken was served, Aemilia got the distinct impression that Valeria no more liked her husband than she did.

"Why marry him then?" Aemilia asked. "Or at least, why *stay* married to him?"

"You're young," she said, holding her cup of wine for a servant to fill. "The scion of a wealthy family. You haven't known what it's like to be poor. Although I think I would have preferred to have been born poor than to become poor. Perhaps then I would have had true friends—friends that would never see me as below them."

Valeria paused, sipping her diluted wine.

"You're a follower of the *Bona Dea*?" Valeria asked, changing the subject.

"I haven't been initiated in her cult," Aemilia said. "Why do you ask?"

"I believe a friend of yours is having a party in honor of the goddess tomorrow, is she not? Servillia Geminus?"

Servillia had, in fact, planned a large party. She enjoyed them a lot more than Aemilia, but this was not to be an ordinary party. They had invited influential women of all ages and political perspectives to Servillia's country home to discuss the *lex Oppia*. As Fabius advised her, she was trying to add weight to her side of the scales.

Valeria, however, was not extended an invitation.

"Word gets around," Aemilia said, a tad embarrassed.

"Indeed, it does."

"It's a relatively small gathering," Aemilia told her. "I'm surprised you—"

"Please," Valeria interrupted her. "No need for an invitation. I'm leaving for Sicily in the morning."

"Oh... Visiting family, right?"

"Something like that," Valeria replied, a sly smile playing on her lips. "Anyway, you wouldn't want me there if you're planning to discuss the *lex Oppia*."

"I'm afraid you've been misinformed," Aemilia lied. "It's just a modest holiday gathering to honor the goddess."

Valeria reached over and put her hand over Aemilia's. Their faces now close, Valeria looked her guest in the eyes.

"You don't have to worry," she told Aemilia. "My husband doesn't know; and neither does Marcus Cato or any of the rest of the Senators that favor it."

She leaned back and sipped some more wine. Aemilia got the feeling that she wanted a reply, but she declined to give her one. No matter what she said, Valeria was Varro's wife. She had to assume she was his agent and not to be trusted.

"Even if they did," Valeria continued, "they wouldn't think anything of it. Only one woman really matters to them."

"Who might that be?" Aemilia asked.

Valeria raised her eyebrows, seemingly surprised Aemilia did not know to whom she referred, as if it should have been obvious.

"Busa of Canusium," Valeria said. "You've heard of her, of course."

"Should I have?"

"I was told you're interested in politics."

"I'm interested in making a difference," Aemilia said.

Valeria gave a condescending single snigger and said, "That's sweet."

"Mmm-hmm," Aemilia said, sipping the wine she now wanted to throw in her hostess' face. "Who is she?"

"A very wealthy woman."

"A rich as your husband?"

"Oh, yes," Valeria said. "Much richer, in fact. She's also probably a murderer."

"Really?"

"They say she murdered two of her husbands," Valeria said. "No one knows how the first died, or if he did at all. He just...

vanished."

"Why wasn't she tried?"

"This is Rome, dear. Anything can be bought, and magistrates come cheap. Busa is also somewhat of a recluse. She rarely leaves Canusium and almost never comes to Rome, but she owns a great deal of this city, and I don't mean land. She owns half the Senate—your half, or your father's half, I should say."

"Liberals?" Aemilia asked.

"Indeed," Valeria replied.

When they finished the almonds, the servants brought a selection of grapes.

"I like you, Aemilia," Valeria said, once the plates were down and the servants out of the way. "You're different than most of the women I've encountered. The rich ones, especially. They have no interest in things like politics and law. All they ever seem to want to talk about is jewelry from Egypt, wine from Greece, stud slaves from Numidia. Oh, and the parties... Eck."

She made a sour face and stuck her tongue out, and Aemilia laughed. Against her better judgment, she felt herself being taken in by the women.

"Do you know my stepson, Aulus?" Valeria asked.

"Not well, I'm afraid," Aemilia said, and sipped her strong wine. In truth, she did know him, or of him. He was his father's disciple. A younger and slimmer version of Varro, she found him equally repugnant. "Is he here?"

"He'll be returning from Greece after the Consular elections," she said as Aemilia put a grape in her mouth. "Perhaps you should marry him."

Aemilia nearly spit the grape out in shock at the audacity of the suggestion, but she managed to cover her mouth just in time and choke it down. Valeria smiled, as if reading her thoughts and finding them amusing. She suspected that this was her game, to use Aemilia's family to advance her own. Marrying her son into a well-connected political family like hers was a time-honored tradition for rising families.

"You and I share at least one thing," Valeria said. "We don't underestimate my husband, even if the rest of the world might. He *will* be a Consul; if not this year, then the next, or the one after. Your family is old Rome, Aemilia. Mine is the new Rome. You can either be part of it, or... "

"Or what?" Aemilia prompted her, anticipating some sort of implied threat.

"Or just keep fading away," her host said.

Aemilia wanted to feel defiant, or at least to say something defiant, but she found herself unable. There was some truth in what she said. Her family, though still powerful and revered, was aging and in decline. Her father was in semi-retirement, and the only other family member of any importance was a Censor whose only surviving son had shown no political inclinations. Aemilia's only brother, whose birth had presaged their mother's death, was fully ten years her junior. Much rested on his shoulders already. Aemilia would add to the load if she did not marry into a family that extended her own's influence through the elaborate networks of clients, patrons, and relations that ran like veins through the body politic of the republic.

Gaudiness aside, Varro's home had a rare feature—a flushable latrine connected to the city's sewage system. Valeria went to make use of it after the two ladies returned from an afternoon stroll through her autumn garden. She left Aemilia by the fountain where she had spoken with Fabius just days before, just down the hall from Varro's study.

She took a few steps toward it, thinking about what she'd heard that day at the party when she'd been eavesdropping for gossip. She thought of the slave, and the few words she heard. *Lilybeaum...* She knew that was a place in Sicily, but what about it? Was it where Valeria was going?

Looking around carefully before going, she crept over and peeked inside to see a mess. Wax tablets, ink, and scrolls littered the furniture and floor. One thing stood out. Hanging from the table was a long narrow strip of what looked like cotton cloth hanging off the table in plain view, with letters written on it. A small bronze statuette of a horse rested on it, keeping it from falling. She glanced both ways down the empty hall, trying to hear or see any sign indicating Valeria's host or servants were around, but she was alone. Stepping closer, Aemilia saw the letters were Greek, but they didn't form any words. They seemed to go down the strip randomly.

She wanted it. She didn't know why, but she did. She got a sense that it was important and, more interestingly, secret. Valeria took time in the middle of a party she and her husband were hosting to do whatever she was doing, which indicted the matter was urgent. She was doing it in her husband's study—a room in which women like her would rarely be interested in entering.

She checked the hallway again, then stepped into the study and snatched the strip of cotton so quickly that she didn't think the bronze horse would move at all; but it did, and her eyes went wide in horror as it fell from the table and clanged on the tiled floor. She wadded up the cotton strip and stuffed it inside her *strophium* against her bosom.

She stepped back out into the hall, looked down, and straightened her *himation* and tried to see if one breast seemed larger than the other.

"My dear," Valeria called to her, making her jerk her head up. "Are you alright?"

"Yes," Aemilia answered with a nervous laugh. "I was just looking for a mirror."

Valeria looked past her to Varro's study. Aemilia saw her eyes move to the floor, where the fallen statuette lay. They lingered there for a long moment, and Aemilia held her breath.

"Elusco... " Valeria called to a slave the slave. Aemilia recognized him as the slave that had been writing that evening as she dictated to him. *Elusco...* she would have to remember the name.

"Yes, *Domina*," he said with a slight bow.

"Fix that ghastly statue and then fetch my hand mirror," she said.

"Yes, *Domina*," he answered, and went about the task.

Valeria took Aemilia's hands in hers.

"I've had fun," she told Aemilia.

"As did I," Aemilia replied, worried Valeria's eyes would move down and see something strange about her chest.

"Perhaps we could do this again after I return from Sicily," she said.

"I would be honored to host you at our home next time we meet," Aemilia stammered, glancing inside the study where she Elusco put the statue back onto the table. He then looked around the floor and moved scrolls. He glanced at Aemilia, and their eyes met briefly before Valeria turned her head to him.

"Are you quite done?" she barked.

"Yes, *Domina*," he answered, coming out of the study while

256

keeping his eyes averted from her.

Valeria glanced at Aemilia, then looked back at the top of her crouched slave's bald head.

"Is everything in order?" she asked him.

Aemilia held her breath as they waited for his answer. The man twitched—not much, just a jerk of the head turning slightly to the right, and she thought for a moment he would give her away.

"Of course, Domina," he finally answered, and hurried away to fetch her mirror.

HANNIBAL

Hannibal was sick with a wet cough. The day after they had picked up the Salluvi guides, his Greek physician had put his hear to Hannibal's chest and reported hearing "water." He'd then made the absurd suggestion of bed rest as they headed toward an imposing mountain.

He coughed up phlegm and cast a leery gaze on his Salluvi hostages. They occupied men day and night to ensure they didn't slip away should their new guides betray them. The Salluvi tribe seemed extremely hostile, according to the soldiers he had sent to their village to collect the human collateral now before him, but that was understandable. His soldiers had been there, after all, to take hostages. Still, Hannibal hoped they would prefer taking money to fighting after what they had seen him inflict on their neighbors to the northwest.

The guides told him that the pass to the east was wide but took a winding path around the mountain. The pass to the west was narrower but more direct. They urged Hannibal to split the army into two columns, send his elephants and cavalry east, and lead the infantry and pack animals to the west. There was a valley on the far side where they could regroup. Hannibal decided against it. Even if they were correct, he reasoned, it would make them more vulnerable to ambush; not to mention risking becoming hopelessly lost in this wooded rocky labyrinth.

"Make sure they keep decent spacing," Hannibal told Gisgo as they watched the men labor to set up their shelters for the night. "If there's a fire, we'll never get it out if we're all bunched up."

Gisgo nodded and left to pass the order on.

Hannibal looked through the gently falling snow up at the mountain that, as far as they knew, had no name. The men had taken to calling it Back Breaker. At last count they had lost, since the battle, 283 men, 34 horses, and 16 pack animals to sickness and accidents. No one knew how many dead Allobrogian slaves they left on the trail. Luckily, desertions were not a factor. While in the mountains, the best hope any of them had was staying with the army. The terrain was so treacherous that the best place they found to set up their shelters was little more than a nearly frozen slope with a steep incline on one side leading to gray boulders looming over them, and sharp decline into a dense pine forest on the other.

As his wariness of the guides grew, Hannibal had taken to sending the cavalry and skirmishers farther ahead to forage, scout, and hopefully sniff out any ambushes. Their losses to accidents were mounting.

Maharbal found him as Hannibal was using a pile of dry pine needles and leaves as kindling beneath thicker branches, stirring his budding fire with a stick. He guessed that he probably looked terrible, though he had no way to see for himself. His hair and beard were growing thick and unkempt, his feet, legs, and backside hurt from riding. Maharbal sat next to him without a word at the end of a coughing fit. For the first time since the news of his nephew's death had reached him in Gaul, Hannibal felt truly miserable. Not even banishing his brother had gotten him to such a desperate place. He tried to make being confident look easy for the sake of his army. Sometimes it *was* easy. Now was not one of those times.

"I wonder what they're doing at this very moment," Hannibal said, squinting into the flickering light of the growing flames.

"Who?" Maharbal asked him.

"My family."

"Oh... "

"At least I know they're warm," Hannibal mused, coughed again, and spat greenish-yellow mucus onto the forest floor.

"If I had a wife, I might have brought her with us," Maharbal told him.

"Not if you loved her," Hannibal countered quietly.

Maharbal opened a wineskin and took a drink before offering it to Hannibal.

"I managed to hide some fresh wine from your brother," he said. "I need it for cold nights, like this."

Hannibal took an uncharacteristically large gulp before handing it back to him and coughing once more.

"This was never Kara's burden to bear," Hannibal said, laying a hand on the grip of his father's sword. "This is for us to do... My brothers and me."

"And if we die in these mountains?" Maharbal asked, squinting as the snowflakes fell on his eyelids. "Will it pass to your son to fight Rome to the death?"

Maharbal may have had expected a yes, but the thought of

259

failure had never seriously occurred to Hannibal. The notion was so foreign, the concept so abstract, that he hadn't devoted serious thought to its possibility; and so Hannibal didn't answer. He couldn't.

"The, uh... good news is the terrain levels out and declines up ahead," Maharbal told him.

"I don't celebrate until I see both sides of the coin," Hannibal told him.

Maharbal frowned.

"By midday tomorrow," he said, "we'll reach a gorge."

Hannibal cursed and coughed. A gorge was the perfect place to be ambushed—better even than the ravine where the Allobroges had attacked, since the army would be at the bottom of it. He wanted to stand up, find Gisgo, and have all the Salluvi hostages executed. But the ground was probably too frozen to dig holes for crosses, anyway. He didn't want to give them any less painful deaths.

"How bad?"

"Narrow, deep, long," Maharbal replied, putting together the exact three words Hannibal was loath to hear. "The walls aren't as steep, either. We were able to climb the eastern side without too much trouble."

"What did you see?"

"Campfires," Maharbal said. "Hundreds of them."

Hannibal cursed himself again, but this time for having been so foolish. If he made it through this, he told himself, he would find his own way to Italy.

"Any way around?"

"We looked all day," Maharbal answered, with a shake of his head.

Hannibal looked out at the camp, ruminating. *Long...* *Narrow... Deep.* The Salluvi knew just where to lead them to neutralize his advantages, but he wouldn't make the same mistake as he'd made with the Allobroges. He would assume they would attack, no matter the odds.

In the morning, he summoned Gisgo, Mago, and Maharbal while the men were still eating.

"Reform the column," he told them.

"You're joking," Mago said. "How?"

"Maharbal takes the cavalry and elephants to the front," Hannibal answered. "Gisgo controls the middle with light infantry, Gauls, and Iberians. Mago, take the African infantry to the rear. All the baggage stays in the middle of the column."

"Elephants to the front?" Mago asked. "You're sure about this?"

It was unorthodox, to say the least. Elephants were suited for attacking along a wide front. Line them up behind one another, and they were far less effective.

"I need an aggressive cavalry leader in the front," Hannibal said.

"Sikarbaal," Maharbal answered. "He's been eager to redeem himself since the... incident in Gaul."

"Fine," Hannibal replied, coughed up and spat mucus, then cussed at it.

"What sort of column formation is this?" Gisgo asked.

"Not a column," Hannibal told them, wiping his lips with his sleeve. "A battering-ram."

***

Hannibal needed to win and win decisively, and that meant getting all his people and equipment through the trap the Salluvi and their allies had set for them. He expected some casualties, but he needed to keep them as low as possible to consider this march a success. He was certain that the clash with Allobroges had dimmed his aura of invincibility with his army, and this situation looked far more dangerous to him. There were more enemy warriors and more avenues for them to attack. This time, however, the army was in a column configured much differently than when they had faced the Allobroges on their road.

The ravine was just as Maharbal has described it. The sides were too steep for Hannibal's men to fight and maneuver as units while protecting the column, but not steep enough to prevent foot soldiers from coming down to raid the column and retreat at will.

Hannibal had placed himself near the front of the column with the war elephants. Rather than riding Suru alone, he had his guards mount the howdah on his back. The small carriage was large enough for three people, including the driver, allowing him to take one of his guards and Vernon with him. In addition to placing him in a good position to control what he anticipated to be his decisive maneuver in battle, being able to stand on Suru gave him a commanding view of the column behind him. In front of him were about three hundred Numidian and Carthaginian cavalrymen, with Sikarbaal at its front.

As the cavalry and elephants passed the entrance to the gorge, Hannibal looked back to see the infantrymen behind him, gripping their weapons and shields tightly, their heads swiveling. He could see bearded, shirtless warriors sprinkled among the pines on either side of the army, their bodies and faces painted with strange symbols. They were being watched, but he could only guess at the size of the force that had come for them.

The western side of the ravine was getting higher and steeper as they marched. Like a menacing giant from an ancient tale, its shadow seemed to swallow the entire column marching in its shadow.

"What tribe do you suppose they're from?" Hannibal asked Vernon.

"More than one, by their paint," Vernon replied. "These highlanders would probably attack anyone passing through. It's not personal."

"That isn't comforting," Hannibal replied and looked to where the western side wall was now too steep to either scale or descend. Still, each time he looked, it seemed more Gauls were shadowing the column from the ridge above, looking down at the trespassing foreigners.

"What are they waiting for?" he wondered aloud.

"They're waiting for us to all come in," he said.

Hannibal coughed, spat, and looked to the rear again. A group of enemy warriors were now behind them, near where the army had entered the gorge. They were massing at the rear, blocking them from retreating. The mouth of the beast had closed. Carthaginian and highland Gaul were now in close, intimate quarters in its dark belly.

"Come on, Mago... " Hannibal muttered, watching the crouched Gauls approach in an unorderly gaggle that was just large enough for an effective attack, however ill-prepared.

He couldn't see the expressions on their painted faces, but he knew the enemy warriors must have been edgy. Hannibal had placed the African infantry at the rear in part because their fifteen-foot spears tended to intimidate Gauls. The enemy shadowed the rearguard for what seemed like miles, advancing and retreating, banging their weapons against their shields and whooping, but never coming into contact. It seemed they were mentally preparing themselves for attack.

Hannibal looked up once more to the west. Other warriors above were still shadowing them on either side, and he presumed they were waiting for some signal or action from their comrades. Hannibal's chest tightened, as it had before nearly every battle where he felt the initiative lay with the enemy, but his cold made it worse. He forced himself to take deep breaths, trying not to cough, bracing himself for the first assault. The anticipation of it was invariably worse than the attack itself.

He heard the battle cry first—a steady half-crazed scream that rose quickly and echoed through the ravine as if it were a cavern.

"General!"

Vernon pointed to the rear, where Hannibal looked on with pride as his African infantrymen's spears rose and descended as one. He couldn't hear the orders from Mago, only the horrible crunch of the colliding forces as his countrymen took the full force of the first ferocious attack; but he knew whatever orders his brother was giving were being obeyed. Hannibal desperately wanted to be there in the middle of the action, to take charge and make sure the attack was decisively met. He trusted Mago, but he trusted no one more than himself.

The Carthaginians were trying to use the inhospitable terrain to their advantage as much as possible, pushing the attackers' flanks and funneling them to the middle. That would make them fight in an ever-tightening space filled with African spears. Gauls wanted to swing their long swords, axes, and hammers in huge arcs to stun and intimidate their opponents with crashing blows; but squeezed together, they lacked space to do so without hitting their comrades. The African infantry's equipment and discipline gave them the advantage, and the Gauls quickly realized it.

The tribesmen retreated as they had earlier advanced, moving in a gaggle without central direction, trampling over one another to get clear of the congested center. The first attack had been soundly rebuffed. Hannibal pumped his fist in the air, hoping that Mago could see his pride in him. Vernon hooted and slapped his general on the back in raucous laughter.

The gorge narrowed further, and the eastern wall became steeper. The column took a soft right turn, following the terrain. Hannibal could hear some cheers from the cavalry ahead, and soon saw the cause for celebration. The light from the ravine's end was so bright that it momentarily blinded him.

"Shields! Shields!" Maharbal yelled, and the order echoed down the column.

It sounded like rain at first, but Hannibal realized that the Gauls on either side were showering them with small rocks from above. Soon it was a deadly downpour, and all Hannibal could do was cower under his shield. Loud cracks and panicked cries of men heralded larger rocks that shattered wooden shields and maimed their bearers.

"Enemy to the front!" he heard Sikarbaal call out, and the men echoed it backward down the column's spine, striking the nerves of all in it. This was it... the Gauls were moving to stall or stop them.

To his front, Hannibal saw another gaggle of Gauls, bigger than that which attacked the rear of the column, sealing off their exit and waiting with their shields and spears. He clenched his jaw and growled in anger.

"General... " Vernon called, but Hannibal was completely

focused on the end of the gorge and getting out.

"General!"

"What?!"

Vernon pointed back to the middle of the column. Hannibal watched in horror as a boulder the size of a horse rolled down from the western side and smashed a baggage cart to splinters, sending a mule into a panicked fit. Another larger boulder came down and struck both a mule and a slinger, killing them instantly. Tribesman from the eastern side of the ravine charged down toward the gap the boulder had left in its wake.

"They're trying to cut the column in half!"

Hannibal had borne the onslaught long enough with gritted teeth. He didn't care if it was too soon to charge—he could take no more. It was time to use his battering ram to push through.

"Prepare to charge!" Hannibal ordered, and Maharbal echoed the command.

A horn sounded the charge, and the cavalry let out a furious cry as their horses bolted forward, running headlong at the enemy infantry to the front of the column. Behind them, the elephants stampeded, making the earth tremble. It was a sloppy attack, reckless and abrupt, but violently executed thanks to Sikarbaal's aggressive leadership at the head of the column. Unnerved, the enemy tribesmen in front of them barely threw a javelin before fleeing in terror. The cavalry rode through and cut down the enemies within their reach before breaking through. The elephants followed, but the premature timing meant the rest of the column remained in the defile.

"Maharbal!" Hannibal bellowed, triggering yet another coughing fit.

Vernon also called for him, but the cavalry was way out ahead and riding too hard for a sudden stop and turn. Instead, Maharbal was leading them on a wide arc that would circle back toward Hannibal and the gorge. Back inside of it, however, his men were fighting for their lives. Only the elephants and their drivers were within shouting distance.

"Turn around!" Hannibal yelled at the top of his lungs. "Turn around!"

Vernon took up the yelling for him. The drivers, having just escaped the gorge and relieved to be alive, looked back at him dumbfounded.

"I said turn around, damn you!" Hannibal shouted.

As the shock wore off, the drivers closest to him began lining up on Surus. Hannibal watched in desperate anger as the Gauls that had only moments before fled before his cavalry and elephants began rushing back into the gorge, intent on blocking and raiding the rest of his column. Inside that wretched gloom, his men were dying; and he was losing supplies he needed to keep the others alive in the coming winter. He chose to not wait for the drivers to get the elephants into any kind of proper formation or for the cavalry to rejoin them.

"Follow me!" he called and drove Surus forward.

Trumpeting, Surus headed back toward the ravine, picking up speed as he went. Dazed or not, it was simple for the other drivers to follow. One elephant caught up, then another. Three abreast, the maximum they could squeeze between the walls, they attacked the rear of the tribesmen. This time, a few stood their ground and raised their spears against the beasts. The drivers easily cut them down or trampled them underfoot. The rest broke and ran to avoid the same fate.

When the rest of the column was finally pulled from the

ravine, they left several hundred of their dead behind to be picked over and robbed. Many of these lay crushed under the rocks that the enemy had relentlessly hurled down onto them. Aside from a messy but successful charge to clear the exit of the gorge, the one bright spot was that Hannibal's infantry had repelled the enemy's attempts to steal his supplies.

Furious with the loss of his men and animals, Hannibal took his frustration out on the Salluvi hostages and Allobrogian prisoners as soon as they were out of the gorge. He had their necks and ankles shackled and chained them together in groups of five or more. The men would bury the dead, carry the wounded in litters, and haul the baggage carts like pack animals. The women would suffer an even harsher fate. Hannibal gave them over to his men.

Vernon pointed out the cut above Hannibal's left eye and his swollen right cheek. It must have been some stones, he thought, or perhaps he'd been struck with his own shield when something had hit it, though he had no memory of it.

Mago was wounded in a second attack on the rear guard, which took place just after Hannibal had broken through the gorge. A barbed arrowhead had burrowed into his thigh, necessitating a minor operation to cut it out. Hannibal took part in holding him down as they cauterized and bandaged the wound.

These highland tribes had diminished him in the eyes of his men. If he was having this much trouble with the disorganized and ill-equipped Gauls, what chance would they have against the Romans?

AEMILIA

There were many goddesses in the Roman pantheon, but *Bona Dea* was the one to which women took to the most. She was not only associated with fertility, but also with the safety and security of the Roman State—two concepts that were wholly intertwined. The holiday in her honor involved many gatherings of women like the one Servillia hosted at her father's country estate just north of the city. Ostensibly, these parties were to remind women of their duties to their families and the state; but like all religious gatherings and ceremonies, it had an important social function. It brought women across generations, classes, and backgrounds together to celebrate their common Roman identity.

Nearly a hundred of the city's most affluent women were now assembled in Servillia's atrium, where serene, bucolic images of the Italian countryside adorned the walls; but the room was anything but calm. Women spoke with wild gesticulations, pounding their fists on floor and waving their arms in the air when making their points. As soon as Servillia had told them that they were gathered to organize their opposition to the *lex Oppia*, the debate had started; and it raged for hours. Aemilia didn't know whether to feel encouraged by the diversity of opinion expressed by the women in the room, who ranged in ages from late teens to late fifties. They all had their own minds, even those that were equivocating. Still, hearing the voices of her fellow Roman women speaking in support of the *lex Oppia*, something she equated with their own enslavement, turned her stomach. The negative reactions had taken an emotional toll on her, and she was even more upset that she'd been so naïve that she had not anticipated them.

After a few hours, the women that were indifferent or supportive of the bill took their leave. The rest remained with Aemilia and Servillia to plan their course of action.

"By morning, every Senator in the city will know we're planning on speaking against the *lex Oppia* at the *Comitia*," Portitia, a family friend of Servillia's, told the remaining women.

"Every woman here has a father, a brother, an uncle, or someone else close to her in the Senate," Servillia said. "We must petition them to speak for us, and against this law."

"What about your father?" Nautia, a young woman from a prominent family, asked.

"I have asked," Servillia told her.

"And?"

Servillia hesitated to answer, and Aemilia knew the reason why. Servillius was a liberal and would abide by the deal Paullus had helped broker. Allowing the bill to be put before the *Comitia* was the price of keeping Varro off the ballot; but if they admitted that here, it would take much of their credibility away. How could they ask these women to petition the men in their lives, when it was their own fathers that helped create this terrible situation?

"We're doing what we can," Aemilia said.

"Let her answer," Nautia replied.

"He cannot," Servillia admitted. The clucking of tongues and murmuring that followed was embarrassing.

"Why not?" Nautia asked.

"Because they made a deal," announced a voice from the back of the room.

It was Fulvia, the widow of a former Consul and the mother of Scipio's friend, Claudius. Her husband had earned the cognomen "Pulcher" (handsome), but she was a handsome woman herself. Aemilia liked her. Fulvia as tough and smart. She held her head high and made eye contact with everyone, especially those who had ever spoken ill of her late husband, but she was also aloof with nearly everyone. She could be intimidating.

She walked between women seated and lounging on cushions to the front of the room, where Servillia and Aemilia were standing. A female servant offered a cup of wine, but Fulvia held up a hand in refusal without taking her eyes from Servillia.

A woman near the front of the room spoke, saying, "How can you ask our men to do what your father—?"

She abruptly stopped when Fulvia whirled and faced the rest of the women.

"Her father, Servillius, is standing for Consul," Fulvia told them.

"Then why not run against this absurd law?" Nautia asked.

The murmuring in the room seemed to indicate that most of the women agreed.

"Perhaps you'd care to explain, Aemilia," Fulvia said, turning her head to Aemilia.

"Every year, the Senate approves the candidates that may stand for Consul," Aemilia told them, "Deals are made... sometimes for the worse. Servillius and others, including my father, opposed several plebeian candidates they deemed unacceptable. One was Gaius Terentius Varro. In exchange for their exclusion from the ballot, they agreed not to oppose the *lex Oppia*."

The faces Aemilia saw wore frowns of disappointment. This is was what she had feared. She looked over to see Servillia's face had turned red. Nautia got to her feet and headed for the door.

A smattering of other guests also stood up, looking ready to leave.

"Please... " Servillia began, but her guests' voices drowned her out.

Aemilia rushed over to the exit, determined to save this effort from falling apart before it even began.

"We're trying to do what our fathers failed to do," she explained to the women trying to leave. "The time has come to make our own voices heard."

"You should have told us that at the beginning," a woman told her. "Instead you ask us to do what you cannot?"

"Please, stay!" Aemilia pleaded with them, but they pushed past her.

She looked to Servillia in desperation. She saw Fulvia put her arm around Servillia, who seemed surprised and touched by the gesture.

"You rush to judge what you do not understand," Fulvia's voice boomed. The murmuring died back down, and women stopped to listen. "Politics seldom lets one choose between good and bad options. The choice is almost always between two evils."

"What could be eviler than letting this... pile of dung pass to a vote?" Nautia asked, drawing a calm look of annoyed disapproval from Fulvia.

"If you need to ask that, dear, you should sit down and listen," Fulvia told her.

The rebuke drew snickers from some of the other women, and the young Nautia sat on her cushion in a huff.

"People think we're in one war," Fulvia said. "We are in two; one with Carthage, the other with ourselves. This young lady's father is brave enough to lead our soldiers, my son included, against the enemy from without. *She* is brave enough to ask you to fight with her against the enemy within."

"Do you think Varro, Cato, and the rest will stop with us?" Aemilia asked them. "Every chance they get, they strip a little more freedom away; and they do it perversely in the name of protecting it. Make no mistake... This isn't about rich women. This is about whether we will remain a republic or slouch toward tyranny. My father doesn't take this seriously. He doesn't take Varro seriously. Yes, Varro is a fool, a liar, and a braggart. Still, people listen to him."

"Why?" someone asked.

"They're afraid," Aemilia said. "The populists turn that fear into anger. Women feel freer to leave their husbands when their marriage isn't working. They want more from life. On top of that, many men that used to be farmers are having to move to the city for work. They feel they're losing control of their lives, and the populists are offering them a chance to take back power over one part of it—their families."

Appia, a woman about fifty, rose to speak. She was known to be an eloquent orator and had taken to the *Rostrum* several times over the years. She had been one of the most forceful voices for divorce reform more than a decade earlier, making her an object of populist anxieties and ire.

"We should not leave it to men to speak for us," she said. "We must speak for ourselves. Aemilia is right. Fear is the leading killer of reason. Men like Varro know this, and they use it very effectively. If we dole out fear, we'll be playing his game; and we will lose. We must take a more principled approach."

"How, then?" Portitia asked. "We cannot convince men that preserving our rights is somehow their interests. Shouldn't we convince them that their own freedoms are next?"

The women clamored in agreement, but Appia was resolute.

"We appeal to them," Appia told them. "Yes, as our husbands, sons, and brothers, but also as our fellow citizens, fellow Romans."

Aemilia saw the nods in the room, and all the eyes looking up at Appia glowingly. She knew why they all revered Appia, but it worried her. She seemed far too optimistic about their chances of overcoming this populist wave with reasoned argumentation and appealing to the common man's rational sensibilities.

"Respectfully, Appia," she said. "I saw a Vestal Virgin, my cousin, nearly torn apart by a mob Cato had whipped into a frenzy."

"That sort of thing happens," Appia replied. "It's horrible, yes; but when the people think the gods are punishing us... "

"I saw Terentius Varro subvert the rule of law," Aemilia said. "Right in front of the entire Senate. The mob was with him, supporting him, cheering him on... I want to appeal to the best in Romans... I do. But right now, we must see our fellow citizens with clear eyes, at their worst."

The room fell more silent than it had been all day, and Aemilia wondered if she'd just crushed their hopes of resisting the monster they faced.

"We cannot offer a spectacle better than that of Varro," Appia told them, "because that is what Varro does best. We can offer them reasons to support us, and trust that their love of freedom will triumph."

Women snapped their fingers and clapped their hands, waving loose portions of their *stolas* like small flags, and cheered.

***

"I know you were just trying to prepare them," Appia told Aemilia afterward as they sat in the house's study with Servillia and Fulvia. "But you must also keep them inspired."

"Forgive me," Aemilia found herself saying.

"There is nothing to forgive," Appia replied.

She leaned forward, reached out, and took Aemilia's hand. Looking straight into her eyes, she said, "*Never* apologize for saying what you think. A man would not. Why should you? Be strong, confident. Yes?"

Appia made a fist with her right hand and held it to her chest as she said the last few words. Aemilia was touched, so much so that she choked up and could only nod and smile in response. She wiped a tear away and felt Servillia's comforting hand on her back. It was more than women coming together to promote their interests, as politicians would. They knew in their hearts this was about much more. Their fight against the *lex Oppia* was part of many struggles—of women for their rights as citizens, against the tyranny of populist sentiment, for the cause of liberty and justice. For that, they were now sisters-in-arms.

CORNELIUS

Cornelius was running out of time. He wanted to face Hannibal alone and defeat him, if not decisively than soundly; but the chances he would be able to do so were diminishing rapidly. The Senate had quite hastily redeployed his colleague, Sempronius, from Sicily to Cisalpine Gaul. In Cornelius's estimate, it would take a few weeks at most to load the ships, sail to a suitable port, and march to join him at Placentia. If Hannibal came out of the Alps after Sempronius arrived, he would have to share the credit for defeating the Carthaginian. In addition, in less than a month the *Comitium* in Rome would elect two new Consuls to relieve Cornelius and Sempronius and assume command of their armies.

If he left office without a great victory, all his plans were in danger. It would be difficult, if not impossible, for him to win another Consular election before the war was over. The spoils of war would go to generals that contributed the most to defeating Carthage, and the spoils of this war would be particularly lucrative. The entire Carthaginian Empire was up for grabs. Governorships and proconsul positions would make a few families immensely powerful and wealthy. Cornelius was determined that his should be among them. Currently, Calvus was a Legate—an unelected commander of an army that acted with the authority of a Consul. He was in a good position to take Hispania and milk it, just as the Barca clan had done, for their family's benefit as well as that of Rome; but the Senate could decide to replace him if Cornelius's influence over it waned.

All this was on Cornelius's mind when he landed in Stalia, a Raman ally on the west coast of Italy, with a small contingent of cavalry troops and single maniple of a hundred infantrymen. There he was met by the Legate Manlius Vulso, who had been fighting in Cisalpine Gaul for two months. The Boii had been laying siege to Mutina, a Roman colony situated on land seized from the Senones tribe on the south side of the Po River. Vulso had two legions and another six thousand allied axillary conscripts. After a hard eight weeks of fighting, Vulso dealt the Boii a crushing defeat and captured several tribal leaders in the process. The bulk of the enemy's troops had fled the battlefield in disarray, but they were still alive, somewhere...

"You look nervous, Vulso," Cornelius said as they dined the evening of his arrival at the house of a prominent local merchant.

Their host served them mussels from his own personal beds, a fact he had mentioned more than once to his guests.

Cornelius saw Vulso look around at the officers reclining by the tables with him. Metellus was seated at Cornelius's right, and he knew that his son-in-law could be intimidating. It often caused people to hold their tongues if they thought their advice would not be well-received or mistaken for a challenge.

"Speak freely," Cornelius told him.

Vulso took a drink of wine and cleared his throat.

"Consul, I'm very glad that you and your men have come," he said.

"Consider yourself among my men now, Vulso," he replied. "You, your legion, your auxiliaries... even your damned Gauls."

The officers shared a hearty laugh with Cornelius. Vulso, however, looked like he could barely manage a smile.

"My concern," Vulso went on, "lies with Hannibal. There are a dozen tribes in Cisalpine Gaul, half of which are openly hostile. We've managed to keep a balance of power through a system of alliances and agreements."

"I know the politics of this place, Vulso," he said, biting off a piece of bread. "What of it?"

"The most important element in the balance is Rome's military power," Vulso said. "Specifically, the fact that even all the tribes put together can no longer challenge us and our allies."

"And you're afraid Hannibal will upset this," Cornelius said.

"Hannibal will come out of the mountains with a shell of an army," Metellus assured Vulso. "If he comes out at all."

"Shell or not," Vulso replied, "he'll rally the Gauls to his cause."

"There'll be no time," Metellus countered. "As soon as he arrives, we'll attack and destroy him."

"This is a big country, Metellus," Vulso said. "Do you know Hannibal's precise path? Does he even know it? By the time we march an army large enough to attack, he could have won over half these tribes and have tens of thousands of reinforcements."

Cornelius glanced around to quickly gauge the reaction of his staff, who seemed unmoved.

"We've grown too comfortable with the Gauls," Vulso said. "We've subdued them on this side of the mountains for so long that we forget what fierce fighters they can be."

"Fierce, yes," Cornelius said. "Tenacious, no. Gauls are always quick to start a fight; but when they suffer a setback, they're just as quick to lose heart. Would you agree, Metellus?"

"Yes, Consul," Metellus answered with a nod. "That has been my experience with them."

Cornelius appreciated the support. He raised his cup to his son-in-law and drank.

"Then again," Vulso said, "they never seem to quite give up, either."

That was enough. Vulso's presumptuousness was as close to insubordination as it would get. Cornelius put his cup down and looked across at Vulso. Out of the corner of his eye, he saw Metellus glaring at the man. Normally, this look alone would be enough to draw an apology, but Vulso was apparently too stiff-necked.

"Consul," he said, "I feel it is my duty to give you my best-considered advice."

"Consider that duty fulfilled," Cornelius replied tersely.

"I understand you may not agree," Vulso continued, "but I'll gladly run the risk of upsetting you if it means that we'll face Hannibal sufficiently prepared."

"We shall be," Cornelius said, this time raising his cup to Vulso.

The room quieted, and Cornelius was hopeful that Vulso was done voicing concerns. Unfortunately, he didn't get another mussel to his mouth before the fretting Legate spoke again.

"Metellus, you say we'll attack Hannibal as soon as he emerges from the Alps?"

"Of course," Metellus replied. "We shall seek decisive battle while our men are rested and ready, and his are tired and starving. Tactically sound, is it not?"

"It is," Vulso agreed. "But surely that plan is contingent upon the arrival of Consul Sempronius and his army? At least, that's what the Senate clearly intends."

"The Senate is not in command of Roman forces in Cisalpine Gaul," Cornelius said. "Thank the gods... else we'd be fighting a war by a damned committee."

The officers laughed, but again Cornelius noticed that Vulso did not join them. The man seemed intent on spoiling Cornelius's plan to claim victory over Hannibal without Sempronius's aid. However, Cornelius had already considered much of what Vulso was saying—especially about not knowing where Hannibal would come out. He'd lost time in Gaul trying to march his legions. If he'd attacked with his cavalry and skirmishers, he could have won an engagement. Even if it was far from a decisive battle, it would affect the morale of Hannibal's men and would sow doubts about his ability to beat the Romans. Most importantly, it would boost morale in Rome and enhance Cornelius's reputation for military prowess.

He wouldn't make the same mistake twice. His time in command was too short to allow Hannibal to elude him again.

Even if it was just a skirmish, he would meet Hannibal, and do so as the sole Roman commander on that battlefield.

"We'll be fine, Vulso," Cornelius assured him. "*You'll* be fine. I have no intention of disregarding the Senate and attacking in force without my dear colleague... not after what they did to old Claudius Pulcher after Drepana. We'll sharpen the men, recruit some extra cavalry, and when Hannibal comes out, we'll merely send a... *reconnaissance*, in force, to ascertain his disposition."

"And who will lead that reconnaissance, Consul?" Vulso asked.

"I will," Cornelius replied.

HANNIBAL

Mago had been carried atop Surus for the second straight day as the army ascended into another pass. All the other soldiers with wounds that would not heal suffered amputations, and many died regardless. Hannibal would not allow any of the physicians to do that to his youngest brother, and the double-standard was clear to all.

After they emerged from the ravine, the army did not stop long enough to set up a true camp for three days. The men were tired, cold, and increasingly hungry as rations were cut. The horses and mules that had died provided a source of meat, but it was not yet cold enough to prevent it from rotting.

Climbing took a massive amount of energy. They were now above the point where trees grew. The wind was fiercer, the snow deeper, the air more difficult to breathe, and the climb steeper and more treacherous.

Hannibal ordered a camp set up at the first suitably level location. He wanted desperately to go in and see Mago, to see if his fever had broken and if he was, at last, healing; but he had to wait for Gisgo's report on how the rest of the army was faring. It took hours to get, leaving Hannibal to wander the camp alone, mouth and nose covered against the wind. He made a show of randomly checking tent spacing before the fires were lit, though he could barely bring himself to care. The war elephants, which had been mostly quiet during the march until now, were incessantly trumpeting. Like the men and other animals, they were cold and miserable. They needed to grumble. Hannibal let them, though he sincerely hoped they would grow tired of it. His cough was getting worse, and phlegm was coming up more often.

When the count came back, Hannibal was appalled. Since they'd crossed the Rhone three weeks before, he'd lost nearly four thousand men, over a hundred warhorses, and close to two hundred pack animals.

"But," Gisgo interjected as Hannibal brooded over the losses, "all thirty-eight war elephants are still with us."

"The gods must love them," Hannibal said as the trumpeting continued. "I can't say the same right now."

"I tried to get a sense of the causes of our attrition," Gisgo told his commander as they shuffled through the snow toward Mago's tent. "Most haven't died in battle... Not directly, anyway. About half have died from accidents—falling, in most cases. Most of the others succumbed to sickness. We've used up all the healing herbs and vinegars we brought with us."

Hannibal nodded, and they walked the rest of the way in silence. When they arrived, Hannibal stood between Gisgo and the entrance.

"We rest here through tomorrow night," Hannibal declared.

"General," Gisgo said before Hannibal could walk away. "I

know the men need rest, but we can't afford more delay than that."

"We need to rest before the descent."

"I realize that, but if we don't get out of these mountains, they'll get sicker and weaker, until—"

"I know!" Hannibal snapped, bringing on a short coughing fit. Gisgo took a step back.

"Apologies, General," he said with a slight bow. "I shall pass the order."

Hannibal nodded and went inside.

The tent was cold and dark. It had been properly secured, but the wind was still causing the sides to flap around noisily. A single flickering oil lamp provided light to Vernon and Hannibal's physician, a Greek called Nicon, who had joined him in Hispania. Their grave expression and the stench of the wound filled Hannibal was dread.

"How is he?" Hannibal asked, stepping between them.

"Not well," Nicon answered, though Hannibal could see that much himself.

Mago was sweating in the cold night air, and his forehead was hot to the touch.

"We're trying to keep him covered," Nicon said. "But the fever..."

Hannibal motioned to the leg.

"Let me see it," he ordered before turning his head to cough.

Nicon gently took the wool blanket from around Mago's feet and lifted it up. Hannibal winced as the pale-yellow puss came into view. He had seen thousands of wounds up close on soldiers barely old enough to be called men, but this was his baby brother. He wanted to weep, but he wouldn't allow himself to do so in front of Vernon and Nicon.

"What do you recommend?" he asked the physician, who covered the wound.

"A good sacrifice to Tanit," Nicon answered. "And in the morning... "

A set of fingers wrapped around Hannibal's wrist. When he looked down, Mago's eyes were open but glassy, looking up at him. His lids were barely open, and his focus didn't seem quite right.

"Hannibal... " he called to him, and Hannibal knelt at his side.

He cradled Mago's head with his free hand and touched his forehead to his brother's.

"I'm here, brother," he answered, and felt the tears coming up.

"If I die... "

"No," Hannibal objected, sniffling. "No, don't... "

"Don't leave me here in this place."

Hannibal didn't answer. The thought of Mago laying out there in the snow, a frozen corpse, made him cry harder. He coughed worse than he ever had, feeling like he couldn't breathe.

"Don't... " Mago whispered, closing his eyes again. "Don't leave me here."

"Shhh... " Hannibal said, laying Mago's head back on the pillow.

He was still holding his brother's hand, pushing his hair from his forehead and putting them into place, when a soldier entered the tent carrying a bowl of porridge.

"What is this?" Nicon asked. "Wheat porridge?"

"Yes, sir," the soldier answered.

"I made it clear that this man needs meat," he said.

"The horsemeat spoiled, sir," the soldier said.

Nicon mumbled something in Greek and waved the soldier away, but Vernon grabbed him.

"Spoiled how?" he asked.

"Maggots got in, sir," the soldier reported.

"Maggots? You're certain of it?"

"Saw it myself, sir," he said. "I was looking forward to some of that meat, myself."

"Bring them," Vernon ordered.

"Bring what, sir?"

"The maggots. Get a bag, get as many as you can, and bring them here at once," he said. "Go!"

Hannibal squeezed his brother's hand, and Mago opened his eyes again.

"You never told me," Hannibal said, trying to engage his brother. "What the difference is... between us and the Romans."

His brother summoned him closer with his fingers, as if he wanted to whisper a secret in his ear, and said, "They're from Rome."

Hannibal pulled his head back and saw Mago's lips form a grin for the first time in days.

"General," Vernon called. Hannibal turned his head to see him extend a small bag toward him. "I think these may save the leg."

Hannibal stood and took the bag from him. He peered inside and saw a mass of writhing brownish larvae.

"General," Nicon called. "I cannot recommend this. Any more delay in severing the leg will... "

"I've seen it work," Vernon assured him. "This could save him *and* his leg."

"If the wound were not as ripe, I might agree," Nicon said. "But this is an extremity."

"What do we do with them?" Hannibal asked.

"We put them on the wound and wrap it," Vernon told him. "They will eat the rotten flesh, and the wound will heal."

"You've seen it work?"

"Once, yes," Vernon answered.

As confident as Vernon appeared, the physician seemed equally dubious.

"General, this is extremely risky," Nicon explained. "I've seen this as well. It fails as often as it succeeds, and if your brother's condition worsens... "

"And how much blood would he lose when you take the leg?" Vernon challenged him. "Even then, he may still not make it."

"He stands a much better chance than with these insects!" Nicon countered.

Hannibal turned back to Mago, ruminating, and blocking all the voices outside his own mind. Would he do this if it were an ordinary soldier? What if it failed? It was the last question that stopped his pondering. He had made it this far by taking the greater risk with the greater rewards.

"Do it," he ordered.

He watched as Nicon placed the wriggling worm-like larvae onto the puss-filled gash. Vernon then lifted Mago's leg carefully as the physician wrapped it in a fresh linen bandage, loosely sealing the maggots inside.

Hannibal closed his eyes and prayed. He was not the religious man Hasdrubal was, but it was moments like this that believing the gods could steer events gave him some comfort. As much as he could control, there was much more he could not.

SCIPIO

Scipio hadn't asked his soldiers why they'd voted to restore his rank after his father had stripped him of it and ordered him flogged. When they landed at Stalia, there had been scarce time to talk before they were marching to Placentia, the city which would serve as their base of operations until Hannibal emerged from the Alps. Once there, they filled their days with training while Cornelius drilled the infantry he now commanded.

After a hard day of drills with the spears and their *gladius hispaniensis* swords, the cavalry version of which was slightly longer and heavier than the infantry version, Scipio returned his horse to the stables that the cavalry had requisitioned. It was there he saw Claudius speaking with a few other officers by the large fountain in the center of the stable's circular courtyard.

"Why are they calling you the 'Hero of the Rhone'?" he called to Claudius.

Claudius looked over the other officers' heads. He excused himself and walked toward Scipio to meet him half-way.

"Really?" Claudius answered. "We haven't seen each other in nearly two weeks... "

"You can say it," Scipio told him. "Since I was flogged."

"Since you were flogged," Claudius obliged. "And that's the first thing you say to me?"

They hugged, laughing with joy.

"Let's get some wine before I die of thirst," Claudius said dramatically, and they walked toward the gymnasium that was serving as the officer's barracks and dining hall.

"How are you feeling?" Claudius asked as they exited the stables.

"A little stiff, but other than that... What about you, though? What happened at the Rhone?"

"Don't make me tell this story again," Claudius pleaded, rolling his eyes.

"Come on," Scipio chided him. "You love the attention."

"I do," Claudius confessed with a devilish grin.

"Spill it, then."

"After you went after for those stragglers, I stayed put, trying to observe Hannibal's main body crossing," Claudius told him. "Of course, he crossed the river quicker than any of us imagined; but he left some Numidian horsemen to screen his movements, trying to keep us from seeing his progress. We lost sight of the main body, so I decided to move my troops in a little closer. We surprised about twenty of them, took them from their flank and killed six, chased the rest back to the crossing point."

"You took on a Numidian cavalry unit twice your size?" Scipio laughed. "Do you have any idea how stupid that is?"

"Stupid? I wasn't the one who got flogged," Claudius reminded him. "Anyway, they put me in charge of our *turmae*."

The *turmae* was a squadron of three ten-strong cavalry troops. Although he retained the rank of *Decurio*, it was still a promotion of sorts.

"That's fantastic!" Scipio said, thrilled to hear some good news for a change. He clapped his friend on the shoulder. "Congratulations, brother!"

"Mother will be pleased, I'm sure," Claudius said. "By the way, there's a rumor going around that you had a close encounter with some druids."

"Don't even ask," Scipio replied with a wave of his hand.

"You're the first Roman that's met them up close... and lived to tell about it, anyway. This will be your claim to fame."

"I doubt that."

"Did they take your blood for their magic?"

Scipio thought of the roundhouse; of surrendering his talisman to them and the visions he saw.

"No... " he answered. "They took something else."

Claudius made a show of looking at his friend's crotch.

"Oh no... Not Romulus and Remus!" he said.

"Still in place," Scipio assured him.

They entered the gymnasium, which was a long colonnaded building with a high roof. It had both indoor and outdoor areas for exercise and games, latrines, and a bath nearby. In the outdoor area, they saw hundreds of Gauls training with wooden swords and shields, swatting and stabbing at one another, advancing and retreating in formation. Dozens of Roman soldiers were training them. They ignored the shouting and grunting of infantry training and served themselves some water and wine from amphoras.

"I think we'll spend half the war just trying to find out where Hannibal is," Claudius mused as they sat in the spectator area. "Anyway... My mother wants me to return to Rome to stand for Tribune. I haven't decided what to do yet. What do you think, Scipio?"

It was a huge leap from *Decurion* to Tribune. Although Claudius barely had the requisite five years of service, Scipio thought Claudius had a good chance of being elected. He was the type of man others admired—tall, good looking, and now a hero.

His happiness for his friend was genuine, but Scipio found himself feeling a tad envious. He didn't care about high office in the military or politics, but neither did he wish to be left behind.

"I think you should run," Scipio told him.

"Really? I... "

Claudius was distracted by something, and Scipio followed his stare. On the crest of a hill just beyond the city's walls, about a dozen crosses were being erected. Scipio didn't object to crucifixions, but neither did he want to participate in it. It was, he thought, a particularly nasty punishment.

"We learned crucifixion from the Carthaginians, you know," they heard a voice next to them say.

When they saw it was a Legate, they leaped to their feet and saluted. The Legate, however, didn't seem to notice. His attention was focused on his own hands, in which he was whittling a piece of wood with a small knife. They recognized him as Manlius Vulso, the man who'd been in charge of the campaign against the Boii.

"You're the Consul's son, aren't you?" he asked, peeking up at Scipio.

"I am, sir," Scipio answered. "This is Claudius Pulcher."

Vulso paused his carving and gestured with his knife at the crosses on the hill.

"Those were my prisoners," he said. "I was foolish enough to ask the Senate's permission to trade their lives for peace, but there are too many in Rome who believe that fear will keep this region in line."

Looking at the crosses, Scipio couldn't imagine a reason why this sort of punishment wouldn't keep the peace. Who would risk it?

"Tell me something, either of you," Vulso went on, jerking his head toward the Gauls being trained. "If you saw your father hanging on a cross, would you be more likely to fight for or against those who put him there?"

"You'll think they'll betray us?" Claudius asked.

"Think? Gods, no," Vulso laughed. "I *know* they'll betray us, just as soon as they can do it without ending up on crosses. It's obvious to everyone." He looked at Scipio. "Except your father."

"Sir, if you're looking for someone to influence my father, I'd advise you to look elsewhere," Scipio told him.

"Every man both fears and loves his father, Scipio," Vulso said. "The question is which is a greater influence on their actions. Your father believes it better to be feared than loved."

"You disagree?" Claudius asked.

Vulso shrugged.

"I have a son," he said. "Six months old now. If he were in that gymnasium and it was on fire, do you think I would let fear keep me from saving him? Even if it meant I'd almost certainly burn to death in there?"

Again, Scipio's mind returned to the druid's house and the vision he'd had. Not to the gentle light in the dark, but the raging, destructive fire that came before it. He could picture the gymnasium engulfed by that fire. He closed his eyes, and the fire from the vision returned. The furious orange flames, the heat, the smoke; and the cries of people from within growing louder and more desperate. Thousands screamed in terror, trapped together as the flames licked at them. The fire around them grew and fed on the horror until the scene blurred into chaos, and the flickering flames became the flickers of light and the white togas seen among the legs of the panicked masses. In between, in sudden, fleeting glimpses, Lucius was crying...

"Scipio," Claudius said with a nudge.

Scipio opened his eyes, struggling to free himself of the vision.

"Your father needs to hear something that he doesn't wish to hear," Vulso told him. "We will not hold this place, or any other, by fear. The Carthaginians have forgotten more about instilling fear in their subjects than we will ever know. Rome needs allies, more than ever before." He jabbed his knife toward the crosses on the hill. "And they will not be won like this."

Vulso stepped closer to Scipio.

"Your father's headed straight toward a disaster," he said. "He will not listen to me, nor will his staff. Maybe he will not listen to you, either; but the question you must ask yourself is this... Do you love him enough to try to save him from himself? Or will you let your fear of him stop you from it?"

Vulso handed Scipio the figurine he'd carved from the wood. It was a tiny elephant.

"Hannibal is coming," he said. "And we're not ready for him."

VALERIA

The Consul didn't seem to notice the Egyptian slave girl standing in the corner of the elegantly furnished room until he'd climaxed. Even then, Sempronius stayed inside of Valeria as he held out a hand toward her and called for water. Sex had left their bodies glistening with sweat, and the slave had towels sent up midway through their session. After she dried off the naked Consul, Sempronius gave her leave to go.

"Whose house is this?" Valeria asked.

"Some local," Sempronius said as he laid back down next to

her and handed her the cup of water. "Owns a fleet of merchant ships. Biremes, I believe."

"And he allows you to use it?"

"He offered before, probably trying to curry some favor for state contracts. I never had reason to use it... until now, of course."

"Oh, I'm sure," Valeria said, nearly certain that Sempronius had found a new lover the first or second night he had been in Sicily.

He grinned and kissed her breast.

"Though I must confess," he went on, "I like your husband's house better, ugly as it is. I get a thrill fucking you in his bed."

"It seems like you'll have that opportunity again sooner than you thought," she said.

He groaned and rolled off her.

"Don't remind me," he said.

"Why?" she asked. "Don't you miss Rome?"

"That's not the issue."

She smiled and rolled herself on top of him again, kissing his sun-chapped lips. He wasn't the most attractive man in Rome, nor even her most attractive lover; but he had qualities that both drew her to him and repulsed her. Sempronius was ambitious, cold, aggressive, and sometimes cruel. He was exactly what was expected of a Roman man. He exhibited the same qualities as a lover, making him impatient and, at times, sadistic. While she indulged and enjoyed his sadism, the sex was just a means to an end. She gave him something he desperately wanted and could not get elsewhere. It gave her a power over him that she enjoyed far more than sex.

He got up and walked over to the room's large window.

Normally, the windows in a home like this would face the inner courtyard to guard against thieves entering from the street; but this shipping magnate was wealthy enough to have personal guards around his home at all hours of the day and night. He was lucky, Valeria thought. Sicily was brutally hot in the summer. Having windows that faced the shore could let in the cool ocean breezes. It was one of countless comforts and advantages the poor could only dream of having.

He pulled the heavy curtain ever so slightly, letting bright midday sunlight and ocean air stream into the dimly lit room. As she soaked in the cool wind and heard the sound of seagull's squawk as they flew over the Sicilian shore, he squinted out at the harbor.

Though she had found many pleasures here, Valeria would soon have to leave Sicily behind. She had more important people than Sempronius to meet, but she wanted something from him before she left. Communications with Rome were slow. Even the Senate wouldn't have information as up to date as she would have. The trick was to get him talking about the war in a way that made it seem as if he were bringing it up of his own accord.

"Barely a month left in my Consulship," he mused. "And all I've done is load and unload ships."

"Perhaps Cornelius is grabbing the glory for himself," she said, fiddling with the ends of her long hair.

"No... We both knew this was the better assignment."

She raised her eyebrows as he sat next to her and caressed her legs.

"Really?"

"Really," he said.

"Why?" she asked. "Doesn't Hispania have all those silver

mines?"

"Silver?" he chuckled. "Carthage, Lady Varro, is worth ten Hispanias; and it's there, ripe for the plucking. If the Senate weren't so timid, I'd have it under siege now."

"So, no one gets Hispania?"

"Calvus gets it," he replied. "Cornelius is sending his brother on to Hispania with nearly all of his soldiers."

"How does he plan to fight Hannibal without an army?" she asked.

"I suspect he'll take Manlius Vulso's troops," he said as he leaned over, then kissed her neck and chest. "Allies, mostly. Not nearly adequate, but that is why the Senate is dragging me back, aren't they?"

This was new. She assumed Cornelius would take all his soldiers to Cisalpine Gaul to face Hannibal, but there was a Roman army headed to Hispania; or, more likely, there already.

"Ah!" she yelped as he closed his teeth around her nipple. He seemed to have a talent for biting with just enough force that it didn't break the skin but still caused pain. She pouted at him and his grin before pulling his face to hers and kissing him, biting down on his lower lip.

He drew back in pain and she smiled, pleased with herself. He touched his lower lip and tasted the little blood she had drawn. For a moment, she feared he might draw his hand back and hit her, which he'd never shown a proclivity to do; but instead, it just seemed to fill him with lust.

"Careful, Lady Varro," he said in a low voice, half menacing and half flirtatious, touching her chin.

"Don't call me that," she hissed.

He leaned closer to her.

"It pleases me," he said in the same low voice, before rising from the bed and again going to the window.

"If I'd only made it to Africa," he said as he peeked outside again. "I'd have enough to buy and sell your husband like the whore he is."

"I don't think you've ever even mentioned money before," she said. "I thought you didn't care for it."

"I don't," he answered. "But your husband does, the simpleton that he is. I just want to rub his nose in it."

"You don't know what money is for," she told him. "You've always had it."

"So?"

"The world looks very different without it," she said.

He turned to her, and his reaction to her expression told her she had given herself away, just a little bit, for the first time with him. The resentment, the rage, the hunger she harbored deep inside of her was hers alone, she reminded herself. She quickly fixed her expression from angry to sexy.

"So confident you could have taken Carthage, if the Senate hadn't called you back?" she asked.

His gaze returned to the sea.

"They're just beginning to organize any kind of defenses. Utica is completely unprotected."

"What of the vaunted Carthaginian Navy?"

"Absent," he said, handing her the cup he'd poured. "Half combatting pirates near the Balearic Islands, the other half putting down a rebellion near Thapsus. The whole thing is so poorly coordinated, it makes me seriously consider... Perhaps Queen Adonica has no control over her own armies."

He let the curtain fall back into place and sat on the bed once more.

"It's out there... " he murmured, staring out into space. "Like a big, fat, overloaded sack of gold. Mine for the taking."

He lifted his free hand up and reached out into the emptiness of the dim room.

"One thrust of my sword," he said, "would be enough to burst it open for me."

She guided his hand from the air to her thigh, put her other hand on his shoulder and pulled him close.

"One thrust?" she whispered. "Is that all?"

He smiled and put the wine aside.

"Well... " he said, climbing on top of her. "Perhaps a few more."

HANNIBAL

Hannibal guessed that very few of the men in his army dreamed the descent would be the treacherous part of their march through these mountains, but it was. From the pass to the foothills, beyond which lay the green pastures of the Po River Valley, was a steep and icy decline partially covered in snow. The line of men and animals wound around the mountainside, skirting a deep chasm. The soles of his soldiers' boots gave little grip on ice, and they sought out anything that could give them traction.

Before they descended five hundred feet, he began to lose men to the terrain. The first few fell and slid straight off the road and into the yawning defile, hundreds of feet down to oblivion. Then an entire chain gang of Allobrogian slaves, a Numidian and his warhorse, more infantry, and a donkey complete with cart and baggage. It went on this way all morning and part of the afternoon until the column came to a trembling stop and refused to move further.

At considerable risk, Hannibal warily made his way on foot to the front to see what was going on. The men he passed were so near exhaustion that they barely seemed to notice him. They were trembling, he saw, but he hoped the sight of the green foothills before them was giving them hope.

"Brother... " he heard Mago call to him as he passed by.

"Stay here," Hannibal told him.

It had only been four days since they had applied the maggots, but Mago was sitting upright on Surus. Nicon was firm in his belief the gods had intervened on his behalf. Hannibal hadn't argued with the Greek. Gods, men, maggots... What difference did it make? Mago was healing, and Hannibal's cough had nearly gone.

A landslide had brought a pile of rocks and boulders to rest on their path, and it was far too high to climb over for the horses and carts. Most of the rocks were too heavy for the men, in their weakened conditions, to move.

Tired, Hannibal sat on one of the rocks to rest. In front of him, his remaining force of about thirty-four thousand soldiers waited for his order. They stood stomping their feet and doing other exercises to keep warm; or sat about the mountainside as the wind whipped across them and blew snow onto what little exposed skin remained on their faces. Now they waited for Hannibal to solve a problem so seemingly simple that it might have seemed trivial; yet, it seemed to sap the last bit of his mental energy. He just wanted to rest his eyes a little, just for a moment.

It was warm. It was sunny. High white clouds moved lazily in the sky. Birds sung their songs, heedless of where they were and what they had witnessed. Waves lapped the light brown sand that looked so much like the beaches back home. His father's large hands took him by both his shoulders, and his deep, commanding voice echoed in Hannibal's ears.

"Do you swear before the gods, and on your sacred honor as a scion of the House of Barca, eternal enmity to Rome?"

His brothers were too young to understand. They simply held out their hands and recited the pledge. Hannibal alone was mature enough to see the hero that he was. He savored the moment the sword opened the skin of his palm and wet the blade. The blood of the four of them dripped onto the altar. He held the sword with both hands, his own wound still bleeding, and aimed the blade. The hilt he braced to his chest, ready to withstand the weight. No one before or since, Hannibal believed, died with more honor. He could feel his father's hands take him by the shoulders one last time, see the warm smile and brown eyes, nodding once to Hannibal. Did he want to make sure Hannibal was ready, or was the nod to assure him everything was going to be fine? Both, perhaps. He felt the pull he'd felt a thousand times when his father knelt and pulled him close to embrace him. The sword went through, and his father let out not a single cry. There was pain in his eyes, as there had been for days, but no regret, only pride. So much pride...

"Hannibal..."

He didn't know how long he'd been sitting like that when Gisgo found him.

"The air is thin," Gisgo said. "It's not good for... thinking."

Hannibal wiped his leaking nose.

"We need engineers," he said, patting the rock on which he sat.

"I'll get Adherbal," Gisgo replied.

***

"All this way," Mago said, looking up at an immense boulder in front of him, "to be stopped by a rock."

Hannibal couldn't help but laugh, though he still coughed a little whenever he did. After a full day and night of working in shifts, Adherbal and his engineers had used the slaves and animals to painstakingly move the rocks from the landslide. What had been their obstacle became, with care and skill, their salvation as the larger rocks were broken apart and hammered into the ice and snow. With better traction and less fear of falling, his army would regain momentum. It looked like they might make it to the foothills, or close to it, the following day. The last thing they had to do was move the largest of the rocks.

The wily old engineer, Adherbal, stared at it for over an hour. At times, he paced from side to side; other times, he peeked through the small space between it and the mountainside. Hannibal watched, amused, as Adherbal climbed over it to the other side, but the change in perspective evidently hadn't seen to provide him with any useful insights.

Finally, Adherbal seemed to give up and go away. At sixty, he was old to be on campaign, but he was smart and stubborn. It was why Hannibal insisted on taking him everywhere. There would inevitably be a problem only Adherbal was dogged enough to solve. When he returned, he had a group of his engineers in tow, all carrying firewood.

"What's this?" Hannibal asked him.

Adherbal stepped up to the boulder and pointed to one of the many fissures in it.

"You see these cracks, General? If we build a fire under the rock and get it hot enough that these expand, we can use our—"

"Just... do it," Hannibal said.

"Yes, sir," the Adherbal answered. "We just need one more ingredient."

He hesitated, looking at Mago.

"What?" Mago asked.

"Your wine, sir."

"*My* wine?" Mago asked with wide eyes, guarding his wineskin as if Adherbal would snatch it from him at any moment. Hannibal chuckled, amused with his brothers' horror.

"Not just yours, sir," Adherbal replied. "Everyone's, of course. All of it."

Mago looked to Hannibal as if he expected his brother to countermand the request.

"You see," Adherbal went on as Mago took one last swig, "we're going to pour the wine into the cracks and... "

Mago didn't wait for him to explain. Cursing, he handed over his wine and limped away in a huff.

AEMILIA

Of the core group of women that were organizing to oppose the *lex Oppia*, not one was a plebeian. In fact, they were among some of the oldest and wealthiest patrician families in the Republic. It worried them. Searching her mental roster of friends and acquaintances, she couldn't think of anyone that would not be considered wealthy by Roman standards. Suspecting herself a snob wasn't what concerned her, however. She knew that support for the *lex Oppia* among the lower classes, which far outnumbered the elites, was strong if not overwhelming. In fact, support among the lower class for all sumptuary laws was strong. Not only did these laws cost them, they also seemed to bring the elites down a notch.

Luckily, Appia and Fulvia had broader social circles that included many women who were more than capable of spreading word among the lower classes of a meeting. Fully aware that there would be few opportunities to talk to a large group of plebeian women before the *Comitia*, Aemilia prepared for it carefully.

She arranged to use the shrine of Pudicitia, the goddess of chastity, in the Vicus Longus neighborhood of Rome. Aemilia had carefully chosen the site. It was the former home of Virginia, a patrician woman who'd married a plebeian and was consequently shunned from the goddess' patrician-only cult. That was seventy years ago, during the plebeians' struggle to gain full and equal political rights. Virginia built her own shrine to the goddess for all women to worship, and she had since become something of a folk hero for Roman women.

As the women gathered, the shrine's ground quickly crowded. Aemilia and Servillia had brought their slaves to serve bread, wine, and water, but they knew that their hospitality wouldn't keep the women there indefinitely. They were hoping that Fulvia, whose direct and plain-spoken rhetorical style they believed would appeal to the group of women before them, would be able to speak. She'd promised them that she would try to make it there, but Fulvia's attention had shifted in recent days from opposing the *lex Oppia* to supporting her son's run for Military Tribune.

"I think they've waited long enough," Servillia told Aemilia as they looked over the crowd of dully dressed chatting women before them.

Standing on the steps of the shrine looking out at the faces and clothing, Aemilia regretted having dressed so well in light green himation, gold bracelets and earrings. Both she and Servillia stood in stark contrast to the rest of the women. Even the young among them seemed quite old next to the pair of patricians.

Before Aemilia stepped out, Servillia pulled her close.

"I think you should explain the law," she told her.

"Why?"

"A lot of these women don't look like they follow politics, Aemilia."

She was right. These women led very different lives, and she could take nothing for granted. After getting their attention, Aemilia introduced herself and addressed them with as much of a smile as she could summon. She briefly explained the *lex Oppia*, and the wide eyes and hands covering mouths on many of their faces told her that Servillia had been right—many of them didn't have any idea what was coming.

"It is my hope today to follow Virginia's example," Aemilia said, indicating the shrine behind her, "and bring women of all classes together. This shrine was dedicated during what we now call the Conflict of Orders, when plebeians fought for their rights and won them. Today, we are in a new conflict—not of orders, but of gender. We must fight against the *lex Oppia* just as the plebeians fought against the unjust laws that benefitted a few families at the expense of the many."

"You ask us to affect things we have no control over," a young woman near the front called out to her. "This law is horrible, yes, but only the men can vote for or against it."

"Yes, but we can speak out against it," Aemilia replied. "We can make our voices heard."

"Yes!" she heard an excited voice say from somewhere in the crowd. She saw women nodding and talking to one another, but others looked at her askew, as if she were trying to sell them cheap wares in the Forum.

"We all have men in our lives," Servillia said. "Fathers, brothers, husbands, sons... Speak to them. Make them understand what this law means to us."

"We can," a voice said from somewhere in the middle of the crowd. "Should we now?"

The women turned in the direction of the voice, and Aemilia watched as a dark-haired figure made her way toward the front. When she was close enough, Aemilia saw that she was a middle-aged woman in a frayed himation that was probably at some point a shade of white but seemed closer now to a yellowish-brown. She looked up at the two clearly wealthier women at the top of the shrine's steps with a scowl.

"I ain't never see you twos before, 'ere in the *Vicius Longus*," the women said in Latin as course as the fabric of her clothes. "Supposing you live up by Palantine's way, then, don'chas? What with all you've gots without 'avin to lift a finger for yourselves, never seen fit to come down 'ere before, lookin' to give nothing to these ladies nothing. But now 'ere you come, askin' of us."

"This is about *all* women," Aemilia said firmly.

"It about rich women, dearie," the women snapped.

"That's who this law is about, isn't it?" another, younger woman with a baby in her arms asked. "It ain't about us. Gods... ain't nothing they can take from us!"

"That's true!" Aemilia heard someone else in the crowd say, and another said, "She's right about that!"

"Put aside the taxes," Aemilia said. "What about our lives? All women, whatever their means, have the right to divorce their husbands without anyone's permission, whatever their age or order. This law would—"

"This 'ere wouldn't change nothin'," the middle-aged woman said. "You think because our 'usbans beats us or worse, we can runs away 'ome to our fathers or brothers? Theys can't afford to take cares of us. We can't gets no jobs. We leave, we're beggin' on the streets, or sellin' ourselves. Dead within a year, most of us."

"She's right," the women with the baby said. "What do we care if they take all your drachmae? You'll still be sitting up there on the Palatine being pampered while we're down in Suburra, working day and night just to survive."

"But this law will make your lives even harder," Aemilia insisted, but the collective reaction was an incredulous and collective "Oh!", as if she had told them the sky was red. There were some, however, she could see thought differently.

"She's right!" one of them, a middle-aged woman in a blue *tunica talaris*, shouted about the rest. "She's right! If this law passes, I won't even be able to wear what I'm wearing now. The law will forbid us from wearing two colors at a time! That's just ridiculous!"

"Oh, boohoo," the women with bad grammar shot back. "We won'ts be wearin' our finery out to the Forum!"

"It would close the gymnasiums for women," a woman about Aemilia's age, her belly swollen with child, shouted back. "It would basically forbid us from exercising!"

"There's a war on, dearie!" bad grammar shouted back. "More important things than runnin' around. And who has times for exercising, anyways? Don't look like you needs any."

Many women broke out in mocking laughter, and the pregnant women's face turned red with anger.

"And what about our daughters?" she demanded.

Bad grammar swatted the air in her direction.

"Yous can stay 'ere and gives these rich girls your time," she said. "I'm not waistin' anys more of mine. This law's gonna make them bleed money. I say good on it."

She made her way to the street. To Aemilia's dismay, most of the women followed.

"Liberty itself is at stake!" Aemilia said as the chatting women shuffled out. "Do you think the conservatives and populists will stop here? They want freedom only for themselves, and chafe at others having it. This is when a republic can die—when we stop caring about each other's rights and want to punish those not like ourselves. Please... "

A few women stayed behind, but the vast majority either left or were leaving by the time Aemilia had finished speaking.

***

As soon as they returned to Aemilia's house, the women flopped themselves down on the most comfortable couches they had. They needed something to take their mind off the disaster. Deciphering the mysterious strip of letters Aemilia had stolen from Varro's study seemed like the perfect game, but it proved as frustrating as their meeting with the plebeian women.

"Honestly, Aemilia, I just don't think we're going to figure this out... whatever this is... without the help of Valeria's slave."

"She took him with her to Sicily to see her cousins," Aemilia told her.

Servillia burst into laughter, getting a quizzical look from her friend.

"Oh, I'm sorry," she said. "Her cousins... In a war zone. I'm certain that's quite true."

"Why else would she go there?"

Servillia picked up a bunch of grapes from the table and lifted a brow.

"Maybe it has something to do with our illustrious Consul, Tiberius Sempronius," she suggested.

Aemilia frowned, confused, so Servillia enlightened her by holding the grapes be the stem above her, tilting her head back and opening her mouth before dipping the bottom few in her mouth and moaning with eyes closed. *That's* what she was doing? Aemilia drew a shocked breath and covered her mouth.

"Stop!" she said, and threw a small pillow at Servillia, who laughed in delight as she munched on her grapes, then plucked one and returned fire at Aemilia.

Gossip among the Roman elite was ubiquitous, inexhaustible, and mostly untrue. Though sometimes, Aemilia admitted to herself, it carried some nugget of truth waiting to be found.

"How do you know she's sleeping with Sempronius?" she asked Servillia.

Servillia shook her head and said, "I never reveal my sources."

Aemilia pouted a little, making Servillia roll her eyes.

"I can't believe Valeria actually thinks you'd consider her stepson for a husband," Servillia said.

Aemilia rubbed her forehead.

"Don't remind me," she said. "It'll make me retch."

Servillia regarded her friend as she chewed and swallowed her grapes.

"Have you heard from him?" Servillia asked.

"Who?"

"Scipio... The Consul's son."

"Not yet."

"Will you marry him instead?"

"No," Aemilia answered. "I don't know. Maybe."

"Are you worried he won't come back?" Servillia asked.

The mental image of Scipio, so handsome in his armor and cloak, fading into oblivion, nearly stopped Aemilia from breathing. The feeling caught her completely by surprise, and she knew she had been avoiding thinking of it. Her chest tightened abruptly, and she found herself weeping.

Servillia moved over to her and put her arm around Aemilia.

"Sorry," she said.

"There's so much that can happen," Aemilia said. "I just... didn't think I'd miss him like this."

"Are you frightened the war will change him much?"

"No," Aemilia answered. "I'm more afraid he'll come back exactly the same."

Servillia held her tighter and kissed her on the top of her head.

Aemilia saw a female slave peek into the room and then quickly disappear.

"Is your source a slave?" Aemilia asked, sitting up straight and wiping away her tears.

"What?" Servillia asked, sitting back a little.

"How you found out about Valeria."

"What do you mean?"

"It's just... Slaves are around us nearly all the time. They hear things, see things... They must talk to one another, just as we do. Gossip."

"So?"

"Perhaps they can tell us what this message means," Aemilia said. "And... other things."

"And how do you propose we get them to tell us the secrets they keep?"

"The same way anyone gets anything out of anyone else," Aemilia answered. "Money."

SCIPIO

Scipio rehearsed three times before he approached the *hospitia* where his father had set up his command post. It would be the first time he'd spoken to him since he was flogged. Just picturing his father's dower default expression made his stomach queasy, and it would be even worse now that Uncle Calvus was not here. Maybe it was the uniform, he thought. The difference in rank made the gulf between them seem even wider than usual. His power seemed nearly absolute.

Walking past the stables and the contracted carpenters with their slaves making crosses, he muttered his practiced words. He found himself touching his hand to the middle of his chest, but the comet talisman was gone. All he felt was the pounding of his own heart.

His brother-in-law was there to challenge him the moment he entered the main chamber.

"What do you want, Scipio?" Metellus demanded.

"Let him through," Cornelius called out to them.

Cornelius was with a staff officer in a dining room, hunkered over a map of Cisalpine Gaul. After he dismissed the officers,

Cornelius turned his somber and disapproving scowl to his son.

"What is it?" he asked.

Scipio took a deep breath, avoiding eye contact while he tried to gather his thoughts.

"These... punishments... for the rebels... "

"Yes? What about them?" Cornelius asked.

"They are... too much," he finally spat out, raising his father's ire. "We need them on our side when Hannibal—"

"What do you know about putting down a revolt?" Cornelius demanded. "Do you even know what the Boii have done to earn this?"

"N... No, but... " Scipio stammered, feeling his throat closing on him.

Cornelius rubbed his forehead with his eyes shut, as if Scipio's presence had brought on some terrible pain. Metellus took his place at Cornelius's side, staring Scipio down as if he were an extension of his father-in-law.

"Listen to me," Cornelius said. "Fear is a powerful tool in war. I cannot ex—"

"We cannot win allies with fear," Scipio said.

"I was not finished!" Cornelius snapped, and Scipio stood at attention as his father stepped around the table toward him.

"We cannot control who loves Rome," Cornelius said. "But we can control who fears it."

"And what will make them stay with us if that fear is removed?" Scipio countered.

"Enough!" Cornelius snapped and slammed his palm on the table, making Scipio flinch. "I spared you the lash in Gaul because I was the one who was foolish enough to promote you. I don't know what your men see in you, but all I see is an empty uniform. Leave us."

Cornelius turned his back to him, and Scipio stood for a moment, lips quivering in anger. Even the threat of scourging would not hold him back this time.

"Father!" he called. When Cornelius lifted his eyes to see him, however, the words he had intended to speak only moments before disappeared in the maelstrom of anger and grief in his head. He had to speak, though; for the whole room was looking at him now. The only words that came to him, though, were Vulso's. "If it were you hanging on a cross, would you expect me to fight with or against the people that put you there?"

Cornelius stepped around the table, advancing on his son as he spoke.

"I'd expect you to do what is best for you," he said. "Or, at least, what is easiest. All your life, you've been nothing but venal and selfish."

"Consul..." Metellus tried to intervene, but they both ignored him.

"Why do you hate me?" Scipio demanded.

"You know why," his father said in a low voice, and Scipio could see him shaking slightly.

"Why?" Scipio asked again.

He saw his father reach across his body, but for reasons he couldn't explain, it still came as a shock when the back of his father's hand stuck the right side of his face. He stumbled a couple of steps back and to the left, and the realization that his father had struck him had barely registered in his mind when Cornelius was yelling at him again.

"You know why!" he thundered.

310

Scipio rubbed the stinging right side of his face. The single blow had hurt worse than all the centurion's baton strikes in his flogging. He wanted to bawl, but he managed to laugh bitterly as a few tears rolled down his cheeks.

"Of course," he said, pointing down in front of him. "This is about Lucius. It's always about Lucius."

"Of course, it's about Lucius!" Cornelius roared, looking down at his son. "He was your responsibility! If you had one selfless bone in your body... "

"I was seven!"

"Old enough!" Cornelius bellowed. "The gods didn't take Lucius from me. *You* did! In the very moment that you needed to have courage, you showed yourself a coward! Now go! Leave us!"

It was all he could take. Scipio saluted and left as quickly as he could, breezing past the staff officers.

***

The sound of horn blasts marshaling the cavalry in the pre-dawn hours wasn't enough to distract Scipio from packing his remaining belongings for the ride back to Rome. Most important was a scroll his father had sent to his gloomy little quarters in the house of a private citizen. On it were the words that, he hoped, would convince Aemilia and her father that he had conducted himself with honor, and was being discharged for injuries suffered in Gaul.

He planned to see no one before he left, but the early marshaling meant his absence was noted from the formation. Before he could leave the house and make it to the stables, he heard Plinius being escorted from the atrium to his room.

"*Decurio!*" he called as he came through the doorway.

Scipio didn't turn around, not wanting to look his deputy in the eyes.

"Hannibal is here," Plinius said excitedly. "In Gaul. He came out of the mountains near a town called Taurasia, and... What are you doing? What's wrong?"

"My father has given me a discharge," Scipio answered.

"He what?"

Scipio turned with a sigh.

"I'm going home, Plinius."

"Home?" Plinius said, squinting his eyes. "Hannibal is *here, Decurio.*"

"Stop calling me that," Scipio said quietly, closing his bag and making to leave.

Plinius, blocking the way, didn't budge.

"What's the matter with you?" he demanded. "You're just going to abandon your men in the field at the worst possible time?"

"You'll all be better off without me," Scipio told him.

"Is that what you think?"

"It's what my father th—"

"Piss on your father!" Plinius said. "Whatever's going on between you and him has got nothing to do with the men—*your* men, the men that chose you to lead them."

Scipio hurled his bag against the wall, whirled around, and paced a few steps in the small room. Plinius was right, and it made Scipio even more upset than he had been about leaving.

"You don't understand," Scipio said, his head pounding with a volatile mix of shame and anger. "I've let my family down. I let my own brother die right in front of my eyes because I was too afraid to help him."

"When?"

"When I was... " Scipio choked up and fought back a sniffle before he could get the words out. "When I was seven."

Plinius showed no reaction in his expression, but he stepped forward, looking Scipio hard in the eyes.

"You're not a boy anymore," he said.

Plinius stepped back, but Scipio could not let him leave without asking the question.

"Why did they choose me, after everything?"

"They saw someone that put them before himself," Plinius told him. "But I see now that they were wrong."

Then he was gone, and Scipio was alone.

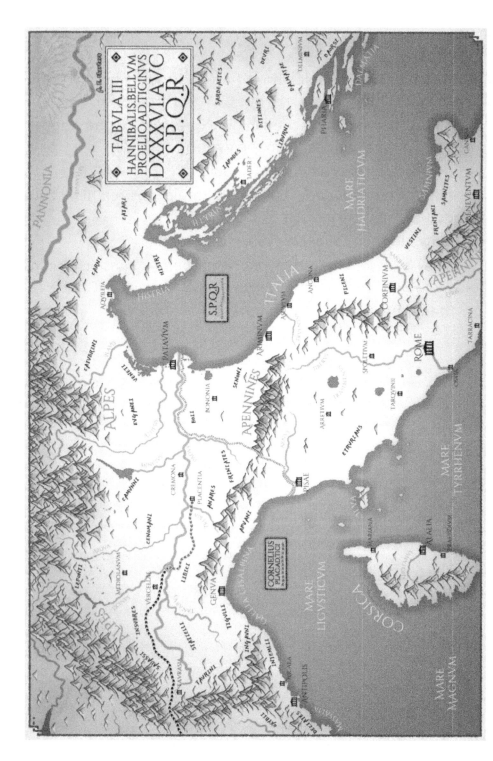

Part IV: Through the Fire

HANNIBAL

Hannibal needed to motivate his men, who were half-starved, battling the effects of exposure in the mountains, and now going into battle well before any of them had expected. Taurasia rebuffed Hannibal's request for food and supplies, fearing that it would inevitably drag them into the war with Rome, whose support they needed against their enemies to the east, the Boii. Hannibal realized the Taurasians were in a precarious position, but he was not in an understanding mood. Instead of moving on, he besieged the town, determined to make an example of them for all the other tribes of Cisalpine Gaul that might hesitate and withhold their support.

Behind the siege line, the animals grazed while Hannibal's army and remaining highland tribe slaves prepared the ladders and battering rams needed to breach the walls of Taurasia. Like their human counterparts that had marched through the Alps, the animals were near starvation when they descended on the wide path Adherbal's engineers had carved for them. But while the animals found a ready supply of vegetation on which to quickly fatten themselves back up, the men's stomachs were still empty.

When darkness fell, Mago, Maharbal and Vernon joined Hannibal around the fire outside his command tent. Through the darkness, they gazed at the walls of the town in bitterness as soldiers passed by. The men, Hannibal noticed, no longer had the glow of awe and admiration in their eyes when they saw him. Most did not bother to look his way, hanging their heads and letting their long hair hide their miserable faces. Hannibal knew that look. It usually preceded desertions, and those came not in dribbles but in surges.

"Not the reception you hoped for," Mago mused. "Is it, brother?"

Hannibal snorted.

"The foragers haven't had much luck," Gisgo reported as he took a place by the fire and warmed his hands. "The men have hardly eaten since we got stuck behind that boulder on the way down."

"Do they even have enough energy for tomorrow?" Maharbal asked no one in particular.

"Sometimes I appreciate your skepticism, Maharbal," Hannibal said, poking the fire with a stick to keep it strong. "When it keeps me honest and on my toes. Other times, I think you're just whining."

"What about my skepticism?" Mago asked.

"Yours is different," Hannibal answered, looking up at his brother's face. "You're *always* whining."

As the officers laughed, an idea came to Hannibal. Nothing helped morale more, he knew, than a little fun. He thought of something that would both entertain them and restore their sense of purpose, without causing undue expenditure of what energy they had left.

"Gather the officers," Hannibal told them, getting to his feet, "and bring me the Allobrogian prisoners."

It took some time, but the few hundred officers from the Numidians, Celtiberians, and Africans finally gathered around a large circle lit with torches that Hannibal had arranged. In the center, Hannibal assembled the slaves in chains before him and his men. They were like walking corpses with overgrown beards. Most didn't even bother looking at their captors as they entered the circle. Joining them in the center of the circle with the slaves, Vernon threw two longswords of the sort the Gauls favored on the ground in front of them.

"Two of you will fight," he told them. "One of you will die. The winner gets some food and a good horse to carry him wherever he wants."

As Vernon translated, Hannibal watched as some of them looked suspiciously at the swords, perhaps thinking it was some sort of trick. Others just remained still, unsteady on their feet and barely aware of what was happening.

"Live or die," Hannibal went on, "those that fight will be free."

Finally, two of the more alert and healthier Gauls stepped forward in their rattling chains. Hannibal gave the nod, and Gisgo unshackled them as the officers formed a circle, murmuring excitedly. This was the first bit of entertainment they had seen since leaving Hispania.

As the captives weakly lifted their swords against one another, the officers cheered them on even before the first clang of metal-on-metal. They watched, spellbound, and screamed for blood as the Gauls fought with every scrap of energy and strength they had left, swinging wildly at one another. The fighters became so tired that their swords hung in the dust after only a few minutes. Exhaustion eventually overtook one of the miserable gladiators, and a strike from his opponent knocked the sword from his hands. He fell to his knees, panting, and the cheers died down to silence. It took a few breaths before the victor could even muster the energy to place his hand on his countryman's shoulder. The vanquished murmured a prayer to his gods as the victor waited, then nodded when he finished. It took all the victor's strength to plunge the sword through the man's heart.

The cheers and applause died down as Vernon escorted the victor away and Hannibal stepped into the ring again. He looked around at the silent officers.

"This is why we're here," he told them. "The only choice we had, we made before we fired our first arrow at Saguntum. Now we must fight and win or die. Either way, we'll remain free men."

He faced the slaves who had chosen not to fight.

"Because we will never live a day as slaves to Rome," he went on. "Go back to your men. Remind them how we shared their hardships; and remind them that tomorrow, we will take this town and show all of Italy who we are! We will put the men and children of this miserable place to the sword, and all that they have—food, wine, gold, women—will be yours!"

The men cheered, slumped and exhausted though they were. Their men responded best when it was easy to explain what they were fighting for. In this case, it was for their very survival. They could literally feel it in their empty bellies. The fall of Rome was still too far into the future to fantasize about, but one good day of fighting would buy all they needed to replenish themselves.

SCIPIO

The tail end of a long line of troops marching from Placentia was nearly a mile outside the city gates before Scipio managed to catch up to them. He rode hard, looking for his troops among the hundreds of cavalrymen riding behind the infantry.

He was nearly numb with fear—not of the battle ahead, for those nerves would come soon enough, but in anticipation of seeing the disgust on the faces of his men. Perhaps, he thought, they'd seen him and hadn't called out because they now wanted him gone.

"Ave, Decurio!" he heard Plinius's voice call to him just before he reached the infantry.

He turned his horse and saw Plinius raise his right hand beside his head. Riding over slowly, Scipio saw a subtle smile across his lips.

"Glad you're feeling better, sir," Appius said.

Scipio nodded to him and took his place in formation beside Plinius and in front of the rest of his men. As his heart settled into a calmer rhythm, he took the scroll with his discharge and handed it to Plinius, who laughed and hurled it as far into the muddy field they were passing as he could.

***

The legions made their camp about one mile from the Ticinus River, one of the Po's tributaries. The news that Taurasia had fallen to Hannibal reached them there. Scipio guessed that the news would quickly spread through Cisalpine Gaul. To prevent them from joining up with the invaders, Cornelius conscripted every able-bodied tribesman he could find from every village they passed.

The scouts returned early the following day with Hannibal's location, and things happened quickly. The heavy infantry was being left at camp while the light infantry *velites* and cavalry went to "reconnoiter" the enemy, though most suspected the Consul's true intent was to bait Hannibal into a fight. The force crossed the river on a pontoon bridge made of small crafts while Cornelius went through the motions of studying bird signs. A trained auger, he was especially watchful for eagles and woodpeckers, which were sacred to Zeus and Mars, respectively.

"Are you nervous?" Claudius asked Scipio as they watched the spectacle.

They were waiting for about half of their men to cross before they themselves made the crossing.

"I'm terrified," Scipio admitted.

"We all are," Claudius said. "Trust me."

Scipio earlier caught himself reaching for his comet talisman, then remembering that whatever was left of it was in the hearth of some druid witches in Gaul. With nothing to squeeze or rub between his fingers, he found himself checking and rechecking his armor and equipment. He needed to do something—anything—to make him feel as though he was as prepared as he could be.

"Let them drink," Claudius said, watching Cornelius and the augers reading bird signs.

"What?" Scipio asked him.

"Just something my father said once," Claudius explained. "Or people told me he said it, anyway. He was commanding the Roman fleet at the battle of Drepana. Apparently, the augers on his ship brought these sacred chickens aboard with them."

"Sacred chickens? They sound delicious."

"Well, the chickens apparently refused to eat their feed," Claudius said. "The augers thought it was a horrible omen of some sort and advised against engaging the enemy."

Scipio couldn't help but laugh at the notion of a gaggle of old augers aghast at a bunch of seasick chickens.

"So, my father says, 'If they don't want to eat, let them drink!' and he tosses them overboard," Claudius said.

Scipio nearly fell from his saddle, holding his aching sides.

"Those priests probably dropped dead from shock, right there on the deck!" Scipio said, wiping tears from his eyes. "Oh, Claudius... . I should have been born into your family."

"Well, it's not all fun and sacrilege," he said. "He lost the battle and was tried for incompetence. The augers had him convicted. He killed himself shortly after. Hemlock, I'm told."

Scipio could see it weighed heavily on his friend, even though he'd been little more than an infant when he'd lost his father. It had been a welcome distraction from the looming fight, but the end of the story reminded him of what was at stake. He imagined how Aemilia might feel if he died. It occurred to him then that his love until he left had been fundamentally selfish. He wanted her to bring happiness and joy into his world. Contemplating death, he now felt as if his own happiness mattered very little if she didn't share in it.

"If I don't make it back," he said to Claudius, "look after Aemilia for me? Whatever she does just... see that she's happy. Will you do that for me, Claudius?"

"I will," Claudius promised.

"Is there anything you'd want me to do?" Scipio asked him.

Claudius took a moment, then said, "Bring me back to Rome and bury me under the brothel on Caelian Hill. You know the one."

"Really? That's all? What about your mother and sisters?"

"They'll be fine," Claudius said. "Just remember—Caelian Hill, and not the brothel near the wall, either. The one near the temple of Venus."

"It shall be done," Scipio told him.

HANNIBAL

A few short miles away, Hannibal received the news of the Roman crossing with cautious optimism. The worst thing that could happen, he thought, was that the Romans would avoid combat except when the numbers and terrain heavily favored them. He expected and needed them to be overly aggressive. All his plans for fighting in Italy depended on it.

Soldiers in Hannibal's personal guards were helping Hannibal and Mago into their armor while Maharbal briefed them on the Romans' movements.

"Only the cavalry and skirmishers crossed the Ticinus," he told them. "Most of their heavy infantry is still in the camp. They're moving fast."

"You're watching them?" Hannibal asked.

"Of course. Their Consul's taken all his cavalry and his skirmishers, and he's headed straight for us."

"Who is in command?"

"The locals say it's Cornelius," Maharbal told him, sounding surprised.

Hannibal looked up at him.

"Again?"

"It might be the same Consul that was after us in Gaul," Maharbal replied, shaking his head. "But I don't think it's the same army."

"Why do you say that?" Mago asked.

"It's smaller, for one... About two legions, at most, and it looks like there are more allies than before."

"Where's the other army, then?" Mago asked.

"Hispania... " Hannibal answered and after a moment added, "... probably."

"Or they're moving in to attack from both sides," Mago countered, eliciting a laugh from Hannibal.

"Always the optimist."

"Why else would he put a river between him and his heavy infantry? It smells like a trap."

"Because you're thinking like a Carthaginian," Hannibal told his brother. "Romans are terrible at deception and aren't capable of patience."

"And if you're wrong?" Mago asked.

"Just keep eyes on that camp," Hannibal told Maharbal. "The last thing we need is to have them show up at our party uninvited. How many horsemen do we have out foraging?"

"About two hundred," Maharbal confirmed.

"Call them back in," Hannibal said, tucking his helmet under his arm. "If Cornelius crosses the Ticinus, he's looking for a fight. We need to be ready to give him one while a river is between him and his heavy infantry."

"Yes, General!"

As Maharbal leaped onto his mount and rode off, Mago began saying something to him about the Numidians. Hannibal wasn't listening. He was too busy picturing the force he was to face, the terrain he wanted to fight them upon, and how they would deploy against him. The battle was playing out in his mind in a dozen different ways as he and Mago fit their horses with bridles and saddles.

SCIPIO

Scipio watched the *velites* form up for the march ahead of them. They were light troops—skirmishers armed with three or four javelins each and a short sword, a wooden shield, and no armor. They would typically wear animal skins and furs to distinguish themselves from the heavy infantry and customized their looks to be conspicuous in battle. They were recruited from among the poorest citizens of the Republic, but their esprit de corps was among the highest in the army. Their lack of armor also meant they could travel farther and faster than the heavy infantry.

The march began.

Even though they were leaving all the heavy infantry behind, the column was an impressive sight. He'd never been part of a formation this large—nearly three hundred *equites*, resplendent in their red cloaks and plumed helmets, with an equal number of allied horsemen riding behind half as many *velites*, whose javelin tips reflected the December sun in lethal beauty. They were in front and along the flanks so they could flush out ambushers, make first contact with the enemy, and keep them occupied while the cavalry positioned themselves to deal a crushing blow.

"We'll stay close," Plinius assured Scipio with a nod.

"We'll crush them," Scipio said, Lars's imperative to project confidence with his men still fresh in his mind. "The one thing my father does well is destroy his enemies."

"From your lips to the gods' ears, *Decurio*."

Marching on a narrow road through the forest, they stopped several times when they spotted enemy scouts among the trees fleeing as the Roman force drew near; but it was never for more than a few moments before Cornelius bellowed the orders to get the formation moving again. They rode for what seemed like hours, and the thought that Hannibal had eluded them again crept into Scipio's mind, but they had moved less than three miles when he saw men speaking to one another and pointing up toward sky ahead of them. He tried to follow their gaze through the bare branches on the winter trees. Then he saw it, as clearly as he had weeks ago in Gaul—the telltale dust cloud of a large force on the march, on a course to collide with his own.

"*Velites!*" a voice cried from up front.

The battle roar and whoops from the light soldiers was rousing, and Scipio was surprised to find himself laughing joyfully at the sound. Nothing could possibly stand against such men, it seemed. They would tear the Carthaginians apart like a lioness.

The column slowed, then stopped. Orders were passed, though Scipio couldn't hear them clearly. Claudius signaled his men to come around through the trees, to take up a position on the right flank. Scipio and his men were part of the line, heading into the forest toward a clearing, up a slight hill.

There they were, across the tall grass littered with leaves, with the tree line at their backs. They stood in sharp contrast to the grandeur of the Roman formation. No red cloaks, no shiny helmets... Just haggard, grizzled horsemen and skirmishers and in dark, dirty sackcloth and sparse armor, carrying well-worn weapons and dented, chipped shields bearing all manner of insignia. The Alps, it seemed, had chewed them up and spit them out.

"Few infantry," Plinius mumbled, barely loud enough for Scipio to hear.

Scipio nodded in agreement, looking at the enemy formation carefully.

"How many are there?" he asked.

Cornelius must have given the order for the *velites* to advance, because Scipio saw them trotting out into the middle of the clearing, javelins and slings ready. About a quarter of the way across the open area, they assembled in a loose line for a skirmish. This, Scipio knew, was meant to screen the movement of the men behind them, so that the Carthaginians could not see clearly how the Romans were forming up their lines. The rest of the Roman cavalry was still coming in from the road and when he heard a horn blast on the other side of the field.

The heavy African cavalry, in the center of the Carthaginian line, was in a full charge before the *velites* were in their formation. Some managed to get a javelin into the air at the charge, but most simply turned and ran for the safety of the Roman cavalry lines.

"Is that supposed to happen?" Scipio asked aloud, though he knew the answer was no.

Claudius rode to the center of his formation and raised his spear.

"Ready!" Scipio called to his men, raising his spear.

"Ready!" they echoed, raising their own.

The *velites* ran between them through their ranks just as Claudius echoed the Roman call to charge. The front rank dashed off like arrows shot from bows. By and large, the second and third ranks managed to avoid the fleeing *velites*, but their hasty retreat still caused considerable confusion and delay in getting the charge going. Scipio struggled with his horse's reigns as *velites* brushed past him with their unused weapons. Their terror was palpable, and he could feel it trying to infect him as he struggled to get free and charge in the direction from which they fled. He finally managed to get clear of them and rode, gripping his spear tightly with his right hand and controlling his mount with his left. When he saw more Carthaginians coming around to the right of the fray, he called to his men.

"Right flank!"

Plinius and Appius echoed the command.

"Shields!" Plinius called, and Scipio realized it was too late for his own.

They collided far too fast for the horses to stop, but the length of his spear gave him the advantage. A Carthaginian was riding straight at him, roaring as he held his shield in front and his battle-ax up to his right. His opponent had to switch hands to try to hit Scipio, but his shield was in the way. Cursing in Punic, he steered toward Scipio, who veered left and thrust as he had done a hundred times in training. The Carthaginian's ax swing missed the shaft of the spear by inches, allowing Scipio to thrust it just above the Carthaginian's hip. Turning his horse while drawing his short sword, Scipio saw the man drop his ax and pull at the spear protruding from his side, but it was stuck in deep. He looked up at Scipio with a pain-filled grimace and fell dead from his saddle.

"*Decurio!*" Appius called from the fray, pointing behind Scipio.

A squad of light infantry from the enemy's side formed not far away—slingers and skirmishers, trying to pick off Romans who strayed from the central mass of bloody confusion. Riding hard back toward his men, he was oblivious to the missiles flung at him as they fell to the ground on either side. He heard his horse make a terrible sound, then found himself on his back on the ground, looking up at a spear tip about to be put through his heart. He rolled to his left, and the spearhead glanced his armor.

Before the Numidian holding it could strike again, Gaius put a spear through his neck just below the jaw, killing him instantly.

Scipio found his sword and shield. Half of his men were already dismounted and fighting. He stepped to the side of an opponent Plinius was engaging and stabbed him in the back. He barely caught an African cavalryman coming up fast to his right, turned and saw the man throw his spear. He turned sideways, letting the spear go by. Sword in hand, the African charged at Scipio, who held his sword at the ready. As Scipio reached back to slash, another Roman's cavalryman charged past him and caught the African in the chest with his spear. Scipio leaped out of the way as the horse flew by him, its rider dead on his back a few feet away from where Scipio had stood.

Suddenly finding himself without an enemy nearby, he scanned beyond the corpses and wounded men crawling back toward the edge of the battlefield to see the Roman *velites* regrouping. In the other direction, it seemed as if the Numidians were advancing unevenly. The farthest man on their flank seemed already past Scipio, and the line extended from him back toward the Carthaginian rear. If the enemy was advancing in a proper line, they should be heavily engaged, yet they were alone. It could only mean that they were coming at them at an angle...

"*Decurio*!" Plinius called, pulling a horse around for him.

He climbed atop the mount and stood in the stirrups, trying to see where he was in relation to the other Roman cavalry units and the enemy. He was on the right flank of the Roman line, and he could only see that the Roman center, where his father was commanding the action, was now farther forward than his own unit but still heavily engaged with the African cavalry. Behind them, it looked as if the left flank were coming toward the center to flank the African cavalry.

"They're calling us to the center!" Appius called out. "We're pushing them back!"

"They Numidians are moving around our flanks!" Scipio told him. "Get word to my father!"

"Yes, sir!" Appius answered, and rode into the thick of battle in the center of the Roman line.

"Scipio!" Claudius called, galloping up. "Get your men to center!"

"We need to break that line," Scipio told him, pointing to the right flank with his sword.

Claudius looked up at the Numidians in confusion.

"Forget them!" Claudius said, pointing the other way. "We're about to break through the center!"

"If we don't break their line, they're going to roll up our flank!" Scipio told him. "They'll surround us and hit the center from behind!"

Claudius looked again, then at the center of the Roman line. Cornelius was directing his men to grind through the African cavalry, but his progress had slowed as reinforcement reached the Carthaginian line.

"Are you sure?" he asked Scipio, looking out at the slow-advancing Numidians.

"Look!" Scipio told him, pointing again to the right and moving his sword in a sweeping arc to show him the angle of the Numidian line.

Finally, Claudius nodded.

"Wedge on me!" Claudius called.

The young soldier carrying his banner gave the signal as Claudius's subordinates echoed the order.

"Gods, I hope you're right," he told Scipio as they formed a wedge of three lines.

When they were ready, Claudius held up his sword. The banner-bearer held up the standard, and the men bellowed a war cry. At Claudius's command, the wedge rumbled forward like a boulder rolling down a hillside, gaining momentum, toward a line of Numidians.

Scipio could only see a small part of their line, but the Numidians seemed confused. They were famously excellent at controlling their horses and improvising in battle. They rode without saddles or bridles, using ropes tied around their steeds' necks to control them, and they wielded their javelins with deadly efficiency. This looked completely different than what he'd been taught to expect. He saw men jerking their heads in different directions, as if they were being given conflicting orders and didn't know what to do. Some of them slowed down while others either sped up or tried to change their formation from a single to a double line.

Claudius tried to slow the formation before they collided, but the momentum was too great on the first pass. Most Numidians barely had their weapons up when the Romans hit them like a battering ram and smashed their line apart.

It was like destroying a beehive. Claudius's *turmae* may have struck a devastating blow, but they now found themselves in a cloud of angry wasps. The Numidians looked far more like hunters than soldiers, but they were the fiercest warriors Scipio had encountered. They engaged and withdrew in turns like a swarm around the Romans, thrusting their javelins like spears and screaming like madmen. As Scipio slashed at the nimble enemies to no avail, he realized that they were herding him and the rest of Claudius's men toward the Roman center.

"We have to fall back while we still can!" Scipio heard a soldier tell Claudius.

"The center is nearly surrounded!" Claudius answered.

"*We're* about to be surrounded if we don't pull back, sir!" the man replied urgently.

Claudius looked around at the chaos of the battlefield.

Finally, he gave the order.

"Fall back!"

Hastily reformed in their wedge, they rode back to the tree line with the Numidians in pursuit. Thankfully, the regrouped *velites* were able to provide them with support. They rained javelins and rocks down on their pursuers, forcing the Numidians to break off their attack. As the injured fell farther back along the road, Claudius gathered his men.

"Get anyone that can fight and rally them here!" he ordered his deputies.

"Are we going to counter-attack?" Scipio asked.

"As soon as we can."

Scipio counted his men and realized Appius was still missing.

"Where's Appius?" he asked Plinius.

"You sent him to the center to find the Consul," his deputy replied.

Scipio looked to see where his father's banner was on the battlefield. Some soldiers from the center were able to break out of the encirclement as Claudius's men had, but most were still there, trying to hold back the Numidians on their flank and rear The Roman left flank had collapsed completely, precipitating a call to general retreat; but the men in the center were now trapped.

Scipio spotted Metellus staggered in from the battlefield nursing a wound on his right forearm. His face and armor were covered in dirt and blood.

"Metellus!" he called, riding up to him. "Where's my father?"

Looking in shock, Metellus seemed to ignore the question and continued walking past the *velites.* Scipio dismounted and grabbed him by his uninjured arm.

"Where is he?" he demanded.

Metellus looked back at the Roman center and motioned toward it.

"Is he alive?" he demanded.

Metellus squinted at him, panting.

"Is he alive?" Scipio asked more forcefully, shaking him.

"I don't know," Metellus answered, rending his arm from Scipio's grip and staggering away.

Scipio remounted and returned to Claudius.

"He's down," he told him.

"What? Who's down?" Claudius asked, but Scipio was staring out at the melee in front of them.

He was there... In between the running, screaming people; in between all the legs and togas fleeing in terror, kneeling on the blood-soaked stones of the forum. The fear had come, as he thought it would. It felt the exact same as it had all those years ago, but, as Plinius reminded him, he was a child no more.

"I'm going back," Scipio declared, drawing his sword.

The suggestion seemed to shock the men around him more than the battle had.

"Scipio, it's a rout," Claudius told him. "We need to regroup before—"

"I'll go alone if I must," he said.

"Scipio... "

Scipio spurred his horse forward. Plinius followed, and before Claudius could fully comprehend what was happening, more were riding past. He cursed Scipio, drew his sword, and followed them in.

HANNIBAL

For Hannibal, the battle had gone far better than had anticipated. He knew the Roman cavalry was a skilled and lethal enemy, with better armor and weapons than his Numidians or heavy African cavalry. Well led, they could be a dangerous foe; but the Romans made several grievous tactical errors, which Hannibal readily exploited.

As soon as he knew the Romans were committed to the center, he sent his Numidians forward on both flanks in oblique lines, intending to keep enough Romans in the center to surround them. The Roman left flank, held by allied cavalry, crumbled quickly, but then part of their right flank had done something he had not anticipated and charged the Numidians before they were ready. The Numidians quickly regrouped and beat them back, but it had allowed part of the Roman right to avoid total encirclement. The ones that escaped seemed too few and too bloodied, however, to rescue their center.

Now the victory was nearly complete. The bulk of the enemy was making a last stand in the middle, while the shattered remains of the right flank were fleeing.

Sikarbaal rode up fast, fresh from battle and holding his blood-soaked sword. He had led the attack on the enemy's left flank and had dealt it a crushing blow.

"General Hannibal!" he called. "The Consul is here! Cornelius is here!"

"What? Where?"

The young cavalry officer pointed to a spot on the field, but all Hannibal could see, even from a slightly elevated spot, were the flashes of swords and spears, a great mess of men and horses, and the corpses and severed limbs that littered the field. He'd have to take the young officer's word for it.

His victory sealed, Hannibal's focus turned toward getting the Consul. Killing him would cap his victory here today, but capturing him... humiliating a Roman Consul would send a powerful message to Roman allies. It would be another victory in and of itself.

"Take him alive, if you can!" he said.

"Yes, General!" Sikarbaal answered and rode back to gather men for the attack.

The Carthaginian center had moved back significantly, bending to accommodate the Roman push as the flanks advanced. Surrounded by his personal guard, Hannibal cautiously approached it and tried to spot the Roman Consul. He scanned the field where Sikarbaal had pointed as he got closer, but the Romans seemed indistinguishable from one another.

When he managed to spot him, it was because the Romans themselves pointed him out. A Roman soldier picked up the Consul's banner off the ground and held high, indicating where he was. Cornelius was on his back on the ground, Hannibal saw; but alive or dead, he couldn't tell.

A small unit of Roman cavalry burst through the Numidians and came to Cornelius's banner. Sikarbaal was leading troops from the Carthaginian right at full speed toward the same spot, with Maharbal close behind him. Hannibal crept closer as the Roman cavalrymen dismounted and made a conspicuous stand directly between the charging Carthaginians and the Consul, who seemed to be struggling to his feet with a soldier on either side supporting him. No matter... Sikarbaal and his men would skewer or mow down the defenders and take the prize he now wanted almost as much as the victory itself—Cornelius.

What followed was terrible and mesmerizing all at once. A young Roman hurled a javelin directly at the attackers with more force and accuracy than Hannibal thought possible. It went straight through Sikarbaal's chest plate and knocked him from his mount. Mortally wounded, Sikarbaal gripped the javelin as if trying to remove it before going limp.

Hannibal looked back to get a better look at the Roman and saw yet more enemy cavalry forming a circle around the Consul. Where were they all coming from? He could only watch in wonder as the same Roman that killed Sikarbaal picked up a spear and thrust it at Maharbal's horse, making it rear up in fright. The Roman stuck his weapon into the animal's chest with enough force to cause it to fall backward and to the left, taking its rider with it and pinning Maharbal's leg under its dying body. A few men dismounted with shields up to protect themselves from the Roman's sudden ferocity. They managed to free Maharbal and carry him away from the enemy. The rest of the Carthaginian cavalry broke off the attack, yielding to the fierce Roman defense. Hannibal watched in horror as Cornelius trotted off the battlefield, slumped over on his horse.

After their Consul escaped, it was a matter of minutes before the remaining Romans surrendered. There was little cheering and hooting from the Carthaginian side as they disarmed and bound the prisoners. Hannibal knew there was much to celebrate, but

Sikarbaal's death and the failure to capture Cornelius irked him.

Mago soon came to him, exhausted but exhilarated with the victory. Hannibal had charged him with leading the Carthaginian center, on whose movements the battle plan largely hinged.

"Should we pursue them?" he asked.

"Reform the cavalry and keep eyes on them," Hannibal answered. "We'll pursue them as far as the river."

CATO

Cato had been skeptical of trying to exploit Cornelius's loss in what becoming known as the Battle of the Ticinus. He had learned, through his education in Greek history and the politicians that came before him, that such tactics were lowly and often hurt their users in the end. Varro intended, however, on making maximum use of this moment to inflict maximum danger on Cornelius's reputation. If it looked like it was working, Cato would exploit the opportunity to deal a blow to the Hellenists just a week before the elections by having the Senate recall Cornelius.

As eager as he was to see their plan work, he still harbored reservations. There were unwritten rules of politics in Rome, and exploiting a military defeat for petty political gain was far outside what was generally considered acceptable. The only person with whom he had discussed it was Fabius, who was staunchly opposed to it.

"Varro is a shameless demagogue," Fabius told him at the baths while two slaves massaged their skin with olive oil. "Arguing policy internally is one thing, but in war we must present a united front—both to our own people as well as to the enemy. You know this, Cato!"

"I know that I'm tired of losing elections to the Hellenists," Cato replied. "They exploit their victories to aggrandize themselves. Why should we not exploit their failures? Besides, politics always inserts itself into military matters. It has ever since we began electing the Military Tribunes."

"Vilifying our opponents isn't a way to win elections," Fabius said. "Varro is a simpleton, a charlatan, and a fear monger. Even if his tactics work, what will it cost Rome? Why would good men— yes, men like Cornelius—get into politics if they think that they'll just be attacked and torn down at every turn?"

Cato rolled his eyes when Fabius asserted that Cornelius was a good man. Good men did not promote the hedonistic ways of the Greeks and Etruscans. This was the old way of thinking—that people could disagree on issues and not doubt the essential goodness of their political opponent. That was what lost elections.

He knew he had made the right decision when he saw the eyes of the enthralled plebeians listening to the words of Sabinus, a talented orator usually found in the courts or citizen assemblies, as he told them of a battle far to the north. Varro had hired him to get their narrative out to the people, and to do it louder and grander than the Hellenists.

"Consul Publius Cornelius has led his army to disastrous defeat at the hands of the barbarian forces on the banks of the River Ticinus! My fellow citizens, those waters now run red with Roman blood! Cornelius cowardly fled the battlefield to save himself and his son, leaving your sons there to die or fall into the hands of African savages... "

Some people had already heard something of the battle, but filling in the details and crafting them into a story that made sense to them was like putting meat on the bone before throwing it to the dogs to eat it up.

Having the crowd on their side was a tremendous advantage. Even Sempronius showing up unexpectedly on his way to Cisalpine Gaul did not ruin the day. While Sabinus spun yarns about the defeat outside the *Curia Hostilia*, the populists were on the verge of victory inside.

"This is ridiculous," Sempronius told the chamber as the debate raged on. "This so-called battle was nothing more than an opening skirmish."

"One for which your colleague was totally unprepared," Cato countered.

Sempronius was clearly fuming as Cato's allies clamored in agreement.

"Clearly he rode out for a reconnaissance, not a battle," Sempronius countered, but Cato ignored him.

"What was Cornelius doing in the north all this time while he should have been preparing our defenses?" Cato asked the Senate. "Perhaps Cornelius thought he could use his learned Greek ways to awe the barbarians into surrender."

The populists and conservatives laughed as Varro stood up.

"I move to immediately recall Cornelius from command of Rome's legions," he said.

Paullus rose, and the Magister called on him to speak.

"Fortune in war is capricious, Senator Varro," Paullus said. "You can have done everything correctly, but if luck is not on your side... "

"Don't presume to lecture me, Paullus!" Varro said. "This is pathetic! If you had finished the job twenty years ago in the first war, we wouldn't be here—"

"You know nothing of war, Varro!" Paullus bellowed.

Cato had never heard Paullus use that tone before, and it had a chilling effect on the room. It fell silent almost immediately. It was as if a lion had just roared, silencing all the lesser beasts around it.

"Apparently, neither does Cornelius," Varro quipped, and the awkward silence broke with laughter.

"Any well-led Roman army, of any size, should be capable of defeating a barbarian attack," Varro continued. "Can anyone disagree with this? Our superiority can only be undermined by incompetence or treachery. So, tell us, Sempronius, which is it? Is Cornelius as stupid as we all think he is, or has he been bribed?"

Sempronius snorted as the populists loudly supported the wild accusations.

"I reject the premise of the question," Sempronius answered simply, shouting over Varro's colleagues.

"That sounds like evasion to me," Varro said when the clamor died down. "Perhaps Adonica's gold found its way into your pockets during your time in Sicily."

"Enough!" Sempronius snapped, standing up and sneering at Varro. "You watch your tongue, you fat, sniveling little worm!"

The chamber was aghast at the breach of etiquette. Cato was surprised as well. Consuls usually tried to stay above the political fray, but Varro had clearly gotten under his skin.

"Crooked Cornelius has had his day," Varro said. "Again, I move for an immediate vote to recall him."

When Cato rose from his seat and seconded the motion, the chamber erupted into shouts, taunts, and recriminations. It was chaos, but Cato could sense it would go their way. To have a sitting Consul recalled in shame! It was his faction's greatest accomplishment in years. When the motion carried, Cato could sense the winds of Fortune at his back; but as the chamber emptied after the congratulatory smiles and embraces from Cato's fellow populists, Fabius approached with the same grim expression he wore when he warned Cato against this very course of action. The old man would not ruin this for him. Not this time.

"I must say, Fabius," Cato said, "for all your warnings about Varro, we seem to score victory after victory with him."

"You can win every battle," Fabius replied, "and still lose the war."

The old man was clearly loath to admit he had been mistaken.

"Cornelius is finished," Cato told him. "He'll never recover from this."

"My concern isn't for Cornelius, but for Rome," Fabius cautioned, sitting down even as the rest of their colleagues filed out. "You think you can ride that... " He pointed to Varro, who surrounded by well-wishers and newfound supporters as he walked out, "... whatever that is, without it coming back to bite you."

"As you saw today, we can," Cato said. "Politics has changed, Fabius. We must change with it."

Cato heard the creak of the door's hinges, then the solid thump against its frame as it shut.

"Forbearance is one of the pillars of democratic government, Marcus," Fabius told him, his voice echoed in the now-empty chamber. "The people elect us because they cannot directly govern themselves. They are too ill-informed, ignorant, and hot-headed."

"Fabius, what is the point of democracy if those elected do not reflect the views and values of those who elected them?"

"They're preoccupied with outcomes, not processes," Fabius answered. "And though they claim to value democracy, they have only the faintest idea of what it is and how it works."

"It works how anything else in life works," Cato said. "There are winners and losers. Varro is a winner."

Fabius looked away. The old man looked sadder than he'd ever seen him before. Cato patted him on the back and strolled toward the exit. Fabius didn't follow.

"Marcus... " he called before Cato reached the exit. "You know as well as I that none of this will end well for Rome."

Cato whirled and left the old man alone, no doubt pining for his long-lost days of civility in politics.

CORNELIUS

It was all a blur. Coming in and out of consciousness as his men staunched the bleeding from the gash on his right arm near the shoulder... Feeling the pain of each breath and the tenderness on his left side—signs of broken ribs, no doubt... Carried on a stretcher across the pontoon bridge, asking what the situation was; no, *demanding* to know what was happening... *Maybe I mumbled it,* he thought. The sight of hundreds of his men on the other side of the Ticinus, abandoned to capture while the men who'd made it across cut the moorings on the pontoon bridge just before the Numidians arrived like screaming spectral visions from a nightmare.

Instead of chasing the Carthaginians back into the mountains, Cornelius was the one being chased, too weak to even ride a horse. He'd lost a lot of blood. He was unconscious for most of the desperate flight to safety across the Po. He was enfeebled... a man not in control of his own destiny for the first time in decades.

When he fully regained consciousness, he was alone in a tent, his arm heavily bandaged and his left side aching. He stumbled out into the daylight wrapped in a wolfskin, feeling like an enfeebled old fool. The first soldier that recognized him brought him to Metellus. After three days and nights of running, the army had found a defensible site overlooking the union of the Trebia and Po Rivers. It was here that Metellus and Vulso had agreed to pause before returning to Placentia.

For Cornelius, it was an unmitigated disaster. He would rather have died on the battlefield than absorb this kind of loss. That had nearly happened, but the Fates took a hand in the unlikely form of his own son.

Scipio

When he saw the smoke in the sky, Scipio feared the Numidians had somehow gotten through in large numbers and raided the camp. He was returning from a two-day patrol, during which he had monitored the eastern-most elements of Hannibal's army. Numidian cavalry had harassed their retreat until the legions crossed the Po River and destroyed the bridges over it. Scipio's now seven-strong troop and other Roman cavalry units had been keeping them at bay by engaging the small Numidian units that had managed to ford the Po, but the skirmishes had always ended in the Numidians retreating.

When he arrived, he was surprised to find his father on his feet. He scarcely recognized him at first. Gone was the tall, proud, stoic father that looked at him with such scorn. In his place stood a wounded old man, wrapped not in his armor and cloak but in furs. If not for his completely bald head, he might have overlooked him entirely. His eyes were soft and tired. They greeted Scipio with a sadness had never seen in them before.

The smoke he saw had been a funeral pyre that was dying down in the frosty December air. Scipio released his men to their tents and dismounted by the pyre's remnants. It was difficult to discern exactly whose bodies were burning, not least because their heads had been separated from their bodies. It was clear from the crimson cloaks in which they were wrapped, however, that they had been Roman soldiers.

Standing before him now, Scipio found himself taller than his father for the first time in his life. It may have been a difference of less than an inch, but it felt as if he towered over him. He saluted Cornelius, who returned the gesture weakly and, for the first time Scipio could remember, greeted him with a warm smile.

"What happened here?" Scipio asked.

His father motioned for Scipio to follow him away from the grisly scene. Scipio felt the eyes of the conscripts follow them. There was a palpable tension in the air between the conscripted tribesman and the Romans that manifested in stares, grumbles, and edgy hands on the hilts of swords. They walked uphill on the Roman side of the camp toward the northeast corner, which afforded a good view of the Po River.

"Some of our Gauls went over to Hannibal during the night," Cornelius told him. "Almost a thousand in all. They attacked one of our cohorts and slaughtered the men in their sleep."

"Gods... "

"Now we face a new dilemma," his father went on. "We can't trust the Gauls to be in our camp, nor can we release them and risk them joining Hannibal."

Scipio said nothing. He didn't need to. It was exactly what

Vulso had warned him about.

"What of the Numidians?" his father asked.

"They largely ceased pursuit at the Po," Scipio answered.

"They were far enough behind us that we had time to destroy the bridges?" Cornelius asked hopefully.

"Actually, they stopped to raid the campsite we left on the other side."

"For what?"

"Food," Scipio said. "What we left behind, anyway... I guess they were hungry. Anyway, it bought us some time."

"Thank the gods for stale bread and turned pork," Cornelius said and laughed dryly. "You lost men?"

"Two injured, one dead," Scipio answered. "Appius... a good man."

Cornelius stopped walking and was silent a long while. He stood gazing out at the Po river with his shoulders stooped. Pain was the likely cause, Scipio thought; but his father's frown and downcast eyes told him it was something more. When Cornelius spoke again, his voice was soft and humble.

"I, um... I ordered a *corona civica* for you," he said.

The civic crown was one of the highest military awards for valor. Still, it seemed a small matter, given everything that had happened. Nearly two thousand men had been killed or captured in the past few days.

"You honor me," Scipio replied. "But... I must refuse it."

"Refuse?"

"I don't want any talk of nepotism," Scipio explained. "Besides... That you're alive and not in enemy hands is reward enough."

Cornelius seemed ready to object when Metellus approached with a soldier Scipio hadn't seen before, but who looked too clean and rested to be part of any unit here. They saluted Cornelius.

"I'm sorry to interrupt, Consul," Metellus said. "This soldier just came from Rome, bearing a message from the Senate."

"I'm to give it to you alone, Consul," the soldier said, and held out the scroll. As soon as it was in Cornelius's hands, the soldier quickly saluted and left.

Cornelius read it, then looked up at his son and son-in-law. He straightened up a bit, as if to regain some of his dignity.

"I've been recalled," he said flatly, and handed the scroll to Scipio.

"You're joking," Metellus said as his father-in-law walked past him into the camp. "Let me see that."

He snatched the scroll from Scipio's hands and read it, going over every word as if there were some hidden letters that might change its meaning. When he finished, he cursed and returned it to Scipio.

"This is bad," was all Metellus could say before following his father-in-law.

HANNIBAL

"They're crossing the River Trebia," Maharbal reported as he walked into the atrium where Hannibal and his closest officers were celebrating. "We're falling behind."

"For the love of the gods, Hasdrubal," an inebriated Mago replied from his seat at the long table. "Sit down and have some wine."

They were in a large country villa in Clastidium. Unlike the more sophisticated Roman homes, this one had a dining table where the guests sat upright in chairs or long benches. The city itself was home to a major grain storage facility that fell without a struggle when the garrison commander, a middle-aged man called Dasius, offered it up to Hannibal at no cost. He was rewarded with a seat at the general's table.

Hannibal could tell that Maharbal was still smarting from his stumble on the battlefield while attempting to capture the Roman Consul. As the men laughed, ate, and drank, Maharbal walked directly up to Hannibal's seat.

"Yesterday, we were nipping at Cornelius's heels," he said. "Now he's almost two days march away. If they make it back to Placentia... "

"Relax, Maharbal," Hannibal replied. "Come... sit."

He motioned for the other officers on the bench to scoot down, and they complied. One of Dasius's slaves brought another cup for him and poured the wine mixed with water. Maharbal looked over the spread and sneered.

"What's wrong with you?" Hannibal asked. "There's bread, olives, fish, grapes... all the things we were dreaming of just a week ago. Did you leave your stomach in the mountains.?"

"Don't worry, Maharbal," Mago said, holding out his cup for more wine. "I'll drink enough for both of us."

"For all of us, probably," Hannibal said to more laughter around the table.

"There is a whole other Roman army out there," Maharbal reminded his comrades. "But by all means, feast away! Drink your fill!"

The words meant to shock his men into sobriety only seemed to amuse them.

"Cornelius is a wounded dog, licking his wounds," Hannibal told him, "and Sempronius Tiberius just left Rome yesterday. We have at least a few days. Now sit down."

As Hannibal picked up his wine and drank, Maharbal leaned in close enough to whisper.

"How do you know this?" he asked in a low tone.

Hannibal ignored the question, put his wine down, and wiped his mouth with the back of his hand.

"This army has earned some rest," Gisgo told Maharbal from across the table.

"This army needs to keep moving," Maharbal countered. "How many days' food will this grain store provide us? We have thirty thousand mouths... "

"Forty-two thousand," Vernon countered, a broad smile on his lips. "And rising."

"What?"

"The tribes of Cisalpine Gaul are coming over to us, just as I said they would," Hannibal said, raising his cup to Vernon. "Some even belonged to Cornelius before last night."

"And Latin allies?" Mago asked, already knowing the answer. "Aside from our excellent host, of course."

"The first of many," Dasius said with a little too much confidence in his voice. "We all suffer under the Roman yoke. Now that General Hannibal has come, we will be free."

"Oh, joy!" Mago laughed, though Dasius seemed unable to tell that he was being mocked. "To Hannibal, liberator of Italy!"

Hannibal gave his clearly drunk brother a sideways look and then returned his attention to Maharbal, who didn't seem at all comforted by the news of their swelling ranks. He leaned in close to Hannibal as the others ate, laughed, and drank themselves into a stupor.

"How do you know about Sempronius?" he asked.

Hannibal could see he needed an answer, but there were some things only he and Mago knew, and no one else. It was the way it had to be.

"We have friends everywhere, Maharbal," was all that he said.

"Even in Rome?"

"Good money buys good friends, just as it buys good soldiers."

Maharbal eased back a bit. Without another word, he emptied his cup, put it down hard on the table, and rose to leave.

"Maharbal," Mago called before he got to the door. "Where are going? Your General told you to sit."

"I have to send scouts south and east," he answered. "That is, unless the gods have given the Barca Brothers the ability to smell Romans before they're in range to strike."

From any other of their soldiers, such sarcasm would have elicited a harsh punishment. Maharbal was different, but he was still a subordinate. All eyes, including Hannibal's, turned to Mago, waiting to see if he would chastise Maharbal or even have him punished. Instead, Mago looked to his older brother.

"Can we do that?" he asked.

"No, Mago," Hannibal answered.

Mago lifted his chin, looked down his nose at Maharbal and said, "Then by all means, man—go! Go! And try to keep your horse upright this time!"

The room erupted in laughter as Maharbal gave a last look at Hannibal and left.

Damn him, Hannibal thought. *Let them celebrate.* They'd

made it over the Alps, captured more than enough supplies for the winter, and had the Romans on their heels. His cherished World Without Rome was closer than ever. The men deserved a little taste of victory.

AEMILIA

The day had come.

A day after the general elections, the *populares* were flush with victory. Several conservative populists had won magistrates, including the Consul-elect Flaminius. Now the *Comitia Tributa* would meet to discuss and vote on new laws.

Aemilia was still angry with her father for being a party to the deal that allowed the *lex Oppia* through to the *Comitia* in the first place. He had been trying to ensure her that the law was doomed by its sheer ridiculousness. She expressed her annoyance with him by leaving for the Forum before he did, walking with Servillia, Appia, and a few servants rather than taking her litter. Although women were not allowed inside the *Comitia* itself, the praetor overseeing the assembly provided the three women places to sit to the left of the Rostrum. The other women who came to show their support were standing in the crowd outside in the Forum.

When the praetor opened debate on the bill, Cato was the first to address the mass of men assembled.

"Who among us knows no trouble these days in preserving the dignity and authority of a man over his family?" Cato asked them. "Our ancestors saw fit to prevent women from engaging in any transactions without a male family member present. If we had been vigilant, we would not be introducing this law to return them to their rightful place. But look! You see them assembled here, ready to participate in politics! This is how permissive we've become... "

As he went on, Aemilia noticed that Servillia seemed to grow deaf to him. Her attention was elsewhere.

"I'm worried," she told Aemilia when she had nudged her.

"We all are," Aemilia replied, putting her arm around her.

"Not just about this," she said. "About my father."

Aemilia had nearly forgotten that her father, Servillius, had been elected Consul just the day before.

"He'll leave within weeks for Placentia," Servillia said. "I know it's selfish, with everything that's going on, but... "

"It's not selfish," Aemilia assured her. "I would feel the same way."

"I know he's an old curmudgeon," she said. "But he's my old curmudgeon. I'm not ready to lose him yet."

"I know," Aemilia replied, and kissed her friend's cheek. "One thing at a time, yes?"

Servillia nodded and tried to put on a brave face, though Aemilia could see her father's impending departure to the front weighing on her.

It took almost half an hour, but Cato finally finished. At the end, most of the people Aemilia could see appeared relieved it was over. The sighs of exhaustion in the audience made her hopeful that he had gone too far.

Appia mounted the Rostrum and faced a crowd already murmuring and casting derisive or dismissive glances toward the women. Her himation was simple and unadorned for the occasion, but she seemed elegant, nonetheless. Speaking to the women earlier, she seemed to brim with confidence; but now Aemilia could see a drastic change as she faced the assembly. Her eyes glanced furtively, her posture deteriorated to a slouch, and her expression could be mistaken for one of surprise.

"Appia... " Aemilia called from the foot of the Rostrum. When Appia's gaze fixed on her at last, Aemilia held a clenched fist to her chest and nodded to the older women. It returned to Appia what she had given to Aemilia the day they first met at Servillia's villa. *Be strong. Be confident. We're with you...*

It seemed to help, if only a little.

"My fellow citizens... " she began. "I believe some of your beards were much shorter when Senator Cato began speaking."

The assembled citizens erupted in laughter. Aemilia looked over to Cato's seat to see him fuming, his face as red as the statue of Jupiter. She savored every second of laughter at his expense.

"I shall therefore endeavor to be briefer, if not quite as eloquent," Appia continued. "I come before you now not as a woman, but as a free citizen whose rights and freedoms are in danger. I come to speak for half of all free citizens, many of whom have so honored me to be their voice today. The women of Rome have come far in their rights not because we have demanded special consideration, but because Rome's laws have become more just in giving us *due* consideration. Our city's founder gave women full citizenship because he recognized how critical we are to the survival and success of the state. This assembly, over time, made all citizens, men and women alike, fully equal in rights of property and civil law. This assembly made our marriages and divorces equitable, and expanded freedom for all in countless other ways. I have no doubt that this assembly will, one day, recognize our place beside our men as one of mutual respect and parity."

It was then the murmuring began and spread through the assembly. *Parity...* Aemilia, for one, would not have used the word. Romans were, by and large, conservative. Appia was right to appeal to their love of liberty, but suggesting too much change so soon could alarm them.

"I stand before you now not asking for your mercy or your charity," Appia went on, doing her best to ignore the murmuring. "But to appeal to you to do only this: your duty. The Senate is not sovereign, nor are the Consuls or any magistrate. In Rome, the *people* are sovereign, and that is who you here to represent: the people... *All* the people. Just as it would be your duty to protect the citizens whose only difference with yourselves is the color of their eyes, skin, hair, or skin, or any other trait whose possessors the state would burden or reward without just cause or due process. I call on you to protect our freedoms now; for if such a thing as this law may happen to women, something much worse may happen to any other group. Because democracy and freedom die not all at once, but little by little, beginning with an assault by the most powerful on the most vulnerable."

Much to Aemilia's relief, there was some applause and even a few cheers of approval as Appia descended the steps. The chatter in the *Comitium* became louder, but as Aemilia scanned the crowd, she saw more nods and aggregable looks than sour faces, folded arms, and shaking heads. All the noise and discussions were soon drowned out as Varro's fanatical admirers cheered wildly when he stepped onto the Rostrum wearing a fine purple-lined toga over his corpulent frame, his bushy eyebrows combed high, and the usual scowl on his face. Many others in the crowd jeered and booed, and some scuffles broke out between some assembly participants who loved and hated the pink-faced aggrieved demagogue before them. He was shaking his head dramatically in either disbelief or anger.

"If you believe all that," he said, "I bet I could sell you a pile of horseshit and convince you it was gold."

His supports laughed and hooted.

"But you know what?" Varro went on. "They said this kind of thing when I was young. Some of you remember... " he stopped and mocked them in a shrill voice, saying "'we want this' and 'we want that!'"

Again, his supporters laughed.

"And everyone gave in," he said. "They just gave in. Not me, though. I spoke against the changes that are now ruining Rome. For twenty years, I've watched these people, these so-called elites have their way unchallenged by the so-called representatives of the people. What has that gotten us? Nothing but corruption and rot!"

Aemilia watched the crowd turn on the mention of "elites."

"The truth is these women... Their money allows them to enjoy all the benefits of citizenship—benefits many of you don't enjoy—without any of the burdens. Oh, they'll fight, and they'll argue, and they'll scream in your ear about 'parity.'"

He shook his head once more.

"No," he said. "Sorry, no... Not what this is about. This is about what they *owe*. They are the most dishonest people in the world, these so-called elites. Liars to the man... or woman. They take from you everything you have, and when you have the temerity to ask for it back, they scream 'what are you doing?'" he said, using the shrill voice again. "Nasty women... I'll tell you what we're doing. We're taking back our country. *Our* country!" he boomed, making his fans and others in the crowd cheer.

He went on nearly as long as Cato had, and when it was over, no one was allowed a rebuttal. The vote moved ahead, and the *lex Oppia* passed, albeit narrowly. The only concession was that it would not go into effect for three months.

The momentum was clearly with the populists, who celebrated two days of electoral victories. Even as the assembly was breaking up, the mood seemed to perceptibly shift. The women with whom she came received sneers from passersby. They heard snickering and mockery, and they felt the hostility.

"I'm sorry," Appia told the group of women.

Aemilia stood on the stones of the Forum in shock and dismay as the women said their goodbyes and went their separate ways. She'd tried to mentally prepare for it, but the moment proved too overwhelming.

"I guess it's over," Servillia said sadly.

Aemilia turned her head toward the sound of laughter nearby. It was Cato, Varro, and a few other populists in a small group lingering by the Rostrum, probably savoring their victory. The sight of Cato's face converted her disappointment to anger, and anger to determination.

"It's only beginning," she told her friend.

"My lady..." she heard someone call from behind her. It was a male's voice, but high and soft. She turned to see a teenaged slave prostrate to her. "My lady, my mistress would like to have a word with you."

He motioned behind him to the Forum, where six brawny well-groomed slaves stood by a covered litter resting on the ground. It was obviously the conveyance of a wealthy woman.

"Who is your mistress?" she asked.

"Lady Busa of Canusium," he answered.

"I do not know her," Aemilia told him. "Tell her if she wishes to make my acquaintance, she will be received at the house of Paullus."

"My mistress regrets she has other appointments before she must return home," he said. "But wished to make your acquaintance."

"Go on," Servillia told her. "I'll see you tomorrow."

Aemilia followed the slave and peeked through the litter's curtains, which she was surprised to find were made of fine silk, to see a woman in her mid-fifties in the subtly perfumed interior. She was elegant and composed, with a serene smile on her carefully painted lips. Her clothing, wig, jewelry, and makeup all signified a woman with a taste for finer things.

"You did a brave thing today," she told Aemilia.

"Appia was the brave one," Aemilia replied.

"So I saw," the woman replied, pursing her lips. "But then she isn't the real leader behind this effort, is she?"

Aemilia didn't answer, and the woman didn't wait for one.

"Please... " she said, bidding Aemilia to enter the litter.

Aemilia sat across from her on a comfortable pillow.

"You know who I am?" Busa asked.

"I have heard your name," Aemilia replied. "Though I don't know why you're here, now."

"I heard about these little meetings of yours," Busa replied. "About the *lex Oppia*."

"Funny that I did not see you at any of them," Aemilia said.

"Well, I did not want to... distract with you with my presence, or bring unwanted attention before I decided if you were ready."

"Ready for what?"

"My support," Busa replied.

"I don't recall asking for it," Aemilia said.

"I offer it nonetheless," Busa told her. "Unless you prefer to be influenced by slanderous rumors that I'm some sort of a witch. That I poisoned both my husbands. Or I'm a fraud, a tax cheat... that I hate Rome and families and enjoy lying with women as much as I do with men... "

"I like to know who my friends are," Aemilia said. "If they are to be my friend, that is."

Busa regarded her a moment, and Aemilia felt she could almost hear her inner deliberations over how much of herself to reveal right now.

"I loved my husbands," she said, breaking the silence. "Mere mortals they were, and neither young when they died. My first husband died in the last war with Carthage, at Drapena. I didn't need to marry again, but I met a lovely, lovely man. He was also much older. He died last year, at seventy-two."

"And now you're rich," Aemilia said.

"I was rich when they were alive as well," Busa responded. "And for all its faults, I love Rome. That is why I want it to live up to its promise of freedom for its people."

"Why did you want to see me, out of all the women here today?" Aemilia asked.

"You all chose Appia to speak for you," Busa said, "and I can understand why. In addition to being a woman, you have the added disadvantage of youth. She has more credibility... gravitas... ."

"She struggled today," Aemilia admitted.

"You would not have."

"You flatter me," Aemilia said, cheeks flushing slightly. "But I have no reason to think I would have spoken better."

"I believe you would have," Busa said, squinting at her.

"Why?"

"Just a feeling... "

Aemilia waited for her to say something else, but Busa just kept looking at her as if she were trying to determine if she was seeing something real or some sort of illusion. It made Aemilia squirm on her pillow.

"My father is waiting at home," Aemilia said at last.

"Of course," Busa said. "Please give the Senator my regards."

"I shall."

"Until next time, then," Busa said as Aemilia went to exit the litter.

"Will there be a next time?" she asked, turning her head and feeling the silk against her cheek.

"Oh yes," Busa said. "We have much work to do. Steel yourself for a long fight, Aemilia. Nothing worth winning is won quickly or cheaply. We'll suffer, and we'll bleed, but I promise you this... *We* will be the ones left standing."

Scipio

To Scipio's surprise, Cornelius asked him to ride with him and his staff to greet his fellow Consul when Sempronius's lead column was in sight of Placentia. They brought Sempronius and one of the Tribunes on his staff, Sergius, to the command tent as Sempronius's legions set up their own camp to the south. Cornelius and Metellus briefed the two newcomers on the worsening situation in Cisalpine Gaul—the Gauls rallying to Hannibal, the lost skirmish at the Ticinus, and now the defection of Clastidium with its grain store.

Scipio's hopes that their fortunes would improve dissipated on hearing the entire situation, as they knew it, described in detail. For the first time, it seemed a real possibility that Rome could lose everything—its dominions, its allies, even its very independence—very quickly.

Sempronius and Sergius listened carefully, but they seemed neither alarmed nor surprised at each piece of bad news. When the briefing was over, they had a simple meal of bread and fish while Sempronius gave them the latest news of the political situation in Sicily, including the key city of Syracuse. Cornelius, however, was preoccupied with Rome.

"You were there when the Senate met?" he asked his colleague.

"I was," Sempronius said. "All your friends supported you to the hilt, but Varro and the rest of the rabble were calling for your head. You know how they are."

"Am I to stand trial?" Cornelius asked.

"Gods, no," Sempronius laughed. "It was a skirmish, Cornelius. Even Cato and Varro know that. They're just making as much use of it as they can. As I said, this is purely political."

"All things are," Cornelius remarked.

Sempronius raised his cup to acknowledge the truth of the point.

"I wonder," Cornelius continued, "what was said in my defense."

Sempronius gulped down his wine.

"Many things," Sempronius assured him, keeping a pleasant smile on his face.

"Such as?"

"But our time is short," Sempronius said. "It is perhaps best spent on discussing the enemy, is it not?"

"Hannibal," Sergius chimed in, as if they wouldn't know of whom Sempronius spoke. "You're the only Romans that have been up against him so far. Did you get a good sense of him?"

"As the Consul mentioned, it was only a skirmish," Metellus answered.

"A consequential one, nevertheless," Sergius countered. "Both commanders were present, were they not?"

"What are you implying?" Metellus asked testily.

"I'm not implying anything," Sergius answered, matching Metellus's tone.

"Certainly, if you had the force you deployed under your brother, Cornelius, you would have gotten the better of him," Sempronius said.

"You think it was an error to deploy my legions to Hispania," Cornelius said. "Perhaps you're correct."

"Error?" Sempronius said and turned his lower lip out. "No... Premature, perhaps."

Scipio saw Cornelius raise his chin and narrow his eyes. It was a look he'd seen from his father all too often, though this time his anger was not directed at his son. Before things could get worse, Scipio blurted out what he'd been thinking.

"He's smart," he said, making all eyes turn to him. It was the first time he'd spoken all evening. "And his army is... different."

"Care to elaborate?" Sergius asked.

"He has more cavalry," Scipio said. "And they're better than we are. They don't dismount to fight like we do."

"Scipio... " Metellus began, but Cornelius interjected.

"Let him speak, Metellus."

They were all waiting for him to continue. Their skeptical gazes made him feel like a child. Still, he'd been going over it in his mind since the day of the battle and talking it over with others. If he noticed something that others didn't, he had to let them know.

He took his scabbarded dagger and drew a line in the dirt, then a parallel line about a foot away.

"We began on either side of the battlefield," he said. "We sent up the *velites* to screen while we lined up, but they charged with their first line of cavalry—heavy cavalry. We met them in the middle, here... "

He drew a new line in the middle of the other two.

"But then they did this... "

Scipio drew two oblique lines on either side of the Roman line.

"That's... odd," Sempronius remarked. "Are you sure?"

"I am, sir," Scipio answered, then drew an arc on either side. "We broke one of their lines, but it wasn't enough. When their wings began to come it, he reinforced his center."

"Like two gates swinging closed," Sempronius murmured.

He nodded to Scipio, obviously impressed with how much he was able to observe even in the heat of battle. Finally, he took a deep breath and rose to his feet.

"Thank you for the dinner, Cornelius, and for, um... sharing your experience."

"It was my pleasure," Cornelius said, rising to see him out. "I'd like my son to escort me back to Rome, if you don't mind."

"How could I?" Sempronius responded.

"About Hannibal," Cornelius said. "A few words of advice."

"Give us a moment," Sempronius told Sergius.

Outside the tent in the cold night air, Scipio and Sergius did their best to eavesdrop inconspicuously; but the ambient noise of the camp thwarted them. Still, they could hear urgency in Cornelius's muffled voice and measured coolness in Sempronius's tone. When they exited, the men embraced for the last time as co-Consuls. Sempronius and Sergius then departed for their own camp.

"What advice did you give him?" Scipio asked.

His father looked in the direction Sempronius had gone.

"I told him to avoid pitched battle, to keep Hannibal locked up in Cisalpine Gaul until we could attack with six or more legions."

"Will he listen?"

"Of course not," Cornelius replied. "He's going to want the same thing that I did. He seems to think it's his last opportunity."

"Perhaps it is," he said.

Cornelius chuckled, amused, and cradled the back of Scipio's head gently in his right hand, then patted his shoulder. It was bizarre... Something only Calvus would have ever done before today. This change in his father had come too swiftly to be genuine and durable.

"Son, this one thing I can promise you, if nothing else," his father told him. "There will always be another war."

ADONICA

Queen Adonica read the letter from Hannibal one last time as the carriage bumped its way along the dirt road. He'd made it clear what he wanted. It was now up to her to deliver. The air was warm and comfortable, but her body was shivering. The butterflies in her stomach were insufferable. She closed her eyes, took a cleansing breath, then another. In... out... in... out... She heard clops of the horses carrying her personal guard alongside the carriage—something she hadn't noticed until now. In... out... Seagulls squawked, birds chirped, leaves on their branches rustled in the wind.

Her stomach was nearly settled when she opened her eyes and met the world in front of her. Yes, this would be fine. Splendid... brilliant, even. She had thought this through from every angle, and it was the perfect way to exploit and maximize one of the best advantages her father had left her.

The carriage stopped, and she listened as the captain of her guard shouted orders to his men. The door opened and the air was filled with a great dust cloud that immediately flooded the carriage. She squinted in the bright daylight.

"My queen... "

The captain of her guard bowed and extended a hand to help her out.

She emerged from the carriage unassisted. Friend or foe, no Roman should be able to detect the slightest hint of weakness, physical or otherwise, from a Carthaginian monarch. The small things, she knew, could be of the highest importance.

Her guards lined the way to the now-hollow temple of Baal and Tanit, where the Roman woman waited, no doubt watching her every movement. Adonica fixed her expression into a well-honed pleasant smile—one that communicated confidence but not enthusiasm, the latter of which could easily be interpreted as neediness. A queen was never in need.

"Your majesty," Valeria said with a bow. "It is a pleasure to make your acquaintance anew, as the queen you were born to be."

"No," Adonica replied. "Let us embrace as we have always known one another—as friends."

"Nothing would please me more, your highness."

They joined in a close but chilly embrace. They had both aged a decade since they last saw one another, but somehow Valeria seemed younger than she had before, or at least more vibrant.

They sat on the cool stone steps in the shade of the temple roof as Adonica's attendants brought wine with water. They ate bread and spoke of Valeria's stepson, Aulus, who was studying in Greece. Adonica had been eager for the pleasantries to be over and business to begin. Valeria had been a solid source of intelligence, but the plan she proposed to end the war required her to be an even better agent of influence. Adonica needed to meet with her in person and see if she had what it took to deliver what Carthage needed to bring this war to a satisfying conclusion.

Adonica wanted to appear warm and welcoming while keeping the disdain she felt for a person who would betray her own people in check, but now she found herself in a much more dangerous position. She liked her. Valeria was flattering without being excessively so, a lost art at Adonica's court. Sophisticated, urbane, charming... she was dangerous indeed.

"This place is called Maleth," Adonica said, looking out toward the coast. "For six hundred years, my people had a thriving colony and trading post right here."

"Remarkable," Valeria said, looking around at the broken columns, statue pieces, and toppled stone ruins scattered about the hill. "What happened?"

"War happened," Adonica said. "During the last war, Rome took it, razed it to the ground, and enslaved fifteen thousand colonists. I come here every so often. It reminds me of what can happen to my people when war is lost."

Adonica's let that settle with her as the servants refilled their cups.

"I must confess, I had my doubts," Adonica said, breaking the silence. "But Sempronius left Sicily, just as you promised."

Valeria bowed her head, though Adonica saw through the faux humility. Whatever the woman and her vulgar husband had done, Hannibal was probably much more responsible for sending Sempronius back to Italy. If Hannibal been turned back in Gaul, Adonica knew she would probably have faced a full-scale invasion of Africa in less than a year.

"My husband will be named dictator," Valeria promised.

"Are the reports that I hear about election preparations false, then? From what I hear, he is not even a candidate for Consul."

"He has the support of the people."

"The people vote to appoint a dictator," Adonica said. "The Senate appoints one. Does he have the support of the Senate?"

The question clearly threw Valeria off balance. Learning about the constitution of Rome had just paid its first dividend.

"The Senate," Valeria explained, "is a pack of old fools. The popular support my husband enjoys is the only thing that can force them to act outside their own narrow interests. Politics is downstream of culture, Queen Adonica, and my husband is a cultural hero."

"I see," Adonica replied, but her tone communicated incredulity.

"I believe I've earned some trust," Valeria said. "Hannibal will be able to keep several steps ahead of Roman armies because of our reports."

"I trust you, of course," Adonica lied. "But the gods can be capricious. What is your plan, should your husband not be named dictator?"

"Then he will be a Consul," Valeria replied simply. "Either way... When the elite lead Rome to defeat after defeat, his popularity will only grow. If there is no dictator, there will be new elections, and he will win."

Adonica was still doubtful, but this was a relatively inexpensive gambit compared to the costs of a long, drawn-out war.

"The price you ask is high," Adonica said. "The money you ask of me could train our rowers, hire new soldiers... "

"Rome is building four hundred new warships," Valeria told her. "That's just the beginning. Cornelius sent his brother to Hispania with an army. My husband is the best chance you have to end this war."

"If your husband manages to win office," Adonica asked her, "what is his intention?"

"He'll raise an army larger than the world has ever seen," Valeria replied. "And attack Hannibal at the first opportunity."

Adonica swallowed, containing her joy. It was exactly what Hannibal wanted—as much of Rome's available military population under the command of a fool willing to come out and fight as aggressively as possible.

"And you?" Adonica asked. "What do you want when this war is over?"

"I want Rome."

"Hannibal will want to raze it," Adonica told her. "Perhaps salt the earth as well. Why should I not let him?"

"Because you and I understand something Hannibal does not," Valeria replied. "Rome is not just another country. It's another *idea*, and those are more powerful than armies, even those led by Hannibal. And you can only destroy an idea from within. *That* is the true value of what I offer."

"So what is it you will take possession of, if Rome is so utterly destroyed."

"Rome will have a monarch again," Valeria replied, "and a glorious new alliance with Carthage, built on the friendship between their queens."

Adonica was taken aback a moment, though she told herself that she should not have been surprised. They drank to their agreement. There would be nothing written, at least not yet. It was fragile and dependent on a great many things, none of which Adonica was confident Valeria could deliver.

Adonica never wanted Hannibal to leave Hispania in the first place, but merely denying him ships hadn't stopped him from doing what he vowed to do. For the sake of at least appearing in complete control of her armies, she now had to support Hannibal, even if his selfishness infuriated her. His vow was to destroy Rome, and he only thought of what could be won by fighting. Hers was to defend Carthage, and she also had to consider what could be lost. This deal with Valeria gave her back some measure of control over events.

AEMILIA

"I need money."

Paullus looked up from his scroll to see his daughter there in the lamplight in the doorway, awaiting his reply.

"Whatever you need," he told her, and went on reading.

"Are you upset with me?" she asked.

He sat back in his chair and rubbed his eyes, looking more tired than she'd seen him in many years.

"Of course not," he said. "Forgive me. Come."

He motioned her over and she put a comforting arm around him, resting her chin on his shoulder and kissing him on the cheek. It brought a smile to his face, but she could tell something was troubling him.

"You're reading Homer?" she asked, reading over his shoulder. "Again?"

"Only parts," he said.

"Aristotle as well?" she asked when she saw another scroll on the table.

"I'm looking for... something," he told her.

"What?"

"I don't know... Inspiration, perhaps."

He looked at the fresco on the wall next to him, and Aemilia followed his gaze there. It depicted the Greek hero Aeneas departing Carthage with the refugees of Troy, bound for Italy. It seemed improbable to her that Carthage's famous circular military and rectangular commercial harbors existed all those centuries ago, but all artists were allowed some creative license. Aemilia wondered why her mother had chosen this scene of all those from Rome's storied history to be indelibly commemorated on their wall. She always thought there would be time to discuss it and a thousand other topics, but there always seemed to be less time than he thought.

"What's troubling you?" Aemilia asked him as she sat on a couch near his table.

He turned in his chair and ran his fingers lightly over the scrolls.

"People don't understand how fragile it is," he replied softly.

"What?"

"The Republic has been here for so long that people assume it will always be here, no matter. They don't know... It all balances on a knife's edge. One good push, one crisis, one scrupulous demagogue and it could all come crashing down."

"Scrupulous demagogue," Aemilia echoed, raising an eyebrow. "You must be speaking of Varro."

He didn't have to answer.

"If we lose the Republic," she told him, "it won't be because Varro stirred the masses against it, or Hannibal trounced it with his soldiers and elephants. It will be because we were too small a people to keep it."

He turned his chair toward her, leaned forward, and took her hands in his.

"I should have listened to you before," he said. "I didn't take Varro seriously."

"It's hard to take someone serious when they're so very stupid," she said, making him chuckle.

"Quite right," he said. "But I won't make that mistake again."

It was the first time he'd ever admitted that she'd known better than he; yet, she derived no great self-satisfaction from it. Rather, she thought of Valeria's comments about her family's influence waning. Looking at her father now, it never seemed more evident.

"*Domina*!" a female slave called from the atrium. "You have a visitor!"

SCIPIO

Scipio saw Rome with new eyes. What seemed like wide avenues before were narrow streets in the crowded confines of the city. The temples and statues that overawed and humbled all who visited seemed to have shrunk in stature and grandeur. He had left and returned before, but this was different. He worried that he would see Aemilia, too, in some different light. Perhaps, he thought, she would seem less stunning, less bright, less warm, and his love less intense. Perhaps it was a boyish crush and not the love he thought it had been. He pondered this possibility while pacing the *vestibulum* in her family home.

When she appeared, however, all the worries evaporated like so much dew in the face of the sun. He wanted to run to her, to pick her up and carry her someplace, make love to her and tell her that he would never leave again; but he couldn't, and she seemed equally restrained. When they were close enough, she reached up and brushed his too-long hair from his face.

"I've missed you," he said.

She smiled and took his hands in hers.

He took a breath.

"There was a slave revolt when I was seven," he said. "I was in the Forum with two of our slaves and my brother, Lucius. He was five. They'd built one of those wooden arenas for games, and we went there nearly every day. I don't know how it started, but suddenly people were screaming and running everywhere. At first, our slaves protected us, but when they realized what was going on, they just left. Men were coming into the forum with knives, swords... anything they could get their hands on. There was just... blood. So much of it that... then... and I was terrified."

Scipio stopped, and she squeezed his hands to remind him of her presence. He realized then that he was trembling, but there was no going back.

"I had his hand, pulling him behind me," he continued. "And I could hear him trying to get my attention, but I was just so fixed on getting through the crowd. He was pulling me back, and I remember just being so scared, Aemilia... I just... lost him."

"Go on," she whispered.

"I got to the stairs by the temple of Jupiter," he went on. "There's a, um... space there behind the sacred lanterns outside— the big ones that look like bowls. Me and Lucius used to call them the flaming piss pots."

She smiled at the name, but the lightness passed quickly.

"I saw him," Scipio said. "From that spot, I saw him there, just for a second, between people running. He was on the ground, on his knees and crying, and I was scared, I remember. So... terrified. I couldn't go out there. I couldn't help him. I closed my eyes, and I prayed the gods would help us both, but... It was only a moment, and then he was gone."

He stopped and she touched his cheek, moving his gaze down to her eyes. It was reassuring and calming.

"What happened to you?" she asked.

"When I didn't come home, a slave in my house came and found me," he said. "We found Lucius... I found him."

She kissed him on the cheek.

"I love you, Aemilia," he told her. "I will take care of you. I will protect you. I know now that I can, and I swear, I—"

She put her finger to his lips.

"I will marry you," she told him.

It took him completely by surprise, and he wasn't quite he'd heard her right.

"I will marry you, Scipio," she said. "First, you need a bath."

He laughed as the feeling of pure joy filled him; he embraced Aemilia and kissed her with more passion than he'd ever felt for her before. It was her father, clearing his throat to get their attention, that interrupted the moment.

"Senator... " Scipio turned to greet him.

"You've changed a little... " he said. "But enough, I hope."

"I believe so," Scipio answered with a slight bow.

"None of us come back the same," Paullus said as he shuffled toward the entrance to the garden. "Each of us leaves some part of ourselves out there, for better or worse, and we return different men."

He stopped in the doorway and turned his head to Scipio.

"In a way, none of us make it home, do we?" he asked.

"No," Scipio agreed. "We don't."

THE END

Printed in Great Britain
by Amazon

18995579R00215